NICOLA THORNE

Affairs of Love

PANTHER
Granada Publishing

Panther Books
Granada Publishing Ltd
8 Grafton Street, London W1X 3LA

Published by Panther Books 1984

First published in Great Britain by
Granada Publishing 1983

Copyright © Nicola Thorne 1983

ISBN 0-583-13625-7

Printed and bound in Great Britain by
Collins, Glasgow

Set in Times

Nicola Thorne was born in Cape Town, South Africa. Her father was English and her mother a New Zealander, and she was brought up and educated in England. She graduated in Sociology at the London School of Economics, but always wanted to pursue a literary career and worked as a reader and editor while writing her first novels. In 1975 she left publishing to write full time. *Affairs of Love* is her eighth novel to be published under the pseudonym Nicola Thorne. She lives in St John's Wood, London.

For Alec and Elisabeth Knowles Fitton
with love, and thanks for happy days at
Appletreewick

Friendship is constant in all other things
Save in the office and affairs of love:
Therefore, all hearts in love use their own tongues:
Let every eye negotiate for itself,
And trust no agent.

Much Ado About Nothing Act 2, Scene 1

PART I

CHAPTER ONE

Gazing at the group on the lawn from under the brim of her wide straw bonnet, Minnie Abercrombie thought how perfect it would be if the pairs playing croquet could pair off in real life, if the two charming men could marry her two enchanting daughters. For to Minnie they were enchanting. Lindsey, it was true, was not strictly beautiful, her nose a trifle too broad, her chin too firm, her mouth usually set and unsmiling.

But if people differed in their assessment of Lindsey there was a general agreement that Estella, the younger sister, was beautiful. The girls were about the same height, had similar colouring and complexion: fair hair, deep blue eyes and rather pale skin. But Estella's features seemed somehow composed to produce an impression of nature in perfect harmony and, despite her uncertain, volatile temperament, she always managed to convey the impression that she found life pleasing by the way her wide mouth curved upwards at each end.

It was such a beautiful afternoon and the partners, wielding their mallets with varying degrees of skill against the croquet ball, either bent or straightened, stood back or exclaimed with amazement, and there was a good deal of laughter. From the profusion of flowers in the herbaceous borders surrounding the well-kept lawn came the somnolent drone of bees, and in the branches of the thick oak tree above her head Minnie felt that the shrill sound of birdsong was positively amorous.

'How handsome they are,' she observed to her husband, who lay on a low-lying wicker chair with an extension on which he could place his feet. His panama hat covered his eyes and from his mouth drooped the stem of a very cold pipe. 'Edmund are you awake?' Minnie stirred her recumbent husband's form with her foot and as he wriggled the pipe fell out of his mouth. Sitting up to retrieve it, his hat tipped forward off his head and his red face looked both comical and annoyed as he groped for his pipe under its crumpled brim.

'Minnie! You know I was fast asleep!'

'I'm sorry, dear.' Minnie was too happy to feel either contrition or regret. Instead she rang the little silver bell on the wicker table by her side to summon tea. 'I was just observing what a handsome quartet they made.' She pointed towards the croquet lawn. 'Our girls with Wykeham and Rayner.'

'Ah, matchmaking.' Edmund slumped back, sticking his cold pipe once again in his mouth and smoothing back the scattered fronds of hair on his almost bald pate.

'Well, what's wrong with that?' Minnie looked up at the maid who appeared at her elbow. 'Could you bring out the tea things please, Jenny?' then, to her husband, 'Lindsey is twenty-two and Estella, well, she has not the ambition or brains of her sister, thank heaven. She is head over heels in love with Rayner Brook.'

'And he with her?' Her husband looked at his wife of twenty-five years whom his younger daughter so resembled, both in looks and temperament.

'Well, he certainly pays her a lot of attention. Why, he is always here!'

'He says he comes to use *my* library. He has a literary bent, you know. I don't know that he has many prospects.'

'The family have money.' Minnie settled back comfortably in her chair. 'Rayner will be a gentleman, like you.'

'Doing nothing, you mean?'

'Well, dear, you never had to work, thanks to your fortune and mine, and I'm sure it has done you no harm.

10

You have your books and your papers and always seem to me to have been a very contented man. No, I think Rayner and Estella well suited. He is a little young but not immature and they both enjoy theatricals. Lindsey . . . ' Minnie bit her lip and frowned. 'I do not think education has improved her. She will be lucky if Wykeham offers for her, but I think he will. In my opinion Wykeham is in love with Lindsey and Estella with Rayner; how the other partners feel I am not so sure. Lindsey of course never speaks to me of intimate things. Ah, Jenny.' Minnie swept some papers aside as the maid, breathing heavily, placed a heavy tea tray on the table. 'That's a good girl. Now fetch the other tray and I will pour. Then perhaps you'd go and tell Miss Lindsey and Miss Estella that tea is ready.'

'Lindsey has no mind to marry.' Her father righted himself. 'You know what she wants to do.'

'Over my dead body,' her mother said firmly. 'And yours too, I hope.'

'Then maybe she will take us both off to the dissecting room.'

'Edmund! I forbid you to mention such a subject.' Minnie's mouth was wide open with horror. 'I will not have my daughter as a doctor. I never heard of anything so common, so unseemly.'

'Mrs Garrett Anderson is a lady of the utmost propriety.'

'So they say. I have not met her; but her father was common. *Some* say he was a pawnbroker in the East End, so what can you expect?'

'Oh, Minnie.'

Edmund sank back and watched the four young people crossing the lawn, Rayner just ahead of Estella; Wykeham close behind Lindsey. The girls wore long white muslin skirts, and Lindsey's blouse was green whereas Estella's was a very soft blue which matched the bow in her broad straw hat. This was tipped on top of her hair which was

11

piled high in a fashion almost too grown up for her. Or was she now grown up, his darling, not yet eighteen? She had the walk of a woman who knew that people admired her and enjoyed their admiration, a slightly swirling gait that had a longer than average step yet was not a stride. Lindsey was altogether different, almost self-effacing with shorter, rather abrupt businesslike steps that seemed indicative of someone with little time to spare.

They reached the oak just as Jenny staggered over with the second tea tray and Wykeham sprang forward and took it from her.

'Allow me, Jenny.'

'Thank you, sir.'

Jenny looked nervously at Minnie, but Minnie was in too serene a mood, too uplifted by her day-dreaming under the tree, to reprimand her servant for letting a guest take a heavy tray. Maybe she would say something to her later when the mood had worn off, but not now.

'There,' Wykeham said. 'Is there anything else you wish me to carry, Jenny?'

'Oh, *no* thank you, sir. Is that all, mum?'

'Bring some more hot water in ten minutes. Thank you, Jenny.'

Minnie smiled graciously and the maid bobbed, her face pink, her cap on one side. She had seldom known her mistress in such a good humour. She scurried back into the kitchen to report it to Cook, who was busy with the dinner for the evening.

'Wykeham, dear, seeing you are so bent on being helpful, would you pass round the sandwiches? Jenny is helping with the dinner and it is Mary's day off. If my husband were not so mean we would have a butler, but . . .'

'Now now, my dear, you know butlers are for grand houses. I don't know what we would do with one here, quite frankly.'

12

'My father had a butler and so did yours.' Minnie, still benign, yet looked reprovingly at him as she passed him his tea. Her expression managed to imply that they had gone down in the world, and indeed at the time this house at the top of Highgate Hill had belonged to Edmund's father it had housed a butler and six other indoor servants, to say nothing of a gardener and a coachman. Now the coachman did the gardening and there were only four indoor servants including the cook; but it was not on account of lack of money, merely that times had changed and servants were not so easy to come by as they had been, nor so docile that they were content to stay with one family for life. Except for Cook, who had been here fourteen years, and her own personal maid who had been Estella's nurse, all the other servants were comparatively new.

'Does anyone mind if I don't put on my jacket?' Rayner mopped his brow with a large white handkerchief and draped his long form in a chair next to Estella.

'No one minds at all,' she replied, smiling at him. 'Only Father wears a jacket on a day like this.' She leaned over and stroked the sleeve of his white alpaca coat. 'It isn't seemly, is it papa, for elderly gentlemen to be seen without jackets?'

'No, my darling, it is not.' He took her hand and planted a kiss on the back of it. 'But for young men it is perfectly in order.'

Wykeham, who had one arm through the sleeve of the coat he had taken from the back of a chair, paused.

'In which category would you put me, sir?'

'Certainly *very* old,' Lindsey interposed, a teasing note in her voice. 'Or perhaps "middle-aged" would be kinder.'

'Nonsense!' Minnie poured tea through a silver strainer into a white porcelain gold-rimmed cup. 'Wykeham, you do no such thing. "Middle-aged" indeed.'

'Thirty is *quite* old,' Estella agreed. 'But maybe you

13

have a year or two left before you need wear a jacket all the time.'

'I'm sure you will tell me when that time comes, my dear Estella.' Wykeham, coatless, sank into his chair and took the cup proffered by Mrs Abercrombie. 'When my hairline starts to recede and my hair begins to fall out.'

Lindsey looked at him critically. 'That time may not be too far off. I advise you to play as much croquet as you can before your limbs start to stiffen into the bargain.'

'Girls, girls.' Mrs Abercrombie finished her task, still smiling, and selected a cucumber sandwich from a plate, studying it before putting it daintily to her mouth. 'That is quite enough levity. Wykeham is in the prime of his life and will be so for a good many years yet. Who won?'

'The game was undecided.' Lindsey refused sandwiches and took one of the little fancy cakes that cook had produced merely an hour before. 'Goodness, these are still hot. Wykeham and I, though, obviously had the edge on the other two.'

'We shall decide it after tea.' Rayner leaned his head back and closed his eyes, his cup and saucer precariously tilted in his hand.

'Not me, I'm afraid.' Lindsey glanced at her mother. 'I have some study to do.'

'Study?' Rayner opened his eyes and stared at her. 'On a day like this?'

'I study every day, rain or fine.'

'It's quite ridiculous.' Her mother's happy smile vanished. 'One would have thought you had done enough study, and could now put all that behind you and enjoy yourself.' The Cambridge Tripos had been weeks ago and Lindsey was awaiting the results.

'I do find study enjoyable Mother, strange as it may seem.'

'I find it very strange for a woman,' her mother said,

14

'but then I was never one for brains myself, for which I thank God.'

'You have brains enough, mother; you have simply not put them to use, and whether or not God would be pleased with that I cannot say.'

'Impertinence,' her Mother said, glaring at her warningly. 'If God had meant women to use their brains he would have made it apparent before now. None of *your* brainy friends that I know of, my dear, are yet married, and my notion is that that is what God intended women for.'

'Oh Mother, you are being stuffy!' Estella took off her hat and ran her hands lightly but expertly over her coiffure, to be sure that none of her blond hairs was out of place. 'You know you are really rather proud of Lindsey, having a mathematician in the family and perhaps a lady doctor, one day!'

'Please don't emphasize the word *lady*,' Lindsey said with some asperity. 'Doctor is both male and female, unlike author or poet or . . .'

'Doctoress!' Estella giggled. 'That's the word. Doctoress.'

'It does not exist, I assure you.'

Wykeham gazed thoughtfully at the tea he was stirring and then his eyes slid towards Lindsey. He was a tall, taciturn young man with the face of a scholar and the somewhat rapt air of an academic. In fact he was a partner in his family's long-established tea business in the city of London. At one time they had owned vast estates in Ceylon and India, but now they were mainly importers and blenders, though Wykeham had spent several years in the Far East learning the business.

'If Lindsey wishes to study, she must,' he said. 'We can finish our game another time.'

'I hope you and Rayner will stay for dinner,' Minnie fanned her face with a podgy white hand. 'Certainly let

15

Lindsey read her books if she wishes, but there is no need for you to go.'

'Mother, you take Lindsey's place,' Estella jumped up, putting on her hat again and securing it at the back with a large pin. 'It will give you an appetite for dinner.'

'Actually I told my family I'd be home.' Rayner produced his watch from his hip pocket and studied it. 'May we not continue the game another day?'

'Oh, I thought we were going to read.' Estella pouted at him, one arm still raised behind her head. 'You said you would read me your new play.'

Rayner's dark cheeks were suddenly suffused with blood and he lowered his eyes.

'Estella, you know . . .'

'Oh I shouldn't have said.' She put her hand to her mouth in an artificial gesture of remorse because her eyes were laughing.

'Rayner's written a play?' Edmund Abercrombie looked up, brushing away the crumbs that had fallen onto his lap.

'Rayner's written a lot of plays.' Estella lowered her hand from her mouth. 'He has shown one to Mr Jerome!'

'And what did that fellow say?'

'You don't like Mr Jerome, sir?' Rayner turned swiftly and stared at his host.

'He is a socialist! I don't know about his criticism of plays, but I don't care for his socialistic views.'

Vincent Jerome was a critic in the local paper, but his influence extended much farther than Highgate. He was an Irishman; a flamboyant, loudly dressed mustachioed character who drank a good deal and was renowned, or rather notorious, for his unorthodox lifestyle and unconventional views.

Rayner found him not only amusing but a fundamentally serious person whose opinions he respected. Jerome often attended the Highgate Amateurs where he massacred Shakespeare's blank verse in a loud exaggeratedly Irish brogue that was greatly deplored by the purists and stylists among the participants.

'Father is a staunch supporter of Mr Gladstone,' Lindsey said gravely. 'That is as far as his liberalism goes.'

'Who thankfully has just been returned to govern us. No, I consider myself an enlightened man; but I do not approve of socialism. Anyone who remembers 1848 as well as I do would be a fool if he did. I hope you are not a socialist, Rayner.'

Edmund looked severely at the young man he had come to regard as a protégé. Edmund had a large library and Rayner made free use of it.

'I do not know what I am, truthfully, Mr Abercrombie.' Rayner got up and smoothed a lock of dark hair away from his brow. 'I am more interested in poetry and the arts than politics; but Mr Jerome is a polymath. He makes everything sound so interesting.'

'He hates Irving so I hate Jerome,' Estella said heatedly.

'That is very unfair,' Rayner's rebuke was delivered mildly. 'He criticizes Irving from a purely professional point of view because he thinks he is a ham. He thinks . . .'

'He is the finest actor in the world,' Estella stamped her foot. 'For Mr Jerome to say he is a ham means he has no judgment.'

'I think Jerome has very good judgment.' Rayner began to struggle into his coat. 'I find him sound in most things. He deserves to be far more widely known than he is. He thinks much current, successful drama is balderdash, and so do I.'

'I don't think I care to read your play in that case.'

'I don't think you will have the chance!'

Rayner's complexion had turned pale and his dark eyes sparkled with anger. He went over to Estella's parents and shook hands, then he bowed towards the company.

I wish you would stay . . .' Minnie gestured rather helplessly. 'If Estella has offended you . . .'

'Mrs Abercrombie, I did promise my parents I would dine with them, It has nothing to do with Estella or her amateurish views. Thank you for a lovely tea and please excuse me.'

'Do come again, dear boy,' Edmund called as he began to cross the lawn to a side gate at the far end of the garden which led onto the street. 'Come again very soon.'

Estella stood watching Rayner, her body quivering, her chin slightly puckered and her eyes very bright. All trace of the smile on her face was gone. She took off her hat again and dashed it to the ground.

'There! Thank goodness he's gone. What an idiot he is!'

'Estella!' Her father looked up.

'I mean it,' Estella cried stamping her foot and inadvertently crushing her straw hat. 'Idiot, idiot, idiot!'

As Rayner paused and then turned to stare at her she ran into the house, leaving the crumpled straw hat, with its gay blue bows, ruined for ever on the ground.

Lindsey sat at the window of her room and looked out over the garden, or what she could see of it in the dusk. The dew was beginning to fall and a very slight breeze disturbed the chintz curtains of her room. As she had come up the stairs from the garden she could hear Estella sobbing in her room, but she passed straight by along the corridor into her own. She had no mind to spend an hour or more listening to the woes of her hot-headed sister when she had a strenuous course of study to get through before entering the London School of Medicine for Women in October. For enter it she would, though her father had yet to give his permission. Her mother, she knew, opposed her and her father would make some token of resistance; but eventually he would agree, as he had agreed to let her go to Cambridge three years before at the entreaty of Miss

Buss, the headmistress of her school. If necessary she would solicit Miss Buss's support again and that of Miss Emily Davies, the head of her Cambridge college and old friend of Mrs Garrett Anderson who had pioneered the way for women to study medicine in England.

Lindsey knew very clearly what she wanted from life and she always had. She was quiet, restrained and avoided argument and polemics. She was no show-off like her sister. She got what she wanted by tenacity rather than words. Her very pertinacity seemed to preclude argument, certainly heated argument of the kind Estella loved to indulge in. Estella had now gone too far on the lawn and she knew it. She wanted to attract Rayner Brook when, in fact, she was doing all she could to antagonize him, however unwittingly. To call him an idiot in front of Wykeham St Clair and her parents made one wonder whether Rayner would ever call at the house again.

It was of little moment to Lindsey whether he did or not. She loved her sister but they shared few things in common; there were five years between them and at their ages it was a big gap and always had been. Whereas Lindsey considered everything beforehand and made a plan, Estella always acted on impulse and relied on her charm and beauty to see her through. Invariably she was successful in a way that Lindsey thought wasn't very fair. She was always thoughtful and controlled, taking care not to offend people; yet she was not loved in the way Estella was, certainly not by her parents, not even by her father whom she so resembled in temperament. Estella was petted and adored. In fact Rayner would call at the house again because he was plainly as mesmerized by Estella as everyone else. And this was not the first tiff they'd had, though probably the most serious, as her parents had been present. Even at school, where the only thing she excelled in was theatricals, Estella was worshipped and admired, encouraging young girls to have crushes on her and

19

cheerfully aping her seniors and peers. Lindsey got through because of her character and intellect, Estella solely through personality.

There was a knock at the door and Lindsey put her book on her lap and rubbed her eyes; she realized she could scarcely see. She called, 'Come in', and then got up to light the lamp that stood on the table in the centre of her room. The handle turned and Wykeham put his head round the door.

'I wondered if you would like a stroll before dinner?'

'Come in,' she said again, going to the door and throwing it wide. 'I thought you were my sister.'

Wykeham still stood on the threshold, his head nearly touching the top of the doorway.

'I don't think I should . . .' he looked nervously at her.

'Oh, don't be silly. I'm sure I shall come to no harm with you.'

'I told your father I would ask you for a walk, not that I would go into your bedroom.'

'It is my study too,' Lindsey gestured around. 'See, my table and books. You may leave the door open if you wish, then I can scream if you touch me.'

'Oh Lindsey . . .'

Wykeham smiled but entered diffidently while Lindsey went over to the table and finished lighting the lamp. turning up the wick so that the pleasant room was softly illuminated. Then she shut the window to keep out the insects that were sure to be attracted by the light. Wykeham stood watching her, the graceful way she moved, the firm purposeful set of her head. Everything she did was decisive and controlled, a woman who knew what she was doing. He was aware of her small neat bed in the corner of the room, almost invisible beyond the gleaming pool of yellow light in the centre of the room. He felt very nervous and, picking up one of the books on the small table by her chair, flicked through it.

20

'*Diseases of the Blood*, so you *were* studying.'

'Of course, what did you think?'

Lindsey, noticing the half-open door with a slight smile on her face, pointed to the chair on the far side of the table.

'I thought that maybe it was an excuse.'

'Why should I make excuses?'

'Why indeed?' Wykeham appeared nonplussed and sat down, balancing his tall body on the edge of the chair. 'Won't you come for a stroll?'

Lindsey looked towards the window beyond which she could see nothing, now that the light inside had made it seem darker without.

'I think it's too cold. Besides, I have to change. I'm sorry if I embarrassed you by asking you into my room, but I feel I know you so well that it doesn't seem indecorous. If you like to wait downstairs I'll join you soon. Is my sister downstairs?'

'She is talking to your mother in the drawing-room. I think your mother is telling her off. I was with your father in the library.'

'Estella makes such a fool of herself. She's always making scenes.'

'She is impulsive, very young.' Wykeham made a gesture of dismissal as though enough had been said about Estella. Lindsey could sense he was nervous and wondered why. Was her bedroom so daunting? She had been mistaken to ask him in. Sometimes she felt she took Wykeham too much for granted.

'I'll just change and then I'll be down directly. If you like to go back to Father . . .'

'No. I . . .' Wykeham swallowed and clenched his hands impulsively in front of him. Then he got up awkwardly and stood facing her. 'I came to talk to you. I wanted to talk to you privately.'

'Then we can talk here.' Lindsey sat down on the chair

21

and stared up at him, her mouth half open, her eyes enquiring. 'Is it something about you?'

'It's something about us.'

Wykeham felt very tall and awkward standing over the seated girl. It was not quite the situation he'd intended – something more like a seat in the garden, or the path through the coppice that led, through a gate in the wooden fence, to Highgate Wood.

'Us?' Lindsey put a finger to her mouth and involuntarily glanced towards the half open door.

'I wondered if you'd become engaged to me?' Wykeham straightened his back and looked towards the back of the room over Lindsey's head. He could see nothing. Indeed he was aware of very little besides himself and Lindsey, here in the room where the bed was; such a personal, intimate place despite what she said about its being her study too. 'No, please don't say anything yet. I know you want to study medicine and I would never stand in your way. We could even be married while you were studying if it was your wish; it would be mine, but I would not insist upon it. I thought the best thing would be for us to become engaged and then . . . if you wish . . . when you wish . . . ' He trailed off and looked at her helplessly.

'*Engaged?*' Lindsey appeared to have difficulty understanding what he was saying

'Had you never realized I loved you, Lindsey?' To her embarrassment Wykeham sank to one knee so that his face was just below hers. She saw that his forehead was bathed in perspiration and his body trembled. His face was aesthetic rather than handsome, pleasing nevertheless with grey eyes set wide apart, a long sculptured nose and a thin rather bloodless mouth which seldom smiled. His fair hair was parted at the side and curled towards the whiskers on his cheeks.

'Loved me?' Lindsey repeated his words as if in wonderment. 'I knew you liked me.'

22

'Love, I love you,' Wykeham said more firmly as though his confidence were flowing back, the confidence of a man of the world of thirty, partner in the family tea business. 'I have loved you for a long time, since before you went to Cambridge, since I came back from India and met you for the first time.'

'You loved me for that long? I must have been eighteen.'

'Yes, you were. You had just left school. I would have asked you then, but knew that while at Cambridge you would not, possibly could not . . .'

'Oh I couldn't entertain the idea of *marriage* even now,' Lindsey said almost with amusement at the idea, although conscious of the pressure he was under, alarmed at the nervous working of his mobile features. 'I want to be a doctor . . .'

'I know that. I told your father so. I said I knew you were determined on it, whatever he says or thinks. I have made enquiries, Lindsey,' his tone quickened breathlessly, 'and some of the women medical students are married. They are accepted at the school. One I knew in India. Mrs Scharlieb. She has two children and is married to a barrister.'

'You've spoken to my father?' Lindsey suddenly felt agitated and sank back in her chair. 'Oh Wykeham, do please get up. You look slightly ridiculous in that position. I feel very embarrassed.'

'So do I.'

Wykeham rose clumsily to his feet, brushing the knees of his trousers. He looked behind him and pulled the chair over so that he sat opposite Lindsey but nearer her, only a foot or two away. He kept glancing towards the open door and lowered his voice. 'I didn't mean to talk to your father before I had spoken to you, except that he has observed my agitation if you did not.'

'I thought I was more observant. I must be stupid; but I saw you as a friend, a very good friend, Wykeham.'

'Only as a friend.' He did not ask a question but seemed

23

to repeat her statement in a flat, rather hopeless voice. 'There is no question then that you return my feelings?'

'None at all, I'm afraid. Oh, I'm sorry.' As he half rose Lindsey stretched a hand towards him. 'Please don't go. I'm terribly sorry to put you in this predicament, but I had no idea. You see my thoughts were not directed at all towards marriage.'

'I can see that.' Wykeham gazed at her bitterly, his hands loosely entwined. 'I had hoped that you liked me enough.'

'I like you very well, you know that; but as a friend, almost a brother. You are here so often that you are almost like one of the family. You know we had a brother, Fred, who died when he was born. He was between Estella and me. I think my parents have always missed him and that's why they encourage young men to call. Father likes having them around to remind him of what Fred might have been. To be frank, I thought you most enjoyed the company of my father!'

She began to laugh but the anguished look on his face made her stop abruptly.

'Yes, I like him very much. We have a lot in common; but to come to see him . . . oh no. It is always you I have come to see Lindsey. I love you and I admire you. The world comes alive for me when I'm near you. I thought when you came down from Cambridge; the pressure of study off your mind . . . Why, you are twenty-two.'

'Very old, I know,' Lindsey said drily.

'No, not old. But many girls, women, do think of marriage at about this time.'

'According to my mother they should all *be* married long before this time.'

'Oh I don't subscribe to that view. I think a woman who is more mature is more interesting. Maybe if I left you to think about what I've said, you might come round to the idea? I can see now that it was quite unexpected and I apologize for being so abrupt. I hoped that you might have concealed your feelings for me under your natural reserve. I see I was mistaken.'

Lindsey studied her hands, aware that they too were shaking, that her composure was deserting her. She liked Wykeham too much to wound him, and somehow it was awful to humiliate a man.

'I'm afraid you were, Wykeham,' she said gently. 'I have never given marriage to you, or anyone, a thought. And I would never come round to the idea, I assure you, as long as my medical studies occupy my mind.'

'But that is for four years!'

Lindsey nodded and, getting up, went again to the lamp, making pretence of trimming the wick.

'At *least* four years. I think you would do well to marry someone else.'

She carefully did not look at him, but was aware that he had risen and stood behind her.

'I would never think of marrying anyone but you.' His voice had broken and she was afraid to look at him.

'It cannot be.'

'Never?'

'Not as far as I can tell. I think if I were to have loved you I would have that feeling now. I don't really know what love is, but I don't think that it's the same emotion I feel for you. I like you. I respect you. I . . .'

She heard Wykeham gulp and when she turned he was walking slowly towards the door. She wanted to stop him and apologize for hurting him because she liked him so much and did not want to lose a friend. When he reached the door and faced her she could see by his demeanour that he had himself very firmly under control.

'Please forgive me, Lindsey, for upsetting you.'

'I assure you I'm not upset,' she moved towards him, a hand extended, wondering how she could feel so calm. 'I'm honoured, very flattered you asked me. Please let us continue to be friends. Now, if you'll excuse me I'll change and see you at dinner. We can forget, if you like, that this conversation ever took place.'

'If you don't mind, Lindsey, I'll make my excuses to your mother. I don't feel I should dine here tonight.'

Wykeham gave a stiff, formal little bow and, withdrawing, shut the door firmly behind him before she could utter another word.

Dinner was a very solemn meal, a large part of it consumed in silence. When Mrs Abercrombie had learned what had happened she had had to sit down and be revived with a stiff brandy. Dinner was, accordingly, half an hour late and cook sent in her apologies because of the overdone beef. The champagne that Edmund had intended to be drunk with the meal was returned to the cellar unopened.

Estella's face still bore the trace of the tears she had shed an hour or two before, but not on account of her sister.

Lindsey had hardly spoken at all and found that her appetite had gone. The interview in the library with her father had been painful. Wykeham had briefly apprised him of what had happened and, sending his apologies to Mrs Abercrombie, had forthwith quit the house. Her father had come upstairs to confront her and, learning that she was dressing, had demanded her presence in the library. There he had told her what he thought of her attitude towards a man who was not only cultured and pleasant tempered, all in fact he could wish for in a son-in-law, but wealthy as well. When Lindsey said she had not meant to be a drain on her father he had replied that he was not talking about money now, but her eventual situation in life. Had she expected Wykeham to wait for her for ever?'

No, she replied, she had and did not. She did not love

26

him, much as she liked him. Moreover, she did not think she would ever wish to marry him. Her father then told her she was a fool and undeserving of either Wykeham's love or his. At that point dinner was announced, very late, by a red-faced Jenny, who had received a sound scolding for all the misdemeanours which, in her erstwhile sunny mood, her mistress had overlooked in the course of the day.

'I thought it was going to be such a happy day,' Minnie said tremulously as the sweet was served, 'and it has been a disaster.'

'No, not a disaster, Mother. Just not the way you intended. I had no idea anyone wished me to marry Wykeham St Clair.'

'You must be very obtuse then,' Estella broke in. 'I have known about it for *years*.'

'But you never said.'

'And you never asked!' Her sister, her nerves still frayed, snapped back. 'Your head in books the whole time. I think you would be very lucky. He is said to have five thousand a year.'

'More,' her father interjected morosely. 'He was good enough to give me a complete account of his finances. Enough for a town house and one in the country. And he was willing to let Lindsey continue her medical studies. Though I can't say for how long because, of course, there would be children.'

'Two coaches doubtless, one for town and one in the country.' Minnie raised a grief-stricken face to the ceiling.

'And a butler . . . ' Estella began to laugh, until her father thumped the table and quelled her with a ferocious look.

'This is no laughing matter, my girl. *You* behave appallingly towards Rayner Brook, and your sister turns down the best offer of marriage she is ever likely to get. I agree with your mother. It has indeed been a disastrous day.' Edmund poured a fresh glass of claret and half emptied it at a gulp.

'You hoped to have us both off your hands, Father, and now you have neither.' Lindsey looked at him, her lids half lowered over eyes which smouldered with resentment. In this year, 1880, she was apparently still regarded by her parents as some sort of chattel to be bartered for by the highest bidder. She felt disappointed in her father, whom she had always considered a most enlightened man.

'I find you impertinent, miss!'

'It was not my intention to be impertinent, Father, merely truthful.'

'Of course I did not wish to have you both off my hands! That is nonsense. I like Wykeham and desire only your happiness. Estella is far too young, so there was no question of her going, but she not only annoyed Rayner Brook; she was rude to him. To call out after a young man that he is an idiot in front of her parents, her sister and a male guest is the height of bad manners. I doubt we shall see him again unless Estella apologizes.'

'I will not apologize. He is an idiot. There, I've said it again. An idiot!'

'Estella! Go to your room.'

Lindsey gazed with concern at her father, who leaned over the table in an attitude that seemed a harbinger of apoplexy, his face red and his chest heaving with the exertion of breathing.

'Father . . .'

'GO TO YOUR ROOM!'

Estella got up and, with her sweeping walk, strode out of the room banging the door behind her so that the glasses and silver on the table danced.

'Really!' Minnie mopped her face with her napkin and passed her glass to her husband. 'Pray give me some claret, Edmund. Never did I think that such a beautiful day would end like this. My daughters are hopeless, quite hopeless. To think you could be married,' she gazed soulfully at Lindsey, 'why, in a very short time, if you had wished. There was nothing to stand in your way. And to what a man – a decent, good man who loved you and would have let you go on with this foolish notion you have about doctoring. That just shows how decent he is, and how he must love you, for few other men I know would have done as much. Even if he was humouring you it was nice of him. You could have had the status of a married woman with your own house, nay *houses*, and servants if what your father says is right. For status is what marriage is all about, my girl. A single woman has no status at all, as one might have thought you would have discovered by now. You are all set to be a spinster, Lindsey, a charge on your father for the rest of your life. Wykeham is very well thought of in the City, a member of the Court of Common Council, maybe one day Lord Mayor, head of the family firm. What is more, he is nice and he loves you. What else can you ask for?'

'To love *him*, Mother.'

Lindsey, not put off by her sister's abrupt exit and the disapproval of her parents, nevertheless felt that the ground was shifting under her. Women of her kind were trying to change things, but her mother was right; unmarried they still enjoyed little status. All the powerful women in the women's movement were married – Mrs Fawcett, Mrs Bodichon, Lady Amberly. Mrs Garrett Anderson was married, and a mother and a doctor to boot.

But Lindsey had never sought status, only personal satisfaction. The excitement of study, of the fresh acquisition of knowledge, far outweighed any temporary kudos she might have had from marriage, especially to a man she did not love, for whom she felt only liking and no attraction at all. She knew nothing about the physical side of marriage, had scarcely ever given it a thought, but she

29

did not think she would even like to touch Wykeham or be touched by him. She was not drawn to him in that way at all.

But ahead of her were years as a spinster, the unmarried daughter at home. At least four more years. Could she endure it, knowing now what her parents felt about her, that she had disgraced herself and let them down? How long had they known about Wykeham's intentions, and why had they not warned her? She realized how free her camaraderie with him had been, how open to misinterpretation.

Suddenly the happy ambience of her home seemed to have changed and grown a cold, hostile place. The eyes of her parents bore down on her accusingly, without love, without forgiveness. Could that past mood ever return again, now that she, now that they, knew the truth?

Putting her napkin in its ring she drew her chair back from the table and got up, smoothing down the front of her hastily donned dress.

'Pray excuse me, Mother, Father,' she inclined her head towards them, 'and forgive me, if you can, because I cannot help myself or be anything other than what I am.'

CHAPTER TWO

BENEDICK: Do not you love me?

BEATRICE: Why, no, no more than reason.

BENEDICK: Why then, your uncle, and the Prince, and Claudio
Have been deceived – they swore you did.

BEATRICE: Do not you love me?

BENEDICK: Troth, no, no more than reason.

BEATRICE: Why then, my cousin, Margaret, and Ursula
Are much deceived; for they did swear you did.

BENEDICK: They swore that you were almost sick for me.

BEATRICE: They swore that you were well-nigh dead for me.

Beatrice and Benedick continue to deny their love until exposed by the evidence of Claudio and Hero. Whereupon Benedick stretches out his hand towards Beatrice:

BENEDICK: Come, I will have thee, but by this light, I take thee for pity.

BEATRICE: I would not deny you, but by this good day I yield upon great persuasion, and partly to save your life, for I was told you were in a consumption.

For a moment she looks tauntingly at Benedick, who, unable to restrain his passion any longer, seizes her hand.

BENEDICK: Peace! I will stop your mouth.

31

Rayner Brook drew Estella to within an inch of his face, puckering his lips in a kiss. Then, letting her go, but still holding her hand, he concluded the reading with Claudio and Leontes:

Strike up, pipers!

called Benedick, lifting his hand, still entwined with that of Beatrice, high above his head.

The small audience sitting on chairs grouped around the makeshift stage at the end of the hall clapped vigorously.

'Bravo!' cried one.

'Bravo, bravo!' echoed the others.

'That was *wonderful*.' Rayner, his face flushed with excitement, breathing fast, looked into Estella's eyes; then he squeezed her hand. 'You were excellent.' He held her hand a moment longer, and, for that lingering moment, they were unaware of anyone else in the hall, their eyes locked. Then abruptly Rayner dropped her hand and turned quickly away. The play was over.

Estella's hand still burned from the firm clasp of Rayner's fingers. Her heart still beating rapidly, she tried to compose herself, turning to smile at the rest of the players clustering round them and then to the audience composed of members of the cast who had finished reading their roles, and friends who had come along to listen. There was a general scraping back of chairs and audience and players mingled, congratulating one another.

A corpulent Leontes mopped his brow, Claudio went to pour water from a jug on a nearby table and Hero threw her arms around Beatrice.

'You are made for Beatrice, Estella. And Rayner you *are* Benedick! Is he not the perfect Benedick, Arthur?'

Leontes, his face still running with perspiration, despite the administrations of his handkerchief, nodded vigorously.

'Excellent; they were both excellent. Edward, could we all have some water please?'

Claudio emptied the contents of the jug into the remaining glasses and the players gathered round the table. Rayner emptied his glass then held up his hand. No one took any notice because they were all busy in the task of mutual congratulation, so, finally, he clapped, and then he jumped on a chair and held up his hands again.

'Could we have silence for a few moments, everybody?'

The chattering ceased and one or two sat down again. There were about fifteen people altogether in the hall as some had doubled up in parts, approximately equal numbers of men and women. 'I just want to thank you all for attending this afternoon. I think it was a very good reading, and you all, *all* entered into the spirit of the thing.' Rayner looked at a piece of paper he had taken from his pocket. 'I want to tell you that our next reading will be *A Midsummer Night's Dream* in about a fortnight's time. I've made a suggested list of parts that I'll pin up on the board and you can consult it before you go; some of the readers are not here today and I'll let them know, if you agree. If anyone is unhappy with their part please tell me. I shall be Oberon. I think we should vary the leads so that everyone has an equal chance to shine. Now, if anyone cares to come back to my house for refreshments you're very welcome. I think you all know where it is, a short walk up the hill.' He jumped off the chair and went to pin the piece of paper he had in his hand on the noticeboard by the door at the end of the hall.

The Highgate Amateurs were a group who met at irregular intervals to read plays, discuss the theatre and, from time to time, put on a performance. There were also regular outings to the theatre, and various London managers, including Irving and Bancroft, let them have special seats for any performance they wished to see. Rayner had been a leading light of the Amateurs since he'd come down from Oxford, but Estella had only started attending in the autumn and Beatrice was her first leading role. Her last had been Jessica in *The Merchant* and, before that, one of the three witches in *Macbeth*. The members were told their parts in advance, which gave them the chance to study the text before they gave dramatic readings like today, standing up and making what actions they could despite the fact that they had to carry the text in their hands. Estella had been almost word perfect for Beatrice, having shut herself in her room studying the part for some hours every day. Beatrice to Rayner's Benedick was an opportunity she felt she could not miss, and she had made the most of it.

Shakespeare's play about the lovers who tried to disguise their feelings for each other beneath a mound of badinage and playful misunderstandings seemed to her to reflect something of the relationship between herself and Rayner, which, too, was partly serious and partly teasing. She had scarcely consulted her words at all during the performance and had thrown herself into her role with passion and conviction. She did not mind a small part in *The Dream*, because to her Beatrice she had given everything.

As it was she was to play Helena. She stood behind Rayner as he pinned the notice on the board but he had told her her part beforehand. There weren't any really good parts for women in *The Dream*, but she saw that Hannah Everest, who had played Hero, was Titania. There was something in Hannah's manner towards Rayner that disturbed Estella, made her feel that in her she had a rival.

She couldn't exactly pin down why she felt this about Hannah, who was a rather self-effacing creature who only came alive when she performed. She knew that a woman attracted to a man often saw rivals where there were none. The Everests were a solidly respectable Highgate family,

34

and Hannah, who was nineteen, was studying at Queen's College in Harley Street to be a teacher. Her mother was a widow and, although the family was not poor, she expected her three daughters to find gainful employment rather than be mere adornments to the house.

Hannah Everest was dark and petite with smooth hair parted in the middle, drawn back in a bun in a rather old-fashioned style. Her face had an almost tubercular pallor, her features were regular but unremarkable except for a pair of large hazel eyes which seemed permanently half-concealed by lowered lids. The effect was thus to make her appear knowing and rather calculating; there was something stealthy, almost feline about her. She spoke very little but those percipient eyes were always on Rayner, and it did not surprise Estella to find her in the small party that climbed up the hill towards the Brook household for afternoon tea.

The readings were usually held on a Sunday afternoon between lunch and teatime because most of the men had occupations and a few of the women, like Hannah and her sisters Esme and Naomi, belonged to that new generation of women who studied. In all there were around seventy members of the Highgate Amateurs, about a third of whom regularly attended meetings or readings and rather more the outings to the theatre, the last of which had been to Irving's celebrated performance as Mathias in *The Bells*.

It was a cold, sunny winter's afternoon, a little snow lingering on the trees and in the hedgerows from the light fall there had been earlier that February, and Estella was glad she had brought her muff and wore thick stockings and high laced boots beneath her red velvet dress.

Arthur Finch, who had played Leontes, and his wife came with them. Eliza Finch, pregnant with her fifth child, had read the part of Margaret; but when she was not pregnant she was slim and statuesque and excelled at theatricals, playing the part of Portia on the stage in the spring production of *The Merchant* before Estella had joined the group. Edward Guthrie who had played Claudio came too, an elegant, dandyish young man who was an Oxford contemporary of Rayner's, and there were five others, another married couple, the Osbornes, and two women and a man. The female sex predominated in the Amateurs, which was a pity, because good female parts were hard to find except in Shakespeare. Although Shakespeare was read more than any other playwright they also occasionally performed modern works by Tom Taylor, Dion Boucicault, H. J. Jones and the popular Frenchman Victorien Sardou – which more or less reflected what was going on on the London stage, where a mixture of high comedy and melodrama predominated.

The Brook residence was a low-lying house approached by a long drive and surrounded by trees. In winter, when they were bare, the house had a good view of Hampstead Heath, but in the summer it could not even be seen from the road. William Brook, Rayner's father, was a prominent physician, a consultant in illnesses of the heart and chest at the Middlesex Hospital, and his mother wrote light novels that enjoyed a wide readership. Rayner had two sisters, one of whom was married and the other still at home, and an elder brother who was also a doctor in America. His mother herself opened the door to welcome the party, standing back as they trooped into the hall and greeting them one by one.

'I was watching out for you! I didn't want you to stand too long in the cold. Isn't it bitter?' She shuddered and rubbed her hands together, evincing the right amount of imagination required of a lady novelist, because it was very warm indoors. There was a large fire in the hall and two in the drawing-room into which she led her guests, one at each end of the long pleasant room that stretched from the front of the house to the back. Rayner's mother

36

was tall and slim, still a beauty in her fifties, very fashion-conscious so that even when she stayed quietly at home working on her latest book she was beautifully dressed. From her it was easy to see where Rayner got his colouring. Her hair was jet black and she had a long aquiline nose, and flashing brown eyes that hinted at a passionate, if not tempestuous, nature. Some people thought she was artificial because she was always smiling, but this seemed to indicate a serenity of temperament rather than dissimulation.

'How was the reading, Rayner darling?'

'It was more like a *performance*, Mother. Estella was word perfect and hardly needed to read her part. Consequently she was all the more convincing.'

Two servants stood by the door waiting to collect the cloaks, coats, bonnets and muffs that were handed to them, and as soon as these were taken away a butler entered carrying a large silver teapot, and behind him were two maids bearing trays. In the centre of the room a large table was already set with sandwiches, cakes, jellies and jugs of cordial.

'Estella really was the star,' Arthur Finch said, after making sure that his pregnant wife was comfortably seated. 'I thought she was remarkable. She is lost to the real stage.'

'But why is she lost?' Mrs Brook said with surprise. 'She is very young yet and, with her beauty, I wonder she has *not* already considered the professional stage.'

'Oh I could never think of that,' Estella suppressed a nervous laugh. 'I am not nearly good enough.'

'Rayner says you are very good. He has spoken to me about you before.'

Rayner, the perfect host, was making sure that his guests had what they required and seemed not to be listening to the conversation behind him, but suddenly he turned and gazed at his Beatrice. 'I think Estella is a natural actress and I've always thought so – both in real life and on the stage.'

The blood rushed to Estella's cheeks and she clasped them between her still cold hands.

'What do you mean by that, Rayner Brook?'

'You see?' He looked at his mother and then at the company. 'She immediately flares up into a tizz. She has all the temperament of an actress.'

'I don't think I find that very complimentary.' Estella accepted with dignity a plate of sandwiches from Henry Custoe, one of the other bachelors in the cast, who had played Don Pedro. 'Thank you, Mr Custoe.'

'Well, it was meant to be, I'm sure, dear.' Mrs Brook, still smiling, bent over Estella, pretending to soothe her. As she stooped there was a delicious fragrance of perfume, and Estella could see the faint traces of powder on her soft cheeks. 'You must know Rayner by now; he likes getting a rise. And how are your dear mother and father?'

'Very well thank you.'

'And Lindsey? Is she still at her medical studies?'

'Oh yes, she is and enjoying them very much. My mother, however, is not yet reconciled to the idea and makes life hard for my sister, though I suppose I shouldn't say it.'

Rayner raised his eyes heavenwards and shook his head, as though silently accusing her of another indiscretion; some further lapse of good manners like losing one's temper or immoderate laughter.

'Well *I'm* not sure that I would like to have a daughter of *mine* pursuing such a career, much as I admire it, and my husband certainly wouldn't approve of it.'

'Father opposed Mrs Anderson, or Miss Garrett as she then was, being a student at the Middlesex. He was one of a number of students who signed a petition to have her removed which was successful. I can't say I regard his

38

action as something of which we have any reason to be proud.' Rayner appeared anxious to disown his parent.

'I must say I would not like to be attended by a woman, however well qualified.' Eliza Finch screwed up her nose and shook her head with evident revulsion at the unnaturalness of such an idea. 'I do not consider the practice of medicine a suitable occupation for those of our sex.'

'I think that's very narrow minded.' Rayner turned his back on her, scanning the table for food while her husband flushed and put an arm protectively around her shoulder.

'Eliza thinks . . . '

'It *is* very naughty of Rayner to speak like that.' Mrs Brook looked reprovingly at her son's back. 'But Rayner is a law to himself. When I have him and my husband in the house together there is an argument all the time. I suppose it is a matter of different generations. I must say the whole problem of women's emancipation is fraught with dissension and thus something which I consider best avoided.' She raised her head and surveyed the company.

'Very clear sighted of you, Mama.' Rayner's tone was sarcastic, but Madeleine Harper, who had merely listened to the reading, as she always did, without hope of a part because she had a stammer and a nervous tic by her left eye, quickly intervened.

'I agree with your mother, Rayner. At least in present company. Could we not discuss instead the idea of putting on a performance of your play for our spring production?' To make up for her physical and emotional disabilities poor Madeleine excelled at making costumes.

'You are to produce one of *Rayner's* plays?' His mother opened her eyes wide with surprise. 'Is the committee agreed?'

'The committee has not been asked,' Rayner replied tensely. 'It is merely an *idea*, Mama. Besides, the committee is really all here and we can discuss it now.'

39

'What a wonderful idea to do one of your plays.' Estella gazed at him with surprise. 'Why have we not heard about it before?'

'I've only discussed with a few people,' Rayner said offhandedly. 'It's a vague idea.'

'I thought it was agreed.' Hannah Everest perched comfortably, but diffidently, her skirt modestly concealing her ankles, on a large cushion by the fire. 'All those I've spoken to think it's an excellent idea.'

'So do I,' Estella said stoutly. 'Though I haven't read it. Have you read it, Hannah?'

'Oh yes. It's marvellous. It has a really great part for a woman.'

'What is it called?' Estella's tone was artificially gay.

'*Who Can Tell?* I mean, that's the name of the play. It really means "who can tell what is in a woman's mind?" Am I right, Rayner?'

'Or, "who can tell about anything?"' Rayner said shrugging his shoulders, an angry frown creasing his brow. 'There's meant to be a play on words.'

'This woman has a conflict between marriage and a career.'

'Oh?' Estella's mouth rounded into an enquiry. 'Is it based on anyone you know?'

'Not at all. She chooses to do charitable work rather than marry the man her parents want her to marry.'

'It is a very modern play,' Hannah insisted, and suddenly Estella felt positive dislike for this quiet, insinuating little black cat sitting on the cushion by the hearth. One could almost hear her purr, such was the satisfaction in her voice, the possessiveness in her eyes, as she looked at Rayner. Despite Hannah's timidity, her lack of beauty, she saw in her personality a real and powerful rival for the man whose affections she so coveted.

'You're very honoured to have read it, Hannah.' Mrs Brook wagged a finger playfully at her son. 'Rayner is so secretive; he doesn't even show his work to his mother. One would have thought he would have valued my professional advice.'

'Rayner was good enough to show it to me because he said he respected my judgment.' Hannah's voice, wishing to offend neither mother nor son, had assumed an obsequious drone.

'So! Does he not respect his mother's?'

'I *do* value your criticism, Mother; but I can't tell you why I couldn't show you my play. Maybe you are too professional, or too close to me. I don't know. Anyway, you will have the chance to find out if it is performed, because we shall all read it together first. I'm having copies made now. Could we change the subject? What with women doctors and my play we seem unable to agree on anything this afternoon.'

'Hasn't the weather been *cold*?' Madeleine Harper said helpfully.

Lindsey crept into Estella's bedroom and stood by the sobbing figure on the bed. It was nearly two in the morning and at first she hadn't known what had woken her up. It had been a very still night and she had lain on her back listening, until she realized the sounds did not come from some bird or animal outside but from her sister's bedroom along the corridor.

Estella was lying on her stomach with her face pressed to the pillow. A low light burned by the side of her bed. She had not even undressed and still wore the red velvet dress she'd only bought the previous week. Lindsey sat on the edge of the bed and put her hand on her sister's shoulder.

'Estella, what is it? Are you ill?'

Estella shook her head and hugged the pillow with her arms.

'You'll wake Mama and Papa.'

41

'Did I wake you?' Estella raised her head and looked at Lindsey with dismay.

'Of course you woke me! I thought it was some animal in pain outside. You'll wake the household if you go on like this. And why are you not undressed?'

'I just fell onto the bed, I was so miserable.'

Estella reluctantly swung her legs over the side and Lindsey was shocked by her appearance; her cheeks were swollen and red and her eyes so puffed up that she looked as though she had a fever.

'But what is the matter?'

'It's nothing.' She vigorously rubbed her eyes with her crumpled handkerchief. Lindsey could see it was soaking wet and useless. Calmly she went to one of the drawers in Estella's dressing table and, getting a clean handkerchief, handed it to her.

'You can't possibly say it's nothing! I never saw you so upset. Is it by any chance Rayner Brook?' Estella flung herself on her back at the name and let out another howl, but this time with dry eyes. Lindsey rapidly began to think of the notes she had taken for the treatment of hysteria. She spoke very rapidly. 'I thought as much. You were in such a temper when you came home. Even Mama commented on your mood. Why do you throw yourself at him if he doesn't want you?'

'I *don't* throw myself at him!' Estella propped herself up and banged a fist into her bed. 'Why do you think he comes here so often?'

'To see Father.' Lindsey lowered her voice, looking nervously at the door. 'They have a lot in common. Yet you are for ever hanging around hoping to see him too. It's so obvious.'

'I tried to show him I was sorry for calling him an idiot in the summer.'

'Well, you showed him; no need to go on doing it, debasing yourself in front of him.'

42

'Did I do that? I never debased myself. I feel I've behaved with dignity. Can I help it if what I feel for him is not returned?'

'No; but you should keep out of his way if you can't control your emotions better than this. You will make yourself ill.'

Estella blew her nose on the fresh handkerchief and glared at her sister. Then she sat up on the bed and fumbled with her hair, as though it were important to keep up appearances even in front of Lindsey.

'I think Rayner *is* attracted to me but will not admit it. He cast me as Beatrice and we were perfectly suited, him playing Benedick. Everyone commented on it, the *rapport* we shared and I *felt* during the performance. Then at the end he grasped my hand and held onto it. Something, I cannot say what it was, but some strong emotion passed between us and I think he has been concealing his affection for me, as Beatrice concealed hers from Benedick. You *know* when you are attracted to someone and he to you. I know I am not deceived. Even the way he avoids me convinces me he feels more than mere friendship for me.'

'But why should he hide it?'

'Because he is confused. He is a rebel. Maybe he is afraid of emotion. He argued with everyone at his home this afternoon; whatever anyone said he said the opposite. The only one he agreed with was a horrible, crawling, snivelling little creature whom he has let read his play.' Estella gave a loud groan again and the omnipresent tears poured down her cheeks. 'He has let *her* read his play and I have so wanted to. He agreed with everything she said and kept on smiling at her. Yet she is not even attractive. She's *very* plain. In fact I think she's ugly.'

'Maybe she has a nice nature.' Lindsey smiled to herself.

'She has a *horrible* nature! She's mean and grasping and

43

sly, like a cat. You never know what's going on in her mind. I hate her. I hate him!'

'I think you should give up the theatricals for a while. Maybe he *is* playing with you. Perhaps Father could speak to him and ask him not to come here so often.'

'No! You must never mention this to Father. I would be too humiliated. I can't give up the theatricals because I love them. Also,' Estella, more in control, dabbed at her eyes. 'I must go on seeing Rayner. I can't help myself. I hope, anyway, that he will cast me as the lead in his play. Whatever his feelings towards me, everyone says I'm the best actress in the whole group. And I am. I know it. When I'm reading a part I feel, so changed, Lindsey. I feel I'm not myself, but the character I'm playing. Today I *was* Beatrice.'

'I think it has upset you.' Lindsey got up and pulled her robe round her, shivering. Estella had let the fire in her room go out and it was very cold. 'Please go to bed and try and get warm, or you'll be ill, staying all night in your dress in this unheated room. I wish I could help you about Rayner Brook, but I don't know what to do.'

'It's because you have never felt passion that you don't know what to do. You are too cold, Lindsey, too unemotional. No wonder you decided to do something as unwomanly as medicine.'

'If that's all the thanks I get for trying to help you,' Lindsey shrugged, 'I might as well go back to my room. Medicine is not the least bit unwomanly, and, furthermore, I do not lack passion, I assure you; but you, you give way to it too easily. Do you know how many times you lose your temper in a week? How much you put this household at odds by your wilfulness, your desire to have your own way, your tantrums? You are not only an actress when you read your roles, Estella, you're always acting a part. Life *is* the stage for you.'

Estella flounced off the bed and began to unfasten her

dress, tugging impatiently at the many velvet-covered buttons which fastened her bodice. She unpinned her hair and flung it over her shoulders, peering in the mirror at her ravaged face in the dim light from the lamp.

'My goodness I do look terrible.' She dabbed some witchhazel on her face from a bottle on the dressing table and, as though her strength were restored, again faced her sister. 'You're the one who's being catty now, Lindsey. You can't think what to say so you give vent to spite. You know I'm very close to Mama, much closer than you. She can't understand you, she says, the way you refuse a nice man like Wykeham St Clair and study something disgusting like medicine. She says you will be an old maid.'

Lindsey tried to turn up the wick in the lamp, but it was short of oil and the light grew even dimmer. 'I know she thinks that,' she said reflectively, 'and I don't care. Isn't it terrible how one's parents consider spinsterhood such an awful fate? Is marriage so marvellous? Miss Nightingale is not married.'

Estella snorted. 'Who wants to be like *her*?'

'She has changed the whole approach to nursing in this country. Her achievements are quite remarkable. Many fine women have remained unmarried to devote themselves to causes.'

Estella was reminded painfully of the subject of Rayner's play. She didn't know why, now, she'd spent so many hours weeping on her bed. The fact that he hadn't let her read the play was wounding, but that didn't mean he didn't intend the main role for her. He was sure to. Who else could play it? Many of the women were married or quite old, and the younger ones plain like Hannah and poor little Madeleine Harper who couldn't say boo to a goose. They would be unthinkable in the leading role. Compared to all these people her talents were considerable; she knew it and Rayner Brook knew it too. She finished undressing and then pulled her long warm flannel nightgown over her head.

'*I* wouldn't like to remain unmarried.'

'I don't expect you will; though I hope whoever marries you realizes what he's in for.'

'Oh, a fine thing to say!' Estella jumped between the sheets and glared at her sister. 'As long as I'm not like *you* I daresay I'll pass. You've become so unfeeling and unkind in these last few months, Lindsey, that I think you're warped. You *are* spinsterish already. You care only for yourself, not about how our parents feel, and yet you pretend to care for others. I pity your patients! You'll become a martinet and they will not dare *not* to get well!'

As Lindsey stormed out of the room without glancing back Estella pulled the bedclothes right over her head and started to giggle, her good humour unexpectedly restored.

In the days that followed the scene between the two girls Edmund Abercrombie, who knew nothing of it, could not fathom what had become of his daughters. Estella's behaviour was characterized by unpredictable moods that swung like a pendulum between elation and melancholy. She dragged her mother on innumerable shopping sprees to purchase clothes that she – already having an extensive wardrobe – did not need. She had teaparties for mere acquaintances as well as her many friends, girls with whom she had been at school and who were now, like her, waiting to be married, few having chosen a career like Lindsey unless they were driven to it by parental need, however delicately concealed. Alternating with these bursts of frenetic activity were periods when she incarcerated herself in her room, reading those works of Shakespeare in which she hoped one day to play leading parts until she almost seemed to become the characters themselves – a distracted Ophelia, a vengeful Lady Macbeth or an aloof and gracious Portia – in her real life as well as in the world of her imagination.

It was very trying for her parents, who also considered the behaviour of their elder daughter to be more disturbing than usual.

Lindsey left the house earlier than ever to attend the medical school and often did not return until dark. Then she would closet herself with her books in the library or her bedroom until it was time for bed. The two girls seemed to go to considerable lengths to avoid each other's company.

In Minnie's opinion Estella's conduct was partly explicable by her age, whereas Lindsey's was definitely eccentric; the unnatural strain of her studies was clearly affecting her health.

'Lindsey should be married,' she said one morning at breakfast. 'She could be Mrs Wykeham St Clair by now, and, maybe, expecting a child.'

Edmund pretended amusement and shook the pages of the morning paper to the arts page. He was a tall, thin man with the lofty brow and bald pate of a thinker. What hair he had left, once fair but now grey, curled round the back of his head into luxuriant sidewhiskers on his cheeks. He had clear blue eyes like his daughters, a broad chiselled nose and a humorous mouth. Edmund had always enjoyed life – his family, his friends and his books – and it showed by the benignity of his countenance.

'So soon?' he gazed at her over his reading glasses.

Minnie spread butter thickly on her toast and covered it with strawberry jam. Although she had enjoyed a good figure as a young woman she liked her food too much to have kept it. She was plump rather than stout and kept her figure rigidly in control with the aid of a good corsetière. She had thick auburn hair, which was still a lovely colour, beautifully coiffeured, and blue-green eyes which, though

47

often petulant, were seldom solemn. She accepted the fact that both her daughters had inherited their father's looks.

'Why not?' she said. 'He proposed to her in July. That is nearly nine months ago; enough time to get to the altar and conceive without it seeming in any way indecorous. I tell you, Edmund, no good can come of women who defy the laws of nature.'

'I daresay this will all happen to her in good time, my dear; you fuss about it too much. But what is wrong with Estella? *That* scarcely explains her behaviour.'

'Estella is at a difficult age,' her mother said sagaciously. 'She is like me and I know her very well. Unlike her sister she would like to be married and I know to whom. She is head over heels in love with Rayner Brook.'

'Rayner Brook?'

'Of course, who else? Are you blind? Does he not haunt the house? He comes to see her, but he will not declare himself. The indecision on his part is affecting her poor nerves which, like mine, have never been strong. She is too volatile for her own good. Marriage will *soon* settle her.' Minnie pursed her mouth firmly.

Edmund put down his paper and removed his gold reading spectacles. It amused Edmund the way marriage seemed, to his wife, a panacea for all ills, bodily and mental. Himself, he had noticed no improvement in her own unpredictable temperament after she'd married him. If anything, freed from the restraining influence of a severe father, she was worse.

'And would you *like* him for a son-in-law? He is a very complex young man.'

'He may be complex but he is charming and I can see why he appeals to her. In a way they are alike. They are so goodlooking and both so keen on theatricals; besides, he is of such very good family, professional people. Could you not talk to him, Edmund? Maybe the thought that we might oppose the match prevents him from declaring himself. Though I don't know why he might think we should.'

'Certainly not,' Edmund said firmly. 'Besides, I'm not at all sure you're right. His mind seems to be taken up with his play. He hopes to have it performed this spring. I have a notion that matrimony is very far from his thoughts.'

'Then *why* does he come here such a lot?' Minnie's tone was aggrieved.

'Because of my extensive collection of annotated editions of Shakespeare. He prepares for his readings very carefully. He selects the plays to read and then studies them as well as he can. At the moment it is *A Midsummer Night's Dream*. Besides, he finds this house conducive to study. His mother writes books and would monopolize his time at home. He confided as much to me.'

Minnie looked out onto the lawn from the breakfast room and considered Rayner Brook as a prospect for her daughter. He was good-looking in an unpredictable way, being not too tall, and thick-set, the build of an athlete. She knew that, besides the theatre, he was addicted to sports and she approved of this, thinking that it gave a man a proper outlet for his physical energies. Rayner liked riding, boxing, and had played cricket for Oxford. She could see why her daughter found him attractive with his black wavy hair that always looked rather tangled and his slightly swarthy complexion. The predominant features of an altogether handsome face were his well-set eyes, the colour of rich brown velvet. He had a large, rather hooked nose and, had she not known the impeccable Aryan ancestry of the Brook family, she would have thought he had Jewish blood. He was decidedly Byronic and dressed with a casual, Bohemian elegance. He wore clothes well, but one had the feeling that he had the suitable masculine attribute of not paying too much attention to them. One did not want a dandy for a son-in-law. She could sense that, one day, Rayner Brook might well be famous. He had the air of a celebrity about him, and that appealed to her too. It would be nice to think of Estella gracing as hostess the salon of a famous man.

'Rayner Brook is coming through the garden gate now,' she cried. 'I thought it was an apparition because I was just thinking of him.'

And, true, the young man occupying her thoughts was sauntering down the path from the entrance to the woods which he nearly always used, because it was the nearest way to and from his house. His hands were thrust deeply into the pockets of his greatcoat and he appeared lost in thought. As he disappeared around the corner of the house Minnie jumped up leaving her breakfast unfinished on the table, cramming a final piece of toast into her mouth.

'What an early hour to call!' she consulted the watch that hung on a chain round her neck. 'It is just past nine.'

'Oh, he said he'd be here early.' Edmund drained the coffee in his cup. 'It is something he is doing on *The Dream*.'

'He looks in a dream already.' Minnie loudly rang the bell and then hurried into the hall to receive their guest.

Rayner, still preoccupied, apologized for the hour of his call but Minnie told him he was expected and ushered him into the library, fussing about to be sure he was comfortable and had what he wanted.

'Please don't put yourself out, Mrs Abercrombie.' He went immediately to one of the shelves lining the wall, obviously familiar with its contents as he ran his finger along the titles. 'I know exactly what I want.'

'My husband said you did. I'll leave you then. Is there anything else you require?'

'Nothing at all, I assure you,' he gave her his grave, thoughtful smile that she found quite melting, and drew out a volume which he took to the large polished table in the centre of the pleasant, sun-filled room. 'What a lovely day it is.'

He gazed through the window. 'I detect signs of spring already. Is Lindsey at school?'

'Oh yes, she left early. She has her first lecture at nine.'

'Ah.'

Sitting down he opened the book before him and nodded at Minnie, not rudely, but brusquely enough for her to interpret the gesture as one of dismissal. What a curious man he was, to be sure, she thought as she tiptoed from the room, closing the door gently behind her. She noticed he did not enquire after her younger daughter.

Estella, having breakfasted in her room, did not get down until nearly eleven. She had been memorizing the part of Helena in bed and always took a long time over her morning toilet. The house was very quiet, the servants having already done their work, and bowls of fresh flowers were reflected in the polished woodwork of the hall. Estella had on her cloak, ready to take a walk, and she opened the library door to tell her father where she was going. Rayner still sat in rapt concentration over his book, occasionally making notes on a pad, and Estella, seeing him, felt her heart leap with delighted shock.

'Oh Rayner! Is Papa not here?'

'Your father has gone into town.' Rayner looked up, smiling. 'I believe he took your mama in the carriage to make some purchases.'

'I was just going for a walk.'

'Yes, it's a beautiful day. I was saying to your mother that it is quite like spring.'

'I don't suppose it interests you to take a walk?' Estella ventured nervously farther into the room. 'Just for a half hour or so?'

'Alas. I am making some notes interpreting *The Dream*. How are you getting on with your part?'

'I nearly know it by heart. I declare there is a lot more in the play than one realizes at first.'

'Indeed that's true.' Rayner sat back and folded his arms. 'Shakespeare was so profound in whatever he did, even his comedies. The rustics in *The Dream* are comparable, are they not, to those in *Much Ado*?'

'Yes, except that Dogberry is more amusing than Bottom.'

'Shakespeare's minor characters are really of importance,' Rayner said, bending forward eagerly. 'He sometimes gives as much weight to the humble as to the great. That's where his genius lies.'

He had on a blue velvet jacket and a high-necked soft shirt with a blue cravat loosely tied under the collar. His hair was tousled as though he had frequently run his hands through it in the course of his reading, and his eyes looked heavy with lack of sleep.

'You look very tired,' Estella remarked. 'Maybe a little walk would perk you up?'

'I have too much to do, Estella, but thank you for asking me. You take a walk as the air today is too good to be missed. I was up most of the night on my play. We start rehearsals quite soon. I had to correct the parts which I had had copied.'

'Oh, is it ready? How exciting.'

Estella immediately slipped off her cloak and sat in a chair opposite him, her back to the sun, her hands firmly clasped with excitement in front of her. 'I can't *wait* to read it Rayner. When do we begin rehearsing?'

She noticed that he flushed because previously his face had been so pale, deep lines of fatigue etched down either side of his mouth.

'Well, rehearsals will begin in a . . . week or so, I dare say. I don't know exactly.'

As he stumbled for words she felt a little chill in her heart as though it had been touched by a cold hand.

'Have you cast the play yet, Rayner?'

'Yes . . . yes I have.' He did not look at her

'And is there a part for me?'

'Estella.' Rayner cleared his throat and sat sideways in his chair, crossing his legs. 'I'm afraid not this time. You are, you know, a very new member of the Amateurs. I didn't think it fair . . . '

'Not think it fair?' she said hotly. 'Are parts awarded on merit or because of long service? It seems a very curious thing to say I am too new. It may seem vain to say it, but everyone tells me I am the best actress you've got. Do I have to wait until I have grey hairs to get a part, for I have a lot of time to catch up on. Some have been members for years. If so all the youthful leads will escape me.'

'It is not *that*, Estella . . . ' Rayner squirmed uncomfortably.

'What is it then, Rayner Brook? You do not want me in your play, is that it? It has nothing at all to do with merit or long service. You simply do not wish it. Is that not more like the truth, Rayner?'

'Indeed it is not. It is simply that,' he passed a hand wearily across his brow, 'there's no part *suitable* for you. My heroine Elizabeth is . . . not suited to your nature. It is true you are a very fine actress; but no actress, however fine, can play every part and you are not my idea of my heroine.'

'Who is then?' She got up, rescuing her cloak and pulling it tight about her shoulders and, as Rayner did not answer, she flung back her head and raised her voice. 'Is it by any chance *Hannah Everest* who is the *ideal* for your part? Is she the *ideal* woman you had in mind?'

'Not ideal.' Rayner crossed and uncrossed his legs. 'Not ideal at all; but yes, since you ask, she is very well suited and I have, as a matter of fact, cast her as Elizabeth.'

'That noble soul who sacrifices all for the cause of serving humanity.' Estella joined her hands as if in prayer and her voice throbbed with scorn. 'You have not the courage to admit that you wrote it for her, have you, Rayner Brook? That you had her in mind all the time?'

'I did not write it for her,' he said indignantly. 'I assure you I had no one in mind.'

'Oh yes you did. Do you think I haven't seen the way she worms herself into your affections, trying, by her air of charming, simpering diffidence, to gain your sympathy and attention. Do you think I have not noticed her cunning when . . .'

'Estella!' Rayner rose magisterially to his feet. 'Please control yourself. My relationship to Miss Everest is entirely proper. In fact there is no relationship, merely a very good working agreement. It is true she is not at all like you. She is a quiet, intense woman and not nearly such an accomplished actress, but, after I had written the part, not before, she did seem to me to embody just those attributes that I was looking for in my heroine.'

'That self-sacrificing, self-effacing, noble creature . . .'

'Yes. Exactly.'

'She can't even *act*.' Estella spat out the words. 'She is pathetic; a little schoolteacher which is what she is and always will be. She hasn't a crumb of talent. How you *could* prefer her to me . . .'

'It is nothing to do with preferment. Miss Everest was cast purely on merit, on suitability. Now you're being hysterical, Estella. You are far too intemperate in your emotions; you must control yourself better.'

'Like Miss Everest.' Estella, dropping her voice, mimicked Hannah's high, rather timid tone, at the same time linking her hands demurely in front of her and lowering her head. In fact for a moment she almost resembled Hannah, despite their disparate looks, and Rayner laughed outright.

'You do her very well. You have caught her expression exactly. But you are unfair to her, Estella; you know she's transformed when she takes part in a reading, and she *is* exactly right for my part.'

'You like these women, don't you, Rayner?' Estella whispered sarcastically. 'These docile, modest women who seek only to do good, like my sister and Miss Everest. There is something in them that attracts you, is there not? Or is it the fact that you can dominate them that pleases you so much? That they have nothing for you but unstinted admiration, almost hero-worship?'

'That is certainly not true of Lindsey!' Rayner exploded. 'There is nothing docile about her. You make a caricature of them. You are too vicious, Estella. But, yes, if you like I do admire women who seek to do something with their lives. It doesn't mean that I'm attached to them emotionally or that I wish to dominate them.'

'You don't realize what you're doing, that's why. Or perhaps you do. You bask in their admiration, poor little creatures being warmed by the sun.'

'Estella, you're making this far too personal.' Rayner paced agitatedly to the fire and back. 'You're going to spoil our friendship if you go on like this. I know you have a volatile nature, but . . . '

'But what?'

'You're overreaching yourself, making yourself ridiculous. You're revealing too much of your own feelings for me, which, I must say, I've suspected. There, I've said it.'

As he stopped pacing, he gazed at her and she immediately drew her cloak tightly round her slim body and stared at him.

'Is that something to be ashamed of? Although you are for the emancipation of women, Mr Brook, you do not think this applies to matters of the heart, is that it? A woman must wait until the man speaks first. Is that what you really think?'

'Yes, it is,' Rayner began to bluster. 'I mean, no it isn't. I believe in equality between the sexes but there is a

55

certain decorum. There has to be. I'm sorry if I led you to think that I had stronger feelings for you than I have. I do like you very much, and I think you are a fine actress. But nothing could be farther from my thoughts than marriage.'

'Marriage?' Estella said haughtily. '*Who* is talking about marriage? You presume too much if you think I want to marry you.'

'But I thought you said, or admitted, that you were attracted . . .'

'I? I admitted no such thing. You accused me of showing feelings for you which, in fact, I do not have. But I said *if* it were the fact I had them, which I deny, should I, as a woman, be ashamed of them? It was merely hypothetical.'

'I'm glad of that.' Rayner looked confused and exhaled loudly as he spoke.

'Quite hypothetical, I assure you. I have no more feeling for you than I have for the cat.' Estella paused and put a finger to her chin. 'In fact, I think I prefer the cat, or maybe I don't, seeing she resembles a little too much that dear Miss Hannah Everest whose own devious, feline nature has not escaped me. I wish you joy with your play, Rayner Brook, and I herewith resign from the Highgate Amateurs. Obviously they have no need of my minuscule talents, since they are held in such little regard. Furthermore, I hope you and I can have as little to do with each other in the future as is humanly possible.'

'But, Estella, that's ridiculous. You *are* being theatrical now. You're making a mountain out of a molehill.'

'Is it? Am I? I think not. One thing I wanted in all my life, Rayner Brook, was to act a good part on a live stage. The chance came and you did not give it to me. When will I get such a chance again?'

'Maybe next year, who knows?' Rayner shrugged offhandedly. 'I shall write more plays if this is a success.'

'I can't wait until next year. I'm not going to waste my time and talents away dancing in the shadow of feeble people like Hannah Everest, Madeleine Harper, Eliza Finch and their like. Apart from yourself, and perhaps Arthur Finch and one or two others, I am the only person in the Highgate Amateurs who has any idea of acting. I have it instinctively whereas I know that, however long they try, they will never acquire it. I know now that you wish to lord it over them all. You do not want opposition. You resented my Beatrice being as good, maybe better, than your Benedick! I will never get a part written for me by you. Never.'

'That is not . . . '

Rayner rushed forward, a hand raised almost as though he would strike her. She caught the hand and held it firmly in her strong young fingers. Momentarily she was reminded of that day they acted together; but how different now. Instead of love, waves of hate seemed to emanate from her, and she would have crushed his fingers between her own had she the strength.

'You are selfish, arrogant and . . . stupid, Rayner Brook,' she burst out. 'Stupid, stupid, stupid.' She dashed his hand against his side and rushed headlong from the room, cannoning into her mother, who, having returned from town and hearing raised voices, had come to see the cause of all the commotion.

'Dear me,' Minnie said, her plump hand fluttering against her well-upholstered bosom. 'What was that all about?'

'I'm damned if I know.' Rayner Brook thrust the book he had been reading into its place on the shelf. Then he gathered up his papers and stuffed them agitatedly in his pockets. 'If you ask me, Mrs Abercrombie, you have a madwoman for a daughter,' and roughly, almost rudely, he swept past Minnie, shouting over his shoulder, 'and I wish you good day!'

CHAPTER THREE

Lindsey's fingers were so cold that, despite warm mittens covering the upper part of her hand, she could no longer hold her scalpel. Even the cadaver seemed frozen and it was with difficulty that she prised the hard flesh away from the bones to expose the main arteries of the arm that she was studying. Finally she put down her scalpel and covered the half-dissected corpse, as though anxious to protect it too from the cold.

The year before, thick snow had covered the ground, and the pipes in the school had frozen for weeks at a time. The students had gathered snow from the lawn outside and boiled it over an open fire to provide water for scrubbing their hands and washing down the dissecting tables after use. This year there was no snow but it was very bleak and, at just after three, the light had nearly gone and the yellow glow from the lamps cast long sepulchral shadows on the walls, outlining the ghoulish remains of the half-dismembered cadavers.

'I think we have done for today. Apart from my frozen fingers I can hardly see anything.'

Her companion working on the table next to her agreed. 'Anyway it is nearly time for tea; thank goodness for that, for I'm starving too.'

Sarah Upchurch raised her head from a close perusal of the cavity in the abdomen of a young child who had died of tuberculosis and gently covered it, tucking in the edges of the calico as though it had been a warm, living infant.

'Poor thing,' she said, 'it was quite healthy otherwise. The mother had the disease too.'

'Mine died of a tumour so large,' Lindsey said enthusiastically, 'that Mrs Anderson is going to present it to the museum.'

The girls went over to the large stone sink and began vigorously to wash their hands, chatting about their findings in their respective corpses with the animation of young girls discussing the latest fashion or a particularly engrossing novel from the circulating library. Then, taking their cloaks from hooks on the wall, they extinguished the lamps and went along to the sitting-room where Miss Heaton, the Assistant Secretary of the School, always presided at tea.

There were few students there that cold day in January 1882. The Christmas holidays were just over and one or two had not yet returned; others were working at the hospital in Gray's Inn Road, some were attending lectures at other colleges of London University, and some of the senior students had leave of absence to study for exams. Miss Heaton was already pouring tea when Lindsey and Sarah entered and, putting their cloaks to one side, went immediately to the fire and warmed their hands.

'I wondered where you were, Lindsey and Sarah.' Miss Heaton smiled in their direction. 'It is not like you to be late for tea.'

'I poked my head round the door of the long room and saw them hard at work.' Mrs Scharlieb, sitting with a plate in her lap and a teacup in her hand on a long low chair near the fire, looked at them approvingly. 'I wonder you were able to see anything. I like to see young students so engrossed.'

Lindsey's face lit up with pleasure at the compliment. Mrs Scharlieb, already a qualified medical practitioner when she joined the School, was one of its most brilliant students. She had lived in India with her husband, who was a practising barrister and her two children, but the sufferings of the Indian women denied male medical help by the strict laws of purdah had proved too much for her

Christian conscience. She had taken the Indian Medical Practitioner's certificate in Madras and returned to London with her children to study for the medical degrees that London University had only recently, and after years of struggle, opened to women.

'You promised you would help us with dissection of uterine and ovarian tissue, Mrs Scharlieb.'

'And so I shall, Miss Abercrombie, as soon as my children return to school. Alas, my days are very hectic until then.'

As though reminding herself of her duties, Mrs Scharlieb finished her tea, got to her feet and hurried out of the room, watched by the admiring eyes of Miss Heaton, who sighed as soon as she had closed the door.

'The dedication of that woman! It is so remarkable, especially in view of her poor health and the fact that her son too has recently been so ill. They despaired of his life.'

'Mrs Anderson says she has the makings of a brilliant doctor.' Lindsey selected a piece of rich cherry cake and put it eagerly to her mouth. The blood had already reached her fingers and was beginning to return to her face. 'She says she already surpasses her in surgery.'

'Mrs Anderson is very generous with her praise; her admiration for Mrs Scharlieb exceeds her judgment.'

Lindsey thoughtfully finished her cake without looking at the speaker who sat in a far corner of the room turning over the pages of a magazine. Then she brushed her fingers and reached for another piece of cake.

'May I, Miss Heaton? Mrs Stubbins makes awfully good cherry cake, better than that of our cook!'

'Of course you may, dear. Mrs Stubbins will be most delighted to hear it. Such praise does not come lightly from you!'

Lindsey looked at the critic of Mrs Scharlieb and went over and sat beside her.

'I don't know why you don't like Mrs Scharlieb, Miss von Harden. She admires you.'

'I don't dislike her at all!' Charlotte von Harden protested indignantly. 'But how could she possibly be as good a surgeon as Mrs Anderson who has had so much more experience?'

'Mrs Anderson is so very *kind*,' Miss Heaton said soothingly. 'She wants to encourage Mrs Scharlieb all she can because she has sacrificed a lot to come here and is, as you observe, not strong. She had to leave India partly for reasons of health. She is a very admirable woman but, despite her sacrifice and her dedication, she does have instinctive and natural talent for her work, especially in obstetrics, as you know I think, Lindsey.'

'It was because of the suffering of Indian women in labour that she determined to become a doctor,' Lindsey said, finishing the second piece of cake with a gulp and looking as though she wondered if she dared ask for a third. 'So she has made midwifery her special subject. I have left the dissection of the uterus entirely until she can assist us. I respect her judgment enormously.'

Miss Heaton, pouring tea for another latecomer, reflected how extraordinary it was to hear genteel young women discussing subjects that a few years before would have been considered unmentionable. The London School of Medicine for Women was a mere eight years old, having been started by Sophia Jex-Blake and a small band of devoted women in the face of vigorous opposition in 1874. It was only since 1877 that the School had become viable, on its affiliation with the Royal Free Hospital in Gray's Inn Road, a short walk away. Then, in 1877, London University had at last admitted women to medical degrees and thus there was no longer any necessity for Englishwomen to go abroad to qualify as Mrs Garrett Anderson, Miss Jex-Blake and others had.

Now, in 1882, the School was on the verge of presenting

61

its first fully qualified women doctors and had close on forty students, studying for degrees of London University or the Irish College of Physicians.

What Miss Heaton knew and Lindsey did not was that Mrs Garrett Anderson had almost as high a regard for Lindsey as she had for Mrs Scharlieb and Miss Edith Shove. Because she had gained high honours in the Cambridge Tripos examinations – had in fact got her degree, though Cambridge refused to award them to women as such – it had not been necessary for her to take the Preliminary Scientific (MB) Examination of the University of London. As soon as she had been accepted as a student by the School Lindsey had applied herself to the study of anatomy, physiology and chemistry and, although there had been no examinations at the end of the first year, she was considered by her teachers the outstanding student of that year.

Yet she was a curious girl. Miss Heaton continued her silent rumination as the students gathered around the fire, chatted and finished their tea. Nothing very much seemed to move her; yet her very lack of temperament was considered an outstanding asset. She was not squeamish in confrontation either with corpses or the diseases of live patients; she was meticulous and diligent in her work and kept long hours, often staying in the dissecting room until late at night. She was always one of the first to arrive in the morning and during holidays was apt to appear at the School to work with specimens in the museum or in the library. She was popular with the girls yet she had no especially close friend, and Miss Heaton had formed the impression that she was someone who did not give her affections easily and also that she was not very happy at home.

'How is your sister, Lindsey?' she said during a lull in the conversation. 'The one on the stage?'

'Oh she's very well,' Lindsey interrupted an energetic

discussion, still presumably about Mrs Scharlieb, with Charlotte. 'We saw her briefly at Christmas, but she was appearing in pantomime in Bolton and had to hurry north.'

'*Pantomime.*' Miss Heaton exaggerated the word. 'I thought she was a serious actress?'

'She *aspires* to be a serious actress certainly, Miss Heaton, but parts are not easy to come by. So far she has achieved no leading role on the legitimate stage, nor any chance of acceptance by a stock company. She takes work when she can get it and, as she has a pleasing singing voice, is very well suited to pantomime and musical comedy though, of course, it is not at all what she wants to do.'

'If I were your mother I would be distraught.' Miss Heaton picked up some sewing to calm her agitation.

'My mother *is* distraught, Miss Heaton. Coming so soon after my own defection to medicine it was almost more than she could take. As I supported my sister she now finds favour with neither of us; we are both disgraced.'

'And your dear father . . . ' Miss Heaton snipped at a piece of cotton, smiling to one or two girls as they got up to leave the room.

'My dear father, alas, is resigned. I think he hoped that my sister at least would be conventional enough to stop at home and make a good match. He never dreamed that she would not only want to go on the stage but leave the nest as well. As least I go home every night, though I am not sure I am so welcome there.'

Lindsey sighed and Charlotte von Harden, still leafing through *The Ladies Journal*, looked at her with a quickened sympathy.

'I had no idea that you had such trouble with your parents, Miss Abercrombie. Do they both disapprove?'

'My mother mainly disapproves; but she is pleased with neither of us. My father is saddened by my sister's behaviour because what she did was in open defiance of them both.'

'And what did she do?' Charlotte drew her chair nearer.

'She ran away.'

'Ran away! Dear dear.' Miss Heaton raised her eyes to the ceiling of the beautiful Adam house in which the School was situated. 'You never told me *that*!'

'I didn't dare tell anyone at the time. Besides, I was too upset myself. I knew what my sister wanted to do and I supported her; but I did *not* encourage her to run away.'

'But where did she go?'

'Eventually to an aunt in Manchester; but she travelled by herself and was some days on the way, which greatly added to my parents' distress. Once there she refused to come home and my father went to see her. She would not listen to reason and when my aunt threatened to turn her out she said she would run away again. So finally he gave in. She was to lodge with my aunt and try and find work; but on condition that she always travelled with a maid and stayed in hotels, not cheap boarding houses. That, at least, she consented to do.'

'And when did this happen?' Charlotte leaned her chin on her wrist, wholly absorbed by Lindsey's tale.

'Nearly a year ago. My sister was disappointed in hopes for something on the amateur stage. A young man . . .' Lindsey paused and lowered her head, 'was also involved.' Seeing the expression on Miss Heaton's face, she hurried on. 'Oh, nothing *disreputable* I hasten to add; but she had certain expectations that were not fulfilled. He was a playwright and she hoped for a part in his play. The realization that he neither loved her nor valued her as an actress was almost too much for her; but out of that sprang a resolve to become a professional actress. She had already shown great aptitude for the stage. The rest is as I have told you.'

'How very singular.' Charlotte rose and put a large

lump of coal on the fire. 'I would like to meet your sister. She shows spirit, which I admire of all things in a woman.'

'They both show spirit.' Sarah Upchurch, who had been listening carefully, now intervened for the first time. 'It cannot be easy for Lindsey either.'

'When you have a vocation nothing else really matters,' Lindsey said, glancing at her watch. 'And now I feel I should stain some slides before I go home.'

She smiled and went out of the room, leaving the three women, now alone, looking after her.

'She is a truly admirable person.' Sarah spoke in a tone that bordered on hero-worship. 'I believe that her mother hardly ever speaks to her and that when the sister, Estella, came home for Christmas the mother would not address one word to her. It is a very unhappy situation. I don't know for how long she can support it.'

'I have this little house off Russell Square,' Charlotte von Harden said. 'I know my mother would be delighted if a companion could share it with me.'

'But where is your mother?' Lindsey, embarrassed and startled by the unexpected proposal, did not know how to answer.

'My mother and father live in Vienna. Did you not know that my father was Austrian?' Charlotte smiled and looked keenly at her companion as they made their way back to the School from a physics lecture at University College in Gower Street.

'Your name . . . ' Lindsey began but, truthfully, though she did not like to admit it, she took little interest in her fellow students or their lives. Her work had become her life and more so than ever since the unhappiness caused by Estella's abrupt departure. It had been a rather frightening experience, finding depths in a sister one had not hitherto suspected.

'I of course was educated in England, at Miss Beale's

school in Cheltenham; but I never dreamed I would come back here to study.'

'Why did you?'

'I felt my life was so empty. I was engaged to be married but soon realized I could not love the man concerned, though he was very kind.' Charlotte stopped as they passed the British Museum and turned into Russell Square. 'Look, my house is so near. Would you like to look at it?'

'Why not? Though I have not said "yes".'

Lindsey smiled and accompanied her companion along Museum Street until she stopped before the terraced house painted white with a shiny black door and a large brass knocker. Charlotte put a key in the lock and ushered Lindsey in. The house smelt of beeswax, and the scent of flowers, even in winter time, reminded her of home. It was a cared-for house, elegant and lived in. The drawing-room into which Charlotte led her was furnished in a style that immediately struck Lindsey as foreign, with pleasant, light sofas and chairs covered in velvet, and small ornate marquetry tables. The pattern of the wall-paper was a delicate motif of tiny leaves and buds and the floor was polished parquet with a tartan rug in the middle.

'You must get your flowers from the same hothouse as my mother,' Lindsey said, sniffing the blooms. 'They are not easy to come by in London in the winter.'

'I think it's somewhere in Hampstead so probably, yes; my housekeeper gets them.' Charlotte put her books on the table and unfastened her bonnet. Then she stooped and stoked the fire smouldering in a recently blackened grate, on which were a brightly burnished assortment of implements: shovel, poker and tongs hanging from a brass holder. Straightening up she said: 'There. Would you like some tea?'

'Thank you,' Lindsey said, taking a seat and looking round. 'It's a lovely room; very spacious.'

'This is all old Viennese furniture that my mother got tired of.'

'Did your father buy this house specially for you?'

'Oh no. He had it when he was a student in case, during the holidays from Oxford, he didn't want to go home. It has been in my family for years; but you can see I'm lonely here on my own. We have a lot in common, have we not? Do you think we'd suit?'

Charlotte von Harden, who was about twenty-six years old, was not beautiful but she had an interesting face. Her thick dark hair was always very carefully dressed as though with the assistance of a maid. Starting from a parting across the head it curled into a fringe on the forehead and at the back ended in a low chignon at the nape of her neck. She had strong features, a broad nose, a wide mouth and arresting grey eyes, and she was always smartly and fashionably dressed, which pleased Mrs Anderson, who liked her students not to forget that they were also women. Charlotte had come to the School at the same time as Lindsey, yet Lindsey felt she knew her less well than any of her fellow students; she had certainly hardly ever had a conversation with her apart from work, and now she was being invited to live with her.

She got up and restlessly crossed the room, staring out of the window which looked onto a small terraced court-yard showing, now, a wintry scene of ivy and brown clematis on the walls with majolica and terracotta pots of dead plants. In the centre was a tiny ornamental pond, in the middle of which was a statue of Cupid caught in perpetuity in the act of shooting an arrow from his bow.

'I don't know that I *should* leave home,' Lindsey said after a while. 'I don't know what my parents would say. After Estella . . . '

'But you're not leaving, are you? Merely lodging. You can go home whenever you like. It is simply so convenient being so near the school.'

Lindsey nodded. 'Yes, it *is* very convenient; also my father hates me coming home in the winter on my own. He is always out looking for me and worrying. Most days when I leave in the morning it is dark and also when I get home at night. But I should like to pay you, if we came to some arrangement. I wouldn't like it to be *gratis* and nor would my father.'

Charlotte vigorously shook her head. 'I'm afraid I couldn't hear of it, and nor would *my* father. I am not, after all, a boarding-house keeper. You would be our guest. You could make it up to me in other ways.'

'Oh?' Lindsey, feeling slightly startled, looked at her.

'We can work together. There are certain subjects in which you are so much better than I am, physics for instance. Wouldn't it be nicer to work here together in the evenings rather than in the cold library at the School?'

Lindsey returned to her seat. 'Yes, I would save time too. I waste hours travelling, because Highgate is a long way off. I will if you like put it to my father, but first you must meet him.'

In eighteen months at the School it was the first time Lindsey had brought a fellow student home. Edmund was delighted and Minnie not only consented to receive her, but to preside at the tea table. There Charlotte had to endure an almost unending monologue concerning Minnie's dissatisfaction with her daughters, the effect their behaviour had had on her health, the worry they had caused their father, the scandal they had created among their friends. But, worst of all: 'They have effectively broken up a happy home,' Minnie concluded sorrowfully, dabbing at her eye with a lace handkerchief which she procured from her heaving bosom.

For a moment there was silence during which the heavy ticking of the grandfather clock in the corner of the dining-room seemed not only to reverberate through the room, but to echo, if imagination permitted it, along the corridors of the large, sad house, empty now, through sheer wilfulness, of the sound of girlish laughter.

'My dear, you really do exaggerate,' Edmund said crossly, laying his napkin on the table. 'This must be very distressing for Miss von Harden.' He had made several attempts to stop his wife but to no avail.

Charlotte eyed her hostess, then, in an impulsive feminine gesture, reached along the table and patted her arm.

'I am sorry to hear of your distress, Mrs Abercrombie; but one day you will be proud of your daughters, maybe Lindsey most of all. She will be a brilliant doctor, an adornment to her profession.'

'I did not want my daughters to be brilliant,' Minnie said mournfully, momentarily pressing the pale, thin hand that lay comfortingly on her arm, 'merely happy women; good wives and mothers. Is this not what women are for? What need have they to compete with men?'

'They do not compete, Mrs Abercrombie, they merely complement. A woman doctor has a lot to offer her own sex. Do you not know that in India many women die rather than consult a male doctor? We also know that it is sometimes the case here. Women conceal serious symptoms because they do not like to be examined by men. Mrs Anderson's hospital in Marylebone Road is full of such patients, and they are the lucky ones because her hospital is only staffed by women.'

'It is true, Mother,' Lindsey said gently, though still angered and humiliated by her mother's outburst. 'Since she started her clinic for women in Seymour Place it has grown to the size of a moderately large hospital, and even now it is bursting at the seams and cannot treat all the patients who have recourse to it.'

'Well, I hope at least you will not go to India!'

'Of course I shan't, Mother, as long as there are sufferers here who need us. But many of our students are destined for India. Mrs Scharlieb will return as soon as she has qualified.'

'Women are on the advance everywhere, Mrs Abercrombie.' Charlotte, having established the rapport she desired, removed her hand. 'You cannot stem the flow. Do they not adorn the acting profession too? Think of the status of Madame Bernhardt and Miss Terry.'

'Pray do not mention those creatures with the immoral lives they lead.' Minnie poured more tea for herself, the teapot trembling in her hand. 'My daughter is already lost as far as I am concerned. For all I know she is one of them too.'

'Oh Mother!' Lindsey burst out. 'How little you know your daughter! To be an actress you do not need to lead an immoral life. Estella is as dedicated to her work as I am to mine.'

'Dedicated to the *pantomime*?' Minnie scoffed, her fine eyes scornful. 'What sort of vocation is *that*, pray?'

'She is merely gaining experience. Father says she has the offer now of a place in a touring company.'

'Why yes, I only heard today.' Edmund took a letter from the inside pocket of his coat, but Minnie waved it away with her hands. 'Pray do not read it again to me, Edmund. I already know the contents by heart.'

'Well, Lindsey and Miss von Harden do not.' Edmund put on his reading glasses and, shaking the letter open, read it aloud:

'Dearest Papa,
I have been interviewed by a Mr Thomas Shipley who has acted with Irving at the Lyceum and is desirous of forming his own company to tour the north of England. My name was mentioned to him by Hettie Leadbetter who recently played Lady Macbeth at the Palace Theatre in Manchester and is a friend of Aunt Catherine's. Mrs Leadbetter is also acquainted with Mr Irving and Miss Terry, through whom she knows Mr Shipley, and has seen me act in small roles.

70

Mr Shipley had me read Portia to him and also Lydia from *The Rivals*. He said he was much impressed and will be in touch with me.

Is not this wonderful news, Father? The pantomime comes to an end this month and I shall then be free for any new engagement.

Your very loving daughter,
Estella.

'There.' His eyes shining, Edmund removed his spectacles and tucked them neatly into their case. 'That is something, is it not?'

'I note she does not send her respects to her mother.' Minnie sniffed, averting her eyes from the sight of the offensive letter.

'She was doubtless in a hurry, my dear.'

'Nor does she mention me.' Lindsey rose to her feet. 'But I am not aggrieved! She is doubtless excited by this splendid prospect. May I ring for the maid to clear, Mother?' As Minnie nodded Lindsey sharply pulled the bellrope by the side of the mantelpiece and stood with her back to the fire. 'I think that is splendid news. Both Portia and Lydia are classical parts. Do you know anything of Mr Shipley, Father?'

Edmund shook his head. 'But Mrs Leadbetter I do know, a friend of your Aunt Catherine's. She has never acted on the London stage, but she is well known in the North of England where she resides with her husband and children. She is a most respectable woman. I have every confidence in her judgment; she would never recommend anyone unsuitable. Let us hope that things start to improve for our poor Estella,' he bowed his head, 'seeing that it is her wish and she will not change her mind. Now, Mrs Abercrombie, may we proceed into the drawing-room and discuss this matter raised by Miss von Harden?'

Minnie rose and, like a ship in full sail, made for the door which Edmund held open for her while, exchanging

71

excited, conspiratorial glances, Charlotte and Lindsey followed in her wake.

A maid had just drawn the curtains in the drawing-room and stoked the fire which burned invitingly, its flames leaping up the chimney. Edmund stood on the hearthrug while his wife went to her accustomed seat and Charlotte and Lindsey sat together on the sofa, their legs tucked under them like nervous schoolgirls. Charlotte was splendidly dressed in a dress of brown grosgrain with a close-fitting bodice and a skirt trimmed with ruffles and bows. The matching coat she had left in the hall together with her brown velvet hat, its flowerpot crown fashionably decked with ribbons and feather trimmings. She had made an immediately favourable impression on Lindsey's parents, particularly the susceptible Mrs Abercrombie, to whom she seemed the very quintessence of gentility.

Lindsey had told her parents of the suggestion the previous week and, expecting the usual storm from her mother, had been surprised to find her quite receptive to the idea, especially if she was to come home at the weekends. The news that Charlotte's father was an Austrian baron was not in his favour – Minnie was of the firm opinion that civilization ended at Dover – but at least he was not Jewish, his wife was an English gentlewoman and he was extraordinarily rich, having houses in Vienna, Paris and London and a *Schloss* in the Hartz mountains.

Charlotte had set out to charm her hostess, and had already achieved some success before tea was finished. Now, her eyes still travelling admiringly over the fashionable dress, Minnie said: 'You are not at all what I had in mind as a medical student, Miss von Harden. What brought you to this strange calling?'

Ignoring the jibe, Charlotte kept her voice low and pleasant. 'I felt the need to do something, Mrs Abercrombie, as Lindsey may already have explained. Women are

72

not so accepted in Vienna as they are here; our medical profession is even more rigid than yours. I was about to be married, but felt I could not go through with it.'

Minnie looked reproachfully at her daughter.

'Oh you too. No wonder you and Lindsey have so much in common.'

'Lindsey was engaged?' Charlotte stared at her companion, eyebrows raised.

Minnie sighed loudly and groped again for her handkerchief. 'Alas, not engaged; but an exceedingly nice man, well known to our family and liked by us, rich too, offered for her. She would not even entertain the idea. He was even willing to permit her to proceed with her medical studies. What more could one ask? He was so brokenhearted he went immediately to India and is still there, and that was eighteen months ago!'

'Oh dear.' Charlotte stifled a smile. 'How very dramatic. Alas, my case was more mundane, but still unfortunate. I had accepted the offer of this gentleman, who was not young, being nearly forty. He had been married and widowed and had two young children to whom I was devoted. He too was well known to my family and comfortably placed in life. I am very fond of children and we had grown close after the sudden death of his wife, who was a friend of mine. When, after a suitable lapse of time, he asked me to marry him, I accepted. But, as preparations for the wedding advanced, I realized it was his children I loved not him.'

'But surely that was enough? You *liked* him, did you not?'

'Oh yes,' Charlotte said quickly. 'And admired him. But,' she shrugged her expressive shoulders, 'but when I came to contemplate matrimony it did not seem sufficient. I cannot explain it exactly. So, the wedding was cancelled, the presents returned and my fiancé quickly married another lady because it seemed all he really wanted was a mother for his children. Meanwhile I returned to England, because my parents too were displeased with me – you see it is not you alone who suffer, dear Mrs Abercrombie. I had read about the setting up of the medical school for women and I began an intensive course of study, for I had to gain matriculation from London University and sit the preliminary exams before I could be accepted.'

Minnie gazed at the rings on her fingers and, once again, sighed loudly.

'Alas, I do not know what has happened to the young women of today. They are not like the youth of my generation. But,' she gave a tired, resigned smile, 'I suppose we must accept it.'

'Well spoken, my dear,' Edmund said cheerfully. 'Then I take it you have no objection if Lindsey lodges for a time with Miss von Harden?'

'I suppose not. What can I say? At least she will not have the tiring journey to and from the School with all its possible dangers in the dark.'

'And I will be home every weekend, Mama.'

'I do hope Miss von Harden will come and stay with us too.'

'I'd like that, Mrs Abercrombie. Please do call me Charlotte.' There was a note of exultation in Charlotte's voice. 'Now when may Lindsey come? I promise I'll take good care of her.'

Charlotte turned to her new friend and impulsively touched her hand. But Lindsey, still distressed by her mother's outburst at tea, sat gazing abstractedly into the fire.

Had they broken up a happy home? Would they ever regret it? Was she selfish? Did she and Estella, in fact, owe a particular duty to their parents for all they had done for them? She didn't know the answers.

But the sad face of her mother, who had always been so

74

cheerful, was a constant reminder of what she
sister had done. She would be glad to get away.

Suddenly she looked at Charlotte and, returning he
smile, gently clasped the hand that still lay on hers.

CHAPTER FOUR

The centre of the stage was littered with half packed prop baskets, and dismantled scenery stacked in the wings shook every time someone with an extra firm tread passed it.

'Careful,' Tom Shipley called cheerfully. 'We don't want to have to reconstruct Pompeii yet again.'

A stagehand righted the tilting painting of Vesuvius belching into a blood red sky and Gerald Saunders, who was the heaviest member of the cast, obligingly sat on top of a basket which Estella was desperately trying to fasten.

'There's too much in it.' She stepped back, panting from her exertions.

'You sit on it.' Gerald jumped up and, as he did, the top flew off and the costumes that had been imprisoned under his weight spilled out again onto the floor, with a jack-in-the-box effect.

Tom Shipley, still engaged in the wings securing the fragile panels of scenery, came abruptly back on the stage, his naturally pale face now red with anger.

'Can't you be more careful, Gerald? Do you think we have money to burn that you can be so careless with our properties?'

He picked up an armful of the clothes scattered on the floor and gazed contemptuously at Gerald and then at Estella, who had started to laugh as, unaware of his presence, she retrieved the lid, balancing it on her head as though it were a large coolie hat. Now she stared at him foolishly, both hands firmly securing the large lid on her head. Silently she lowered her hands, placing the lid on the floor at her feet.

'*You* think it's funny Estella, do you?' Roughly Tom threw the clothes on top of the lid. 'Well *I* consider this no laughing matter, I can tell you.'

'Tom we were only trying . . . ' Gerald began.

'You were larking about, both of you. I'm glad you find the whole thing so amusing. I find it sickening.'

Abashed, Estella meekly bent down quietly and began to gather up the scattered garments.

'Sorry Tom. We didn't mean . . . '

'Fooling! You were fooling about,' Tom shouted and, angrily seizing the clothes from her, thrust them into the basket. 'Either you take this matter seriously or you can go back to London, where you are doubtless accustomed to having maids perform such menial tasks for you!'

Gerald picked up the lid and began once more to try and fasten it on top of the by now bulging basket.

'Don't be unfair on Estella, Tom. I was to blame too. Estella works as hard as any of us. Harder.'

Tom's face paled again as quickly as it had flushed and he bent down to help Gerald secure the basket as Estella stood abjectly by.

'We can do it, Tom,' Gerald said gently, and Tom, as a stage hand called to him, backed away and wiped his face with a large grubby handkerchief.

'Well, I'll leave you to it then.' His tone was conciliatory and he put his handkerchief back in his pocket, looking at Estella.

'Sorry about that, Estella. I know you work as hard as any of us. It's just that,' he gesticulated vaguely around the disordered stage, 'it's just that there is so much to do, so little time to get everything ready. Sorry if I was harsh.'

He smiled at her and Estella, blushing, quickly touched her hair, untidied by its encounter with the basket lid, and passed her hand down her skirt as though involuntarily grooming herself for him. Tom was respected by all his players, liked by most of them, adored by one or two of

77

them – including perhaps herself. After all, had he not given her, an untried player, her chance? On the whole he was fair, didn't bear grudges and worked twice as hard as any of them. But, perhaps due to the many frustrations of his profession, he was prone to violent, unexpected surges of temper when he seemed to turn on anyone near at hand regardless of whether they were guilty or innocent. Consequently most people went warily of Tom and particularly the more susceptible among them, the most easily hurt, and she included herself, went very warily indeed. To have Tom criticize her was insupportable especially when she tried so hard and when, on the other hand, he had given her so much personal attention and coaching in her various parts.

Tom turned away as abruptly as he had appeared and, glancing guiltily at each other but saying nothing in case Tom was still within earshot, she and Gerald once more studied the task of securing the overflowing basket.

'I'll get on top,' she said brightly, her humiliation forgotten, and, clambering onto the lid, sat there pressing firmly with both hands.

Gerald squatted on his knees and, this time, successfully managed to fasten the straps on one side.

'Now the other,' he said and Estella obligingly moved to the far side pressing with all her might, her face puce with the effort. The basket tilted but Gerald secured the far straps and then extended a hand to help Estella off.

'Well done,' he said as she landed on the floor, planting a courtly kiss on the back of her hand, as if to make up for Tom's outburst. Gerald, who had known Tom for years, respected him and ignored his moods. He expected such unpredictability in people with the responsibility for success in an enterprise as difficult as this; and in the present circumstances Tom's outburst – and it hadn't been the first – could be excused.

Elsewhere other couples were similarly engaged and

soon all the baskets stood in a more or less neat row ready to be moved out onto the cart awaiting them. Stage hands began to remove the remains of Pompeii and fiery Vesuvius and a final prop basket was filled with Roman swords, helmets and various household vessels; and three people had to sit on the lid before that was securely fastened and ready to be stowed away.

Tom, in his shirtsleeves, rushed from stage to auditorium and back again, a check list in his hands, as he consulted with Owen Griffiths the stage manager as to the order in which they should be removed and stowed away. The stage curtain had been lifted and the auditorium, which had never been very full during the run, looked more desolate and uninviting than ever.

Wigan had not been perhaps a very good place to stage an ambitious series of plays which ranged from Shakespeare and Sheridan to *Hunted Down* by the prolific Dion Boucicault and *To Parents and Guardians* by the popular and successful Tom Taylor. There were several triple bills with one-act curtain raisers of a sentimental nature by little known authors, many of them hastily improvised by Tom Shipley himself, as was his adaptation of Bulwer Lytton's *The Last Days of Pompeii*, simply called *Pompeii* to avoid unwelcome comparisons with the original three-volume novel. In fact, despite its dramatic qualities and the realism of its final scene – the destruction of the city aided by cans and implements thrown onto the stage from the wings, impressive flashes of lightning and fearsome noises off – *Pompeii* had not been sufficiently appreciated by the unsophisticated populace of Wigan and the neighbouring town of St Helens, who had mostly stayed away on the final night despite a curtain-raiser called *Roses for Me* whose mawkish sentimentality made it almost universally popular.

No, Wigan had not been a success, and as he stood on the now empty stage looking into the deserted auditorium

Tom Shipley, not for the first time, felt his heart sink at the thought of what he had to say to his players, who now began to wander back from packing the prop cart outside and gather round him.

'Would you all go and sit down?' He pointed to the shabby crimson seats of the stalls. 'I have something to say.'

By their grim faces it seemed that his troupe had an inkling of what this might be and they grouped together, some with shoulders slouched, others affecting a nonchalance. Gerald Saunders lit a cigar and puffed at it with the air of a man who had little to worry him in life, certainly not the prospect of a wife and four children depending on him and now lodged in one ramshackle room in a back-street in the outskirts of Manchester.

Estella felt tired; but the theatre exhilarated her, even if one played to a half-empty auditorium like tonight. She had only a small role in *Pompeii*, but the lead in *Roses for Me*, in which she played opposite Tom as the lovelorn bride he deserted for another woman. Since joining Tom's troupe Estella had played more roles than she could count; she had to write them all down, which she did in the letters to her father, increasing in number now that she was happier and more successful. She never addressed them to her mother ever since that awful Christmas when her mother had spoken not one word to her, not even to wish her a happy Christmas. Owen Griffiths, who doubled as stage manager and played some of the leading parts, sat next to her and winked, slipping his hand down the side of his chair in an effort to touch hers. But she was used to Owen and she simply put her hands firmly in her lap, keeping her eyes fixed on Tom who was clearing his throat on stage.

Tom looked at his troupe of strolling players clustered trustingly around him, looking hopefully up at him, and he clasped his hands as if in prayer and gazed momentarily towards heaven. A complicated, troubled man, Tom Shipley was yet a player at heart, a man who could slip easily under the skins of ordinary people. In the case of this assembly, who were actors like himself, it was very important, in order to gain their confidence, to identify with them. It was vital to show that he loved them, that he could have wept for and with them, but that his plight was as grave as theirs – like them he had everything to lose. When he spoke he projected his beautiful voice as he did when he was acting, because he had to cajole them into accepting what he was so reluctant to accept himself: defeat. Here there must be no hint of censoriousness or blame. So, into his performance went all the roles he had played on the stage so many times and in his voice were blended, in various cadences, cajolery, flattery, hope and something else: the possibility of triumph over that very defeat.

Tom pulled out his pockets so that the linings hung empty by his side, and made a gesture of despair. 'Dear people, I suppose you can guess my bad news. Wigan has been a disaster, as you know. We have lost money and I was unwise to come here, or at any rate to put on such an ambitious repertoire. We should have stuck to melodrama or love-sick romances, as we shall have to do in Blackpool. If we cannot pull off full houses in Blackpool we shall have to disband. Now tomorrow we move on to Blackpool and the theatre there is small, so I have a list of light comedies we shall start with and I have adapted two or three French farces which always go down well. Possibly we'll do *The Rivals* and *School for Scandal,* but no Shakespeare. Now some of you will have to learn new parts before Monday night, and I'm giving them to those with the best memories like Gerald, Prudence and Estella, who have never yet let me down. We'll open with *Roses* and then an adaptation I've done of a play by Sardou. Tuesday we might do *School for Scandal* while we learn

81

the parts for Wednesday and Thursday. I'm sorry but that's how it is. After Blackpool no more work unless it's a success. Now go to bed all of you and try and get a good night's sleep. The train tomorrow is at noon and we start rehearsing in the afternoon.'

As he held up his hands in dismissal there was a sprinkling of applause and Albert Lang, who was the business manager and a 'utility' man, that is, he did not play leading roles, stood up and called for silence. Tom was just about to leave the stage and as Albert started to speak he stopped.

'I'd just like to say, Tom,' Albert called, 'how much we all appreciate what you are doing and the hard work you're putting into the company. We know that after each performance you stay up all night writing and rewriting, copying out parts ready for rehearsal the next day. For my part, I don't know about the others, I'm willing to play for less wages if it will help you . . . '

Albert, a single man, abruptly sat down, but this time there was no applause, and the twenty or so members of the troupe began murmuring among themselves.

'I can't take less wages,' Gerald hissed to Estella. 'I only get five pounds a week as it is. How can I support a family and pay for two sets of lodgings and eat and clothe myself for less than that?'

'I agree with you.' Owen spoke across Estella. 'How can we take less when we already get the minimum?'

As though sensing the mood of his players Tom stepped back into the centre of the stage.

'Thank you, Albert, everyone. I appreciate your sentiments and thank you for them and for the trust you place in me; but I know that many of you cannot afford to take a penny less. You are underpaid already. Rather than cut your wages I would see the company disband so that you may have a chance of employment elsewhere.'

Tom stepped off the stage and again there was murmuring as his players began to get up and saunter off in twos and threes towards a side door. No one looked back. It was not a theatre they would remember or wish to see again.

Estella felt no regrets as the train pulled out of Wigan station. She found the North of England depressing enough, but nothing she had seen was as bad as Wigan, surrounded by coal mines with their great slag heaps dominating the town. Even the populace of Wigan was depressed, despite the obvious affluence of those who owned the pits or the various new businesses and industries that were springing up because of the industrial boom of the 1880s. Large houses were being built on the outskirts and there were a few fine carriages in the street; but the mass of the people looked poor and she was appalled by the number of women one saw walking to the mines where they worked – 'pit brow' girls they were called. Estella was half shocked to find that many of them wore breeches and leggings like men. Before Wigan there had been Newcastle, Leeds, Bradford, Manchester, Stockport, Macclesfield, Manchester again and then Wigan. Now it was meant to be Blackpool, Lancaster and Kendal before the tour finished in the autumn. Shortly after she'd written to her father in January she had joined the troupe of players formed by Tom, taking, as she'd promised, her maid and initially staying in hotels away from the others.

But she saw immediately what a bad effect it had, how unpopular it had made her with her fellow players, and how uncongenial this isolation, conveying, as it did, superiority, was to her. In Bradford she dismissed the maid and went into lodgings with Anna York and Sophie Springfield, who were roughly her age. They shared a room, occasionally a bed, and, because Estella could afford to help out, they invariably ate well and their room was heated. It was not the case with others in the troupe, most of whom existed solely on the money they earned from their work. Many of the 'utilities' got as little as fifteen shillings a week and she herself only received twenty, and she played leading parts though she was still strictly speaking a utility player.

As if to atone for his recent outburst, Tom had specifically invited Estella to sit next to him in the carriage. Indeed ever since he had gone out of his way to be nice to her. Now he sat hunched up in a corner of the compartment by the window. His eyes were closed and his hat was tilted over his brow. His face was normally pale but this day it was ashen and his chin had not had the benefit of a razor. She exchanged glances with the others and no one spoke so that Tom could get some much-needed sleep. She half dozed herself so that when they came to Blackpool she woke with pleasure to see that the sun was shining, the sky was blue and there was the welcome sound of gulls as they flew in from the sea.

The theatre, the Gaiety, was in the centre of the small town which after Wigan was pleasantly clean. Its houses were freshly painted to welcome the arrivals that were expected for the summer season, during which Tom's company had been booked for five weeks with an extension promised if they were successful. They were welcomed by the manager of the theatre, Harold Pinchbeck, who told them that their prop cart had arrived and that everything was ready for the afternoon's rehearsal.

'I also have a list of lodging places,' he said, 'and I have taken the liberty of providing refreshments before you commence.'

Harold Pinchbeck looked like a prosperous solicitor. He was well built with a bald pate, a florid face and a large moustache. He exuded confidence and success and his bright, freshly painted little theatre seemed to offer them the chance they'd hoped for. After eating the good plain fare he set before them, they set to with a will, feeling that the fortunes of Tom Shipley and his company of players were about to turn.

But they were wrong. It was a very hot summer and Blackpool had begun to offer many rival attractions to lure those with money in their pockets who came from the cotton mills of Lancashire, the woollen mills of Yorkshire and further afield. There were dockworkers and shipwrights from Tyneside, miners from Northumberland, Durham, and the newly opened pits in Yorkshire and Lancashire. There were shopworkers from Bolton, Leeds, Bradford and Manchester and factory workers from every large town one cared to name. For although wages were low there was full productivity and if all the grown-up members of the family worked, women as well as men, there was a prosperity in some homes they hadn't known before. Boarding houses were springing up all the time in Blackpool to deal with the large numbers that the new railways could bring; but the people preferred to spend their money on cheap food and the sort of frivolous entertainment provided by the circus, the music hall and the many sideshows and entertainments that had been devised on the sea front, where the brisk winds blowing in from the Atlantic were renowned for their therapeutic qualities. Miners with lung disease were said to benefit from the Blackpool air, and so were consumptive girls who worked long hours in factories and shops, and thin undernourished children who were still at school.

For Blackpool, because it was not linked with industry, lacked what Newcastle, Bradford, Leeds, Manchester, Stockport and even Wigan had: a nucleus of prosperous middle-class people who enjoyed going to the theatre. Most of all, of course, they enjoyed going to see plays put on by companies that came from London with stars such as Ellen Terry and Henry Irving, Squire and Marie Bancroft, the Kendals, George Alexander, Frank Benson and Beerbohm-Tree. When the London theatres closed for the summer the leading actors and actresses invariably toured with a sophisticated experienced company. They travelled complete with exotic props, costumes and scenery in a special train, the coaches emblazoned with the initials of the leading actor-managers and would then stay in the best hotels, occupying the best and largest theatres, which were filled to capacity night after night.

This was a very different proposition from the activities of such troupes as that formed by the ambitious but impecunious Thomas Shipley, who, against Irving's advice, had launched himself on the north of England a mere two years before. He engaged local actors, none of whom, despite their talents, had ever appeared on the London stage, and the leading parts were played in second- and third-rate theatres tucked away in back streets by him and the members of his troupe.

Formerly such itinerant companies were the lifeblood of the provincial theatre but, with the arrival of the stars, the new breed of actor-manager and their band of more accomplished professional actors, they began to fade away. They could not compete with star names, with the spectacular dramas they offered but, above all, with the magnificent props and scenery which they brought with them, the startling lighting and sound effects they were able to achieve. In fact their performances were really dramatic spectacles, some with live animals and, even, growing flowers and trees. They also offered new and better plays by established dramatists whose works were not available except under licence. With Irving at the Grand in Bradford as Hamlet or Mathias, what chance had Tom Shipley playing round the corner in a shabby unsanitary theatre, with a cast of supporting players who had never appeared on the London stage in a play written by himself between the hours of midnight and dawn, hastily copied and performed the following day?

Tom Shipley aspired to be a great actor-manager along the lines of Garrick, Bancroft or Irving with whose company he had played from the time Irving took over the Lyceum from the Batemans in 1878. In fact Tom had had a career very similar to Irving's, having acted all sorts of roles, including melodrama, farce, burlesque and even pantomime from the age of eighteen. He was now twenty-eight and when two years before, he had told Irving of his plans to form his own troupe he had ignored the veteran actor's warning that the road to fame was long and narrow.

He pointed out that by the time he himself was thirty he had played 588 parts, that his first success on the London stage had been in 1871 when he was thirty-three, and that before he became manager of the Lyceum he had been its chief actor for seven years. 'I was forty years of age, Tom, and well established. You are not. Stay with me, boy, and I will see to it your parts get better.'

The kind avuncular actor had taken him out to dinner to warn him of his prospects if he left London, but Tom refused to heed him and handed in his notice after accepting an offer of repertoire in Manchester where he met the fashionable Hettie Leadbetter and where his ideas began to take shape.

In his first year he had broken even; but Mrs Leadbetter, who was well known in the north, had taken leading parts to help to get him established. For his second season he was on his own. She could not tour with him and suggested young Estella Abercrombie instead. But this second season was not as successful as the first, and already it was a financial disaster.

'Tom, might I have a word with you?'

Tom Shipley turned as he was leaving the theatre after rehearsal by a side door, his shoulders hunched and his hands thrust deep in the pockets of his greatcoat. Estella, her cloak round her shoulders, looked round to make sure they were alone. She felt very afraid, not only on account of what she was about to do, but in case it had the opposite effect to the one she intended and provoked Tom into one of his rages. But he smiled at her, politely doffing his hat and bending his head to show she had all his attention.

'Of course, Estella. Is it something to do with your part?'

'No, it's something private.'

'Then come for a walk with me. I was about to take a turn along the front to get some air.'

He stood back for her to precede him and together they walked along the narrow road that led to the sea. It was a warm but blustery day and Estella was glad she had had the foresight to seize her warm cloak before she had impulsively run after Tom. The beach was already crowded with people; some were braving the cold of the Irish Sea from the shelter of the bathing tents that stretched along the sand, and groups of children were waiting eagerly for their turns on the donkey rides, or to watch the Punch and Judy shows. Purveyors of whelks, ice-creams, drinks and sweets were selling their wares from barrows and stalls and at the end of the promenade a fun fair was tempting revellers with its carousel. Everywhere there was colour and bustle, while a group of nigger minstrels strumming their banjos mingled with the crowds.

'Let's walk towards the north shore where it's quieter.' Tom put a penny into a hat proffered by a minstrel, and pointed ahead of him as Estella fell into step beside him trying to keep up with his long strides. 'Now, what is it you want to talk about?'

'I wish to say, Tom, that I am prepared to act for nothing, if it will help. I don't really need the money.'

Tom impulsively touched her arm with his hand but did not let it linger. 'That's kind of you, Estella. Don't think I don't appreciate it, but not paying your wages won't save us. We shall have to close after next week if things don't improve and even cheerful Harry Pinchbeck doesn't think they will. He's already trying to book a musical comedy to take over from us.'

'Why don't *we* play musical comedy? I can sing.'

Tom looked into her eager face and wished he could share her optimism.

'I couldn't devise a musical comedy if I wanted to, just like that. Anyway I don't. Besides, I can't sing a note. That's certainly something for you to consider if you want work; but you don't need to work do you?'

'Yes. I do.' She gazed up at him, lowering her eyes when she saw the surprise in his. 'I mean I need to work, not for money though it may come to that one day. I want to be an actress, to succeed on the legitimate stage.'

'And you will. You have more talent than anyone else in my company. Why don't you go back to London? Come to that, I may go back to London too, though I doubt that Irving would employ me again. I don't think I'd like to confess my failure to him anyway.'

'You're not a failure. There's just too much against you. But I can't go back to London either and face my family. It is as much a matter of pride to me as it is to you.'

'Where will you go?'

'Back to my aunt in Manchester; but I'd rather stay with you.'

He glanced at her and suddenly he realized that the colour in her face was not due solely to the wind.

'With me?'

'I mean, your company. I admire you enormously, Tom, and what you're doing.'

'Well, it's nice to have your admiration. I know I'm tetchy at times, but I never mean any harm.' Tom looked at her, but she thought it wisest to say nothing. Tom too remained silent and they climbed steadily towards the cliff

89

walk on the north shore of the town, leaving the crowds behind. Below them the beach stretched in a line from Fleetwood in the north to Lytham in the south and the choppy grey sea was crested with white foam on which, here and there, seagulls were happily riding.

Despite some bickering and disagreement among the women players Tom inevitably cast Estella in the leading roles, with himself playing opposite her. She not only had talent, but her amazing looks guaranteed her popularity with his audiences. But more than that she was a real professional. She was word perfect in all her parts, even those she was given the morning before a performance. She could not only learn them, but quickly assimilate the nuances of the various characters she was called upon to play. She was as adept as Kate Hardcastle in *She Stoops to Conquer* as she was as Jessica in *The Merchant,* and she had a fine gift for comedy and an innate sense of tragedy. He had known her only six months, but the personal admiration he felt for her he concealed beneath the rather chilly professional manner with which he managed his troupe. He was not a man given to making intimates of his actors. He lodged alone and he invariably ate alone. In this way, by withholding camaraderie, he expected people to respect him, in a way to fear him, and they did. He was scrupulously just, very hardworking and courageous. Above all he had a masterful sense of theatre. If people did not love him they admired him, and they wanted to work for him again. The bitterness he felt now was that his lack of means prevented him from exercising his true gifts as a writer and flair as an actor.

'Irving was right,' he said as they paused for a moment to admire the breathtaking view. 'I tried to spread my wings before I was ready to fly. Irving waited and worked until he had the resources to go on his own. How can I go back to him now?'

Estella wanted to tuck her arm in his and perhaps kiss

his cheek. She thought he was the most fascinating man she had ever known, certainly more fascinating, clever and nice than Rayner Brook. Besides his dedication, his poverty gave him an added glamour that Rayner, with his comfortable circumstances, lacked. Rayner appeared cosseted and self-indulgent compared to Tom. Tom was also more handsome than Rayner; having the classical good looks of an actor in the mould of Irving or George Alexander. He was very tall and thin with straight black hair which he brushed back from his head, dark jowls and heavy lidded eyes which burned with the intensity of dedication and suffering. His manner was theatrical, but not affected, as though he'd been born with a love of the boards. He always wore a top hat in the street and carried a malacca cane.

She knew nothing about him, because off stage he gave nothing of himself, yet when he took her in his arms as a stage lover she would often close her eyes and half open her mouth wishing it could be real.

'My family have money,' Estella said suddenly. 'Maybe not enough to support a theatre but quite a lot.'

'But would they *give* it to you?'

'My father might. But it would depend . . . '

'On what?'

He looked at her eagerly, his animation depriving his face of its customary pallor. He took her hand and pressed it.

'On what would it depend, Estella?'

She dropped her eyes, her pounding heart making her feel slightly giddy. 'I can't say.'

She thought of her conversation with Rayner and how bold he had thought her, how nearly she had betrayed her feelings to him, denying them at the last moment. She couldn't possibly tell Tom now about the wild thought that had suddenly intruded itself in her mind. Even though he was an actor and unconventional he

91

might disapprove of any display of feeling from her as much as Rayner had.

He looked at her a moment longer, his eyes quizzical and then, gently taking her arm, he guided her carefully along the path at the top of the cliff.

But from that moment they were both aware of a new intimacy and harmony and, even though the audiences continued to fall, they both seemed buoyed up by the personal feeling between them that had been established so unexpectedly at the top of the north shore.

They worked together on their parts. Tom started eating with her and her friends. He waited for her after the performances and saw her, with the girls she shared a room with, back to their lodgings. His manner changed; there were never any harsh words now, and he became gayer despite the continuing downward spiral of the box office takings. They were never alone, but he could make her feel they were. There was a tenderness in his gestures on the stage, an unspoken, amorous quality that had not hitherto been there. It seemed only a short time before everyone felt that the detached, emotionless, short tempered Tom was very much in love.

Anna York's coughing frequently disturbed her room mates at night. Sometimes Estella would get up and refill the jug of water she kept by her bedside. Sophie Springfield was a very sound sleeper and if she was disturbed she said nothing, perhaps because she did not want to leave the comforting warmth of her bed.

The little boarding house was behind Blackpool station, a short walk from the theatre. Their room was on the top floor and from the narrow window with its thin, frayed curtain they could see only the tiled roofs of other small houses like theirs huddled so close together that a cat could walk along without having to jump. It was one of the most uncomfortable digs they had had, worse than

Wigan, but both the girls lived on what they earned and came from poor homes. In order not to draw attention to herself Estella was quite happy to cut her purse to the size of theirs.

She did what she could, however, to help them, especially Anne, without appearing patronizing. How ashamed she was of the days she used to travel alone with her maid, stay in a comfortable hotel and meet them at the theatre. Thank goodness few remembered them now and none seemed to hold it against her because Estella, by her very normality, her lack of side, her sheer grit and hard work, had won universal affection. She shared all the menial tasks expected of the company and proved an excellent dresser to the others when she wasn't on stage. And although she was given the leading parts and inevitably there was a little jealousy among the less gifted, she was so kind and considerate, such a good trouper that resentment couldn't last. She scarcely ever talked about her home and, despite her refinement, even those who knew forgot that she had been born to money, to a life of servants and ease.

Anna York adored Estella, was glad to play any bit part to her lead, to serve as her dresser, her chaperone and her friend. And if at night she started to cough she tried to stifle it in her pillow so that Estella would not be disturbed. But if she did awake then she was glad to feel the warm vibrant body of her friend beside the bed, her firm hand gently touching her brow.

'I didn't mean to wake you,' Anna gasped as Estella tenderly lowered her head after giving her a sip of fresh water. She lay panting, trying to make out Estella's face outlined against the night sky beyond the window. The girls didn't draw the curtain in order to allow Anna as much fresh air as possible, but the nights were cold as the breeze blew in from the sea.

'I know you didn't, but if you try and stifle your

coughing you will make it worse. I don't mind getting up and I can easily get to sleep again.'

'You're so kind, Estella.' Anna grasped her hand and, pressing it to her mouth, kissed it. Her lips were dry and hot and Estella, alarmed, sat on the bed and tried to feel the pulse at Anna's wrist.

'I think you have a fever,' she said anxiously. 'Anna, have you seen a doctor about this cough?'

'*I* cannot afford a doctor! It has only become bad recently. I think the warm weather doesn't suit me. Never mind, I shall soon be able to rest, and much thanks my mother will give me for that!'

It was true that Anna's cough had only got worse since they had been in Blackpool; but she never seemed to Estella to be a healthy girl. She was tall and very thin, pale and tense, and a highly strung, nervous energy enabled her to play the character and minor parts which she was given very well. She specialized in comedy and was a wonderful nurse when they were able to do *Romeo*, or a marvellous Mrs Malaprop in *The Rivals*. She came from a village in Cumberland and had contrived, by her own efforts, to achieve some sort of education, intended to provide her with a career as a governess or teacher. But she was always drawn to the stage and had managed to enlist in a company playing in Penrith, who had taken her with them when they left. Like Estella she had incurred parental wrath by her behaviour, and the two girls were drawn to each other from the beginning though Anna, at twenty-seven, was a good deal older.

'You must come and stay with me in Manchester if we break up. Your parents will only make you work on the farm.' Estella sighed. 'It's sad that neither of us can go to our real homes for fear they will stop our careers. How much we have in common, dearest Anna.' She put her arm around her and kissed her cheek. 'Try and go back to sleep now. It's nearly morning and we have another long day. But I worry about you. I wish my sister were here and she would tell you whether your cough is serious or not.'

'The one who's a doctor?'

'Well, not yet. She finishes her second year this summer.'

'Do you miss her?'

Estella clasped her knees between her hands and gazed towards the horizon where dawn was just beginning to break. The dim light enabled Anna to see her face quite clearly, outlined the sheen on her blond hair that tumbled about her shoulders. But she could not see the sadness in her eyes, though she could hear it in her voice.

'Oh yes, I miss her. We had many arguments, especially before I left home, but we loved each other. I see now qualities in Lindsey that I could not perceive before. She always seemed to me so determined that it made her appear harsh; but she had to be to get what she wanted. I see that now. I had to be hard too to wound my mama the way I did. I bitterly regretted that and I still do.'

'But was it worth it?' Anna propped herself on one elbow and gazed at her friend, her hand still clasping Estella's. 'When I think that you had a loving home and family, plenty of money, servants, everything you wished and you gave it up . . . for this! I think if I had had your circumstances I should never have gone on the stage. My life was so hard that I was always making believe it was different, that, by pretending I could become a lady. But you *were* a lady, and now you are just like me.' Anna still retained a pleasant Cumbrian accent which she managed to shed on the stage, except for a few broad vowels now and then.

She sank back and her breathing became stertorous again. 'I had nothing to give up. My life could only get better, not worse. I was one of eight children and, as the youngest, always felt in the way. Then when I didn't even want to marry a local farmworker . . . My parents lost all interest in me.'

'Well now you have *me*,' Estella said comfortingly and, rising, tucked the sheet and thin blanket round Anna's slight form. She was getting thinner too.

'But for how much longer?' Anna's tone was wistful.

'I tell you we shall not lose touch. My aunt is a very generous person and would love to have you to stay. But we will soon get work again. Besides, I believe in Tom . . . ' Estella's voice faltered and Anna quickly intervened.

'I know you do. That's what I meant by asking for how much longer you will be with us.'

'Whatever do you mean?'

Estella was grateful for the gloom so that Anna couldn't see the expression in her eyes. Even the mention of Tom's name these days made her tremble inwardly, whether with joy or fear she couldn't say. No, it wasn't exactly fear but apprehension. Yes, apprehension was the right word. A sort of thrilling fear of the unknown.

'Everyone says Tom is in love with you, and I know you are with him.'

'Oh Anna, is it so obvious?' All thoughts of sleep forgotten, Estella sank on the bed again and bent over to try to see Anna's face.

'Very obvious, especially to those who love you as I do, not as a man loves a woman but love nevertheless. I think you have been in love with him from the beginning.'

'I think I have.' Estella caught her breath. 'Oh yes I have; but I never dreamt he would be interested in me.'

'Whyever not? You are not only the most talented girl in the troupe, but the most beautiful too.'

'Someone once said that about me,' Estella's voice was hardly above a whisper, 'and it meant nothing. I dared not let myself hope that Tom would feel the same. I felt because of this man, this other man, I was destined always to be disappointed in love.'

'Well you won't be. Tom loves you. I can tell you that,' Anna said firmly. 'And we are all delighted for it. It has improved Tom and made you so happy. Do you not see how his face glows, particularly when he looks at you?'

Estella blushed in the dark. 'Yes I do. Oh Anna, is it not *the* most wonderful thing to be in love? And the thought that he loves me . . . oh, I can hardly support it. When he looks at me on the stage, takes my hand, I feel my veins will burst and I almost forget my lines. Then I remember we are actors and the moment passes.'

'But has he said nothing to you privately?'

'Oh no. He would not. He is too much a gentleman. Besides he has no fortune and I have. I realize now that if I am to get anywhere with Tom, especially before we break up, the initiative must come from me. Otherwise we'll part and I'll never see him again. I nearly spoke to him some time ago on the cliff, but I dared not.'

'What did you say?' Giggling, Anna sat up on her pillows, cough forgotten.

'I said I might be able to get some money to help the troupe from my family. He asked me how.'

'And . . . ?'

'I didn't say.' Now that the light was increasing Anna saw the excitement in Estella's face and was not deceived by dropped eyes and an uncharacteristically demure look. 'Well, I couldn't say, could I?'

'How do you mean?'

'I was thinking of my dowry,' Estella said.

CHAPTER FIVE

The room was as high and almost as narrow as the digs in Blackpool, and there was also a solitary window which overlooked a similar cluster of slate-covered roofs with uniform chimneys from which little wisps of smoke spiralled upwards to the sky. But this time dominating the roofs was the great purple mass of Mount Skiddaw and beyond that, out of sight, Lake Derwentwater stretched luminously as far as the foothills of the crags that towered above Borrowdale.

But this Estella saw only in her mind's eye as she lay in bed, contemplating Skiddaw dotted with the tough little Herdwick sheep grazing precariously upon its steep slope. From this distance they looked like tiny gleaming white boulders until one moved and then the whole flock assumed a leisurely, uniform pace in search of more succulent pastures. Estella put her arms behind her head, sighing so deeply that the man beside her stirred and threw an arm around her waist caressing the underside of her bare breast. Tom's touch, more thrilling in reality than any promise on the stage, drew her eyes away from the mountainside and she snuggled close to him, planting a kiss on the side of the cheek nearest to her, his face being still pressed into the pillow encircled by his other arm.

'That was a sad sigh,' Tom murmured, raising his head and clasping her breast more firmly in his hand as though this sensual awakening surprised him. He turned towards her and the hair on his chest – still springy and unfamiliar – brushing against her nipples aroused in Estella newly erotic thoughts that were not only disturbing but wildly exciting to a woman who had only been married three days, and was therefore able to indulge them.

Farther down there was a stirring and his flesh tapped against her body. Fearful at first, she took him very eagerly now and, as her hips enclosed him and he began the gentle rhythm of lovemaking, she realized that it was a sensation the delights of which she had almost instinctively known, although as ignorant of the physical side of marriage as any other well brought up Victorian young lady. Tom gripped her buttocks, pushing himself more firmly into her, and she entwined her arms round his back, pressing him, urging him, writhing with the torment of desire, the longing for release that only the achievement of their mutual pleasure would bring. Longing – yet a wish to postpone it too; so she lowered her limbs and eased her hands to his waist, pushing him lightly from her so that she could see both him and the instrument of his love as his long, lean body supported by his hands on either side of her, moved to and fro. Tom's face was contorted, his brow and cheeks covered with moisture, his eyes closed; and then he opened them and stared at her, at her face, her breasts, her widespread thighs, at himself emerging and disappearing as the rhythm quickened. He suddenly threw back his head and gave a loud cry and as he fell on Estella she clasped him tightly in her arms while her limbs seemed aflame, the sensation spreading from her loins to her belly, finally penetrating her heart.

Tom lay for a long time upon her and she thought he was asleep again. He was very heavy and she eased herself sideways because of the weight on her heart. The sticky sensation where he still adhered to her had frightened her at first and she had expected to discover some haemorrhage. Then she had wished she had had the opportunity to ask some questions of her sister before her hasty marriage, but when she looked there was nothing except a clear transparent liquid which, Tom had explained very carefully to her, came from both herself and him.

'It is how we make babies,' Tom had said after the first time, when she had also hurt a little, which also made her think it was blood.

'Oh!' Estella had felt terribly ignorant, yet still transported by the experience and not the least bit ashamed. She wasn't ashamed of anything to do with Tom, neither showing herself nor seeing him, because all this she had known when they were on the stage together and she had wanted so badly to hold him in her arms.

Tom had mopped her a little and explained about the semen that came from him, then he'd urged her to wash because they didn't want to start a family yet. They hardly had enough money for a honeymoon never mind a home. The first time he washed her himself, his fingers delicately intruding into the cavity he had widened; and his exploration encouraged further delights, so that the first day of their honeymoon they didn't leave their hotel room despite the glorious weather outside, a fact meaningfully commented upon by the wife of the hotel proprietor at breakfast the next morning, when they ate ravenously.

Tom and Estella thought of nothing but being alone together during those first days in Keswick, where they had journeyed after their hurried wedding in Blackpool. It was attended only by Gerald Saunders and Anna York, who wept so copiously at the time that the Registrar had thought at first she was the bride and lined her and Tom up together before he realized his mistake.

It was Anna who had pointed out what a suitable place for a honeymoon the Lake District was, how near yet how remote and romantic, especially if the weather were fine, and there was a better chance of this in August than at any other time in the year. She had given them the address of the little hotel in Keswick in the shadow of Mount

100

Skiddaw and then she, still tearful, and Gerald had seen them on their way, waving until the train was out of sight, as if she could see it setting off, as the bridal pair were, into an unknown future.

But Tom and Estella had no doubts at all, not from the moment they decided to marry and Tom obtained a special licence and she lied about her age, claiming twenty-two years (one added to the majority for extra safety) instead of nineteen. The theatre had closed the night before, the troupe disbanded except for Gerald and Anna, and no one else in the cast told about their intentions.

Indeed, as the train steamed away from Blackpool for Lancaster, where they had to change, it seemed that nothing very much could be predicted with certainty about them from now on.

Except their love. The frantic beating of his heart steadied and his breathing grew deep and regular. His eyes were closed, his mouth puckered, and she thought how beautiful he was, even in repose, with his grave, tormented, rather vulnerable looking face which seemed so much at variance with the strong yet comforting masculinity of his body. If she left him he would sleep for an hour or more, and then he might wake and want to start again as he had all that first day when they had never left their room. They had had some stale sandwiches and half a bottle of wine left over from the train. These they had consumed late at night, with much giggling, and in a sort of stupor of bodily satiety – the animal in man being satisfied on all fronts, as Tom had observed to renewed paroxysms of mirth from them both. Were they drunk on love? It seemed like it.

The next day, with a good breakfast in their stomachs, they had gone in the steamer from Keswick to the end of the lake, had alighted at a jetty and then climbed up by Catbells and Manesty Moor and made love again among thick green ferns, behind a large stone right on top of the hill. Tucking up her skirts and making love roughly in the open, with Tom almost fully clothed, was an even more erotic experience than doing it when they were both naked in bed; and she had looked over his shoulder at that deep, innocent sky above them and wondered if she would ever again know such happiness, such glorious abandonment.

It was very hot in the room now, no breeze disturbed the cheap cotton curtain, and Estella was hungry. She realized that if they didn't get up they'd miss breakfast, so she slid gently from under Tom and he flopped, still fast asleep, onto the crumpled sheet.

She got out of bed and went to the window, raising it and drawing a deep gulp of air into her lungs as if inhaling all the lovely fresh smells and sights of Lakeland. Then she poured icy water from the jug on the tallboy into a basin she had set on the floor and washed between her legs very carefully as Tom had taught her, swishing the water around so that it went as deeply inside her as possible and even squatting in it for a minute or two, letting the cold slake her hot thighs.

When she looked up Tom was lying on his back gazing at her and, jumping up, she pulled a towel around her and began vigorously to dry herself. He held out a hand but she shook her head.

'I'm starving.'

'You look wonderfully attractive, Estella. I can't believe you're my wife. Give me a kiss. Just a little one,' he wheedled, still holding out his hand.

Estella ran to the bed and he seized her, wrenching the towel away from her and exposing the newly washed hair that burst from her pubis like a thick bush of broom in the spring, all fragrant, gold and gleaming in the little patch of sunlight that streamed upon it through the window. Tom gave an exclamation and buried his dark face in it, prising

102

her legs apart, but she tumbled away from him laughing and, jumping off the bed, ran lightly across the room where she pretended to cower in terror.

'Save me, oh kind sir, from another violation. Have care for my maidenly sensibilities!'

'Maidenly!' Tom said derisively, lying back upon the bed, his expression fond and contented. 'I would like to know, young woman, when you lost your maidenhead. I am certain it was not with me!'

'Tom!' Estella straightened herself and put her hand on her hips indignantly, her breasts thrust out provocatively, though she was still innocent enough not to realize it. 'How *can* you say such a thing! You know you are the first man that has taken me. Did you not have to tell me the facts of life?'

'Aye and show them you too,' Tom said lasciviously, eyeing her as she reached for her bodice and began to dress. As she stooped, her long blond hair covered her breasts with their elongated nipples and her face, animated and rosy from his kisses, had an expression of rapt detachment as though she still could not rid herself of the memory of their lovemaking, but knew that the time had come to be practical.

'Well then,' Estella threw back her hair and, enclosing her breasts in her bodice, began quickly to fasten the buttons until she stood there merely in her top with her lower parts, the mop of gold-brown body hair, still exposed. Tom groaned and felt his crotch.

'Pray dress quickly or I will take you as you are. You cannot imagine the sensation of looking at you half naked in a man used to celibacy.'

Estella quickly snatched up her petticoat, put it over her head and then reached for her skirt. Her light, white bodice had short sleeves and a pretty ruched square neckline that showed a good deal of the top of her bosom. Her skirt was of red check cotton, and she secured it to her waist with a red bandeau. Then she applied herself to her hair, turning to the mirror and beginning to brush it before she started to twine it elaborately into the smart chignon which she had decided was more suitable for a married woman than a fringe and curls.

'*Used* to celibacy,' Estella murmured looking at herself as she draped the thick strands of hair around her hand. 'I wonder. You did not appear to fumble much to me, Mr Shipley.'

'How else could I make love such a pleasure, Mrs Shipley?' Tom said, reluctantly getting off the bed. 'You would not like a lover who knew nothing about it. It can be a very brutal experience which few women enjoy, I can tell you. You are fortunate that in me you have a man who is no stranger to love, and thankful for it if, eventually, it enabled him to give pleasure to a woman like you. Yet I am no philanderer, I can promise you, and when I say I have been celibate for a long time, you may believe it.'

Estella listened in silence, plaiting the carefully coiled braids about her head, some pins in her mouth until, one by one, she put them expertly into her completed coiffure. She had never questioned him on his past, a natural reticence remaining part of their relationship which, despite their intimacy, still made them in many ways strangers to each other.

'I have always heard love was painful,' she said after a while. 'My mother implied as much. But I knew it would not be for me if I found the right man. I had no dread about marriage, but no knowledge of it either, I assure you. You know you took me as a virgin, Tom. Only I am an actress too and there were many things I could imagine, especially as I faced you on the stage so often and yearned for you.'

Tom, still naked, stood behind her, and put his arms around her, pressing his cheek with its harsh black stubble against hers, his arms once more encircling her bosom.

104

'And I yearned for you. I could visualize you quite naked as you were a minute ago; but I never thought I could have you. How was it possible? I, a penniless wandering actor, and you the daughter of a gentleman, playing merely for fun? I thought one day we would part and I would never see you again.'

She turned to him and, taking his face between her hands, kissed the tip of his nose. He closed his eyes in an expression half of gratification, half of a kind of bovine contentment. Indeed he looked supremely at peace, as she went on:

'I thought the same about you. I knew that if I did not suggest marriage you would not either. I thought I might offend you, but I had to do it.'

'How glad I am that you did, my darling.' Tom kissed her gently on the mouth and she ran her hand down his naked body until it rested against his belly. She did not want to stir him to desire again, not just yet, but she could feel his flesh tremble. 'Because I can always say, if things do not work out between us, that it was you who suggested it!'

Estella removed her hand and drew back, startled. 'Things not work out? How could that be possible?'

Tom shrugged, reached for the basin she had washed in, threw the contents into a bucket and poured himself fresh water, turning his back on her.

'It's just an expression. Forget it as soon as you can. Things will work out, I can see that. But we didn't know it did we, for sure?' He gazed at her over his shoulder then rubbed his hand along the stubble of his face, examining it carefully in the mirror. 'Women are not always as pleased as you are by love. Many fear it and hate it. What else have we got, I thought, but that? A woman, happy in love, might forget our situation. One, afraid and discontented, hating her husband's caresses, can console herself with other things. But we have nothing *but* love – no money, no prospects, no chance of a home, yet.'

'Until I have talked to my father.'

'Until you have told him we're *married*!' Tom said sharply, glancing at her again. 'I'm not sure you did the right thing in not telling him that.'

'He would never have consented. I am under age and he would have withheld his permission. He would have sent me away, abroad, somewhere I would never see you again. Now that we are married, man and wife, bedded well and truly, what can he do? He would want you, as his son-in-law, to prosper. I am sure he will let bygones be bygones and give me a portion of my dowry. My sister will help me, I know.'

'Then you'd better write to her quickly,' Tom said, 'and get her to pave the way. We can't exist on love – not for ever, not with the comforts you're used to. Now, would you go down, my darling, and get some hot shaving water for me? I've a terrible beard today.'

Estella took up the enamel shaving jug that stood on the floor and turned to the door, a frown on her face. There was a harsh, rather ugly note in Tom's voice that reminded her sharply of his uncertain temper, evidence of which she had not yet seen on their honeymoon. Just then, just at that instant, coming as it did after such passionate moments of love, such a feeling of union, it frightened her.

Harriet Leadbetter was a tall regal looking woman of thirty-eight who had been on the stage since she was eight years of age. Her father had been a magician and, assisted by his wife and a band of growing children, had toured the music halls ekeing out a living that left his family permanently on the verge of penury, until his sudden death from typhoid pushed them over the brink altogether. His widow had put her younger children in an orphanage and gathered her elder ones about her, telling them that they were now the breadwinners. Harriet, thirteen at the time,

106

was used to being sawn in two, roped in an iron box, half drowned in a tank, or disappearing in a wardrobe twice nightly, with a matinée on Wednesdays and Saturdays. Her mother Phyllis, also a regal lady with a will and heart of steel, had managed the act and helped her husband produce rabbits from hats, streams of coloured handkerchiefs from his sleeve and smoke from out of nowhere. In between times, and sometimes almost in the wings, she had, apparently also magically, borne her husband a child every two years without ever appearing to be pregnant, or, certainly, not permitting it to inconvenience her or stop her working.

Consequently the children were sharp, adept at managing without apparent means of support, self-sufficient and completely uneducated. Harriet's elder brother Albert, fifteen, had gone into the Merchant Navy while she, her mother and sister Ellie, eleven, had formed themselves into an act which included singing, dancing and rudimentary conjuring tricks. They were known as the Three Graces but they didn't do very well, and the younger children stayed in the orphanage until they had forgotten who their parents were. When Harriet was sixteen Phyllis gave up the struggle and succumbed to an attack of pneumonia almost as quickly as her husband had died of typhoid. One minute she was alive and the next minute she was dead. Harriet and Ellie were beautiful, nubile girls and on their own they seemed to do better without their mother, who, with prematurely raddled skin and wrinkles, had never resembled one of the daughters of Zeus, even at her best. They were also prey to unscrupulous men with dishonourable intentions.

Ellie was seduced by one soon after their mother died, and nine months later she herself died in childbirth without the consolation of a wedding licence. Harriet put her sister's baby into the orphanage with her younger brothers and sisters, and at seventeen married a man twice her age who toured with an act of performing fleas. In a year or two there was nothing that Harriet didn't know about fleas and their habits but she never grew to like them, nor her husband, whom she had married in preference to sharing the fate of her sister.

She ran away from him when she was nineteen, and at twenty bigamously married a circus lion tamer who also had a family that he had neglected to tell Harriet about. Harriet liked the lion tamer and was happy with him, but she disliked lions as much as she had fleas; and when she discovered he had a wife and four children she was only too relieved to find that her marriage was not only illegal twice over but also void. She determined to put it out of her mind for ever and resumed a career as a singer until she met a magician, like her father, who was looking for someone to assist him with his act. His name was Bob Shawcross and he wanted to marry her, but she told him she wasn't free, and it was true that she had lost trace of the husband with the performing fleas.

She lived with Bob Shawcross for three years and had a child by him, in between conjuring acts as her mother had. They were known as Bob and Harriet Shawcross and might have lived like that for a long time if Harriet had not met Jack Leadbetter who was something she had never known: a gentleman. He was also very wealthy, a lawyer by training but a speculator by inclination and ability, and he fell madly in love with the young woman whose beauty was still intact despite the rigours of her peripatetic existence. He had gone to the music hall on a night out with the boys and there she was: smiling, regal, beautiful, and he decided she was for him.

To Jack Leadbetter Harriet was able to confide all the errors and mistakes of her past. She even revealed the existence of her child to him, who by now was in the same orphanage as her sister's child and her own youngest brother Arthur, then aged eleven, the others having grown up and fled the nest, no one knew where to.

Harriet was very fortunate in meeting a man like Jack when she did. He managed to find the flea trainer and get her divorced. He not only married her but offered a home to her son, Edward, known as Eddie, her sister's daughter, Claudia, and her young brother. When all this good fortune fell into her lap Harriet was twenty-four and seemed condemned henceforth to a life of the utmost respectability in a large house in the Manchester suburb of Withington.

But despite her duties as the wife of a successful businessman, her concern for the young children in her care – the number very soon augmented by a new baby of her own – Harriet grew restless. She loved the travelling life and the greasepaint, and Jack, who could deny her nothing, rented a small theatre for her and helped to launch her on the legitimate stage which had always been her ambition.

Harriet under her new, respectable name of Leadbetter, was almost an overnight success. She had never acted in straight drama before, but she had a real feel for it and the melodramatic parts which were in vogue at the time – indeed throughout most of the nineteenth century – suited her rather flamboyant style admirably. Despite her origins she had a very ladylike air, and soon became one of the principal actresses of the northern theatre.

The only stipulation that her indulgent husband made was that she was not to leave him to appear in London whatever the inducements, and in time there were some. But Harriet had known too much poverty, uncertainty and misery to disobey Jack. She confined herself to the north, preferably Manchester and places like Leeds and Bradford within easy reach and, as her mother had before her, she did not neglect her duty by her husband. Within ten years she had presented him with four more children, two boys and two girls, making three girls in all.

With a background like hers it was therefore not surprising that, viewing Tom and Estella sitting demurely on the sofa in her large drawing room, which was over-furnished like the rest of the house but very fashionable nevertheless, the expression on her face was formidable rather than friendly. She looked particularly regal in a dress of purple brocade with a pleated corsage decked with little black ribbons that emphasized the proportions of her celebrated bust, which men, it was rumoured, came to see rather than her acting. A large bustle swept imperiously up at the back emphasizing her shapely hips which were almost as famous as her bosom. Her hair was auburn, though it had not been so when she was young or even when she married Jack Leadbetter, and her clear matt complexion owed much to the ministrations of a beautician who visited the house daily and travelled with her when she was on tour. She had brilliant green eyes, whose luminosity could adapt so well to the various histrionic roles she was called upon to perform, but were particularly remarkable when filled with tears.

She paced up and down and when she reached the end of the room would stop and sweep back her short train with a forceful flourish before walking back the way she had come, rather as the captain on a ship might pace the deck.

'Why, why did you have to *marry*?' she said at last, pausing melodramatically and throwing up her expressive arms.

'We were in love,' Estella replied, seeing that Tom remained tongue-tied.

'*Love* is no reason for marriage! Love in fact is a reason *not* to marry because it soon passes and, believe me, with you it will be very soon if you are as poor as you say.'

'Our love will not pass.' Tom at last found his voice. 'It will endure as long as we do.' He looked at his wife and protectively took her hand, enclosing it between his.

110

Harriet gave a mirthless smile and inclined her head.

'You are not in the theatre now, Tom. You know that's nonsense. You are a man of over thirty and should be past that sort of thing. You should know better, even if Estella does not.'

'Estella wouldn't; that is . . . ' Tom cleared his throat. 'I mean there was no question of . . . without marriage.'

'Oh I see!' Harriet clapped her hands together and laughed, again without merriment. 'How very touching I'm sure. You could not take her to bed without wedding her, is that it?'

Estella blushed and only the pressure of Tom's hand kept her from showing her anger. They had already been back in Manchester for two weeks, lodging in a miserable room in the working class district of Ancoats, and Tom had been out every day looking for work. 'I hope it is not that you are with child?' Harriet stared accusingly at Estella's flat stomach.

'Indeed not, Mrs Leadbetter. Moreover we are anxious not to have a child until we can provide it with a home.'

'I hope you know what you are about then,' Harriet said severely. 'You had better have a word in private with me later. There is no need to blush, child. One must be practical about these things.'

Estella lowered her eyes to the floor and her head swam. The way Harriet talked seemed somehow to make a mockery of their love for each other, made it something rather common and sordid, a hole-in-the-corner disgusting business rather than the beautiful experience she knew it for. Tom had told her something of Harriet's past, although he did not know everything, so maybe her crudeness came from unhappy experience.

'Practical, practical,' Harriet went on, beating her open hand with a clenched fist. 'You must *not* have babies, you must have somewhere to live that is decent, and you must have work. Now, how are we to achieve all this?'

111

She gazed at Tom, her mouth pursed. 'You are responsible for a lot, you know, Tom. This young girl's welfare is no light matter. She is also an actress of considerable merit and you may have ruined her chances of a career, though, I must say, an early and ill considered marriage did not ruin mine. However, I was fortunate,' she looked gratefully at the closed door. 'There are not many men in this world like Jack Leadbetter.'

'My marriage was not "ill considered", Mrs Leadbetter.' Estella let go of Tom's hand and got to her feet. She was as tall as Harriet, but more slender, nineteen years younger, and looked, now, every bit as regal. She squared her shoulders and tossed back her head, and the passion in her dark blue eyes seemed a reflection of the high colour on her cheeks. 'I have loved Tom since I've known him, and he me. I may be young, but I am not as foolish as you seem to think me and he is a very capable man, a talented actor and writer, who has simply been unlucky. His luck will change and I will help him. My family are not without fortune, and it is my intention to travel south to tell my parents of my marriage and introduce Tom to them. I know they will love him – not as I do, but as a son-in-law – and will help him to establish a new company adequately financed.'

As she spoke Harriet's mobile face registered many differing emotions, among which could briefly be detected admiration, pity, incredulity and maybe just a trace of envy at being in the presence of such youthful beauty and spirit. However she now sank into a chair, clasping both arms, as though for support, and saying when Estella had finished: 'You mean you have not told your father of your marriage?'

'No, I have not.'

'But is that not the most incredible folly?'

'I did what I thought best. You see I am under age.'

Harriet passed a hand across her brow and then dabbed at it with a wisp of a handkerchief.

'Then you are not legally married, if you are under age and you have not told your father. Did you not know you had to have his permission? Did *you* not know this, Tom?'

Tom stood up and put an arm around Estella's waist.

'She told them she was twenty-two. I begged her not to, but she said her father would never give his permission. I wanted to do the right thing, but she would not let me.'

'Not *let* you! That is not a word you would hear in this house where, despite my experience and abilities, my husband has always been the master. It is never I who *let* him do anything, but he who *lets* me. You are too modern for your own good, Tom Shipley. You should have had more sense.'

'I *persuaded* Tom,' Estella said, her certainty evaporating, looking at him anxiously. 'That is a better word than "let". I said it was common sense. Once we were married my father could not possibly object. It would shame him too much.'

'And do you expect that that sense of shame will be enough to make him agree to part with some of his fortune? I think you are very naïve, my dear Estella, if you do. He may forgive you; he may feel he has to. But he will not forget. I would be very surprised if he reacted as you think he will. If you take my advice you will not tell him yet. You will try and establish yourselves on the stage and then present him with a *fait accompli*. He may support success, but if he is a wise man he will never throw his money away on failure. That has always been a principle of Mr Leadbetter, instilled into me.'

Harriet too rose to her feet, her expression a little kinder, and stretched out a hand, touching Estella's shoulder. 'How beautiful you are, my dear, and I know you're talented. Headstrong, though, and, doubtless, passionate as I was at your age. Whatever wrong you have done is done and, because I had so much good fortune in my own youth, I will do all I can to help you both. Now it

113

occurs to me there is a young man, not without fortune of his own, who is currently in Manchester looking for a cast to try out a new play. I believe he has cast all the female roles, but not the male ones. He is young and talented and Bancroft has already put on one of his plays at the Haymarket. It had mixed reviews, but those that were good were very good. As you know, Mr Leadbetter and I are sailing to America on Sunday – you were fortunate to find me here – but I will give you a note for him and you may introduce yourselves. Tell me, have either of you ever heard of a young man called Rayner Brook?'

CHAPTER SIX

Lindsey sat gazing out of the carriage window, her hand loosely in that of her father. The flat, uninteresting countryside through which their train passed provided a kind of neutral background against which she could visualize her thoughts, and her fears.

What had happened to Estella? She was an intermittent letter writer but, since hearing from the Lake District where she had said she was holidaying with a friend, there had been silence. Then came panic when Aunt Catherine wrote to say that she had heard Tom Shipley was back in Manchester, his troupe having disbanded. Lindsey agreed to go at once to Manchester with her father.

'Do you not know the name of the friend she was with in the Lake District, Papa? Did she not say?'

'No.' Edmund shook his head, loose fleshy bags, caused by sleeplessness, trembling beneath his eyes. 'It was very sudden. I thought they were touring until the autumn. Oh what have I done to deserve losing my daughter like this? Where did I go wrong?'

'You mustn't blame yourself, Papa. Estella is nearly twenty. She knew quite well what she was about. She has surely come to no harm or we'd have heard. People don't just disappear – not people of our class, Papa. Maybe Tom Shipley will know more. How curious that Aunt Catherine says he has been in contact with Rayner Brook.'

'Coincidence is a funny thing.' Her father, comforted by her words, rested his head against the well-upholstered seat of the first-class carriage. 'It has happened many times to me in my life that coincidence has changed my

115

fortune. For instance, it was very coincidental that I met your mother. We were both staying in the same hotel unknown to each other except through mutual friends who finally, again coincidentally, bumped into one another and then introduced us. But for that singular coincidence you would never have been born.'

Edmund looked lovingly at his daughter and pressed her hand. How close she was to him, closer than ever since Estella had left them. They had just returned from a happy holiday in France at Deauville. He and Lindsey cycled about the countryside every day while Minnie sat on a deckchair in the garden of the comfortable hotel they had stayed in, the sun and sea air completely restoring all their spirits. But the fact that Estella had not written for well over a month had immediately caused consternation, and it was Lindsey who, practical as always, had quietly suggested travelling north to consult with Aunt Catherine.

'It *is* a coincidence that Rayner Brook is there,' Lindsey murmured, gazing once more at the passing scenery, the flat Cheshire plains, now that they had left Crewe, interspersed by the smoking chimneys and towering slag heaps of the grey industrial towns of the Midlands. 'His play cannot have been altogether a success if he had to come to Manchester to put on another.'

'He has contacts there, I believe, friends with money. His plays are unusual, you know; they are not quite what people expect and they have to get used to them. I liked his play myself, but it was not to everyone's taste because he deals with contemporary human issues and eschews melodrama. He was hoping to induce Harriet Leadbetter, whom he knows well, to appear in his play.'

'A pity he could not offer a part to Estella.'

'Do you think she would have taken it? You know as well as I what a hot-tempered young woman she is; too volatile, indeed, for her own good. Oh how I wish she

116

would settle down, and abandon this foolish ambition to be a great actress. What chance has she got?'

Edmund sighed and momentarily closed his eyes as if in pain.

Tom turned restlessly in bed and Estella knew he was not asleep. The room was hot and stuffy and they dared not open the window because of the horrible smell that came up from the back yard. She had begun to itch and Tom was scratching too. She thought of those lovely days of their honeymoon, only a few weeks away, and the calm beautiful landscape of Lakeland which was such an incongruous contrast to the grimy backstreets of the Manchester slum. Next door she could hear Anna coughing; the day before she had not got up at all, and Estella had sat with her while Tom had gone to rehearsal. Once again she was running a fever.

She thought of Anna lying there, maybe too tired to get water, so she crept out of bed and, donning her gown, opened the door and slipped quietly into the room next door. A lamp glowed by Anna's bedside, but even in the gloom she looked as pale as the sheet on which lay her thin clenched hands, a soiled handkerchief crumpled in her palm. She did not seem aware that Estella was there until she sat on her bed, gazing anxiously at her face.

'Anna are you all right?' Anna clasped her handkerchief to her mouth and started coughing again while two large tears from each eye rolled down her cheeks. 'Anna, are you ill?' She saw that the water jug was nearly empty, but put what there was in a glass and held it to the sufferer's lips. Anna could hardly raise her head to drink, and then let it fall back after a few feeble sips.

'I'm done for, Estella.'

'Nonsense! I will go for the doctor myself tomorrow. Don't worry about the money. Somehow we'll find enough . . .'

'But you said your allowance . . .

'It simply hasn't come because my poor father doesn't know where I am. When I get in touch with him, he will send it.'

'But what will you tell them?'

'I'll think of something.' She stroked Anna's brow, tucking back the long damp fronds of hair behind Anna's ears. She was terribly hot and Estella was convinced that she was seriously ill. 'Look, I'll get some fresh water from our room and come back.'

When she returned to the room she shared with Tom he had lit the light and was sitting up in bed scratching under his armpits. His hair was tousled and his dark face bad tempered.

'Where have you been?'

'Anna isn't well. She needs water. I'll have to get a doctor to see her.'

'You worry too much about Anna, and not enough about me,' he said petulantly.

Estella calmly refilled the water jug from the large jug in the basin on the tallboy and then, setting it down, sat on ths side of the bed.

'Why should I worry about you? You're not ill, are you? You have work. You have something to do all day. I haven't.'

'It's your fault; you should have gone to see Brook. He might have found something. I hate the man, but he knows everyone.'

'I told you you were better off without him knowing you had a wife to support. He's hardly likely to find work for two people. Besides, why do you hate him so much?'

'He's so arrogant. All right it *is* his play, but he controls everything and he thinks he can tell me how to act. He is nothing but a spoiled dilettante with too much money and no talent. I despise him.'

'Well you'll have to put up with him until you get

something else. I'll just take this water to Anna, and come straight back.'

Anna seemed to have fallen asleep, so Estella refilled her glass and was about to tiptoe away when a thin hot hand plucked at her arm.

'Don't leave me, Estella. I get so afraid. I think I'm going to die.'

'That *is* nonsense. You are not dying, but you certainly are very ill. I shall go myself tomorrow and fetch the doctor. Now I must go back to Tom.'

Anna held onto her hand, her large eyes anxious. 'Is he angry again?'

'He's not angry, but he's upset. He's perpetually bad tempered these days – because of his small part, his lack of prospects. We can't sleep because the room is too hot and the bed lumpy and uncomfortable. There is such a smell from outside that we daren't open the window.'

Estella freed her hand and, going to the tiny window, tried again to pull it down but the sash was stuck. The cord was broken and the window, half open, would not budge. Estella held her nose against the smell from outside and firmly tugged the tattered curtains together. 'We must get out of this place or we'll all die of typhoid. Gerald's youngest child has already been quite ill. I'm sure that's it.'

She bent and stroked Anna's hot brow, trying to smooth the creases on it with her thumb. 'I think you may have to go back to your family, Anna dear. This is no place for you and the air of your lovely countryside will do you the world of good. As for me, I think I may have to go back to my aunt.' She stood upright and looked gravely at a spot beyond Anna's head.

'For good?'

'Oh no, not for good, but for a while. I must have some money and then, maybe, after a while I can tell her about Tom. I think I made a terrible mistake marrying in such a hurry, but it is too late now for regrets.'

'Do you regret it?'

'Not marrying Tom. Not that. But now I do regret doing it so hastily, without my father's permission. How do I know he would not have agreed? I think it seemed rather daring at the time, rather naughty; silly and impulsive, anyway. Now I think it was a bit foolish and so does Tom.' She bent down and kissed the invalid. Anna blinked up at her in the gloomy light of the oil lamp. 'Good night, my dear. I'll see you in the morning.'

'I love you, Estella.'

'I know.'

Estella gazed back, her eyes filling with tears. Perhaps Anna loved her more than Tom.

By the time dawn came she felt she had hardly closed her eyes. Tom continued to be restless and soon it seemed that her whole body itched. Maybe she did sleep because she was haunted by dreams about her mother and father, about Rayner Brook and her calm contented schooldays in London. But she wondered if these were thoughts that haunted her waking mind and prevented her from sleeping.

Finally Tom stopped moving and she knew he was awake. She glanced at him and saw that his eyes were wide open, staring at the ceiling. His body smelt and she wondered if hers did too. Oh for those happy Lakeland days when, after a good night's refreshing sleep, they would move together in an embrace as soon as they awakened. It seemed like a paradise now.

'I've hardly slept at all,' Tom said rubbing his eyes. 'I feel terrible.'

'I don't think I closed my eyes.'

'Poor Estella, you've made a mistake, haven't you?' His flat voice contained no hint of mockery.

'How do you mean?' She, too, kept her eyes on the ceiling, lying quite still beside him.

'Marrying me. You never thought you'd know such poverty, did you?'

120

'It won't last. It's all good experience, for an actress.'

She turned to him, her mouth close to his. She felt no desire, but she wanted to comfort him. He put an arm weakly around her but it lacked strength. He was truly exhausted.

'You know I don't regret marrying you, Tom Shipley. I love you and, as Ruth said to Naomi in the Bible, whither thou goest I go. I am your wife and, although we have not made vows in church, I have taken you for better or for worse.'

'I hope this is the worst! I never thought I'd bring you to a place like this. Gerald must be mad to stay here. I never dreamed his digs were as bad as this.'

'It's no good for Anna either. I'm very worried about her, Tom. Seriously.'

'Anna always worried too much about her health.'

'But she is ill. She can hardly stand.'

'I still think she exaggerates.'

She could feel Tom stirring beside her, but the thought of their bodies joined was suddenly abhorrent to her. She felt she wanted to have a bath and cleanse herself, inside and out, put on fresh clothes and wander through the sweet smelling garden towards Highgate Wood. She crinkled her nostrils, as though suddenly assailed by the fragrances of the roses, of the lavender and sweet william that proliferated in the herbaceous borders.

Tom put a hand between her legs but she moved away.

'It's too hot,' she said. 'I feel dirty.'

'But you're married to me,' he said roughly, keeping his hand on her thigh.

'I don't mean dirty in *that* way, Tom. I mean physically dirty. I don't feel I've had a good wash for days.' She hesitated a moment, then raised her voice firmly. 'Tom, I think I should go back to my aunt. I must have some money because I want Anna to see a doctor, and I think we should move out of here before we're all ill.'

'Alone?'

'Well, alone at first, of course. I have to tell her about you. It won't be for long, but we can't go on like this – no money and,' she waved a hand around the room, 'such squalor.'

'You want to run away, don't you?' he said accusingly.

'Don't be silly. But I think it is wise, for the time being. Aunt is full of good sense and perhaps she can help us.'

'You'll have our marriage annulled because you were under age, and you'll . . .'

'Tom, don't torment yourself . . .'

But Tom's nails dug savagely into her thigh and he began to rub the finger of one hand against that pleasurable place between her legs. She shut her eyes because she could not feel desire, only irritation and, somehow, disgust. She thought that there was probably grime under his fingernail, and the smell from his body was of stale semen from the night before. She had washed, as she always did, but the cold water could not wash away the dirt and grime, the sense she had of ingrained filth. Tom wore protection now when they made love, but she still washed because in this sordid room she felt unclean. She longed with all her being for a warm bath and fresh fragrant clothes.

Tom was now on top of her and their bodies seemed to congeal together. There was a pool of sweat between her breasts and Tom's armpits smelled strongly of body odour. He wasn't gentle with her and she felt even more pain than she had on the first night of their honeymoon.

'You're not at all wet, you little bitch,' he growled. 'You don't love me any more, do you?'

'Of course I love you,' she gasped into his hair. 'But how can I, if you don't give me time . . . ?'

'You didn't need time before. You don't want me, that's all.'

As though to emphasize the savagery of his feeling he

began to move vigorously in and out, not trying to please her, not attempting to kiss her, as though she were merely an object for his lust. She felt like an object, but she spread her legs to try and make it easier, less painful, for herself. She reminded herself of how much she loved Tom, but he abruptly grasped her buttocks and raised her legs high in the air, emptying himself as though she really were a receptacle and not a human being, not a woman, not a wife at all. She felt ridiculous and humiliated with her legs still in the air until her gasping husband, trembling, fell supine across her body. No wonder, she thought bitterly, some women thought love was disgusting. Like this it was. When one became a thing and not a person, it was terrible. Maybe this happened to some people all the time; maybe she'd been lucky to know the happiness she had.

Quite roughly she shifted Tom over and staggered to her feet, feeling angry and sore as though she had been raped. But rape wasn't possible in marriage; what her husband had done was lawful and he could do it any time he liked. She saw now that some blood came from between her legs and there were spots on the sheet. He had penetrated her so harshly that he must have torn her delicate flesh. God knew what other harm he'd done, both physically and emotionally.

Estella poured water in the bowl and squatted, thankful for its cool, healing qualities. When she dried herself there was fresh blood on the towel, and she knew her monthly time was not due.

She poured fresh water and washed herself all over, while Tom still lay spreadeagled across the bed, across the stains and the dirty sheets, snoring, She couldn't smell him now and guessed that their bodily smells had merged and she was as bad as he. She washed vigorously under her armpits and then she put on a fresh white lawn nightdress that she had not used for weeks. They'd always slept

123

together naked. She brushed her hair, standing at the window, looking out onto the level, uniformly tiled roofs of hundreds of tiny houses that stretched as far as the eye could see.

At home the dew would be sparkling on the grass and the goldfish would be swimming among the lilies in the pond, popping up in the water expectantly for the gardener to come and feed them. Soon Mama and Papa would be in the breakfast room, facing each other across a table laid with a white lace cloth with silver rings enclosing starched linen napkins. Mama's dress would be freshly pressed, as would be Father's shirt and suit, his shoes gleaming with polish . . .

She put down the brush and coiled her hair into a single thick strand; then her eyes roamed around the room over the peeling brown wallpaper which was stained near the ceiling. Every single item of furniture in the room tilted, as though either the floorboards sloped or the legs on which they stood were of uneven length.

Despite the mugginess in the room, Estella shivered. Never in her life had she thought she would live in a place like this. Despair and an almost unbearable feeling of isolation swept over her, despite the presence – now only a terrible reminder of the experience she had just endured – of her husband still slumbering on their nuptial bed.

There was no chair in the room so Estella went slowly over to the bed, sitting as far away from Tom's body as she could, her eyes transfixed on a stain on the crumpled sheet. Then slowly, to her horror, the stain started to move, lurching drunkenly, sightlessly, in an erratic direction towards nowhere. Then she knew what the blot was and that, if she turned the mattress over, she would find others like it. The whole bed was probably crawling with them, and her itchiness, the reason for her feelings of squalor and dirt, became immediately apparent. She would find more creatures like this, tucked in the crannies of the bed, under the mattress ticking, lodged in the blankets and between the sheets. The whole room suddenly seemed to be crawling with fat satiated bugs, their bodies engorged with her blood and that of Tom.

She put her hands to her head and, standing up, started to scream.

The Hackney carriage stopped outside the large imposing house where Uncle George and Aunt Catherine lived, and Estella got out. The cabbie jumped off his box taking her two light valises cheerfully under one arm.

'These aren't heavy, miss. Staying long?'

'I live here.' Estella looked nervously at the wrought iron gates which stood open onto the circular drive; those at the other end were shut.

The cabbie took her bags to the door and she paid him and gave him a large tip at which he gratefully touched his cap. Estella straightened her hat, adjusted her cloak and rang the doorbell.

Minnie's sister Catherine was thought to be marrying beneath her when she accepted George Henshaw, a mere clerk in a bank in Broadstairs, Kent, where her family came from. But George Henshaw had been young, ambitious and clever and, in time, he rose in the hierarchy of the bank to become manager of its large branch in Manchester. At forty he had quit banking to go into business where his financial expertise had quickly secured him a number of directorships. Now, at fifty-four, he was a man of considerable wealth, a member of the City council, a Justice of the Peace and patron of a large number of charitable and artistic foundations. His two children, a son and a daughter, were grown up and married and his wife was accordingly able to devote her time to the many good causes in which her husband was interested. Aunt Catherine was a plain, sensible woman

125

with little pretension. She had a practical streak which her sister Minnie lacked and, because she had not expected much from life, she was grateful for the many good things it had given her.

Although the Henshaws employed a large number of servants, it was Aunt Catherine who now opened the door, because she happened to be passing when the bell rang.

'Estella!' She extended her arms and Estella ran into them, feeling that she had indeed come home after an adventure that had transformed her from a girl into a woman. Would that it had been a nightmare from which the sensible, reassuring presence of her aunt now awakened her. She leaned her head on her aunt's homely bosom. 'Why Estella,' Aunt Catherine stood back and gazed at her, her arms still around the girl's shoulders. 'You're crying.'

'I'm glad to be back, Aunt. They're tears of happiness.' Estella brushed the tears from her eyes with her hand, but they continued to well up and she extracted a handkerchief from her pocket and gave her nose a good blow. 'There! I'm better now.'

'But where have you been, child? We were out of our minds with worry.'

'It's a long story, Aunt. May I come in?'

'Of course, of course. Leave your bags. I'll ask Frank to take them to your room. Do you know that your sister and father are here? They have come to look for you. Lindsey was about to set out to find Mr Shipley.'

'Why Mr Shipley?' Estella paused, the blood draining guiltily from her face.

'Because child, as far as anyone knew, he was the last person who knew where you were. Anyway, thank God you're here, and no harm done.'

Aunt Catherine drew her into the hall and helped her to remove her cloak and hat. She looked at herself in the

126

hall mirror, patting her hair and pinching her cheeks in an effort to restore her colour. She had taken off her wedding ring and it lay in the pocket of her skirt, a last-minute gesture before the cab stopped in front of the house. Now she frantically rubbed her finger to try and remove the circular mark left by the band.

'Come, they're in the drawing room.'

Drawing a deep breath, Estella obediently followed her aunt.

Lindsey and her father were drinking tea with Uncle George who had met them at the station, having left his office early. As Estella came through the door they all put down their cups simultaneously and stared at her, while Aunt Catherine stood back and said with a smile, 'Look who's here.'

Estella gazed at her sister and father, whom she had not seen for nearly nine months, and suddenly the enormity of what had happened to her seemed to draw down a barrier between her and them that, although invisible, was impenetrable too. She shut her eyes and took another deep breath, and then she felt tender hands about her shoulders and a soft familiar cheek against hers.

'Oh Estella, we have been so worried.'

Lindsey kissed her sister and Estella put her arms around her and held her, reliving in her mind's eye the horrible scene that morning when Tom had hit her to stop her screaming and then squashed the bed bug between the finger and thumb of his right hand. She'd fallen to the floor and was still there when Grace Saunders, Gerald's wife, came up, having heard the commotion, and Anna started banging anxiously on the wall next door. Tom had dragged her to her feet and hit her again and Grace had tried to stop him and been hit too. She ran to the door and screamed for Gerald, and at one time it seemed that the whole house was in uproar with doors opening and banging and people running in and out of the room.

Finally she and Tom were left alone again and he'd called her a spoiled tramp and burst out that he bitterly regretted he'd ever married her.

She held Lindsey tighter and when she opened her eyes the horrible vision had gone, and she saw the clear calm brow of her sister and the soft, understanding expression in her blue eyes.

Then Papa came over and she embraced him and cried a little once again, but with joy, she assured them, with joy. When they asked where she'd been she told them that, after the troupe had disbanded, she'd stayed with her friend in the Lake District and had now travelled back with her to Manchester because she was very ill and needed medical help.

Listening to her Lindsey was convinced that her sister was hiding something; she looked so worn and so anxious that it seemed scarcely credible that a tale as simple as this could have made her so wretched. For Estella looked wretched. She was not only as pale as death, but her eyes had lost their opalescent glow, her hair was lacklustre and she had shed so much weight that her dress hung from her as from a scarecrow. It was Lindsey too, trained now to notice things other people did not, who first observed the circular impress on the third finger of Estella's left hand and a terrible suspicion began to form in her mind.

'But where *is* your friend?' Aunt Catherine exclaimed, having listened to the story with horror. 'Should she have been dragged all the way back to Manchester when she is evidently so ill? Is not her mother the best person to care for her?'

'Her mother doesn't want her. She . . . ' Estella continued to rub at her finger and then she kept it hidden in her right hand in case anybody noticed.

'I think I had best come and see your friend,' Lindsey said practically. 'Obviously you are very concerned about her.'

'You should have brought her straight here, dear,' Aunt Catherine was soothing. 'We have a large house with plenty of room.'

'I did not like to, Aunt . . .'

'But where is she now?'

'With other . . . friends. In Ancoats.'

'*Ancoats*!' Aunt Catherine spoke the word as though it was already synonymous with the plague, as, indeed, to many it was. It was the sort of place that one skirted if one had business nearby, and that no lady ever visited unless in the course of charitable works, and then always escorted by a male, her husband or a member of her staff.

'She, we have friends there living in theatrical lodgings.'

'I see we have much to speak about,' Lindsey said, firmly clasping her sister's hand. Yes, she saw very clearly now the impress of a ring and her eyes flickered from it to Estella's face. 'Do you feel up to accompanying me there now, or are you too tired?'

'Oh no, I'm not too tired.' Estella removed her hand from Lindsey's and put it behind her back. 'I came to see if Aunt could let me have some money and then I was going to go back for a doctor. But now that you are here . . .' A great weight was suddenly lifted from Estella's heart. Capable, compassionate Lindsey would know what to do. The tears formed behind her eyes again and she swayed momentarily, while Lindsey steadied her with a firm arm and held her tight.

'We are all here, my darling,' Edmund said standing beside Lindsey. 'You must have had an upsetting experience. You don't look well at all. You've no idea how worried we have been about you. Why did you not write, at least?'

'I knew you were in France, Papa. I didn't know when you were returning. I was so worried too, about Anna and the failure of the company in Blackpool. I was quite miserable about that. I didn't really think about writing letters.'

And it was true she had not. But not for the reasons she said. She had been far too much in love with her husband to think about anything else. Together they had seemed aloof and inviolate, cocooned and protected by their mutual love. Yet that very morning Tom had taken hold of her windpipe as he shook her and yelled: 'Spoiled bitch! Spoiled bitch! Did you never see a bed-bug before? Then you were lucky. Never had them on your fine white sheets at home, did you? No, nor a man either. Well you've learned something of life in these few weeks my girl, and high time if you ask me.' Then he'd shaken her again and hurled her across the room.

'Come, we will all go together to see your friend,' Aunt Catherine said. 'You need protection in a place like Ancoats. Oh my dear it is full of prostitutes and thieves.'

'Please no, Aunt!' Estella looked at her in alarm, then at Lindsey. 'Please let Lindsey and me go alone. We shall be quite all right.'

'I don't like it.' Edmund looked doubtfully at his brother-in-law.

'Well, if they want to go alone, let them,' George said sensibly, reluctant to leave the comfort of his home. 'Perhaps it will be best for the young lady concerned. But they will take my coach; and my coachman, Robert, is a good sturdy fellow with plenty of muscle, and I will tell him to wait at the ready with his whip should trouble occur.' He wagged a finger sternly at Estella. 'But be sure you return here straight away, and bring your poor friend with you. Doctor Openshaw will attend her at once, and at my expense.'

Lindsey said little to her sister as the coach made its way from prosperous Withington, with its big houses well set

130

back from the road, through the centre of Manchester past the new Town Hall and into the narrow streets of the slum areas, with their tiny terraced houses clustered in unending rows back to back. Estella seemed grateful for the silence, for the lack of questions, for the warm, comforting presence of her sister who would soon know all the sordid details of her recent life. Lindsey held her hand throughout the journey, only exclaiming once or twice about some passing scene or something happening in the street. But when they stopped at the house and Robert got down to open the carriage door she could scarcely believe they had arrived.

'Here?' she queried. 'Your friend is *here*?'

'Yes. The house belongs to a couple who used to be in the music hall and were forced out by ill health and the growing competition of the professionals, which is also what happened to,' Estella gulped and compulsively clasped her finger even though now it was safely gloved, 'Tom. Tom Shipley.'

'Well, I hope Mr Shipley doesn't end up keeping a place like this. For his sake.' Lindsey descended from the carriage, taking care where she placed her feet on the cobbled street, and turned round to help her sister. 'Would you wait here, Robert, and keep an eye on the house? We may need your assistance in bringing Miss York out. I don't yet know quite how ill she is.'

'Yes miss.' Robert touched his hat and wrinkled his nose, wondering how his employer could possibly let his nieces come to a place like this.

They could hear Anna's cough as soon as they entered the house. There was a threadbare carpet on the hall floor and from the far end they could hear the noises made by the four small children of Gerald Saunders, who spent most of the day cooped up indoors with their mother. Grace now appeared at the top of the staircase, one arm on the banister. She was a tall gaunt woman, only thirty, but her face was deeply lined by years of hardship and embitterment. Her wispy blond hair was uncombed, and her scraggy arms and thin breasts showed through the cheap cotton dress she was wearing. Like Estella Grace had started out as an actress and also, like Estella, she had made the mistake of marrying too young. She was quite sure that Estella would end up as she had, especially after the scene she had witnessed in the morning.

'I never saw Tom in such a rage,' she had said to her husband. 'He was like a man possessed. Hit her twice he did, while I was there and powerless to stop him.'

'Tom always had a temper,' Gerald replied. 'Especially when thwarted. He has all the charm in the world, but I don't think Estella knew what she was marrying, even though she'd been the victim of his moods. She was too blindly in love with him to think he could harm her. I never saw a woman so stricken with a man, even from the beginning.'

As they went up the stairs Grace stood back for them, trying to smooth back her hair and brush some stains made by the baby from her bodice. The elegant young woman behind Estella could only be her sister, they resembled each other so much. There was, however, something very imperious about her as though she were used to commanding and being obeyed. She seemed to have come from another world.

'You'll be the doctor,' she said half curtseying, she did not know why.

'No I'm not a doctor yet,' Lindsey replied kindly, sensing the woman's unease. 'I'm Miss Abercrombie's sister.'

'*Miss* Abercrombie,' Grace smiled to herself. 'Miss Abercrombie' indeed. But aloud she said, 'I know that, miss, you look so alike. But Estella has often talked about you. How proud she is of you.'

'Really?' Lindsey glanced up at Estella's back. 'I'm glad to hear it. She must have changed her views.'

'I've not changed my views,' Estella retorted, some of her old asperity returning. 'I was always proud of you, but concerned for you too. Anyway, all that was a long time ago. I have grown up since.'

She led the way into Anna's bedroom and was immediately conscious of the stench that came through the half open window. Lindsey at once went over to try and close it, but to no avail. Then she turned and looked at the patient with her calm clinical eyes, drawing off her long grey gloves as she did and unfastening her grey cloak in which she had travelled up from London. As she bent down to examine the woman lying on the bed Lindsey was suddenly conscious of an extreme weariness, an exhaustion of mind and body that she sometimes saw in the doctors who had spent all day and sometimes half the night in the clinics and wards of the women's hospital. She would see them momentarily sag and then straighten up and smile, as if this act forced them to find the strength to go on. And they did. So would she; but the worry about her sister, the length and tedium of the journey and now this, combined with the fears she had about Estella, had seemed to drain her energy, cause an overwhelming tiredness.

'This is my sister Lindsey.' Estella had sat on the side of Anna's bed and taken her hand. 'I found her there when I got to my aunt's. We have come to fetch you.'

Anna peered at Estella through half closed eyes and even then she seemed not to see her. The hand that Estella held was limp and so hot that it appeared to have seared her flesh, which hung loosely from her bones. Her mouth was half open and a rasping sound came from her throat.

'She has been like this since you left.' Grace stood dispiritedly behind Lindsey, looking at Estella. 'I thought she was dead at one time; then she opened her eyes again, but she has not spoken a word.'

133

Lindsey put her ear to Anna's chest and took her pulse. Then she lifted her eyelids and peered at her eyes.

'I wish I had better light,' she said looking at the flickering lamp. 'Never mind. Would you please get off the bed, Estella? You should stand as far back as you can anyway.'

As Estella got up Lindsey drew back the bedclothes and, lifting Anna's pathetic nightdress, carefully prodded her stomach, feeling her, her head thoughtfully on one side as though she were interpreting the message passed through her fingers. Then she drew down her nightdress, put back the bedclothes and tucked them round the patient.

'This woman is very ill,' she said gravely. 'She cannot possibly be moved to Aunt's house for, it is hard to be sure, but I fear she is suffering from the fever, her spleen is so swollen.' Lindsey straightened up and looked around her. 'Typhoid. That evil smell from the windows means infected drains. Anyone who lives here is in deadly danger.'

'Then what can we do?' Estella flew across the room and placed her hand on Lindsey's arm.

'We must fetch the doctor and someone must nurse her. I don't think it will be for very long. You cannot have crossed the north of England recently with this woman, Estella. I would say she has been deteriorating like this for weeks. The fever is far advanced and she could not possibly have travelled in such a state.'

Estella looked at Grace, who inclined her head and moved towards the door. Suddenly there was the sound of firm steps running up the stairs and coming quickly along the corridor. Grace peered out and then rushed back into the room, stifling her mouth with her apron, gazing at Estella, her face comically miming a warning.

There was a sense of quiet everywhere; one of those pregnant moments people sometimes recall in retrospect.

134

The footsteps had ceased and only Anna's stertorous breathing disturbed the unnatural calm.

Taking care not to look at her sister Estella went to the door as Tom emerged from their room, stopping when he saw her.

'Someone said they'd seen you come in,' he said, opening his arms. 'Oh my darling, can you ever forgive me? I never thought I'd see you again.' Tom fell on his knees and clutched her around the hips, pressing his face into her thighs. And that was how Lindsey found them as she came to the door of Anna's room, quietly fastening her cloak.

Estella gestured towards the man at her feet but no words came and Lindsey's grave eyes were not so much accusatory as sad. She looked at Tom, unaware of her presence, and then at her sister.

'This is Tom,' Estella said at last in a voice that surprised her by its strength. 'Tom Shipley. He's my husband.'

Lindsey gazed first at Estella and then at the man whose face was so abjectly pressed against her body, almost lost in the folds of her skirt.

'I know,' she said at last. 'It was as I feared. Well, how do you do, Mr Shipley?' She extended a hand, but Tom was too far gone to observe the courtesies; it is doubtful if he even heard her voice.

CHAPTER SEVEN

Anna's coughing had stopped and she now spent most of the time either unconscious or in a delirium, punctuated by rare moments of lucidity. The doctor had confirmed Lindsey's diagnosis of typhoid, congratulating her at the same time even though it was obvious he considered women medical students a very strange species. He held out no hope for the patient at all as the illness was too far gone. He said he didn't know who would nurse Anna in these conditions but, as there was plenty of money available, he would do what he could. He was surprised when Lindsey offered her own services, saying that it would give her experience. He left with the remark that women were much more suited to nursing than doctoring, and said he would call again. But, more important, he promised to send the sanitary authorities to do their best to eliminate the cause of the contagion and clean up the drains.

All this had now been done and Lindsey lay upon the bed, fully clothed, that Estella had shared with Tom. It had now been deloused and fumigated, as had the whole house. Every floor had been scrubbed and every ragged curtain and item of linen washed by an army of maids paid for by George Henshaw, who had also come personally to reprimand the landlord, only to find he did not live on the premises and owned not one but hundreds of miserable dwellings like this. George was inspired to make a note of his name and address and set off with enthusiasm to track the scoundrel down and, if he could, prosecute him.

The smell of carbolic still hung about the house but at least it was better than the awful stench that had come from the drains. The window in Anna's room had also been repaired and there were vases of sweet smelling flowers in her room, and a supply of bowls and napkins for her vomit and diarrhoea. It was not pleasant to tend such a patient in the last stages of typhus fever, but Lindsey revelled in it. She had loved cleaning up the house, applying to it those standards of hygiene which Dr Jex-Blake made such a feature of her course on the subject at the women's medical school. She changed her patient several times a day, wiping away the faeces and washing her as though she were someone beloved and not a person she scarcely knew at all. Grace Saunders was glad to help her for the money and good things that she gave her and her family, and eagerly did all the washing that came relentlessly from the first floor room. It was quite certain now that one of her children had had the fever too but had recovered, maybe due to familiarity with the germs, having been brought up in perpetually unhygienic conditions.

The house was peaceful at last. Anna slept next door, and Lindsey closed her eyes, her mind running back over the past few days, the realization that not only was Estella married, but that her husband had not a penny to his name, no family of his own and no home to take her to. When she'd seen the mark of the ring on Estella's hand Lindsey had feared that her sister might have been living with a man, pretending to be married. But her relief at learning that she had gone through a form of marriage ceremony was tempered by the knowledge of what Tom was and how little he had to give her. Knowing what she knew now she wondered whether it would not have been better if her sister had not married, but had lived openly with her lover in sin?

Lindsey's eyelids flickered and she opened them again In sin. Well, Estella was living in sin according to their father because she was improperly married. There had

137

been a terrible scene with Tom at the house where Lindsey had led him, together with Estella, on the day she found him on his knees. Edmund said he would never recognize him and that, given the chance, he would prosecute him for seducing his daughter; but Estella had clung to Tom's arm and pronounced that, whatever her father did or said, she was his wife in body and soul and wished to remain so.

After this had come a family council at which neither Tom nor Estella was present, and where a lot of good sense had been spoken by George and Catherine Henshaw in turn, and also by Lindsey. She pointed out that, although the circumstances of her sister's marriage had scarcely been auspicious, the couple should be given time to work things out and, if necessary, go through a proper marriage in a church with their father's blessing.

Uncle George said that this would take time; they had been married legally in the sense that they had gone through a form of marriage in front of a registrar. But he did agree that a proper marriage was essential, especially, he said gravely, if Estella were to find herself with child. Lindsey remembered the profound silence that had fallen at this remark, as if the reality of what had happened had suddenly dawned on her father. His precious daughter, though still a child to him, had now known a man, his love and his lust. It was a difficult enough thing for any father to contemplate, never mind one who felt his daughter, his pearl, had been stolen from him. Uncle George hurried on to say that Edmund should leave everything to him; that he would try and devise a solution that did not incriminate Estella, and Aunt Catherine hastily intimated that Tom and Estella were welcome to stay with her. Lindsey meanwhile said she wished to take care of Anna, who was not long for this world, and that her father should return home to break the news personally to their mother. Edmund agreed, but he refused to say goodbye to his

138

daughter and the man that he still refused to call her husband.

Lindsey made her head more comfortable on the pillow and thought of that word 'husband' and what it meant. On this very bed Estella had known the greatest intimacy with a person that it was possible to know; yet the two gave her the impression of scarcely knowing each other. She knew that Tom and Estella had quarrelled the day she had arrived, and there was certainly a willingness on both their parts to forgive and forget. Yet Estella eyed her husband warily, almost fearfully, and Tom seemed distanced by the abrupt change in his fortunes, the awful confrontation with her father. It appeared to Lindsey that they had very reluctantly gone into the same room together, despite Estella's vehement protestations of love. It really was a fraught situation and one that she was glad to escape from, preferring this house of disease and incipient death to the strife-torn mansion in Withington.

There was a tap at the door and Grace put her head round. Grace had smartened herself up since the arrival of Lindsey, whom she deeply admired. Lindsey had naturally assumed that rather distant manner of the physician, that is based partly on arrogance and partly on superior knowledge, and which people respect because they have no alternative in the face of terrible and unpredictable illness. But Lindsey's essential kindness showed beneath her brisk, professional manner and the capable way she had set about having the house cleaned up. Above all, the way she personally had cared for the dying woman next door had been one of the noblest deeds Grace had ever witnessed. Lindsey seemed to give no thought for herself or the danger of contagion from the disgusting faeces or vomit that covered her hands when she attended Anna in a way that she, Grace, could never have brought herself to do, even as a mother who had frequently to wipe the bottoms of her children or cleanse their pewking mouths.

That was one thing, but a strange woman was quite another. To do what Lindsey did was heroic.

'Would you like a cup of tea, Miss Abercrombie?'

Seeing the tray in Grace's hand, the little egg cup of flowers by the old enamel pot, the plate of biscuits neatly on a doily, Lindsey sat up and smiled.

'Oh thank you, Grace. How thoughtful.'

'It's a pleasure, miss,' Grace said humbly, her face flushing with pleasure as she put the tray on the rickety table by the side of the bed.

'You do look after me.' Lindsey propped herself on an elbow as Grace poured. 'Didn't you bring a cup for yourself, Grace?'

'I had it downstairs, miss,' Grace said in a shocked tone, as though the idea of eating or drinking in the presence of such a being was not to be considered. She thought of her in quite a different way from Estella who, to her, was an ordinary mortal, whereas Lindsey had a touch of the divine. 'The children have a bite at about this time. I had it with them; thanks to you, Miss Abercrombie, we have had enough to eat these past few days. We shall miss you when you go.'

'I wish I could do something more for you, Grace.' Lindsey thoughtfully accepted her cup of tea with a gracious nod. 'It seems to me the world is full of men who cannot provide for their families.'

'My husband is a *good* man,' Grace said defensively. 'He has just had hard luck; but that is the lot of a profession like ours. I was an actress too, you know, when I married Mr Saunders. I didn't really give it up until our fourth was born and then it was too hard moving around with all the children. I thought I'd stay put until they were a bit older, but I'll have to work again. We had great hopes of Mr Shipley's company and they thought the world of him, Miss Abercrombie, they really did.'

'But he let them down too, did he not?' Lindsey said

coldly. 'Offered them prospects he couldn't realize? Led them all, as it were, up the garden path?'

'You mustn't be hard on the poor man, miss.' Grace leaned against the door, her arms akimbo. 'I know there's a lot about him you disapprove of, on account of Estella, and I don't say that I blame you. My husband said he'd never known a harder worker and he did not fail for lack of trying. Everyone liked him; but I must say, here, I found him a hard man to understand. There he had a lovely young woman and he didn't seem to appreciate her. Estella said that his anxiety made him so bad tempered, but . . .'

'My sister is certainly very loyal to Mr Shipley.' Lindsey placed her cup delicately in its saucer as though she were in the drawing room in Withington or Highgate. 'And, who knows, all may turn out well for them. I scarcely know him myself.' She handed the cup to Grace and got off the bed. 'Now we mustn't gossip, Grace. It's time to look at Anna again.'

She consulted her watch and then walked to the door, smiling at Grace who moved quickly to one side, eyes downcast, as if worshipping the boards on which Lindsey trod.

'And I say to you, Mr Abtree, that I will not tolerate such interference.'

'It is not I who interfere, ma'am, but the people who demand their rights. For if you continue to oppose them they will find other means to exact vengeance.'

'No, no, *no*!' Rayner Brook called, hurrying to the front of the house. 'Please, Mr Shipley, a little more *strength* in your voice. "It is not *I* who interfere, ma'am," emphasize the "I". "*I* who interfere, ma'am". Then: "if you continue to oppose them", emphasize the *you*. Again please, Mr Shipley. Joanna, dear, do you mind giving him his cue?'

141

Joanna Nesbitt pouted and raised her eyes to the ceiling giving as she did an impatient little stamp on the floor with a dainty foot. This was the fourth time they'd been called on to play the scene, and it was scarcely an important one.

'And I say to you, Mr Abtree . . . '

Tom Shipley abruptly threw down his script and folded his arms, turning to stare down at the man who gazed at him from the front row of the stalls.

'I'm damned if I'm going to do *that* again, Brook. I'll have you know that I was acting when you and Miss Nesbitt here were in rompers. As my standards go this is a very mean part and . . . '

'Then maybe it is beneath you, Mr Shipley, seeing that you play it so badly. If you do not like it, perhaps you do not want it?'

Rayner paused, an air of menace belying the silky tone of his voice, and the question seemed to echo and re-echo throughout the empty theatre.

Tom Shipley and Rayner Brook had never got on. Rayner hadn't even liked him when he read for the part and would never have considered him for it, but he wished to do a favour for Harriet Leadbetter, who he still hoped would arrive in time to take over the part of the imperious Lady Courtmander, now being played by her understudy Joanna Nesbitt. Her letter had extolled the virtues of Mr Shipley and also indicated that it would be such a kindly, Christian act to give him work, for reasons unspecified, that Rayner felt he dared not refuse. As it was he thought nobody could spoil such a small part, the leader of the coalminers who were threatening to strike, but Shipley was doing his best. Well, he would sack him and make his case to Harriet when she returned from the United States. He couldn't tolerate such an insubordinate, arrogant man who always appeared to know best, belittling everything he, Rayner Brook, said or did.

142

None of the rehearsals for the play had gone well and Rayner kept on postponing the opening date, also waiting anxiously for word from Harriet about her return. He'd given her the play to study on the boat. He had not had the bills printed in the hope that her name would still appear on the top, together with himself as the leading man – a local coalowner who was sympathetic to the claims of the miners.

The Rights of Man?, rather a bold play for the time with no romantic interest, had been read by Jerome and highly praised. But Jerome recommended him to try putting it on in the north, where it might receive a more sympathetic reception than in London. It was a play with a message, its essential cynicism suggested by the question mark at the end of the title. Had these poor striving miners any real rights when they depended entirely on the owners for their wages? Everyone knew that Jerome was a Socialist and many feared that Rayner Brook was becoming one too. However, he had money of his own and backing for the play from his friend Hilary Cliff-Archer, who lived not far from the Henshaws and owned some of the best property in Manchester including valuable sites in the centre of the city.

Tom had slowly descended the steps leading from the stage to the auditorium, watched with bated breath by the rest of the cast, both those who were still on the stage taking part and those who sat waiting for their cues in the stalls. Rayner felt a slight tremor of alarm and put down his script on the seat behind him so that he had both hands, both fists rather, free.

'I said, Mr Shipley . . . ' he began.

Almost before Rayner could anticipate him Tom reached out and seized the collar of his coat.

'I heard what you said, Brook. You think I'm going to quit this part, don't you? You'd be glad to see me leave, wouldn't you? It would be nice to put it about that Tom

Shipley couldn't act even a mean part like this, wouldn't it? Not content with knocking a man when he's down you'll stamp on his head too.'

Tom slowly put the other hand on Rayner's right lapel and began to shake him.

'Well . . . Rayner . . . Brook . . . Mr Socialist, defender of the rights of man, I'm not going to let you. I'm not going to walk out and make it easy for you. Nor am I going to go, even if I'm fired. I'm going to blacken your name throughout the theatrical world for the no-good, rotten, talentless bastard that you are.'

Enraged by his words no less than by his action, Rayner grasped both Tom's hands and flung him away from him. As Tom staggered against the stage Rayner leapt on him, beginning to pummel him with clenched fists.

'"Bastard" did you call me? I'll tell you what you are, you rotten weed. You have no acting ability at all, yet you have such an opinion of yourself that you can't see the boards you walk on. You . . . '

One of the actors ran up and started to pull Rayner away from Tom; but Rayner had him pinned against the stage and with every word he spoke he hit him in the face or on the chest. However the action distracted him and Tom seized the opportunity to get away from the stage, facing Rayner on more open ground with an exit behind him rather than a solid wall. As Rayner shook the actor off him, Tom now threw himself upon Rayner and together they fell, grappling with each other on the floor while the cast grouped themselves about the protagonists, those on the stage peering eagerly from the edge, uttering sounds of encouragement. No one dared encourage Tom, had they wished to, and those the most eager for preferment from the man who held their livelihoods in his hands cried the loudest:

'Get him Rayner, get him man!'

Estella, coming into the back of the auditorium,

144

thought at first that the action was part of the play though it was odd that it should take place offstage. As she walked along the centre aisle and saw what was happening, and who was fighting, she flung aside her bag and umbrella and began to run towards the crowd gathered between the stalls and the stage. With horror she realized that Rayner and Tom were at each other's throats, their faces contorted either with agony or hatred.

'Can no one stop them?' she cried, but everyone had their excited eyes on the men wrestling on the ground. Then Tom was on his back, Rayner straddling him, whereupon Estella, putting out her hand, grabbed Rayner's thick mop of curly hair and pulled at it for all she was worth.

Rayner abruptly released Tom and, giving a cry of pain, jerked backwards while Tom, seeing Estella, struggled to his feet, shaking himself like a dog rescued from an encounter with a bear. Estella kept hold of Rayner's hair until he was on his feet and as he turned painfully to see who this new attacker was she let go and backed swiftly away, out of his reach.

Rayner looked angrily about him, rubbing his head, his face scarlet with rage.

'Who on *earth* did that! Come forward please.'

Estella took a deep breath and, her bosom heaving, walked into the clearing the cast had instinctively made for her, her eyes fearlessly upon Rayner.

'I'm sorry, Rayner, but it was I.'

'What are *you* doing here?' Rayner gasped at her in astonishment and then sank onto one of the front row chairs, his right hand still tenderly rubbing the back of his head.

'I came to see Tom, and you if you like.'

'You know Tom Shipley?'

'I'm married to him.'

Rayner closed his eyes and his head fell back, his mouth

145

open. Tom meanwhile was straightening his coat and his tie and smoothing down his hair with both hands.

'Married to Tom Shipley!' Rayner moaned, twisting his head from side to side. 'Oh God and no one told me. No one told me, Estella.' He had opened his eyes, the distress in them plainly showing as he looked at her. 'How could I know?'

'You couldn't.'

'But why didn't someone *tell* me?'

'I thought Tom would have a better chance of getting a part in his own right if you didn't know he was married to me. He didn't know I knew you and neither did Harriet Leadbetter. It's quite simple really.'

'But you must have known I'd find out sooner or later.'

'I'd rather it were later,' Estella said, putting an arm round Tom's waist. 'It was worth a try. You've never really known what it's like to be desperate for work, have you Rayner Brook? You pose as such a kindly, concerned man; but all you do is think of yourself. I told you years ago that you were selfish and you've scarcely changed, not one little bit. Well, I love Tom and I'm married to him, but he needs to work. I'd rather have one Tom than ten of you. Tom is a real man; he knows what it's like to be a real actor: travelling, writing, working, managing a cast. He's a fine man and has more talent in one little finger than you in the whole of your body. There.' She let go her arm and turned to Tom. 'Get your hat, Tom. You don't need to work for a slug like this.'

Tom's eyes, moving from Estella to Rayner, finally settled upon Estella. She didn't know whether the anger still on his face – anger mixed with incredulity – was because of Rayner or because of what he'd just learned.

Eventually Tom said: 'You mean you've *known* Rayner Brook all the time?'

Estella nodded, speaking quickly to hide a sudden sense of fear. 'I've known him for years. His family lived near

146

mine in London. I've even acted with him as an amateur. I'm sorry but what I did was for the best. Now I know it was wrong. I should have told you I knew him because you were both bound to find out the truth.'

'But *why* are you here today?'

'I wanted to peep in and see how things were going, standing at the back. I thought if things were going well, I might . . . Well, I was wrong again. Everything I seem to do these days is wrong, wrong . . . ' She began to wring her hands, signifying distress, but Tom went on glaring at her and now she grew more alarmed because she thought that in his eyes she could see humiliation as well as rage.

'You never said a truer word, Estella Shipley, and God only knows how unhappy I am that I have to call you by my name. Good-day to you.'

Without even taking up his hat or looking for his coat, Tom walked with grave dignity up the long aisle and out of the theatre.

Lindsey sat on the bed in the room she had now occupied for a week writing up her notes. The new mattress was covered by a white counterpane only, the sheets and blankets having been taken by Grace to be washed. Grace promised also to scrub the room out again and the one next door where Anna's body lay, covered by a white sheet, waiting for the undertaker. Lindsey would see the body go and then return to Aunt Catherine's house, and then?

She looked up from her notes out of the window at the grey, rain-filled Manchester sky. Why, she must return home. The school term would soon commence, the beginning of her third year. She had done her job; nursed a sick woman and done what she could to comfort Estella, who had daily visited her dying friend. She had also talked with Estella about her marriage, and about her future but, really, what Estella made of her life was now up to her.

Much as she loved her, Lindsey had herself to consider. Moreover, she doubted whether she would make such a fine mess of it as Estella had. But understanding the vagaries of people's minds was as much a part of a doctor's profession as healing their bodies – or so it seemed to Lindsey, in the many hours she'd had for reflection as she sat alone in her room, or by Anna's bedside.

Lindsey continued with her work, her small fine handwriting carefully covering page after page. She had noted down every symptom, every stage of poor Anna's illness without much thought for the person herself beyond that dictated by Christian compassion, the kind of feeling she had for any suffering creature. But that, too, was part of a doctor's training.

For, early on in the medical course, the students were taught the importance of detachment. It was vital, Mrs Garrett Anderson had stressed, not to become involved with patients other than was strictly necessary in medical terms. One girl had had to be sent home because her personal involvement with the sick had threatened her own health.

Yes, Lindsey knew very little about the personality of Anna York, about her background or the life that had preceded her death in that quiet back room in a Manchester slum. But she knew now a great deal about the progression of typhus fever. Every day she had made meticulous notes, and she had an hourly account of the course of the disease from when she had made her diagnosis to its fateful culmination. She even noted how she had briefly been misled by her sister into thinking Anna had consumption, due to reports of a previous illness in the summer. But bronchitis was also a symptom of typhoid, as was a high fever, the enlargement of the spleen and other internal organs. Despite all she had done to save the patient, aided by frequent visits from the doctor, Anna York had died. Yet here was an important indeed almost priceless, account of the course of the disease as minutely observed by her. It had been valuable experience.

Now Lindsey, having concluded her account of Anna's death, was writing about the steps she had taken to disinfect the house, the elimination of the contagion from the drains, the scrubbing of floors, the washing of bed linen. She raised her head from her work and thought of the terrible story Estella had told about finding bugs in this very bed; there were some in Anna's bed too and new mattresses had been procured, the old ones burned. The thought of her sister sleeping in a bed crawling with bugs . . . Lindsey shuddered and looked up to see Tom standing at the door.

'Mr Shipley? Are you looking for Estella? She was here this morning to take farewell of Anna. She . . . '

'No, I'm not looking for Estella. I know where she is.' Tom looked back along the corridor. 'Anna's dead?'

'I'm afraid so. Her death was inevitable. She died during the night. We have washed her body and are awaiting the undertaker.'

'You're a plucky girl, Lindsey,' Tom said. 'I may call you Lindsey, may I not?'

'Of course.'

'After all,' Tom came slowly into the room, 'we're related.' As she didn't reply he went on. 'Or do you think that's a matter of opinion?'

Lindsey's expression remained polite, giving little clue to her feelings. There was something about Tom's tone that worried her; it was as though he were challenging her to make some sort of admission. Then what? She felt she had to be careful because there was a brooding, threatening quality about Tom now, and she knew he was a violent man.

'Insomuch as you are married to Estella you are my brother-in-law.'

149

'*Insomuch*?' Tom placed heavy emphasis on the word. 'You think we're not married then?'

'In the sight of God I think you are.'

'Your father would have us unwed.' Tom slumped on the mattress beside her, the menace suddenly gone from his voice. He looked tired and put his face in his hands.

'That's understandable, Mr Shipley. What you did was not right. Estella has caused her parents enough suffering without this.'

'Yet you forgive her, but not me?'

'You are that much older, Mr Shipley.' Lindsey chose her words with care. 'You should have known better.' She shut her notebook firmly, placing it on the bed, and got to her feet. She felt uncomfortable sitting next to him, and standing in front of him, looking down at him, gave her an advantage. She was not so afraid of him now. 'You should have controlled your lust for my sister and, if you loved her as much as you say, made a really honest woman of her by asking permission of my father.'

'She said he would not allow it.' Tom shook his head. 'Do you not think I've repented of it time enough already? It was not mere lust, as you suggest, though I know a spinster likes to think that lust is evil. I loved Estella passionately and I wanted to marry her. She said your father would not entertain my suit and would send her away.'

'But was there not something else, Mr Shipley?'

Lindsey went to the window and drew back the curtain so that she could see the bleak landscape beyond. She was offended by his derogatory implication that she, as an unmarried woman, knew nothing about lust. She saw enough of the results of lust in the wards of the hospitals – unhappy, tormented women and unwanted babies. But she would not let him rile her.

'And what is that, pray?' he said after a moment's pause.

150

'Money,' she replied, letting the curtain fall. Leaning against the windowsill she folded her arms and stared at him, quite unafraid now. 'I understood that you thought my sister could produce some money to finance your theatrical ventures. I may say that it was not Estella who told me this but poor Anna before she fell into a coma. Anna told me, in snatches, the whole story.'

'I see.' Tom hung his head as if deflated and something in Lindsey went out to him in pity. She did not dislike Tom Shipley; she could see his attraction for her sister, or any woman, for that matter. He was not only handsome, he was a nice looking man. He looked as though it was his nature to be kind and both Anna and Grace had spoken well of him. Surely not even her wayward sister would have fallen in love with a brute? Yet he had a terrible temper and this was put down to his heritage, which was part Irish. No one knew a lot about Tom Shipley's background apart from the fact that his mother was Irish, that he'd been born in England of an English father.

Tom raised his head, and spoke again: 'You think, then, that I married Estella for money?'

'Partly, maybe.'

'Well, I didn't.'

'Maybe you didn't realize quite why you went along with her madcap scheme, which could, according to my Uncle George, land you both in prison for deception. All I can tell you, Mr Shipley, is this. My father is not a poor man, he is what you may call comfortably well off; but he has nothing *like* the money to back any theatrical venture even if he had the inclination, which, as you know, he has not. Most of his money is inherited and in trust for us. He lives on the income from the various investments made on his behalf and, as a dowry, Estella would have enough money to see that she lived in the style to which she was accustomed; but no more. There is one point, however, on which I do agree with Estella. I doubt my father would have given her permission to marry a penniless adventurer about whom absolutely nothing is known.'

Tom rose to his feet and crossed over to where Lindsey was standing by the window. For a moment the expression on his dark face frightened her again and she felt moisture on the palms of her hands. A lock of hair fell over his brow and she could hardly see his eyes for the fierce concentration of his brows. She could see then how very attractive he was and, at the same time, how fearsome. It was an unfortunate combination. He was a tall man, and this menacing air coupled with his dark hair and saturnine features seemed to give him something of the attributes that poor Emily Brontë had invested in that product of her tormented imagination: Heathcliff.

She found she was trembling, but he stopped before he got to her and, tilting his head, put his hands on both his hips.

'Miss Abercrombie, I see you are under some delusion about me. I am not a penniless adventurer, or rather I am certainly penniless but not an adventurer. I am an actor and have played for my livelihood in this way since I was eighteen years of age. My father was an Englishman, a businessman who did fairly well but died when I was ten. My mother was Irish and her parents had been on the stage. She was related by marriage to Dion Boucicault, of whom you have no doubt heard, and I acted for some time with him and also with Bancroft and Irving. My fortunes, like those of many actors, have fluctuated over the years; but I have always been devoted to the stage and I have always worked. I have never married because I have never had the time, but I have had the opportunity, and to marry wealthy women if I chose. I have not done so before. Why should I now?'

Lindsey lowered her head, carefully wiping the palms of her hands on her sleeves, despising herself for the enhanced beat of her heart. She was glad, however, that he had spoken so gently, and her fear of him evaporated.

'I'm sorry, Mr Shipley, if I did you an injustice. We are all upset and the circumstances here have not helped, have they? I apologize for what I said. I am sure my uncle will straighten everything out. Now, when the coach comes will you return with me to his house?'

'No I will not.' Tom folded his arms and teetered back on his feet, growing even taller. 'I have just had a fight with Rayner Brook and Estella found us. Fancy never telling me she knew Brook! What a fool she made of me. What a fool he must think me. I am going to stay here, in this house, until I get another job, or I might return at once to London, I'm not sure which. Whatever I do I will not return to your uncle's house, where I am patronized, or seek to live again with Estella until I can support her and say to her: "a fig for all your family!"' Tom snapped his fingers in Lindsey's face and then stepped back.

Lindsey wasn't sure whether her heart leapt with joy or dismay; but there certainly was a renewed commotion in her breast such as she was unaccustomed to.

'You are *not* going back to Estella?'

'No, I am not. The whole thing has been a mistake, a terrible folly. I can see her father hates me and she soon will come to despise me if she feels I depend on her family. I hated living at your aunt's house. The only happiness Estella and I had was on our honeymoon and that lasted just two short weeks. Since then our life has been a misery and I have not always treated her as I should. I am sorry for that, but let your uncle take what action he likes. I shall pack my things up there and try and make my name on my own.'

'But have you told Estella all this?'

'*You* tell her,' Tom said roughly.

'Don't you think you should, at least, explain?'

'Explain what? Why should I explain anything?'

153

'Because I'm afraid she loves you,' Lindsey said sadly, more than ever convinced that, like Heathcliff, he was an upstart and certainly not a gentleman. 'Whatever you have done to her has not been enough to make her hate you. She still loves you very much.'

Harriet gazed at his profile, at his face staring thoughtfully into the fire. She went over to him and put an arm on his shoulder, then she encircled his neck and drew his cheek towards her for a kiss.

'Did I upset you, my darling? I'm sorry; but if I can't tell you the truth to whom can I tell it? I know it's wounding to hear your precious work criticized, but I am trying to be helpful and I think the remedy is very simple.'

'What remedy is that?' Rayner said sulkily, refusing to respond to her caresses.

'You must make it more romantic. Why, Rayner, it has no romance at all! It is all stark unremitting drama, and the dialogue . . . Some of the miners' speeches go on for *pages*. They are like political tracts. Now, if you made Lady Courtmander *younger* and Sir Terence Brett a little *older*, why you would have a real drama. Not only does he convert her to his point of view – that the miners have souls as well as bodies – but he marries her as well.'

'Who wants romantic nonsense!' Rayner stepped away from her and threw himself petulantly into a chair.

'The *people* do, Rayner. The public, who see your plays, do. I tell you this will not succeed on any stage without romance. It is too stark, too long, too dreary . . . and, Rayner dear,' she went over to him and, kneeling by his side, took his hand, 'I am too old for the part as I envisage it now, and you are too young.'

Suddenly he leaned forward and grasping her hand kissed it.

'Don't speak like that, Harriet!'

'But my dear it's true. I am fifteen years older than you, in life as well as on stage. I am enormously flattered by your admiration and your love, my darling, believe me I am. I know you have written a part for me, because you wanted to act with me too. And for this reason you have ruined your play. We can have romance in real life, but not on the stage, eh Rayner? It would ruin the play? So you left out romance altogether.'

'That's not true at all!' Rayner protested, drawing her face towards him, kissing her passionately on the mouth. 'You're the most wonderful woman, the most vital . . .'

'I know darling, I know and I thank you for it.' Harriet got gracefully to her feet. 'I do not feel old and I must say people tell me I do not look my age. But you are twenty-three and I am thirty-eight. Some people consider that *very* old indeed. Immorally old. I have had two husbands and five children. But that is a fact. On the stage it is a fact. It would be ridiculous for young Sir Terence to consider marrying Lady Courtmander, besides which she is married already.'

'So are you.' As Rayner relaxed, she could sense the tension leave his body and she smiled.

'Darling, if you think Mr Leadbetter has not had his amusements these past thirteen years you are very much mistaken. He has a young girl now whom he actually *keeps* in an apartment in Audenshaw. I believe she was a *shop* assistant before he raised her above her station. Or is being a kept woman below it? I confess I'm not sure. When he goes away on business he either takes her with him, or he pretends and does not go away but stays with her. No matter. I am devoted to Jack and he to me. We suit each other as things are and neither fears a rival to threaten our marriage.'

'Does he know about me?'

'Of course not, you silly boy! It is quite all right for a *husband* to have affairs, but he expects fidelity in his wife.

155

If he did know that I had affairs too then it might be different.'

'*Affairs*? You have other men?'

'I have *had* affairs in the past, Rayner. I have not hidden that from you. But you are the only other man in my life at the moment, apart from Jack.'

Rayner turned his head away. He was a jealous man and he hated to think that she had relations with her husband, as he supposed she did. He never asked. He hoped that the need to attend a nubile young shop girl made them very rare.

His affair with Harriet Leadbetter was a year old. He had met her through his friend, Hilary Cliff-Archer, and he thought she was the most fascinating woman he had ever met, more fascinating even than Ellen Terry with whom he had imagined himself half in love. Harriet was not the first woman older than he with whom Rayner had fallen in love. He liked older women, their poise, sophistication, above all their expertise when it came to making love. They knew how to satisfy a man, and it was not hard to satisfy such a woman. By that time the affections of their husbands were usually engaged elsewhere, as Jack Leadbetter's were; but they retained their normal, womanly appetite for love, whetted, inevitably, by enforced abstinence.

It was difficult, but not too difficult, to find opportunities to make love, and this gave heightened excitement to the affair. Hilary's house was always available to the lovers; but there were not many opportunities for them both to slip away. Thus the anticipation of making love to Harriet was so delicious that it almost surpassed the ecstasy of the actual event itself. Furtiveness made a liaison so much more exciting.

From where he sat he could see the deep cleavage between her full breasts and the sight was enough to arouse in him such a longing that he attempted to unbutton her corsage and slip his hand down to caress her. Harriet leaned foward, her lips parted, the light in her green eyes amorous, inviting, but her hand very firmly drew his away and, with a lightning kiss, she rose to her feet, fastening the buttons he had undone.

'Rayner, darling! Anyone could come in.'

'Lock the door.'

'Don't be silly. They'd wonder why it was locked. We don't want to be discovered, Rayner, not if Jack is going to back you in a tour with your play.' His proximity, the clarity of his intentions, had excited her and she went to the mirror and examined the high colour of her cheeks, putting her cool palms upon them and straightening her hair. Rayner was so physical. She could hardly be alone with him for a few minutes without imagining herself in bed with him, and wishing they were there. But expediency came first, and caution. She had so much to lose, and Rayner had very little to offer apart from his magnificent body. She did not underestimate that prize; but he was so young that if their liaison were revealed she would look ridiculous. She would lose her exalted position in Manchester society. Who knew what Jack would do if he found out?

'And I tell you another thing, Rayner Brook,' she said, turning to him. 'You must change that play or Jack won't back it.'

'Hilary will.'

'Hilary won't like it either. Hilary will only lose money on it and who wants to throw money away? Now, my love, I tell you what you must do.' She moved over to him and, drawing up a chair by his side, firmly clasped his hand in a gesture that was almost maternal. 'You must rewrite it. You must make Lady Courtmander young and lovely, and you must make Sir Terence older than she. The rest you can keep, cut a few speeches here and there, that sort of thing. And you must *not* star Harriet Leadbetter in the leading role.'

157

'What do you mean?' Rayner seized both her hands and drew them to his breast.

'I am too old. Besides I do not really want a long tour. My family needs me, you know. My youngest child is still only three years of age. I don't fancy a long tour, maybe a season in London, which Jack has always forbidden anyway. I tell you who you must cast in the part now that she is free and all that business about her marriage is cleared up, or, at least, shelved.'

'You don't mean Estella Abercrombie?' Rayner gasped, suddenly overwhelmed by misery, by thwarted love. What chances would he and Harriet not have had, alone together on tour? But even as she'd spoken he'd seen the sense of her argument. He must change his play.

'I mean her exactly,' Harriet said, nodding serenely. 'She is a *very* talented young woman; she is just right for the part. As I envisage it, you might even have written it for her.'

PART II

CHAPTER EIGHT

'I've heard so much about you, child,' Miss Terry said. 'I simply *had* to come and see you for myself.'

Estella felt like curtseying in the presence of the Queen of the English stage, but Miss Terry's benevolent smile and extended open arms seemed to preclude such formality as she swept into Estella's dressing room. Instead she found herself partly smothered in a warm, maternal embrace such that she scarcely felt she was meeting a stranger.

Ellen Terry's charm was legendary, as was her generosity to young actors and actresses, her selflessness when it came to bestowing praise. She was tall and well built but her delicate, well moulded features had an elfin quality; the slightly pert, retroussé nose a confirmation of her reputation for mischievousness. Her blond hair beneath the rim of her wide black hat enhanced the impression she conveyed of a sweet, natural womanliness, while her long brown cloak emphasized her graciousness.

Estella, still in the wig and black robe she had worn as Portia, raised her head and stared into the famed blue Terry eyes that she had only ever seen from the stalls in the Lyceum when she was a girl, and to see them from that far was not to perceive their alluring quality. To be so near, embraced by the star, seemed so unreal that, were it not for the enveloping arms, she would have thought she was dreaming. Miss Terry returned her gaze, her bewitching eyes searching the face of the young actress, and then she held her away from her, her head on one side, the appraisal over.

'You are very like me, do you know that dear? We have

the same colouring. I knew I had a rival, but not one that so mirrored my looks.'

Terry brushed her own soft cheek as though lamenting the passage of time and then, tucking Estella's hand in hers, led her to the sofa at the back of the dressing room, sitting the younger woman close beside her.

'How old are you, Estella? May I call you by your Christian name?'

'Of course you may. I was twenty-one in March, Miss Terry.'

'Twenty-one!' Miss Terry looked up at Rayner Brook and Grant Nicholson, who had played Shylock. 'How very talented you are. I wonder if I could have played Portia so well at your age.'

'You're very generous, Miss Terry.' Estella's shyness began to evaporate and, feeling hot in her robes, she gently disengaged her hand from that of the great actress and removed her wig, shaking out her blond hair which fell across the shoulders of her gown. 'I could not hope to rival your Portia or, indeed, anything else you do. I have seen your Beatrice, your Lady Macbeth and your Juliet. Had I known you were here tonight I don't think I should have dared to go on.'

'Did you not tell her I was here, Grant?' Miss Terry looked at the celebrated actor with whom she had often played before her partnership with Irving.

'I didn't dare, Ellen. I thought it might spoil her performance.'

'You *knew*!' Estella mockingly shook a fist at him, but she was too happy for it to appear anything but a game. Portia, achieved only this year, had indeed been her triumph; and now the great Terry had been in her audience and approved. Then she held out a hand, beckoning to Rayner who had stood quietly by the half-open door. 'Do you know Rayner Brook, Miss Terry? May I introduce him to you?'

'I have heard of Mr Brook and, of course, Grant introduced us before we came in to see you. I believe he is a very talented playwright and his Bassanio was excellent. You are very accomplished, Mr Brook.' Ellen Terry gave a regal nod and Rayner bowed, squeezing Estella's hand as though drawing both comfort and support from it. He was clearly as nervous as she was.

'Thank you, Miss Terry. I wish you had seen one of my own plays.'

'I wish I had and I shall, although I know they're considered very modern. You must send one to Mr Irving. He is for ever on the lookout for new talent. Why, he spends *thousands* of pounds on commissioning works which are never performed.'

'I did send Mr Irving one of my plays, Miss Terry, and he returned it.'

'Oh.' Miss Terry's mobile features registered dismay, as though she had made a *gaffe*. Quickly she recovered. 'Then *I* will ask him to read it again. Pray send it to me at the Adelphi.'

'I do not think my plays are quite what Mr Irving is looking for, knowing his repertoire so well, although I would love to try and write one for you, Miss Terry.' Rayner's tone implied criticism of Irving's bad judgment, but became reverential when he spoke her name.

'I do wish you would.' Ellen clasped her hands and leaned foward earnestly as though discussing a point of great mutual interest. She was clearly adept at putting people at their ease. 'There are not enough good parts for actresses, are there Estella? What would we do without Shakespeare? How often have I asked myself that question. Time and time again.' She took Estella's hand and abruptly stood up. 'I must go. Grant is taking me to supper. Will you have lunch with me tomorrow at the hotel my dear? I have to return to London in the afternoon.'

163

That night, two floors up from Ellen Terry, in another room in the hotel where she was staying during the run of Shakespearean plays at the Theatre Royal, Liverpool, Estella hardly slept. The days of sordid theatrical lodgings were happily over and, with the other leads in the company touring the North, she stayed at the best hotels in each town they visited. She lay propped up on pillows in her bed reliving each moment of the interview with the woman who was a model for every actress of her age, observing the Liverpool skyline which glowed permanently through the night from the lights in the docks and the large industrial complexes which had mushroomed in that prosperous, hard working city. Towards dawn the hotel came alive with the noise made by early risers, and the sounds of trains arriving in and departing from the busy railway station nearby contributed to the atmosphere of energy, excitement and bustle.

Eighteen months had passed since Estella had taken the lead in Rayner Brook's latest play *The Rights of Man?*. Despite the fact that he had almost entirely rewritten it to accommodate her, it was an instant flop except for one thing: all the critics (and, unfortunately for Rayner but fortunately for her, there were plenty) noticed her acting and paid tribute to it.

It is a pity that Miss Estella Abercrombie makes her serious *début* in a play of such little merit because it could almost have cut short a career that augurs to be one of great promise. As it is, she is the only good thing about it.

The only thing to be said about Mr Rayner Brook's new play *The Rights of Man?* is that it should never have been put on, but for one thing: Miss Estella Abercrombie, making her *début* in the role of Lady Courtmander, is the sort of find that makes a jaded critic like the present writer rub his eyes and wonder if he's dreaming. She is sensational not only for her ability, but for her beauty and intelligence, all of which somehow contrive to bring a sparkle to a dull and stupid play, and make it an evening to remember.

I nearly left after the first act of *The Rights of Man?* at the Palace Theatre last night, but the acting of Estella Abercrombie (a newcomer, though she has appeared in less exalted company) held me spellbound. Had she just been left alone standing on the stage for two hours (and, indeed, it would have been preferable to what we had to endure) without uttering a word I would still have stayed, riveted, in my seat.

Estella's grief at the uniformly bad notices Rayner's play received was tempered, therefore, by her joy in the excellence of her notices, their confirmation that she had a place on the legitimate stage.

This was largely due to Grant Nicholson, who was looking for someone to play Viola in his new production of *Twelfth Night*. He had not seen her act, but he asked her to audition for him and, from then on, he took her into the company which he had successfully established in his own theatre, The Playhouse, Manchester. From there they toured the whole of England and Scotland but left out London, where it was difficult for a provincial company to get a suitable theatre.

Many had considered Grant Nicholson a failure when he left London five years before, driven out by lack of money and poor plays. But he owed his resurgence in the north to the efforts of that well known patroness of the arts Harriet Leadbetter, who had acted with him when they were both younger and always remained loyal to her friends. Some said they had been lovers, but Harriet gave no clue. She persuaded her husband and a group of other businessmen to support Grant Nicholson and he purchased the lease of the Playhouse, off Market Street in the centre of the town, refurbished it to a high standard, and then set about attracting the best players he could find.

Lying in bed now Estella felt they had been eighteen

months very well spent. She had consolidated all the experience she had gathered in the previous less happy period on the stage; and she felt that she was now an established player, a member of a well-respected company who gave her top billing under Grant and Rayner when Harriet Leadbetter was not in the cast. But Portia had been her triumph. How Had Ellen Terry got to hear about her?

'Of course I've known Grant for years,' Ellen confided across the small table that had been laid just for two in the sitting room of her hotel suite. 'I came up here really on a little nostalgic tour because my parents, you know, acted here at the Theatre Royal together. My father, Ben, was under contract when my sister, Kate, was first taken on by Mr and Mrs Kean at the Princess's Theatre London, and I stayed behind to look after Father. I was only eight years of age, so who looked after who is not quite certain. Liverpool is full of fond memories for me. I had been promising myself a flying visit and then I saw that Grant was appearing there with his company, and that you were Portia.'

Miss Terry wore a white cotton dress with one enormous flower embroidered on the skirt, the bodice plain but with large gigot sleeves and white lace at her throat and wrists.

'I played Portia, you know, in our recent tour of America. It is one of my favourite roles, one of the best written for women, I think. Tell me, my dear,' Miss Terry broke off and leaned across the table, putting a hand on her wrist. She seemed very much at the whim of impulse, as a person. 'Are you in love with Rayner Brook? He is such a *handsome* young man and it seemed to me that he never took his eyes off you, on stage and off. I hope you don't think I'm being too personal but I do like to *know* about people, don't you?'

Estella smiled nervously. Miss Terry had hardly stopped talking since lunch had begun, but it was all quite fascinating to a young actress alone in the presence of such a celebrity. Besides, she loved hearing about the lavish productions staged at the Lyceum and how their private train in America had consisted of eight coaches, two box cars and an open 'gondola' all packed with costumes, props, poles, rigging and fold-away scenery. Miss Terry had said they had simply transported the Lyceum to America and their six-month tour, which included *Charles I, Faust*, Irving of course in *The Bells*, as well as *The Merchant*, had been such a fabulous success that they were to go again in September, though she personally hated ships and always felt she would never return. 'One can make such a lot of *money* in America,' Miss Terry had said, her eyes sparkling. 'And they treat one so *well*.'

But, if Miss Terry was interested in her private life, Estella was equally intrigued by hers. The scandal of her past had helped to contribute to her aura. She had been married twice, the first time to the famous painter G. F. Watts, but after that she had lived openly with the architect Edward Godwin by whom she had two children.

'*I* in love with Rayner Brook!' Estella was able to answer the question with a laugh of genuine incredulity. 'Oh no. Nor is he in love with me.'

'Good. Then I can ask you the next question.' Miss Terry seemed satisfied and kept her hand firmly on Estella's wrist. 'What has happened to Tom Shipley?'

Estella gazed at the hand on her wrist, a hand that was large and capable yet capable of infinitely expressive gestures. She raised her eyes to meet those enquiring ones of her companion.

'Do you *know* about Tom and me?'

'Indeed I do.' Miss Terry sat back and raised a glass of white wine to her lips, but did not drink. 'I do not know the whole story, but I know that you and he were married

167

and that it finished after three months. Tom used to act at the Lyceum, you know, and we, Henry and I, were very fond of him. He was extremely talented, but headstrong and, ignoring Henry's warnings, went off without sufficient money or experience – fatal to lack both! We heard that he had married a beautiful actress and then that his company had failed and his marriage too. Henry thought that Tom might get in touch with him about work, but he never did. It was only recently I learned that the young actress he married was *you*.'

'Our marriage was annulled, Miss Terry.' Estella spoke slowly, attempting to practise the deep breathing she had learned in order to conquer her nerves on the stage. But despite this she felt her heartbeat quicken, and knew that the telltale colour was rising on her cheeks. 'I was under age when I married Tom and I lied about it. But that was not why our marriage foundered.'

'Ah.' Miss Terry gave her the knowing, insinuating look of a woman of the world and Estella blushed even more deeply.

'No nor *that* either, I think I know what you imply. Tom had no money and my parents violently opposed him. My father made him feel small. He left me, quite simply, that is all. He told my sister we had made a mistake and he wanted to give me a fresh start.'

Estella could feel tears pricking behind her eyes and she swallowed hard.

'Oh dear.' Miss Terry put down her untouched glass and leaned back, her own luminous, sympathetic eyes brimming with tears. 'How sad you make it sound.'

'It *was* very sad.' Estella dabbed openly at her eyes. 'I couldn't forgive Tom for leaving without speaking to me. I was so angry with him that for a time I didn't care, but then I missed him and . . .'

'And you still do?'

'Yes. I have never got over Tom because what was

between us was unfinished. We were married such a short time. I loved him and I know he loved me. But there was too much against us – or so it seemed. Looking back now, I think neither of us tried hard enough. We gave in too quickly. So of course I don't love Rayner Brook or anyone else, though Rayner has become a very good friend to me. Anyway, he has engaged the affections of another woman, so that is that.'

'I see.' Miss Terry put her napkin on the table and folded her arms, gazing at Estella. 'You may have thought that question very personal my dear, and indeed it was. But it had a purpose, and that was not to pry into your personal life. I wondered, naturally, if there were news of Tom; but mainly I wished to know whether or not you would consider yourself free for another engagement, if one were offered.'

'Another engagement?'

'How would you like to appear at the Lyceum? You have never acted on the London stage have you?'

'The Lyceum!' Estella clasped her burning cheeks. 'Does Mr Irving know?'

'Mr Irving knows that we need good actresses. I cannot take *all* the parts myself. I get too tired. I think the Lyceum could well form a springboard from which you could leap into a splendid future, Estella. You are still very young. After that, you will become a rival indeed but, I hope, always a friend.'

'I'm honoured, of course, but I'd have to think about it,' Estella said cautiously, playing with a ring on her hand, a gift from Grant to celebrate the first lead she had taken in his company. 'I owe a lot of loyalty to Grant.'

'Grant does not wish to stand in your way. I've spoken to him already.'

'There *are* other factors.' Estella gazed at her hand. 'I'm estranged from my parents, so I have kept away from London.'

169

'Is it because of Tom?'

'Before then, though Tom was the culmination of our discord. I ran away from home to become an actress and greatly upset my mother. Then, of course, my marrying Tom upset my father. I refused to forgive him for the attitude he took. I have seen neither of my parents since.'

'That is very sad, but, alas, understandable.' Miss Terry sighed and tasted a little of the wine in her glass. 'The older generation never understands the younger. I daresay I am well placed between your parents and yourself to see both points of view. I too was alienated from my own dear family by my relationship with Mr Godwin. But when I married and became respectable again they welcomed me with open arms. No doubt when you are at the Lyceum they will be so proud of you . . . '

'That is not the point, Miss Terry,' Estella said acidly. '*I* am not proud of *them*. I think they behaved shabbily towards me and I feel I can do without them.'

Miss Terry looked astonished. 'Then have you *no* family?'

'Yes, a sister and also a dear kind uncle and aunt with whom I live in Manchester. It was my uncle who arranged, with some difficulty, the annulment of my marriage with Tom. He did it, he said, so that I should not suffer if either Tom or I wished to marry again. I often hope I will see Tom again and, if I do and we both feel the same, then I can marry him without the permission of anyone.'

'Oh dear.' Miss Terry impulsively extended the sympathetic hand yet again. 'How you *must* long for Tom. If only he knew. You have no idea where he is?'

'He has vanished from the face of the earth. My uncle tried to find him for the annulment process but couldn't. In the event, Tom's absence helped to speed the proceedings. We think he went abroad, maybe to Australia.'

'Well, if I see him again or hear from him I shall tell him that there is a young lady still very much in love with him. And where is your sister? Is she married?'

'She lives in London and is qualifying this summer as a doctor. She is going to be a surgeon.'

'My goodness, how exciting! How I admire the young women of today. In my youth I was considered a pioneer; but then only the stage was really open to women wishing for an independent life, as you have found for yourself, my dear Estella.'

The gracious lady drew back her chair and, bending over Estella, kissed her cheek and then clasped her to her bosom, enveloping her in the mystique of her charm, the subtle fragrance of her perfume, so that both seemed synonymous. 'I am *just* old enough to be your mother – I was first married at sixteen you know – and I want you to feel that you have in me, if not a mother, then a person to whom you can always come with the certainty that you will find love, a welcome and a sympathetic ear.'

'It's only for a season, Rayner.' Estella, still too excited to believe it, had flown to his room to show him the letter from Irving. They were playing in Preston on their way back to Manchester and the letter from Irving had been forwarded to her by her aunt:

Dear Miss Abercrombie, (it read)

Miss Terry tells me you are a most accomplished actress. I have reason to have great faith in her judgment. Could I, do you think, tempt you to consider a season with us at the Lyceum when we return from our next tour to America, in April or May? In the meantime could you manage a journey to London to discuss details with me if you are interested? We leave in September.

      With kind regards,
         Yours sincerely,
            Henry Irving.

171

PS. Miss Terry, alas, is ill with blood poisoning but recovered sufficiently to send you her best wishes.

'It will be the end of you if you go to London, Estella. You will be completely eclipsed by Terry. Mark my words.'

'It's a wonderful chance for me,' Estella took the letter from Rayner. 'Miss Terry called it a great leap forward. Oh Rayner, I don't want to leave you and Grant, Elspeth, Harriet and all our friends. But I do need to stretch my wings. I feel that something great is happening to me, that I am being called and cannot say "no".'

'You're dramatizing your life, Estella,' Rayner said bitterly. 'You can't live apart from make-believe. Consider, what parts can you play with Terry, the leading lady, the greatest star in the firmament of the British theatre? The critics will ignore you whereas here you are always noticed. Besides, Grant is thinking of renting a theatre in London and you will be his star.'

'Yes, I know.' Estella knew, too, that Rayner was hard at work on a new play, hoping that Grant would take it with him to London. In it, she knew too, was a leading part for her. The reasons for Rayner's disappointment were all too obvious.

'Think about it, Estella. Think of your future.'

Estella put the letter on a table and stood at the window looking onto the main street of this bustling Lancashire cotton town. The Theatre Royal, Preston had not the status of the Theatre Royal, Liverpool or the Theatre Royal, Manchester, but they had had a good run, with the house full of prosperous bourgeoisie most nights of the week. Many were farmers who owned vast acreages of the fertile land in the basin of the River Ribble which bisected the town. But most of them were industrialists who had opened up the cotton trade for which the wet Lancashire climate was so suitable. There were mills in practically every back street in Preston, and at six o'clock in the morning the cobblestones reverberated with the sound of the clogs of those who worked in them walking to work. Yet parts of Preston were pretty. It had a lovely park which sloped down to the banks of the river, and many fine houses with large gardens on the outskirts.

'I *have* thought about it, and I intend to accept. I can always come back if I'm wrong.'

'Of *course* Estella must accept,' Harriet said a few days later when Estella, back in Manchester, paid her a visit. 'It will be the silliest thing she has ever done if she declines.'

As usual Rayner was there. Estella knew all about their affair, having connived many times in arranging for them to meet. She liked Harriet and what people did with their lives was, she thought, no business of hers. But somehow she felt sorry for Rayner because she knew how little this form of love satisfied him. He had told her that, despite the difference in their ages, he wanted to marry Harriet, but she refused to hear of it and had started to mock him instead, emphasizing the gap between them.

'I have written back that I'll go and see him,' Estella replied. 'I'm leaving for London on Monday.'

'And taking a short holiday I hope.' Harriet put her head on one side. 'You've been working so hard. Rayner, why don't you go back to London with Estella? Maybe you could help reconcile her to her parents?'

'I think you want to get rid of me, Harriet,' Rayner said shortly. 'As for reconciling her with her father, what chance have I got? I wouldn't care to try.'

'I'm staying with my sister.' Estella looked from Rayner to Harriet, sensing that her arrival had interrupted a row. 'There is certainly nothing that Rayner can do for me with my parents. Besides, he does not approve of my going to the Lyceum.'

'He's jealous that's all,' Harriet said tauntingly. 'He wishes dear Henry wanted to employ *him*.'

'That's not true, Harriet!' Rayner snapped back.

'Isn't it?' Harriet had taken to smoking cigarettes in private and now put one in her mouth, lit it and exhaled a long thin trail of fragrant smoke in his direction. 'I wonder. Don't you feel a little on the rocks, Rayner Brook? The young genius who hasn't quite arrived, who has somehow "missed the boat"?'

'I most certainly don't.' Rayner, his face convulsed with rage, took up his hat which he had thrown on the couch, so eager had he been for sight of his beloved that he had forgotten to leave it in the hall. 'If that's what you think about me good day to you, Mrs Leadbetter.'

'Good day, good day, Mr Brook.' Harriet neatly stepped to one side and inclined her head, smiling sweetly as he brushed past her. Then she slammed the door after him and her face bore a smile of satisfaction. 'Well, that's got rid of him!'

'Did you *want* to get rid of him?' The scene had astonished and dismayed Estella.

'Of course I do, my dear; but he won't take the hint.'

'But I thought you were madly in love with him?'

'I *was*,' Harriet gestured vaguely in the air with her cigarette. 'But these things pass, don't they? Our affair has been going on for nearly three years, which is a long time for me. I wonder Rayner is still interested too. When there is a beautiful young girl like you about why does he prefer a raddled old hag like me?' Harriet fluttered her large eyes at Estella, quite openly fishing for compliments.

'You are a very attractive woman,' Estella obediently took up the cue, 'and don't you know it!'

'Thirty-nine, my dear, nearly forty.'

'Miss Terry is thirty-seven and she dazzled all the men in our cast, including Anthony Kitchin who is nineteen. Rayner has told me that he always prefers *mature* women

– apart from which he means nothing to me.'

'I wonder why not?' Harriet tipped the ash neatly in an ashtray and gave one of her mysterious smiles. 'I should have thought you *very* well suited.'

'Because he is in love with you, that's why. And I . . . '

'You are still in love with Tom Shipley, I'll wager.'

'Yes, I am in love with Tom.'

'But how? Why? He treated you so badly.'

'And we treated him badly, my family and I! We humiliated him. Tom had such pride. Only a man as proud as he was would behave as he did. At first I hated him, but now I admire him for it.'

'And would you like to see him again?'

The note of intrigue in Harriet's voice made Estella draw in her breath.

'You know where he is?'

Harriet nodded. 'I have known for some time where he is. He's in Manchester.'

'Oh Harriet!' Estella sank onto a chair, letting her body go limp. 'Does he want to see me?'

'Of course. He did not know how you felt about him. I said I'd ask you. He's been touring in Australia. Now he is once again looking for work. The first thing he asked me was how you were. He's heard of your success.'

'How long has he been here?'

'Only a few days. But first, my dear, you must go to London.'

'No, first I must see Tom.'

'No.' Harriet held up a hand. 'I want you to fix up the next stage in your career before you get involved with that man again. It is vital for you to go to the Lyceum.'

'It is vital for me to see Tom,' Estella said stubbornly. 'Do you realize that it is two years since we were married?'

'And you've not had a man since that time? Oh, dear, don't look so shocked. I know what it's like. When Mr

Leadbetter first took up with his mistresses I nearly went mad, but in time, of course, I found my own consolation. Any sensible woman should have at least two strings to her bow. As it is Mr Leadbetter scarcely ever troubles me now. No, mature women, my dear, of a passionate disposition, as you and I undoubtedly are, cannot do without men. I wonder you have not succumbed. I tried, you know, to put you and Rayner together; but I did not guess what a faithful soul he was, or how steadfast you could be to your Tom.'

'You *tried* to put us together?' Estella could hardly believe her ears, though she should have learned by now not to be shocked by anything Harriet said or did.

'Well, I thought you were more suitable than he and I. Besides I now have another lover. I can't say who he is for his name is too well known, locally at any rate. But he has wealth and connections as well as great charm and he is nearer my own age. A young man palls after a time. They lack sophistication. I think if poor Rayner found out about it he would kill him, and certainly if my "friend" knew about him he might do the same. He is intensely jealous.' Harriet moistened her lips and her eyes gleamed with excitement. 'So you see I am in something of a predicament. But I suppose, now that Tom's here, there's no chance you'd take poor dear Rayner away?'

CHAPTER NINE

The audience cheered and clapped and, one hand in Rayner's, the other in Grant's, Estella bowed low with the rest of the cast. Rayner and Grant spontaneously pushed her forward on her own, and she sank into a deep curtsey before rejoining the line and acknowledging the applause of the full house who had gathered for the last night of the season.

Then they left her alone on the stage and the audience rose as one while the curtain fell behind her and she curtsied again and again, first to the stalls, then to the circle and finally, blowing kisses, to the gallery. A footman came in carrying several bouquets which he put in her arms, and single flowers were thrown on the stage from the auditorium.

Estella's eyes filled with tears as she looked at the massed, excited crowd; she blew them more kisses and then she stepped behind the curtain and the whole cast reassembled around her as it rose again.

On the table in her dressing room was a letter, propped up against a vase containing a dozen red roses. She quickly shut the door to keep out the noise of revelry and Nan, her dresser, looked at her with shining eyes as she picked up the letter, her finger tearing through the envelope.

My dearest Estella,
    If you would like to see me again I shall be waiting in a coach opposite the stage door. Then I can tell you all the things I meant to tell you for so long. You were magnificent tonight.
Tom.

Estella brought the letter to her lips and looked at Nan. 'Did he bring it himself?'

'He gave it to me, miss, handing the letter and the roses through the door. He scarcely said a thing.'

'Oh Nan, help me out of my things, quickly.'

As she dressed those in the cast who thought they were seeing her on the Manchester stage for the last time came in to kiss and congratulate her. Some wept. They all knew she had seen Irving, who had offered her a place at the Lyceum. They all knew that, in Estella Abercrombie, a new star was on the ascendant and very few begrudged her her success. She received them courteously and calmly, hiding the extreme agitation she felt in her breast. Harriet had told her that Tom would be watching the play and would contact her afterwards.

'No Grant, I can't dine,' she said as he appeared behind her in white tie and tails. 'I have an appointment.'

'Ah?' he smiled. 'Something special?'

'Very special.'

'Maybe later, at the Windsor Rooms? You promised.'

'I'm sorry, this time I can't.' Estella shook her head and stood up, smoothing her long dress, patting her hair, dabbing some perfume behind her ears. Just the little makeup she wore was enough, she thought.

'Rayner and Harriet have gone off to the Windsor. Try to come.'

Nan slipped her cloak around her and gave her her bag.

'I'm sorry, Grant. It's too important. But we shall all meet again. I promise.'

'What shall I tell them?'

Grant was clearly upset because the party had been arranged for weeks.

'Tell them . . . ' her eyes flew to the door; he was sitting outside in the carriage waiting for her. Maybe if she were late he'd think she didn't want to see him and leave. 'Tell them I'll see them all again. Very soon.'

She kissed Grant on the cheek and ran along the corridor out of the stage door, clutching her long evening cloak around her.

There was the coach under the light of the street lamp. It was like a fairy story: she was going to her prince. The horse pawing at the cobbles of the narrow side street seemed an expression of her own agitation, and the coachman called to it sharply and pulled at his reins. As she ran towards it the door opened and two arms reached out for her, drawing her in.

'Estella!'

'Tom!'

And then the face that had haunted her dreams for so long was between her hands, the lips she had kissed so many times were hers once again. He folded her into his arms and the familiarity of his embrace made her feel they had never been apart, that the long months since their last meeting were a dream. At last he drew away from her and slipped a hand beneath her cloak, feeling her breast before letting it rest on her heart. The intimacy of the gesture thrilled her. This was a man she had known, and who had known her. It was even more romantic, more erotic than a fairy story. Now it began to seem real.

'I wondered if you'd come,' he said.

'Of course I came.' She looked at him, trying to smile, and he put up a finger to catch a tear that had slipped away from her eye down her cheek.

She leaned back against the seat and Tom tapped on the partition that divided them from the driver.

'Where are we going?' she said.

'Wherever you like.'

'I want to be with you.'

'I'm staying at a little house not far from here.'

'Let's go there.'

'Harriet talked about a party for the cast . . .'

'I want to be alone with you.' Her voice was firm

because she was quite decided about what she wanted to do. She had no doubts at all.

Tom gave instructions to the driver who drove forward slowly, then took a right turn while his horse broke into a trot. Estella nestled up to Tom, her face resting against his breast.

'I can't think you've forgiven me,' he said. 'This must be a dream.'

'Let's not talk about the past.'

'It was good for you anyway; you've become a success. I knew you would. I don't want to spoil your life now, Estella.'

She felt a tremor of fear and slipped a hand through his shirt to feel his bare flesh, to reinforce the intimacy begun by him. 'You'll spoil my life if you ever go away again.'

For a while he said nothing, and when the coach stopped he quickly jumped out, turning to help her onto the pavement. He had a few words with the cabbie and paid him, then he put his arm through hers and took her into the house.

'I told him to come back in an hour.'

'I want to stay with you all night.'

'What will your aunt and uncle say?'

'I don't care what they say. I'm of age now to do as I please. Besides, as far as I'm concerned, you're still my husband.'

The room was cold and impersonal as lodgings are, but not as bad as the one they'd shared before. A fire burned in the grate and the sheets were turned back on the large double bed. As soon as he closed the door behind them they embraced and, slipping off her cloak, he drew her over to the bed, laying her on it before he removed his own coat and lay beside her.

'Let's go away,' she said, turning to unfasten his tie.

'Where to?' His eyes were troubled, but he didn't stop her.

'Keswick. We were very happy there.'

'Estella . . .' He sat up as though to say something, but she pulled him down and kissed him, drawing on his tie until it lay in her hands. Steadily she undid his shirt and put her lips to his nipple surrounded by fine dark hairs. As she stroked him her body started to burn with passion. Tom groaned and suddenly he pulled his shirt wide open, exposing his naked torso. Quite roughly he turned her on her back and brutally kissed her face and her neck, wrenching at her low bodice and pulling down her dress, then her petticoat and stockings until she was quite naked. He finished undressing and knelt beside her, outlining her breasts with his hands.

'They've grown,' he said, opening his eyes wide.

'Then I was a girl, now I'm a woman.'

'Show me,' Tom said gazing at her thighs, which she opened wide to accommodate him.

When the dawn came they were still awake. Making love had eased the pressure, soothed the constraint between them, and he poured out all his adventures while she told him about Grant and Rayner and the stage. They made plans to go away together that very day. But she didn't say a word about Ellen Terry or Irving and the Lyceum. Because it seemed to her that Tom was more or less where he had been two years before, while she had progressed much farther. She didn't want to do or say anything to hurt him, because she remembered his pride and recalled his violence – a little hint of which she'd had as he undressed her.

As the blackbirds sang they made love again and then they slept. She was the first to awake and she quickly got up and dressed, leaving him slumbering on the bed. She wrote a note to say that she'd meet him at the station as they'd planned and then she slipped quietly out to look for a cab. She felt grown up and serene, at peace.

Her aunt and uncle were about to breakfast when she

got home and they looked up astonished to see her in her evening clothes.

'Estella, where have you been? We thought you were upstairs asleep.'

'I've been with Tom,' Estella said bluntly. 'He's back.'

She didn't want to phrase the announcement in a way that made it seem she was ashamed of herself, because she wasn't. She didn't want to hide the truth because she was so proud of her love for Tom. Imagining herself as Portia when she declared her love for Bassanio ('You see me, lord Bassanio, where I stand'), she gazed quite fearlessly at her uncle, who rose from his chair, and then quickly sat down again and looked in astonishment at his wife.

'I knew it would happen,' he said after a while. 'Just when you were launched that man would come back into your life again and ruin it.'

'He's my husband,' Estella said, accepting a cup of tea from her aunt. 'Thank you, Aunt Catherine.'

'Estella, he is *not* your husband,' her aunt said, reproving her. 'He is not and he never has been. He can only bring unhappiness to you. I know quite well what kind of man he is. He's mesmerized you.'

'You don't know him at all.' Estella sipped the tea, thinking of their bodies joined, of the rapture that even she could not describe; nor could she say how its memory lay lodged in her heart like a diamond which she would polish and cherish so that it would shine for ever. 'You don't know that he really is the kindest, most tender man on earth.'

'I would hardly call the way he behaved to you during your so-called marriage tender,' her uncle said mildly, tucking his napkin once more into the front of his waistcoat and trying to resume his breakfast. 'You have too short a memory, my dear. Your own gentleness does you credit; but I beg of you consider the advice of myself and your aunt. Do not see Mr Shipley again. Will you not breakfast with us, by the way?'

He held out a hand to her, but Estella placed her cup and saucer down gently on the table and joined her hands in her lap.

'I am not hungry, thank you, and I do appreciate your kindness Uncle, and that of Aunt Catherine. I do know how concerned you are for my welfare.' Slowly she stood up and, passing her hands down either side of her form, gazed at herself in the long mirror that hung over the mantelpiece in the breakfast room – a low pleasant room that led directly from the kitchen onto a conservatory, the doors of which were now open. 'But I am a woman now, am I not? Twenty-one, of age, is that not so? I agree I have made mistakes in the past but I hope I have profited from them.'

'You will make the biggest mistake of your life if you go off with Tom Shipley again,' her uncle said shortly. 'I can tell you that without any hesitation at all.'

'I concur, my dear.' Aunt Catherine shook her head sadly. She had observed Estella's gesture as she looked at her shapely womanly body in the mirror and understood its meaning. 'Mr Shipley is not a man to whom you should entrust your life and happiness.'

'Nor your fortune.' George Henshaw glanced at his wife, who avoided his eyes.

Estella looked sorrowfully at two people for whom she had a very real affection and regard, then she took up her cloak which she had laid on a chair as she came in and put it about her shoulders.

'What I have *is* Tom's, Uncle. He is my husband, my lover. Please do not be shocked because, before long, we shall regularize our union, this time for good. But in the meantime we're going away. I have finished, as you know, with Grant and his players and Tom and I have time to get to know each other again before we go to London.'

'Then you will take up your place with Mr Irving?'

'Of course I shall.' Estella smiled and bent to kiss her

183

aunt's fragrant cheek. 'With Tom by my side and a part in the Lyceum shall I not be the happiest, luckiest woman in the world?' Impulsively, theatrically, Estella knelt by her aunt's side and bowed her head. 'Oh Aunt Catherine, please give me your blessing, say you wish us both well.'

She raised her eyes to meet those of her aunt, and the contrast between the one pair, which sparkled with youthful hope, and the other, which was full of doubts occasioned by the wisdom of age, was noted by her uncle who looked helplessly at them both, his breakfast still untasted before him. Brusquely he pushed his plate away. Slowly her aunt put one hand on Estella's head and then, falteringly, joined the other to it in a silent benediction. But she spoke no words.

They didn't stay at the same hotel in Keswick, but at a farmhouse in Borrowdale where they had a large low-ceilinged bedroom with a view of the distant lake. They spent a lot of time in their room, as they had on their honeymoon two years before; but their landlady was indulgent and didn't make sly remarks or give knowing winks, but brought them up large trays of food for sustenance. Estella wore the ring that she had always kept and they said they were on their honeymoon.

When they did leave their room they climbed the beautiful Borrowdale hills or walked along the banks of the lake, hands entwined, arm in arm; lovers who had quite deliberately cast aside all care or concern with the world.

A week passed in this fashion and then another and they didn't discuss the future, although Estella wanted to. She remained unconcerned because she knew now that Tom was in her heart for ever. After a reunion like this nothing could part them again. She gave so freely of herself that it was like giving away her life, putting it completely, and with trust, in the care of another. Estella was so hungry for love that Tom didn't dare say what was on his mind, or tell her the thoughts that kept him awake while she slept by his side.

'What a perfect day it is, again.' Estella ran to the window and gazed across the marshy stretch that separated the farmhouse from the lake. The purple hills and brown crags on either side of Derwentwater were reflected in the clear waters of the lake so that they seemed to be a continuous mass falling into the depths. Estella stretched and drew her arms above her head quite wantonly, knowing well the effect this would have on Tom, shaking loose her blond hair and then running her hands through it.

Tom's eyes travelled along her body and he reached out his arms for her, putting back the sheets so that she could climb in beside him.

'What shall we do today?' Estella said, willingly lying back and abandoning herself to his caresses.

'This.' Tom kissed her.

She put a hand on the back of his head and drew him on to her; then she lowered her arm to his neck and enclosed him tightly between her thighs.

'I wish I could keep you like this for ever in my prison,' she murmured. 'Are you happy, Tom?'

'Happy, happy,' he said.

That morning they breakfasted downstairs by the window of the small dining room that looked up the valley, past Lingy Bank and High Scawdell to Seatoller Fell and Honister Pass. There were a few other guests staying, but they had all gone out. They were mostly older people who liked walking. Estella and Tom had a map between them and, heads close together, Estella's finger traced a path that led over Honister to Buttermere at the other side.

'It's a long walk,' Mrs Hardcastle glanced over their shoulders as she put two large plates of eggs and Cumber-

185

land sausages in front of them. 'You best take care not to go too far, or you'll be caught by nightfall, now that the evenings are drawing in.'

'That won't matter,' Tom said, smiling at the farmer's wife. 'We shall know what to do.'

'I'm sure of that,' their hostess chuckled, gathering up the porridge plates they'd put to one side. 'Tea or coffee?'

'Coffee please, Mrs Hardcastle, as usual.'

They ate for a while in silence and when they'd finished Tom leaned back and gazed at her.

'I think I'm utterly content,' he said. 'Lovely scenery, good food, beautiful weather, you . . . '

Estella put her knife and fork together and reached for his hand.

'Tom, let's talk about the future some time? What we're going to do?'

'Do?' Tom said as if the idea of 'doing' anything were quite alien to him.

'About ourselves.'

'Oh, I see.' Tom frowned and wiped his lips with a napkin.

'We could get married again any time you liked.'

'It seems very funny to say "married again",' Tom said in a way that didn't sound at all amused.

'I wish you'd say what you have on your mind Tom?'

'I've nothing on my mind.' Tom shook out the previous day's paper that had lain untouched by his side. 'Why spoil a beautiful day by looking into the future?'

Scowling he looked at the paper and, suddenly nervous, Estella got up and went upstairs to put on her walking skirt and heavy boots. She remembered how Rayner had reacted so many years ago when she was about to declare her love for him. She'd proposed to Tom two years before, and now she was about to do the same thing again, make the same mistake. She was too impulsive. But what made Tom hesitate? Was he afraid of interrupting this idyll? Tom was so different now from the man who had once frightened her, who had raped her, whose fear had been translated into violence towards himself and another. She understood all the reasons for that now. Seeing him scowl reminded her quite painfully of how he could change and turn to violence. Because he was a violent man; even his lovemaking wasn't gentle but forceful. It seemed as though he were governed by forces he could scarcely keep under control; yet his passion matched her own temperament and she found his frenzy exciting, erotic and deeply satisfying.

Such memories made her forget her misgivings and her happiness slowly returned as she brushed her hair and coiled it at the nape of her neck, securing it with two long pins. Tom liked it loose, so she hardly ever made an elaborate coiffure. She looked for some cold cream to smooth lightly on her face, because her complexion was so vital to her career and the weather could suddenly change in Lakeland. Then she remembered Tom had put the small jar in the pocket of his coat the day before because the wind chapped his lips during the day. She picked up her bag and stick and then saw that the coat Tom had worn the day before was hanging in the wardrobe, so she ran her hand through the pockets looking for the cream.

In an inside pocket her fingers encountered a solitary piece of paper. It was quite thick and folded in half. There had been nothing else in his pockets, but just this paper and, as she touched it, she knew instinctively that it had a message for her that would change her life. Afterwards she would think she was being dramatic, but nevertheless it was true. She knew with certainty, as she drew the paper out and slowly unfolded it, that something momentous and crucial was happening. She could put it back, but she knew she wouldn't. The paper seemed there for her to touch and open, and she did.

There was a Melbourne address and the date: 24 July

1884, nearly two months ago. Estella had assimilated its entire contents in a single glance, but she backed onto the bed and sat down, beginning again, reading slowly:

Dearest Tommy, *(the letter ran, in an immature script)*
I have sorted out all our things and packed up and I've booked a passage on the *SS Themistocles* which leaves Melbourne on 14 August. The doctor says the baby isn't due until November, by which time I will be with you well and truly, Tommy dear.

I wish you would write me an address where I can reach you rather than the post office. I hope all your problems are sorted out, and you are finding work and a nice little home for us. All friends here send their love and kind regards.

    Your very loving little 'wifie',
              Tilly.

PS. Baby jumping inside me sends Daddy a great big kiss.

Estella let the paper fall and lay back on the bed. She felt suddenly surrounded by intense cold as though someone were laying her in her tomb. She shut her eyes and the room turned round, the cold penetrating her body so that even her lips were numb. She trembled with the cold and the rigour of her body prevented her from moving her limbs.

She didn't know how long she lay there and when she opened her eyes it seemed dark, but then she realized that a large form standing at the window, his back to her, blocked out the sun. Her lips were very dry and when she tried to speak no words came because her tongue stuck to the roof of her mouth. She made a sound and Tom turned round. Two deep grooves bracketed either side of his mouth, and his lips had disappeared beneath a recently grown moustache. Heavy lids drooped across his eyes. Altogether he looked menacing as he sat beside her without attempting to touch her. However, his voice was gentle when he spoke.

'I'm sorry you found out this way. I tried to tell you but I couldn't. The words just wouldn't come. I should have thrown the letter away, but . . . I suppose I wanted you to find it. You had to some time.'

Estella lay where she was, staring at the ceiling. She wished the ceiling would fall and bury them, or the house would sink under the earth, entombing their love for ever. She wished she could go back to the time before she had read the letter, but something had happened that could never be undone, and it lay beside her on the bed – a testimony to infidelity. She tried to moisten her lips, but her tongue was so dry it only made a clacking noise against her mouth, as a dead branch beats against the walls of a house. She wondered if she'd had a stroke because it was impossible to move and her stricken eyes looked out at Tom, begging him to have pity.

She saw the consternation on his face and he leaned over her and said: 'Are you all right?'

Her tongue clacked helplessly again and she made a gasping noise with her throat. Quickly he got up and poured her some water from a jug that stood by the side of the bed. Then he raised her head as though she were a baby and gave her nourishment. Estella sipped greedily and the water of life flowed through her body, freeing her limbs. She took a deep breath and sat up. Her head was throbbing and she held it between her hands.

'I'm terribly, terribly sorry, Estella. Believe me, I didn't know this would happen. I mean, I didn't know we'd fall so madly in love again. I thought maybe it was all over.'

'But why did you try and see me?' Her voice was very low and sounded unfamiliar to her.

'I had to see you. I wanted to know; but I didn't ever think it could be like this. I was curious if you like. What man can resist seeing a pretty woman he has once loved?' The 'once' hurt her, but she didn't interrupt and he continued: 'I didn't in my wildest dreams, think you'd react like you did. You actually *seduced* me, Estella.'

Tom began to sound rather indignant now and he got up

189

and returned to the window moodily staring out. She realized then that men and women, whatever the degree of intimacy between them, always remained strangers to each other. That no trust was possible between them because one or the other was always capable of deception. That, now, she believed to be true.

Estella took another sip of water and rose unsteadily from the bed. The letter fell with her, and she kicked it under the bed. Then she went to the dressing table and uncoiled her hair, brushing it before dividing it into three plaits and very carefully making an elaborate coiffure of it again.

The honeymoon was over.

They didn't go out again until afternoon, when they took a long walk by the side of the lake, not hand in hand and not very close together. Tom had told her about the woman he'd met on the boat going out to Australia. How depressed he'd been and what a good companion she'd become to him. He'd never dreamed that Estella would ever forgive him and he became very fond of Matilda, or Tilly as she called herself, who was a kind, good person, an orphan who'd gone to Australia to look for a job. She was no one, Tom said, not even very pretty and with no talent such as Estella had. Estella knew the effect that someone like Tom would have on a penniless young girl without family, adrift and looking for work.

Tilly had been very good and faithful to Tom and, feeling the future had nothing to offer him, he married her when she knew she was pregnant and before returning to England. He didn't want it, but she did. When Estella asked him why he wanted to come home alone he said he had to be sure he was free, because if he were a bigamist Tilly couldn't enter Britain. He told her he'd a lot of business problems to see to. It was Harriet who'd informed him that his marriage to Estella had been annulled, but he didn't tell her about Tilly. She had told him, however, that Estella talked about him and, she thought, still loved him.

'Then you should have left me alone,' Estella had said.

'How could I?' Tom replied. 'I would have had to be superhuman not to want at least to see you again. Besides, the passion we've shared surpasses anything I've known with Tilly . . .'

'Shared'. The past tense again, and she had begged him to stop before she once again lost control of herself.

The sun had sunk behind the hills and a breeze disturbed the calm water of the lake. Estella felt she had never seen anything so beautiful, or ever felt such desolation.

'Look,' Tom said desperately, turning to her. 'I'll tell her what has happened and ask her to divorce me.'

'Is that a nice thing to do to a woman expecting your child?'

For the first time Estella was able to feel contempt for the man at her side, which relieved her because all she'd felt during the day was a terrible sense of deprivation and loss. How could you feel anything else when something like this had happened so suddenly? It was worse than death, because a dead person was no longer there, while living, breathing Tom had shared a bed with her last night and would do so again if she allowed him. He had never at any time seemed to her to register the enormity of what he'd done. Lindsey would say that was just like a man. But Lindsey didn't know men as she did, didn't know this man.

'No, it's not, but we . . . ' Tom stared at her as though hoping she'd tell him what to say.

'*We* haven't got anything left now, Tom. Not after you've done this to me. It is Tilly and your baby you must think about.'

'Please, Estella, don't say that.'

'What else can I say? I'd be hideously selfish if I thought only of me and not of them.'

'I didn't mean to *do* anything to you. It just happened.'

Estella stopped and broke a twig full of red leaves from the low lying branch of a tree. The leaves seemed like the autumn of her life, beautiful but dead and brittle, without hope.

'I see how weak you are, now, Tom Shipley. Everything "just happens" to you, doesn't it? The only thing that puzzled me about these past two weeks was that you never wanted to discuss the future. The only time you frowned was this morning at breakfast when I brought it up. I wore my ring and I wanted to talk about our remarriage; but something about you held me back. I wanted the suggestion to come from you. Rayner Brook once said that because I am an actress, I dramatize everything. Yet your arrival seemed the culmination of my recent successes. I imagined a wonderful future for us on the London stage. Because I'm going to the Lyceum, Tom.' He tried to interrupt her, but she held up a hand. 'Mr Irving has asked me, and I'm starting next spring. In my dreams, and knowing how well they thought of you, I imagined us both acting there, Mr and Mrs Shipley like Mr and Mrs Bancroft, Mr and Mrs Kean or Mr and Mrs Kendall. I imagined a great theatrical partnership, with you acting, writing and directing and me playing all the fine roles.'

'Then why didn't you *say* . . .' Tom began, but she threw the branch upon the water and watched it drift away, dusting her hands.

'It's dead, Tom. I thought you were a fine, proud man. I admired you for *not* kow-towing to my father. I thought this separation between us was a preparation for the rest of our life together. But now I see you are very weak, pitifully weak. I could forgive you almost everything, even infidelity; but I cannot forgive you marrying another woman and coming back to *me* when *she* is expecting your child! I cannot ever, ever forgive that.'

Tom's eyes had almost disappeared beneath his thick

brows and she could feel the storm rising within him. He stepped forward and, thrusting her against the thick trunk of a fir tree, leaned the full weight of his body against hers.

'Estella, if you say anything more you'll drive me mad, do you hear?' He took her chin between his hands, his warm breath fanning her face. 'Do you hear that, Estella? With you I've known a tremendous love and if I've hurt Tilly by it I'm sorry. But I want you and I'm not going to let you go. By God, I shan't let you go!'

He pressed his lips upon hers and put his knee between her legs. The terrible memory of the rape came back, and she struck at him with her fists, summoning all her strength to push him away from her. Then she hit him across the face, backwards and forwards, as she sometimes had in a play. The drama of her own life was so vivid now that she could scarcely tell what was acting and what was real. The actions and the dialogue were like a stage performance, yet her emotional turmoil was like nothing she ever knew on the stage.

'Tom Shipley, if I have to go to the far side of the world I will get away from you. You're treacherous, Tom, vile and false. You came from another woman straight to me and yet you say *I* seduced you! You gave me roses, Tom, red roses. Rosemary, that's for remembrance, but red roses are for love. You welcomed me with open arms and yet you never gave me any hint of the truth.'

'The truth was that I loved you, Estella! Why do you have to be so stupid that you can't realize that? Why can't you help me with my problem and not torment me?'

She'd marked Tom's face but he seemed to feel no pain, no anger. He was like a man in a daze continuing to gaze at her as though unaware of what she had done.

'Because you *lied* to me,' Estella hissed. 'All those stories you told me about Australia were lies.'

'They were true.'

'You never once mentioned that all the time you were

accompanied by a woman. You left out the parts that didn't suit you. You can never win with lies, Tom. The truth will always come out.'

'Did you expect me to tell you about Tilly when I was with you? Tilly means nothing to me, compared to you. I'll provide for her and the child. I'll . . . '

Estella felt herself overwhelmed by a really terrible rage, and restrained herself with difficulty from hitting him once more.

'Tom, what are you saying? Are you quite mad? That woman will kill herself if you do as you say. She is coming over here in all trust expecting to see you, to have you with her when she has her child. What sort of woman do you think *I* am to connive at such behaviour? I tell you, Tom Shipley, I am much too proud to want you now . . . '

Tom put his arms on either side of her, his palms against the tree, his face almost touching hers. The desperation in his eyes was more frightening than the threat of real physical abuse; slowly Estella interposed a hand between herself and his chest and began to push him away.

'Don't kiss me, Tom. Let me go now. Let me walk away . . . '

Her eyes mesmerized him and she pushed him gently until she felt his body yield and he stood quietly back to let her pass.

Estella walked quickly along by the side of the lake, the path where they'd walked so often, sharing so many happy confidences about the theatre, about life, but never about the future. Never ever about the future. She didn't look behind to see if he was following her because she'd seen the expression in his eyes. It was as though a fire had been quenched, as he quietly stepped aside, out of her path, out of her life. She rubbed her painful wrists and when she was out of sight of Tom she dipped them in the cool water of the lake, and then she rubbed water on her face and down her neck.

Once back at the farm she quickly packed her things and asked their landlady to find her transport back to Keswick. She didn't explain why and Mrs Hardcastle didn't ask, though her face was troubled.

Estella stood by the door and took a quick look round the room: at their bed, at the almost empty wardrobe still with the jacket hanging there whose pockets she had so thoughtlessly ransacked that morning. She looked at the view from the window and saw that it was almost dark. She took the ring from her finger and placed it on the table on Tom's side of the bed.

Then she shut the door firmly behind her.

CHAPTER TEN

The young woman's stomach was distended and her breasts were swollen. She lay on the demonstration couch with her eyes vacant as though quite unaware of, and unconcerned by, the interested students surrounding her. Mrs Atkins, who lectured in diseases of women at the School, gently palpated her belly, tracing the blue milk veins on her breasts, talking in a quiet voice. Then she invited the students to examine the patient.

'How many months pregnant would you say she was?' Mrs Atkins enquired of Mary Rossi, a fourth year student who was trying to listen to the foetal heart.

'Seven months?' Mary, puzzled, straightened up and Mrs Atkins, smiling, covered the supine patient and turned away, leaving the cubicle before proceeding to the next. Outside she stopped and the party gathered round her.

'She is not pregnant at all,' Mrs Atkins whispered. 'This is a very interesting case of pseudocyesis, or phantom pregnancy. She is a patient at the psychiatric department of University College and they lent her to us so that I could demonstrate the case to you.'

'What will happen to her?' Lindsey was attending Mrs Atkins as assistant gynaecologist.

'She will go into labour in two months' time. Of course nothing will happen, except that her stomach will subsequently return to its normal shape. This is her third phantom pregnancy which reproduces all the symptoms of actual pregnancy except that there is no foetus in her uterus.'

'But the uterus *was* distended,' Mary Rossi, who had made the diagnosis of seven months, protested.

'Exactly.'

'What causes this condition?' Lindsey was writing busily in a large blue notebook.

'Who knows? You will have to ask the professor of psychiatry that. It is certainly a most interesting phenomenon. Now the next case is quite genuine; however, there are some interesting factors,' and she parted the curtains of the cubicle and went in followed by her small escort.

Lindsey thought about the patient with the pseudocyesis as she made her way home that night. According to Mrs Atkins the girl was a virgin, a quiet, rather timid young person who lived with her parents in Camberwell and worked as a clerk in an Oxford Street store during the day. She was twenty-eight years of age, pale and dark and quite pretty. Lindsey would have given a great deal to know further details, and made a note to contact the psychiatric department of University College Hospital and find out more about her if she could.

Lindsey had graduated from the London School of Medicine for Women in the summer, obtaining high marks in all her papers and honours in obstetrics and gynaecology. The practical clinical year came at the end of three years' study of the theory and practice of medicine, and soon she would be presented by the Dean to Lord Granville, the Chancellor, at Burlington House, London, to receive her degrees of Bachelor of Medicine and Bachelor of Surgery. Mrs Garrett Anderson had offered her the post of assistant gynaecologist at her hospital in Euston Road, which had, as yet, no obstetric department; and Lindsey now spent her days in looking after the women patients at the hospital, assisting at operations and helping to instruct the students.

Yet Lindsey's heart was not in gynaecology, not even, she felt, in the practice of physical medicine. Although her surgical and diagnostic skills had received high praise, she

197

felt that what she did was mechanical, like riding a bicycle, or exercising some other skill that had taken more time to acquire. Her mind, she sometimes felt, was like that of an automaton, stuffed full of facts, learned by rote, which it repeated over and over again.

When she got in Charlotte, as usual, was waiting for her with the tea tray laid by the fire, and as she relaxed she told her about the curious case of the phantom pregnancy which interested her so much because of its rarity. It was so different from the usual organic diseases she encountered every day. Charlotte had given up the study of medicine at the end of her second year because her squeamishness had threatened her mental equilibrium; and now she devoted her time to the study of history and music, embroidery and, occasionally, the practice of good works. Lindsey was frequently moved by the plight of the many poor women who attended the hospital and occasionally she would bring a particularly bad case to Charlotte's attention, and Charlotte would do all she could to bring some relief, either by offers of food or money or by improving the conditions of the patient. Usually this was impossible due to the overcrowded houses in which the mass of Londoners still lived. But sometimes she was able to send the patient to the country to convalesce, or arrange for her children to be looked after during the duration of her illness.

But over-riding every other interest in life was Lindsey: her comfort and her welfare. Nothing at all was ever allowed to interfere with that, and Lindsey, cared for like a husband, always had exactly the conditions she needed to work at home. Occasionally, or as her finals had drawn near, Charlotte had insisted on taking her abroad to Switzerland, to her father's *Schloss* in Austria in the mountains, or to the seaside.

Every day, too, like a good spouse, Charlotte made a point of being home to welcome her, attend to her needs and listen to her after a hard day at the hospital. Sometimes she had to return at night for a difficult or dangerous case, and Charlotte would get up with her and wait for her, be there to welcome her when she returned, with hot milk or tea and a warm fire.

'What brings about this condition in a young woman?' Charlotte enquired as Lindsey sipped her tea, gazing into the fire.

'Very little is known about it, for it falls within the category of diseases classified under hysteria. The subject is much despised by the medical fraternity – they call it malingering – but I am convinced it is genuine and remain fascinated by its many different manifestations. I have seen patients paralysed and in constant pain, no organic reason ever being found for their distressing conditions. Hysteria is *supposed* to be due to some malfunctioning of the womb – hence the name, you see – and so a hysterical pregnancy is perhaps not so very extraordinary, after all. But I am not convinced of this, myself, as it is quite certain men are affected as well as women and that hysterical symptoms can arise from shock.

'The paralysis of the limbs in hysterics is a fact, and the swollen belly and large-veined breasts of the woman I told you about were facts too. This strengthens my view that the origin of many illnesses is psychological, and if we knew more about it we could either cure or prevent a number of conditions that we classify now as organic. Take Estella.' Lindsey lowered her voice, instinctively raising her eyes to the ceiling. 'She is quite surely not *ill*, and yet she has many of the symptoms of a wasting illness, say a cancerous growth, or tuberculosis. She coughs, she has lost weight, she eats very little, she sleeps badly. She is frequently sick and nauseous, but no one at the hospital could find anything seriously amiss with her.'

'We know what's wrong with Estella.' Charlotte glanced up from her knitting. 'It's her experience with that terrible man.'

'Yes, Tom Shipley has to answer for a lot,' Lindsey replied. 'But Estella should have got over it by now. She has been here more than three months. I wish to God Irving would come back and the Lyceum season could begin.'

'You think she will be all right then?'

'Without a doubt. She has nothing to take her mind off her humiliation and, perhaps, remorse and guilt. I wish she would agree to see my parents too. She insists on leading a life that is unnaturally abnormal – no close friends, no contact with relatives except me and no entertainment. For a successful actress it is, indeed, a strange and rather terrifying existence.'

Lindsey got up and put her teacup on the tray, glancing at her watch. Everything at the hospital was governed by time and she was for ever consulting it – a large timepiece given to her by her father when she took her Cambridge degree. Then she went over to Charlotte and perched on the arm of her chair, her hand carelessly on Charlotte's shoulder.

'There's a man in Paris called Professor Charcot. He's a famous neurologist who has transformed his treatment of the insane at the Salpêtrière hospital. Dr Digby told me of him, and lent me papers written by Dr Charcot and others about his work. He has successfully treated many cases of hysteria by hypnotism, which, of course, is anathema to the main body of the medical profession. I would like to see him at work.'

'You would like to visit Paris?'

'I'd like to *live* in Paris.' Lindsey wound a piece of Charlotte's hair about her fingers. 'I'd like to work under Dr Charcot for a year; but I dread letting Mrs Anderson down.'

'I don't wonder.'

'I know she has great hopes of me at the hospital. I'm one of the first graduates of her school, and she expects me to repay in kind what I have gained.'

Charlotte turned and gazed up at Lindsey, lightly touching her hand. 'She has a point. It would seem such a waste.'

'Why *waste*?'

'What exactly are you talking about, my dear, the treatment of the insane?'

'No, you simply don't understand.' Lindsey got impatiently off the chair and walked to the window, gazing at the little patio illuminated on this cold November evening only by the light from the drawing room. She pressed her head against the window and stared for a long time at the reflection of herself. 'Medical research, the nervous system, functions of the brain, interest me more than the behaviour of the womb or diseased organs of reproduction. Neurology is the key to mental abnormality, to states such as depression, melancholia and hysteria. In many ways our treatment of these conditions is mediaeval. Why do we subordinate them to the care of the physically sick? No expense is spared on research of this kind. I would like to study neurology in Paris and see how far the neurones influence mental dysfunction. Are the neurones not involved at all, and the illness purely psychological? What is the relationship between neurology and psychology – or is there one at all? I have had many interesting conversations with Dr Digby at the Royal Free about it. Might I ask him to dinner some time, Charlotte dear?'

As Lindsey turned from the window Charlotte looked at her. Lindsey at twenty-six was tall, striking and extraordinarily composed. It was difficult to imagine Lindsey ever losing her head, letting her control slip and panicking. It was also very difficult – for one who knew her well – to imagine Lindsey losing her heart and falling in love. Yet it was not at all difficult to see why men were attracted to her. She had never been conventionally beautiful, and she wasn't now, but she was arresting. People noticed her and then looked at her again. She held herself well and dressed with style; and that capable air, that unruffled appearance, that serene brow and those thoughtful, intelligent blue eyes, made many a man feel that Lindsey would be a very suitable person to preside over their home, and many of them pursued her.

Lindsey always had a special friend among the men she met; some medical student or doctor who became fascinated by her, courted her and sent her flowers. She liked men, especially their minds; but she had never had a lover, and would never permit an intimate relationship to intervene between herself and her career. Charlotte always dreaded the time when that should happen, because it was inevitable that it would, and as long as Lindsey was a student she felt she was safe. But now that she was qualified, what was to prevent her giving her heart as so many other women like her did? What would Charlotte do then?

So the mention of another new name, Mortimer Digby, which cropped up more and more these days, sent a tremor of apprehension through Charlotte in case this should be the one who would ultimately take Lindsey from her. But the idea of further research and study could postpone this eventuality for longer. Maybe Dr Digby should be encouraged?

'Pray *do* ask Dr Digby to dinner,' she said cheerfully. 'Maybe he will also be good for our dear Estella.'

Dr Mortimer Jethro Spencer Digby was a New Englander of good family, a most intelligent man of thirty-six years of age endowed with considerable charm. Since graduating in medicine at Harvard thirteen years before he had applied himself solely to medical research, and had gradually decided that neurology should be his speciality. He had studied in Vienna under Professor Meynert and in Paris with Professor Charcot before coming to London to take up an appointment at University College as lecturer and demonstrator in neuropathology.

Dr Digby was very tall, so tall in fact that he had a slight stoop as though he had perpetually to bend when entering a room, as indeed he had. His frame, though spare, had a muscularity that one would not expect but which enabled him to move not awkwardly, as some tall people do, but with a certain elegance. Although he showed all the confidence that wealth, security and the certainty of excellence in his chosen profession gave to a man, there was an appealing sensitivity about him that made him pleasing to men and attractive to women. He seemed, even at a glance, to possess a most well rounded and affecting personality. In colouring he was fair, his hairline receding, not much but just enough to emphasize the qualities of his considerable brain, which seemed to manifest itself in a lofty forehead beneath which was an alert, interesting and humorous face. He wore gold-rimmed spectacles, maybe for affectation because he did not need them all the time, or maybe because they enhanced the undoubted intelligence of his pale blue eyes.

Despite the morbid nature of much of his research, the pathology, for instance, of the nervous system and the brain, he appeared to derive a good deal of pleasure from life. He positively exuded enjoyment, and perhaps it was the attraction of opposite personalities that drew him to the intense young woman opposite him, as she peered through a microscope in the pathology laboratory in the hospital which she had special permission to work in when her normal duties allowed.

Lindsey fascinated Dr Digby, the more so the less he saw of her. She did not have any of the flirtatious attributes of most of the matrimonially inclined young women he encountered, and a woman doctor was still enough of a rarity to fill him with admiration and some awe. It was not, he considered, as though she were dowdy, plain or bowed down by the weight of cerebral activity as many of the academic women he came into contact with were. On the contrary, her clothes were extremely smart, and her blond hair was also dressed with an eye to fashion. It lay on her forehead in a fringe of curls from a centre parting across the head and rose at the back to a large chignon secured by a tortoiseshell comb. Her skin was particularly good, giving the impression not only of care, but of a healthy, active life with plenty of good food and fresh air.

But more than anything it was not the quality of her mind, not the grace of her carriage nor the style of her clothes, but a peculiar and distinctive aura that emanated from her that attracted Dr Digby. One had the sensation of a tightly coiled spring that held the promise of infinite and rewarding possibilities when it was allowed, or maybe permitted itself, to unwind.

Mortimer Digby had very quickly summed up in his mind exactly the rare sort of woman Lindsey was, and he knew too – being something of a psychologist – that she might be more intrigued by apparent indifference than excessive admiration. Accordingly he reluctantly rationed himself in taking advantage of the delights of her presence and of conversation with her. He was often missing from the laboratory when he knew she would be there and he never invited her out, despite the fact that they increasingly became aware of common interests apart from medicine: a love of cycling and the out of doors, and an interest in the theatre and opera. He knew her sister was an actress and it was when, after a number of months, he said he would like to meet her that Lindsey, to his surprise and gratification, invited him to dinner.

Mortimer Digby knew about Charlotte because Lindsey

frequently mentioned her name. After spending an hour in their company he had made up his mind about their relationship; it was not uncommon in women who either voluntarily or involuntarily were deprived of male company. Seeing that they were both attractive, personable young women he imagined it to be voluntary and based on Lindsey's passion to be a doctor which matrimony would have ruined. Here, he knew, was a special friendship, but one that was not in any way unnatural or physical. He knew this as much by Lindsey's intense reserve as by the protective way Charlotte regarded her. He had come across many women who passionately enjoyed the company of their own sex in an age when a more natural, normal relationship between the sexes was not encouraged. Men had recourse to lower-class women, or brothels; but there was no such release possible for well brought up females. As a doctor Mortimer knew more than most men about these things, and it had made him a passionate advocate of women's emancipation. Usually, however, when the time came such cloistered women were not averse to matrimony. He felt sure this was the case with Lindsey, but he had not the same certainty about the watchful Charlotte. He knew he would have to make a friend of her if he were ever to try and prise Lindsey away.

Their visitor was most entertaining company. He was amusing, erudite and had travelled widely. Even Charlotte could not but help approving of him but, in particular, she encouraged him to discourse about Paris and the celebrated Professor Charcot.

'My father has a house in Paris, in the Parc Monceau. Should Lindsey care to study there, there would be a home for her.'

'Lindsey is going to study in Paris?' Estella had not been listening much to the conversation, nibbling her food, wrapped up in her own problems. But now she came alive. 'When?'

'Oh nothing's settled,' Lindsey said quickly. 'It is just a notion I'm toying with.'

'Paris is magnificent!' Dr Digby exclaimed enthusiastically. 'London is so dreary in the winter, but in Paris there is too much to do.'

'There's quite a lot to do here if one has the mind for it, the Bancrofts at the Haymarket, and Melba at the opera.' Charlotte nodded to the maid to serve the sweet. 'But yes, Paris would be attractive. Lindsey dear?'

'It's not the attractions of Paris I'm thinking about. Unlike Dr Digby, I have much to learn.'

'But *I* have much to learn too, Dr Abercrombie.' Dr Digby's ebullience gave place to gravity. 'I don't think I shall ever learn enough however long I live. But is this not one of the hazards as well as the charms of our profession? Sometimes we seem to be still in the dark ages, at others on the threshold of great discoveries, and this applies particularly to neurology and the study of the brain. In Vienna a certain Doctor Breuer has already applied hypnotism to cases of hysteria and even in America the science of psychopathology is making vast strides.'

'I didn't know you were even contemplating moving to Paris. Whatever shall I do?' Estella was overcome by a wave of anxiety and, as she gazed at the apple pie that had been set before her, topped by a blob of rich, thick cream, she experienced a sudden feeling of nausea that caused her to sway in her chair.

'Are you quite well, Miss Abercrombie?' Dr Digby leaned forward anxiously and Lindsey hastily intervened.

'I assure you we're not thinking of going to Paris just yet. I would never dream of leaving you until Mr Irving has returned and you are settled. Besides, I have my own problems with Mrs Anderson to sort out.'

Suddenly Dr Digby leapt to his feet as Estella fell forward over the table, contriving to catch her before she hit her head. As he supported her with his arms, he professionally took her pulse.

'My sister has not been well,' Lindsey hastened to add her support to that of Dr Digby as Estella's eyelids fluttered and opened again. 'She has been over-tired and prey to nervous prostration.' Lindsey put a glass of water to Estella's lips and then helped her to rise from her chair.

'I'm so sorry,' Estella murmured, her eyes vague as though she did not know where she was. 'I felt faint. Would it be all right if I went to my room?'

'Of course.' Charlotte anxiously fluttered around the table while Lindsey put an arm round her sister's waist and guided her to the door.

'Pray excuse me. I shan't be a minute.'

While Lindsey was away Charlotte took Dr Digby into the drawing room, calling for the maid to bring coffee. She felt uneasy and, begging him to sit down, paced agitatedly about the room. 'Lindsey is very concerned about her sister.'

'But what is the cause of the trouble exactly? Does anybody know?'

'She is suffering from the unsatisfactory conclusion to an affair of the heart.'

'Ah, depression.' Dr Digby sagely nodded his head. 'Maybe some neurasthenia. She also looks anaemic to me.'

He confided his diagnosis to Lindsey when at last she returned, saying that Estella was settled and resting.

'Anaemia?' Lindsey shook her head. 'She has had a complete examination at our hospital. Neurasthenia, what is that?'

'Nervous exhaustion, a breakdown of the system, a term coined by George Beard, a New York neurologist, to indicate nervous debility brought on by overwork or stress. An unrequited love affair might have precipitated your sister's condition.'

207

'Oh it *was* requited,' Lindsey's eyes flashed. 'Unfortunately. But in total it was most unsatisfactory, and damaging to Estella. I think I may ask Mrs Anderson to examine her again. She has certainly made very little progress in the time she's been here; she is quite unlike her former self. Our reference to Paris distressed her because she has been engaged to appear at the Lyceum. Unfortunately she is estranged from my parents and would have nowhere to go if we were to leave.'

'She could stay here,' Charlotte said. 'She can treat it as her home.'

'That's very kind of you, Charlotte dear.' Lindsey leaned foward and pressed her hand. 'But I could never leave Estella, not until she's better. Maybe we can talk about Dr Charcot another day, Dr Digby? It is useless to plan anything until my sister is well again.'

Dr Digby lowered his head in concurrence. He would be very happy if Lindsey stayed in London as long as possible but, if she did go to Paris, he would contrive to be there too.

The curtains were raised and she came forward again and again, bowing to the applause of the massed audience. She was alone on the stage, her feet covered in flowers, facing the packed house who seemed simultaneously to rise to their feet and begin to descend upon her. Now she stood knee deep in flowers whose sweet perfume engulfed her senses. People rushed on to the stage, pawing at her and shaking her hands until she sank beneath the flowers, only her head borne above them by those who clung onto her. Suddenly Tom appeared from the wings and, as she began to sink, he swiftly raised her head and held a glass of water to her lips . . .

Estella woke up suddenly, her face running with sweat, her heart beating wildly. Her lips were dry and her mouth parched. The lamp glowed by the side of her bed, casting a single triangular shadow on the ceiling. She put her hand to her stomach imagining that it had suddenly grown, but it was flat, even concave, her hip bones protruding sharply. She sipped water from the glass by the bed and took deep breaths, as she had taught herself on the stage, to induce a feeling of calm.

Estella had spent such a lot of time lying on this bed in the small narrow room which overlooked the walls of the British Museum. She scarcely ever merely sat or read, but lay on the bed thinking. She had seen the room in all its aspects, in all its varieties of light, from the first glimmerings of dawn to the onset of night. She loved the room because it was her home and her refuge, the only one she had. Yet every night, and sometimes during the day, she dreamed about the theatre and, more often than not, her hand was held high above her head by Irving as they acknowledged the applause – her Portia to his Shylock. She knew with certainty that when Irving returned she would be quite well and life would begin again, because her only reality was in the drama. She dreamed of Tom, but she had no sense of longing for him, no regrets for what she had done or for what had happened between them. She tried to see it as a play, a production in her life that was behind her, like her season with Grant Nicholson's company.

She must have been day-dreaming again because, when she looked up, Lindsey was standing by her bed, concern on her face.

'Are you all right?'

'Perfectly all right. I'm sorry about dinner. I felt terribly tired, slightly unwell. What a nice person Dr Digby is.'

Lindsey sat on the edge of the bed, her hands folded in her lap.

'Yes, he's very nice. He was also concerned about you. He thinks you should have more tests, that maybe you are anaemic.'

Estella took her sister's hand and gently laid it on her abdomen. 'There is no need for tests. I know quite well what is wrong with me. I am carrying a baby. I wonder you did not know it too, with all your experience.'

Lindsey closed her eyes, aware only of her hand and the thin fabric of her sister's dress beneath which there was a layer of skin covering her uterus and reproductive organs. She could see it all quite clinically and with detachment, so familiar was she with this part of the female anatomy. Yet, because this was her sister, there was a complicating factor that seemed to obscure her judgment and render impossible an accurate diagnosis. Lindsey opened her eyes and shook her head.

'It isn't possible,' she said. 'You're imagining it.'

'I'm not.' Estella placed her hand on top of Lindsey's. 'See, you can feel it.'

Lindsey probed carefully. 'It's too early to feel anything, even if there's anything there. Have you not been menstruating?'

'No.'

'Then why didn't you tell me?'

'Can't you guess?'

'You know you can confide in me.'

'It's still a terrible thing to tell one's sister, even if she is a doctor.'

'I might have helped to allay your fears. There may be other reasons for not menstruating: if you're anaemic, if you're run down and underweight as you most definitely are.'

'Pregnant, pregnant,' Estella banged her head against the pillow.

'Do you *want* to be pregnant?'

'Of course I don't. It would ruin my career and I think of nothing but the theatre. The theatre *is* my life, Lindsey.'

'I know. The theatre and . . . ' Lindsey paused because

they had never mentioned his name since Estella had arrived in such a distressed condition in London nearly three months before and told her the story.

'Tom Shipley is no longer my life, Lindsey. I hate him.'

Lindsey removed her hand from under Estella's and, getting to her feet, began to pace the room.

'I wish I could believe you. Having loved him so much I feel you hate him too much now; it's not natural. You never speak of him; yet I suppose you think of him a lot?'

'I dream of him, but I never think of him. He's gone from my life for good. He's now with another woman and she's having his baby too.' Estella screwed up her nose. 'Is it not *disgusting* that a man can impregnate two women to bear children at the same time?'

'Nature ordained things in a very curious way,' Lindsey agreed. 'It was to ensure the preservation of the species. It seems that no account was taken of human emotions.'

'I don't want Tom's child.' Estella's voice became a little shrill. 'I don't want it, I don't want it. How could I love a child that belonged to Tom? I don't want it to be born and, if it is born, I want it to die.'

'Please don't say that.' Lindsey felt once more in a practical frame of mind. It was necessary to think ahead again, to plan. But first one had to be sure. 'We must have more tests to see if there is a baby; then we will decide what to do. You need never see it; you can have it adopted. But, first, you must bear it. In a year you'll have forgotten all this.'

Estella stared at her, and Lindsey, abruptly stopping her pacing, stared back. Each seemed to know what the other was thinking.

How could one ever possibly forget something like this?

'I was the first woman surgeon to perform an ovariotomy.' Mrs Garrett Anderson dried her hands on a towel and then carefully examined her well-pared finger nails to be

211

sure they were perfectly clean. 'Did I tell you, Lindsey? In those days it had such a high mortality rate that the hospital management committee refused to let it be done in the hospital. I had the patient transferred to a private house, the room scrubbed and whitewashed and then I performed it myself, although Dr Smith of St Bartholomew's kindly agreed to be present. My husband Skelton met all the expenses out of his own pocket and said we should be well on the way to bankruptcy if my surgical practice continued. Well, all that was well over ten years ago and now the operation is a matter of routine.'

Mrs Garrett Anderson had indeed told this story before, but Lindsey listened politely. The great woman, who was now Dean of the Medical School in addition to doing all the major surgery at the New Hospital which had been founded by her, was allowed to repeat herself. No one would dare intervene or interrupt her. In this winter of 1884 Elizabeth Garrett Anderson was forty-eight; a small, rather plain, beautifully dressed woman who was both loved and feared in equal measure. So exacting had been the standards she required of herself in her long struggle to the top that lesser mortals sometimes regarded her as too brusque and intolerant; but she was respected, and admired almost to the point of veneration.

Mrs Anderson had said she'd always known that Charlotte would never complete the course. In her opinion the daughter of an Austrian father might well not have had the necessary fibre such as was expected of English girls. This was possessed in full measure by Lindsey who, because of her gifts of thoroughness coupled with a suitable detachment, would make a brilliant surgeon. Consequently she almost always called upon Lindsey to assist her in major surgery and allowed her to administer chloroform and perform many minor operations both general and gynaecological. Lindsey had a good eye and a steady hand that never wavered; she was observant, methodical and neat, quite rigorous in her attention to detail. Mrs Anderson joked that her expertise at needlework had enabled her to be such a good surgeon but, more realistically, that this was due to her remarkable grasp of clinical procedures and the theory of medicine.

Mrs Anderson chatted away as they scrubbed their hands and removed their rubber aprons. Then with a final look round the operation theatre where a student and two nurses were clearing up, she beckoned to Lindsey.

'A word with you in my room, if I may, Lindsey dear.'

Lindsey followed Mrs Anderson along the narrow passage of the two small houses that formed the women's hospital, now so full of patients that there was urgent talk of finding new premises.

Mrs Anderson briskly indicated a chair and then sat herself behind the large desk that occupied most of the tiny room, drawing some papers towards her.

'Your sister is fourteen weeks pregnant, Lindsey,' and then she added 'at least' for good measure, as if that added insult to injury. 'And you had no idea?'

Lindsey studied her clean scrubbed hands that still smelt faintly of the carbolic she had sprayed on the patient's wound during the operation.

'No, Mrs Anderson.'

'Of course we didn't look for pregnancy when you brought her to me in September. We never considered it. Did it *never* cross your mind?' Mrs Anderson sounded distinctly peeved as though this lapse called into question her whole standing as a diagnostician.

'No.' Lindsey kept her head bowed.

'Nor mine, not knowing the circumstances. I wish you had told me that a man was involved then, Lindsey. I wish you had told me the whole story. One cannot make a proper diagnosis unless *all* the facts are known, as I frequently tell you.'

'Would you have agreed to terminate it if you'd known, Mrs Anderson?'

Mrs Anderson's eyes flickered and she studied the papers with a frown. 'Certainly not, seeing that it is quite illegal. I might, however, have *advised* your sister on what to do to try and attempt a miscarriage by her own means. Now it is too late.'

'My sister was once married to the man in question,' Lindsey said, colouring faintly, as if it made a difference.

'Well, she isn't now, is she?'

'She's an actress.' Lindsey's tone was defensive rather than apologetic. 'They do lead irregular lives.'

'More's the pity.' Mrs Anderson's tone was unforgiving. As a woman and a doctor she did not lack compassion, but her sympathies were mainly reserved for the virtuous, the ignorant and the poor, for victims of fortune rather than those creating disasters for themselves. Among the latter she included well brought up girls who should have known better. 'I can't think what your poor father will say.'

'Estella won't tell my father, Mrs Anderson. She has had no contact with him for over two years.'

'I'm *very* sorry to hear that. I must say I found her extraordinarily reticent when I examined her. She vouchsafed nothing about herself at all. She is almost in a state of . . .' Mrs Anderson groped for the word. 'Trance.'

'She is like that all the time. I have never seen anyone change so much as my poor young sister. She has been so deeply wounded by this man to whom she gave herself. I'm afraid she talks frequently of termination.'

'That is quite impossible,' Mrs Anderson said, 'and I trust you will do nothing to help or encourage her. She is far too advanced for it to be anything but extremely dangerous. No, she must pay the price, as have other silly young women who do not foresee the consequences of their actions.'

'She feels it will destroy her career.'

'*That* is an exaggeration,' Mrs Anderson said a little more kindly. Though she had little sympathy for a flighty actress, who she knew had already caused immeasurable distress to her parents, she was deeply attached to her serious, dedicated sister. 'She can go somewhere to have the baby; it can easily be adopted and . . . no one will be the wiser. I know just the place in the country.'

'Thank you, Mrs Anderson,' Lindsey nervously joined and unjoined her hands. 'But we, Charlotte and I that is, have other plans.' Lindsey cleared her throat and wished someone would bring in a cup of tea as they often did after surgery.

'Oh, what are they?' Mrs Anderson kept her voice low and calm because she felt Lindsey was on the threshold of some other disturbing revelation.

'I have told you, Mrs Anderson, that I am not happy with surgery . . . ' Lindsey began.

'That's quite ridiculous.' Mrs Anderson let her calm slip.

'Well, ridiculous or no it is the case.' Lindsey raised her eyes to meet those of the older woman. 'I find myself drawn towards the study of psychiatry, the care of the mentally sick. I have been attending Dr Mercier's lectures on mental pathology and insanity and he has invited me several times to visit his asylum at Beckenham. Hysteria, in particular, interests me because it is a condition which seems to lend itself more readily to effective treatment. I have heard of the work of Professor Charcot in Paris and I would like to study under him. I'm sorry, Mrs Anderson, because I know how much this distresses you; but my mind is made up. My sister's condition has only confirmed my desire to leave England and go and live for a while in Paris. She will come with us; then, if she wishes, she can return to the English stage when she is safely delivered of her baby, which will be due in May. She might even make the Lyceum season. I have come, most regretfully, to ask for my release, Mrs Anderson.'

Mrs Anderson thoughtfully eyed the young woman of whom she had had such hopes. Then she sighed and pulled a sheet of paper towards her on which to record her notes on the operation.

'What you say saddens me, Lindsey. I had greater expectations of you than any other student at the school, even of dear Mary Scharlieb before she returned to India. You have such potential as a practical surgeon that I feel you are throwing yourself away on the illnesses of the mind, some of the cures for which strike me as little better than quackery. Surgical skills, if correctly carried out, almost always bring about a lasting cure. In the realms of psychiatry and neurology it is often not possible to tell whether one has been successful or not. With surgery one *always* knows. The removal of diseased tissue unfailingly brings about health, and the patient recovers. I feel you are throwing your great gifts away in taking the course you propose. Furthermore, Lindsey,' Mrs Anderson's pale face flushed slightly, 'and please do not misunderstand me if I speak frankly. I do it for your own good, as you know. The fact is that your relationship with Charlotte von Harden strikes me as unusual. It is almost as though you were a married couple, which you decidedly are not. It is not wise, my dear Lindsey, for women to live too long together, to be too close. It may give people a false idea. I am thinking of the unfavourable impression Miss Jex-Blake made because of her emotional attachments to various young ladies. I know I can speak confidentially to you. I have had many close women friends and know the great boon of female companionship; but the joy of marriage is incomparable and not incompatible with being a doctor, Lindsey. I hope it is something you may soon start to think about.'

Lindsey smiled, feeling almost relieved now that the subject had turned to her, and rose from her chair, placing her hands over the back.

'I do assure you, Mrs Anderson, that your fears about Charlotte and myself are quite unfounded. She has been a very dear friend to me, replacing my mother who long ago withdrew from me her love and support. Charlotte has made life so easy for me these past four years that I owe her an enormous debt; but I assure you that my affection for her, or hers for me, is as sisters and dear friends, nothing more. I do not expect it for a moment to supplant the affection that I may one day anticipate for a man. But, until that day comes, Charlotte and I will stay together and we are certainly going together to Paris, and will take my sister with us.'

When Lindsey returned to the house, exhausted both from the rigours of the day and the ordeal of talking to Mrs Anderson, she found the door, unusually because it was dark, wide open. As she went inside Charlotte flew down the stairs towards her, her arms outstretched.

'Oh Lindsey, thank God. I've sent Mabel for the doctor, but please come quickly.'

'What is it? What has happened?' Lindsey, used to emergencies, felt her heart turn cold, because she knew it was something to do with Estella.

'Come and see.' Charlotte seized her hand, dragging her up the stairs, and Lindsey had scarcely time to unfasten her hat and let it fall into the hall below.

The door to the bathroom next to Estella's room stood open and, to her horror, she saw her sister lying inert and naked on the linoleum, her thighs and upper limbs covered with blood. There was also blood in the bath and on the edge. Charlotte, pale with shock, covered her mouth with her hands, and pushed Lindsey forwards.

Lindsey ran into the bathroom and saw immediately the long bloodstained needle on the floor next to her sister. She put a hand on Estella's heart and raised her eyelids; then, rolling up her sleeves, she drew water from the newly installed gas geyser over the bath and soaked a towel in it. Gently she began to sponge Estella down before attempting to discover how much damage she had inflicted on herself. To her relief the blood had stopped flowing, there were no abdominal contractions, and when she was able to make a proper examination she raised her eyes to heaven and turned to Charlotte, who had remained outside the door.

'Thank God she appears to have done herself no real harm, as far as I can tell. She was obviously attempting to abort herself with this dreadful object but merely perforated her vagina and must have fainted with the shock. The doctor will make a more detailed examination, but that is my diagnosis. I should have expected as much, and I reproach myself for not anticipating this. However, I don't know how I could have prevented it.'

Lindsey's diagnosis proved correct. The doctor examined his patient, by then washed and resting in bed, and thought that no lasting harm had been done. He advised frequent syringing of the vagina with Condy's fluid and water and said he would call again. During the examination Estella, who had quickly recovered consciousness, kept her eyes on the ceiling, her expression remaining impassive and detached, even calm. Charlotte saw the doctor to the door and Lindsey sat for a long time on the chair beside the bed, recovering, she now realized, from the considerable shock inflicted on herself.

'I'm sorry,' Estella said at last, reaching for Lindsey's hand.

'That's all right. Thank God I was in time.'

'I mean, I'm sorry I didn't succeed. It was so ghastly. I never realized it would be so painful, so difficult.'

'It's not a portion of our anatomy that we know much about.' Lindsey returned the pressure of her sister's hand. 'Don't speak about it. Try and rest.'

'I *want* to speak about it. I don't want to have the baby.'

218

'I know that; but you'll have to go through with it. If you did this again you might kill yourself. I have seen many victims of self-induced abortion and the resultant septicaemia is often fatal. I *beg* you, never do it again.' As Estella remained silent Lindsey put an arm behind her head and bent to embrace her. Suddenly Estella gave a convulsive groan and threw her arms around Lindsey's head, thrusting her face in her hair. Lindsey, close to tears herself, hugged her tightly, realizing, at last, how precious to her was the life of the person she held in her arms. Sisters, they were really alone together; all they had in the world was each other. Charlotte didn't count; medical studies didn't count. But the deep, blood bond between them counted more, now, than she had ever known. Gently, at last, she laid Estella's head on the pillow and stroked her brow. 'You'll have me, darling, to look after you. Maybe I've been rather a strict sister, overcritical, not as understanding as I might have been. Maybe I left you too much by yourself and did not talk enough, or tell you that, in reality, I sympathized and understood. Maybe you found me too unsympathetic to confide in. I'm an old maid, you know. I've never known passion or the love of a man, and it's something I don't really under-stand. I am beginning to understand it, but it's hard for me because all my life has been devoted to one thing: medicine.

'Maybe the study of human emotions should be taught at the School, for we have too little experience of them. I realize now that much that is essential for the full under-standing of life has passed me by, and others like me. We are to be pitied. You, my poor darling, have had too many. You already have a lifetime of experiences and you are younger than I, yet so much wiser in the world. Forgive me?'

Estella, who had been listening to her sister with some amazement, used the top of her sheet to brush away her tears. Then she took Lindsey's practical, clever hand firmly in hers, contrasting it with hers. One was blunt and red with frequent scrubbing; the other was white and tapering, fragile. Their hands seemed so expressive of their personalities – conflicting, yet basically in harmony. She felt possessed by a sense of peace that she had not known for months, by a feeling of resignation she never thought she would have. Her sister loved her and would look after her. She brought Lindsey's hand to her lips, her eyes brimming with gratitude. 'Thank you,' she said, and kissed it.

CHAPTER ELEVEN

Professor Charcot, in common with a preponderance of the male medical profession, world wide, did not approve of women doctors. Although the University of Paris had shown great liberality in being among the first to grant medical degrees to women – Elizabeth Garrett Anderson had taken her MD there in 1870 – the distinguished Professor of Diseases of the Nervous System did not believe their place was in the dissecting room, the laboratory or the wards of a busy hospital.

The great hospital of Salpêtrière, near the banks of the Seine, had seemed quite daunting to Lindsey when Dr Digby had first taken her there in the summer of 1885 soon after the move to Paris. He had personally introduced her to the great man, who had greeted her civilly, but with so marked a degree of reserve that she was not deceived. He was impressed with her credentials, with her obvious sincerity, but shook his great head slowly as he remarked:

'The study of neuropathology is not for women, Mademoiselle, nor, to my mind, is the study of medicine itself. Death and disease are not subjects that should trouble the heads of charming ladies such as yourself. However, since you are here and my good friend and colleague Dr Digby speaks so well of you, please avail yourself of all the facilities you need but, pray, make yourself as inconspicuous as possible.'

He had then turned pointedly to Mortimer Digby, as though in a gesture of dismissal, and began to discuss with him some learned aspect of his work.

Jean Martin Charcot was sixty years of age in 1885 and

one of the most eminent doctors in the world, from whose far corners patients travelled to consult him about their nervous disorders. He had transformed the great, ancient hospital of Salpêtrière – built in the sixteenth century on the site of an arsenal, hence its name, Saltpeter (one of the ingredients of gunpowder) – into a modern complex using the most up-to-date methods in the treatment of neurological disorders. As well as patients he attracted students from all over Europe and America to study and learn his innovative techniques.

For centuries the Salpêtrière had housed paralytics, cancer patients, old people and lunatics as well as beggars, prostitutes and the dregs of human society collected from the streets of Paris by the Bureau for the Poor. Charcot himself had once called it a 'grand asylum of human misery' but, as a young doctor, he had seen the chance that its permanent inhabitants afforded for the detailed study and treatment of chronic nervous diseases of the sick. In its time the Salpêtrière had also been a prison, and La Grande Prison de la Force had branded a 'V' or a *fleur de lis* on the shoulders of those unfortunates incarcerated in its grim walls.

Yet, despite its modern improvements, its pre-eminence in its field, Lindsey found the vast hospital, which had once been capable of housing around eight thousand inhabitants, a depressing place and she was glad to escape from it at night to the pleasant house which the Baron von Harden owned in the more elegant quarter of the Parc Monceau.

For some time Professor Charcot had felt that he had exhausted all that was known about the physiology of the nervous system and had concentrated on the study of hysteria, the symptoms of which, he had discovered, were responsive to suggestion and treatment by hypnosis. By the use of such means he could induce the stigmata of hysterical symptoms: paralysis, twitches and tremors and

222

the various vaso motor disturbances in patients who were free from them, simply by putting them into a trance and telling them they had them. Thus he could eliminate these symptoms by the same method in patients who were in the throes of 'la grande hystérie', a major hysterical attack.

Symptoms which formerly had been thought to be organic in origin were now clearly demonstrated to be due to processes which were only just beginning to be understood. In other words, they came not from lesions of the brain or injury to the nervous system, as had been accepted for years, but from the mysterious workings of the mind, since they could be summoned up or relieved by mental processes alone. Charcot found that patients could create their illnesses by auto suggestion and, by the same means, he was able to relieve them or, in cases, cure them completely.

Charcot's Tuesday lectures, during which he demonstrated his patients and his theories of hypnotism, were famous throughout Paris and, being open to the public, were attended by doctors, men of letters, journalists, writers and philosophers interested in psychological problems as well as members of the beau monde, actresses, demi- mondaines and such as were attracted by the prospect of the sort of spectacle that was more often seen in the music hall or the circus. The presence of Charcot on this occasion, however, bestowed on it respectability. To his admirers these demonstrations showed his diagnostic skills to perfection, to his critics they were merely a manifestation of an absurd charlatanism; and so they brought him praise and abuse in equal proportions.

The huge amphitheatre where Charcot gave his demonstrations was packed with people seated, standing in the aisles, jamming the doors, jostling and peering eagerly over the heads of those obstructing their view. Below, on the platform, the Professor and his assistants had gathered together a number of patients who were by now clearly exhibiting his famous three stages of deep hypnotic states ('*le grand hypnotisme*') namely lethargy, catalepsy and somnambulism. The lethargic patients exhibited a neuromuscular hyperexcitability, the manifestations of which were the grotesque contractions of facial or other muscles. The cataleptic and somnambulistic subjects on the other hand maintained a plasticity of muscular sensation that made them especially amenable to the suggestions which the doctor now made to them.

Charcot used mimicry and imitative gestures of his own to enhance the effects he produced, adopting here the mannerisms of the sleepwalker or the sweeping *arc-en-ciel* of the major attack. Some of his patients sat about drooping, others sank to the floor, and yet others of the unfortunates were adorned with brightly coloured feathers in their hair to show the degree of tremor in their bodies. While these absurd and demeaning head-dresses fluttered in the background, as though the wearers were participating in the *Folies Bergères*, in the foreground Charcot would offer one hypnotized patient a bottle of ammonia telling her it was rosewater and, as she smelt it with delight, a beatific expression on her face, the audience rustled with amusement. Another was commanded to crawl on all fours and started barking furiously when the master told her she was a dog; then she vainly flapped her arms in an attempt to fly when told she was a pigeon. To another a top hat was given and she rocked it in her arms when informed it was a baby, made cooing noises to it and, at one stage, until stopped abruptly by an assistant, attempted to give it suck. A glove was thrown at the foot of yet another hapless victim and she raised her skirts in horror at being told it was a snake.

All these bizarre manifestations elicited various exclamations from the audience and, when he was not darting about attempting to influence or imitate his patients' hysterics, were accompanied by a commentary from the

224

master, his deep-set compelling eyes intent on observing the reactions of his audience. Abandoning his customary top hat he wore a velvet skull cap which seemed to enhance all the more the overall impression not of a medical lecture but of some consummate art of showman-ship.

'You see,' Charcot said, stepping forward like a master conjurer who had just produced a rabbit from his hat, 'how one imitates the other. If one swoons so does the patient next in the line. The hysterical syndrome is contagious in groups – for example the inhabitants of a convent come to mind; you are doubtless familiar with the devils of Loudun when all the inmates believed them-selves possessed. If I break up or scatter this group,' he clapped his hands above his head and his assistants came forward to disperse those on the platform, 'you will find that their symptoms disappear because they have no one whom they can now imitate.'

As the lecture proceeded Lindsey found many aspects, though undoubtedly absorbing, more and more distasteful and occasionally lowered her eyes when the sight of some absurd and pathetic female grovelling on the floor at the feet of her tormentor – for Lindsey could only think of him in this role as a tormentor, not a physician – became too painful.

Suddenly Charcot clapped his hands again and all on the stage became locked in the various attitudes of their distressing symptoms. At a word of instruction from him his assistants proceeded to make the various mesmeric passes that released the patients from their trances. Thus released, they looked both bewildered and foolish as one woman realized she was carrying not a baby but a top hat in her arms, her bodice partly undone in a futile attempt to feed it, and another saw the glove for what it was and not an evil slithering snake. They were then ushered from the platform, those with the pink, blue and yellow feathers in their hair still shaking from their tremors. Charcot, going to the front of the platform, addressed himself solely to his audience, most of whom were by now leaning forward eagerly in their seats, thoroughly entertained.

'What I have demonstrated to you today, learned colleagues, ladies and gentlemen, is that these hysterio-traumatisms you have seen, although entirely real, are nevertheless of psychic not physical origin. I can make symptoms appear and disappear; and many of these unfortunates you have seen before you, and no doubt found amusing as well as pitiable, are capable of being completely cured by means which I and my assistants have developed at this great hospital. Thus they will be released from the torments of their neuroses, and returned, cured, to their homes and the bosoms of their families once again.'

As he bowed low the audience rose to its feet and then, gathering together the papers he had placed on a lectern but never consulted, he left the room with élan, accompanied by his customary obsequious retinue, who bowed and smiled to their friends in the room as though sharing in the glory of the master.

Lindsey, sombrely dressed as always so as to remain inconspicuous and in her accustomed place at the back of the hall, did not applaud the professor but stared at the scene before her, a frown on her face, her chin resting in her hand. Beautifully dressed actresses and well-known writers rose to their feet loudly and ostentatiously greeting one another, the scene resembling more and more a fashionable night at the theatre.

She knew Charcot was a man of genius and she knew the skill and care with which he examined patients brought to him from the wards to his small sparsely furnished room at the hospital which, together with all the furnishings, was painted in black. She herself had obser-

226

ved the famous silences of Dr Charcot as he studied a patient for several minutes after an assistant had read the summary of the case, not touching him or her but looking, his eyebrows drawn over his eyes deep-set in the shadows of their orbits. Short of stature, and thick-set, he was nevertheless known as the Caesar of the Salpêtrière because of his commanding, brooding air. He would tap his hand on the table while studying the patient, and then he would ask him to say something or make a movement, or request an assistant to test the patient's reflexes. Then, abruptly, he would summon the next one and so on, often saying nothing at all about his diagnoses of the cases. Many said that intuition played a great part in the skills of Dr Charcot. More often than not he didn't trouble to enlighten his colleagues as to what he had decided, but left on the stroke of noon to return to his home for lunch and an afternoon spent writing or examining private patients, many of them distinguished. It was said that he possessed second sight, that he could sense a disease; and in this much of his fame lay.

But the performance she had just witnessed distressed Lindsey unaccountably; its theatricality, the helplessness of the patients, most of them poor, ignorant and quite defenceless, certainly prone to suggestibility. In these performances before the public Charcot seemed more like a showman, a poseur, than the great physician she knew him to be. She was disillusioned. She sighed and gathered together the papers on which she had nevertheless made copious notes during the demonstration.

'The sight distressed you, mademoiselle?'

The young man who sat beside her had also made notes and, like her, had withheld his applause at the end of the lecture. He was soberly dressed in grey, but his eyes above his full black beard were alert and somehow sympathetic. However, he appeared very cold and withdrawn, not one to start a conversation with a stranger. He had a pronounced

German accent and spoke now in faltering tones. She had seen him at some of Charcot's private clinics and at lectures but had never spoken to him. Indeed she spoke to few of her fellow students.

'I think it is, perhaps, unnecessary,' she replied carefully, knowing how fragile her status in the hospital was. It would never do to be heard criticizing Charcot.

'I agree with you.' The young man also gathered his papers together. 'These demonstrations are quite unnecessary. They demean a great man.'

'Then why does he do it?'

The stranger shrugged. He had heavy black brows and his hair was beginning to recede.

'I think he wants all the world to know about his discoveries, which are indeed remarkable. Fancy, a psychological basis to hysteria! In mediaeval times the poor wretches were considered possessed and burned at the stake. Dr Charcot has introduced us to the subtleties of the mind in a way which, I must confess, has profoundly influenced me. I find his methods quite extraordinary and riveting, so much so that I am considering abandoning my own field.'

'And that is?'

Despite his remoteness, Lindsey felt drawn to the serious young man and smiled encouragingly.

'I am a neuropathologist, from Vienna, mademoiselle. My name is Sigmund Freud. In coming to the Salpêtrière my intention was to study the secondary atrophies and degenerations that follow on affections of the brain in children. Indeed some extremely valuable pathologic material was put at my disposal. Professor Charcot himself was kind enough to have me supplied with a fresh supply of young, immature brains. But the clinics have such a plethora of new and interesting material that I find myself sidetracked. You have, of course, observed the way the professor studies his patients. He is like an artist, a *visuel*, a man who sees. He has remarked again and again that in medicine people only see what they have learned to see. If one looks for long enough, and with a fresh eye, one suddenly perceives a new state of illness that one may have overlooked for many many years; a new understanding dawns on one . . . '

'Ah I see you know Freud,' Mortimer Digby made his way along the fast emptying benches, spectacles on the edge of his nose, his face flushed with excitement. 'I was late for the lecture and stood at the back.' He bowed towards Lindsey and stood smiling at the bearded man, who looked at him with surprise, then extended his hand.

'Dr Digby. How nice to see you again.' Dr Freud spoke in English and turned to Lindsey. 'I did not realize you were an acquaintance of Dr Digby, with whom I have worked in Vienna.'

'In fact we have only just started talking about the subject of the Maître's lecture,' Lindsey smiled awkwardly. 'And Dr Freud was kind enough to introduce himself.'

'Then, Sigmund, may I present Dr Lindsey Abercrombie from London.'

Lindsey took Freud's hand, aware of the firm clasp as his fingers curled round hers. 'I have seen you, of course, about the hospital.'

'And I have seen *you*, Dr Abercrombie. How could one miss a lady among such a concourse of sombre medical men? Had I known of your acquaintanceship with Dr Digby I would have made myself known to you sooner. But, being a foreigner here, I am shy. Tell me, Digby, are you permanently in Paris again?'

'Only temporarily, I fear. I had a post in London until the summer, but I returned to Paris to see Dr Abercrombie settled with Professor Charcot. I have also been to Nancy to see Professor Bernheim's investigations into the phenomena of animal magnetism which he also bases on psychological principles. He and Dr Charcot do not quite agree. However, I must soon abandon Europe and return to America, for I have not seen my family for nearly three years. For how long are you in Paris, Dr Freud?'

'Only a few months,' the Viennese said. 'I am on a bursary from the University of Vienna. I was just saying to Dr Abercrombie how much my visit here had changed my own views.'

'Oh, how?' Mortimer Digby pushed his spectacles up his nose with one hand and mopped his brow with the other.

'A change of emphasis from the physical basis of hysteria to the psychological, the power of suggestion as we have seen demonstrated here today. In fact I wrote to my fiancée . . .'

Mortimer appeared to see a friend, because he smiled over the doctor's shoulder and put a hand on his arm.

'Freud, forgive me but I have seen someone I know. We must dine together. Look let's fix a date.' He produced his diary and began hurriedly flicking through the pages. 'Lindsey, do you see your sister over there with Lagrange? How about Tuesday week, that is the . . .'

'I assure you there will be another opportunity . . .' Dr Freud said nervously, looking around him as Estella, beautifully gowned, wearing a large hat and carrying a long parasol, stopped in the aisle parallel to where her sister and colleagues were standing. Beside her was a tall man with grey flowing hair, elegantly but casually dressed in a green velvet suit, a loosely knotted bow tie at his neck.

'You didn't tell me you were coming to Professor Charcot's lecture.' Lindsey kissed her sister's cheek. 'Had I known I could have saved a place for you.'

'Oh Marc had places right at the front. What an enthralling experience. Is not the man a genius? Marc tells me that many of his patients are paid performers, hired for the occasion.'

'That's not quite true,' Mortimer Digby said hastily. 'They are patients in the hospital, all of them.'

'But still, they know what to do. And I have heard that they do receive payment.' Marc Lagrange's tone was adamant as he shook hands with Mortimer and looked enquiringly over his shoulder to the stranger who stood diffidently behind them.

'This is Dr Freud from Vienna,' Mortimer ushered his friend forward. 'He is a distinguished neurologist in his own right.'

'And a *great* admirer of Dr Charcot,' Freud said firmly as though to establish once and for all his position.

'He has changed Dr Freud's life,' Lindsey said lightly. Then, 'May I introduce my sister, Estella Abercrombie?' As Freud bowed and shook Estella's hand Lindsey went on. 'And this is Monsieur Lagrange, a critic and novelist of whom you may have heard.'

Freud looked vague, but Estella smiled bewitchingly at him.

'*How* has Professor Charcot changed your life, Dr Freud?'

'It is rather too complicated to explain in these circumstances, Miss Abercrombie. It is a long story.'

'You must come to dinner,' Estella said impulsively, taking Marc's arm. 'Marc loves to meet new people and hear interesting theories. Unfortunately we have to hurry away now, but hope to see you again. Good day, Dr Freud.'

'Good day, Miss Abercrombie.' Freud inclined his head as Estella swept up the steps closely followed by her companion.

'What a fascinating woman your sister is.' Sigmund Freud watched her progress up the steps until she passed out of sight through the door at the top. 'Is she, by any chance, an actress?'

'I see you are a keen observer of people,' Lindsey followed his gaze. 'Yes, she is.'

'She is very beautiful. I imagine she has quite a success on the stage. What a curious combination!' he turned to Lindsey, giving her the benefit of his alert, dark eyes. 'A doctor and an actress. Have you other siblings?'

'No, there are just the two of us.'

'How singular.' Dr Freud paused for a moment as though raking his memory. 'I have scarcely ever met a professional woman in my life and today I have met two. What attracted you to medicine, Dr Abercrombie?'

As his eyes searched hers Lindsey felt a frisson, whether of alarm or excitement she could not immediately tell. He was not unattractive and yet he had no immediate appeal, because his manner was brusque, rather peremptory. He seemed to be a man totally in control of himself, a scientist rather than a clinician. Facts and phenomena would interest him more than people. Or would they? He was certainly enigmatic and she found him intriguing. She would be very bold and renew her sister's invitation to dinner.

'Why do we not have this discussion, as my sister suggested, at dinner, Dr Freud? We share a house with another in the Parc Monceau. Would you care to name a day you are free? And Mortimer, since you intend to dine together, perhaps you would join us too?'

Once more Mortimer Digby began eagerly turning the pages of his diary, his broad intelligent forehead furrowed in a frown.

Ellen Terry was the last fond memory that Estella had of England, and she had named her baby after her. Ellen had been born in May shortly after the young women had taken up residence in the Parc Monceau, and for several days Estella had refused to look at her daughter, who was cared for devotedly by Charlotte, who employed a nanny as well as a wet nurse to feed her.

They had been very hard, difficult days, those days

232

when Charlotte, Lindsey and Estella had first come to Paris, and the memory, the taint of them, still informed the atmosphere of the three-storeyed house which over-looked the fashionable Parc.

For Estella, Ellen represented Tom, and Tom she had blotted from her mind. It was not difficult either to see the features of her former husband in their daughter, for she had his dark colouring and did not in any way resemble her mother.

When Lindsey first showed Ellen to Estella she put a woollen bonnet over her head to hide her black curls, but nothing made any difference to Estella's feelings for her child. 'Let her be named after Miss Terry,' she said. 'That may help the poor thing to have some chance in life.' Then she turned her face away, for she couldn't bear the sight of her and wished her to be adopted.

So as Estella recovered her strength, which she quickly did having had a short and easy labour and being so well cared for during and after her confinement by her sister, a strange dichotomy established itself in the gracious, spacious house. Part of it became the living quarters of the young women, and part a nursery suite for the baby, who was kept almost exclusively in it, cared for by her two devoted nurses and visited only by Charlotte and Lindsey. Both of them thought that, given time, Estella would come round to the idea of acknowledging and loving her daughter, to whom, when all was said and done, she had given a name that was precious to her.

But nothing moved Estella from her determination to remain apart from her baby. As soon as she was up and able to go about she bought herself a completely new wardrobe of clothes, giving all her old garments to the maids in the house as though they represented a life that she now wished to discard.

Charlotte had many acquaintances in Paris all of whom she cultivated in order to entertain Lindsey; but, Lindsey was devoted to her studies at the Salpêtrière, and it was Estella who cultivated Charlotte's friends, most of whom, men and women, immediately became entranced by her. Motherhood, whether she wished it or not, had bestowed on Estella a dimension she had not possessed before. It was difficult to define or give it a name; it had something to do with personality rather than appearance and a lot to do with the enhancement of her beauty and a sense of allure. At twenty-two Estella was indeed a woman, now a mother, one who had known love and the sorrow that goes with love. Her experiences had made her emotionally richer, not poorer; philosophical not bitter – except in her attitude towards her daughter – and this showed in her deportment, in the grace, ease and elegance with which she seemed to think, speak and move.

As soon as she entered the house or salon of a friend of Charlotte's she was welcomed to it like an old habituée. She was drawn into the circle of clever, articulate men and women who were interested in music, the arts, science and letters.

And she quickly had a lover. By August her liaison with Marc Lagrange was so well known that they were invited everywhere together. They moved about with the ease and acceptability of an established couple and thus life became even more interesting and alluring for the woman who still would not look into the eyes of her baby and acknowledge her as her own.

It was Charlotte who clung to Ellen. Charlotte who loved children with the desperation of a woman who never expected to have any of her own. It was Charlotte who supervised Ellen's daily routine, saw that she had plenty of fresh air and played with her for many hours of the day. It was Charlotte who walked behind the pram with the nurse or took her in her carriage to the Bois de Boulogne as those beautiful spring days ripened into summer.

Charlotte it was who refused to part with Ellen, refused to entertain the idea of having her adopted or, at least, by anyone but herself.

But it was impossible for an unmarried woman to adopt a child. However much she longed to strengthen the bond between herself and Ellen she knew she could not. She was, therefore, content to remain grateful for Estella's preoccupation with her social life and with her love affair, and Lindsey's absorption in her studies.

And so the months passed. Autumn came and with it the approach of winter. The Paris season reached its zenith as *le tout Paris* returned from houses in the country to throng once again the salons, the boulevards and the fashionable cafés and restaurants of the Boulevard St Germaine and the Left Bank.

Le tout Paris, those who had not met Estella in the late spring and early summer, who had not invited her to their summer houses or châteaux, were delighted to find this star in their midst – this beautiful, elegant charmer who was an established actress and whose private life was acknowledged to be scandalous. Yet none of them knew about the baby in the Parc Monceau, for Estella, although concealing nothing about her private life or her past, revealed nothing either. She refused to discuss herself, and so Paris, like any other society small or large, provincial and international, throve on gossip and speculation.

Estella was 'la grande inconnue', the great unknown, a delicious mystery to excite, titillate and entertain the rich, the beautiful or the simply bored.

Lindsey turned from the window overlooking the neat garden that led directly into the little park. There had been a fall of snow the night before and the laden branches of the skeletal trees dipped and swung, blown by the gentle wind that scattered the snow onto the white, phosphorescent surface below.

'How can you be content with the life you lead?' She looked at Estella, getting ready to go out. 'It is not only boring and idle. It is . . . '

'Yes?' Estella, taking a final critical look at her new hat in the mirror, gazed past her reflection at her sister.

'Immoral.' Lindsey sank onto a chair and tucked her chin into her hand, her eyes returning Estella's gaze through the mirror.

'Oh, my life is immoral, is it?' Estella anchored the hat more securely by repositioning a large pin with an amber head. She wore a long velvet cloak, covering her dress, and a hat of the same material adorned with small stuffed birds and tiny black feathers. She appeared, for the instant, more interested in her appearance than the state of her soul; but a high colour had risen slowly to her cheeks and, her toilet completed, she turned and stared directly at her sister.

'I wondered when I was going to have a little lecture about my life. If you like I can move out and live with Marc. It is what *he* wants. He practically supports me now, buying my clothes and so on, as, to all intents and purposes, I am a pauper. He would like nothing more than to share his house with me as well. Would that suit you better? Then you and Charlotte can enjoy your lives untainted by my presence.'

'You know that's not what *I* want. At least while we are under the same roof I can keep an eye on you. I worry about you, Estella. I don't mean to be censorious, you know that.'

'You certainly *sound* censorious.' Estella glanced at the gold Empire clock that ticked away slowly on the marbled mantelpiece. 'Boring, idle *and* immoral. Is not that a rather strong judgment?'

'Of sorts. I suppose it is.'

'You consider your own life so important and mine futile? Is that it?'

'In a way, I must confess I do. Oh, I know you have never conformed, done what was expected of you but, believe me, my sole wish is your happiness. I would like nothing better than to see you settled and happy.'

'I am settled and happy.'

'I don't think you are. You may think you are; but you seem to me to be very restless. You don't see the anguish and discontent on your face in quiet unguarded moments, as I do.'

'It is true,' Estella agreed. 'I would like to return to the stage; but I don't wish to go back to London. Madame Bernhardt has told me that when my French improves she will consider me for her company again. I like the life in Paris and the people I meet. What has London to offer me? I never had a social life there and, estranged from my parents . . . '

'You could write to Mr Irving again.'

'After I have let him down once? I would have to tell him the reason I left London so abruptly, and that is something I'm not prepared to do, not yet anyway. If only Ellen had been adopted I would feel so free. You have no idea what an encumbrance she is to my spirit.'

'Estella, how *could* you say that?' Lindsey got up and, with an uncharacteristic movement, flounced across the floor angrily throwing a piece of paper, a note or a letter of some description, she had in her hand into the fire. 'What an encumbrance indeed. When did you last see her, pray?'

Estella gazed absently at the ceiling and then quite unexpectedly two tears stole from under her eyelids, progressing slowly down her cheeks. Lindsey, stricken, gazed at her and then hurried to her side, putting an arm round her shoulder.

'My dear, you *are* unhappy, aren't you? All you try and put on every day is a brave front. I knew it. I'm sorry I spoke so harshly!' She left her hand for a moment and

237

then removed it, moving away. 'I don't think I understand you, really.'

Estella dabbed carefully at her eyes with a handkerchief, her trembling hands making the flash of jewels on her fingers gleam like fireflies in the twinkling glow of the chandeliers, the bright flames of the fire.

'I'm not un . . . unhappy,' Estella gave her nose a good, unladylike blow. 'I'm confused. I don't know what I do want from life. I've lost my direction which seemed at one time so secure and certain. Yes, I do feel guilty about Ellen. Did yóu think I would really have let her go?' She smiled tremulously at her sister. 'If I really hated her do you think I would have tolerated staying in the same house with her? Do you think my heart, the heart of her mother, is not moved by the sight of her adorable little face, her pink dimpled cheeks and black curly hair? Do you think I do not want to stretch out my arms to her and give her the love that is in me?'

'Then why don't you do it? Why don't you *do* it?' Lindsey put both arms round her again and hugged her, looking into her face.

'Because I can't. I want to but I can't. If she were not so like Tom I think I could forget him. My memories of him are still too painful and vivid. If only she were not so like him . . . '

'That isn't her fault.' Lindsey abruptly took her own handkerchief to dab gently at her sister's eyes. 'She's quite blameless, the poor darling angel.'

'I know it and that's what makes it worse. I am making her suffer for something she didn't do, something I did. But the fact torments me when I look at her and so I can't show her the love I feel. I try to, but when it comes to it, I can't.'

'But you *do* love her, that's what's important. Oh I'm so glad, Estella, that you love her. Once again you have shown me how selfish and self-centred I am. I am so concerned with my studies that I seem to sense nothing of the real life around me. What a poor doctor I'll make. Maybe I should stick to the anatomy of the brain after all, or, maybe, I should go back to Mrs Anderson and be a good gynaecologist, though – like Mr Irving – I doubt she would have me now after all this time.'

Estella, always a prey to her swiftly changing emotions but feeling calmer now, took her sister's hand and led her to the sofa. The knowledge that they were once again united in spirit was more of a relief to her than her confession of love for Ellen. How she had missed the true companionship of her sister in the nine months since her baby had been born. How she regretted her apparently hedonistic pursuit of pleasure. What strangers they had become!

'Are you serious?'

'I'm serious in a way.' Lindsey joined her hands and looked into the fire. 'I do not like Professor Charcot or his methods. I can admire him as a physician but not as a man. Since I attended that public lecture that you went to I have turned against him completely. I see now that he is cold and arrogant, not really concerned with the patients in his care. He is more interested in them as symptoms than as people, as ways of making himself more famous, his work better known. Hence his notion of throwing previously private lectures open to the public. Did you not find it nauseating the way he humiliated his poor patients? Who know how much or how little they care? Charcot certainly does not. People call him the Caesar of the Salpêtrière, you know, both on account of his manner and his looks. His assistants are so terrified of contradicting him that they will say anything to please him. They fawn upon him. But some people really hate him.'

'But he has got such a wonderful reputation.'

'In many ways deserved,' Lindsey acknowledged. 'He has opened new frontiers in medicine, changed ideas, banished stereotypes; but he has grown so used to power that he has lost the humility that is essential for every good physician. You should see the way he examines his patients, has them stripped stark naked and looks at them coldly, poking them from time to time as though they were objects, never saying a word. Dr Freud admires his technique, and so does Mortimer, and others do too. But I am a woman and I think he treats women disgracefully. In shaming these poor souls he shames me too. He considers the female sex inferior and it shows in his attitude towards me, never addressing a word to me if he can help it, behaving as though I did not exist.

'Mortimer says that in America, and England too, doctors are becoming more interested in the treatment of the neuroses, like hysteria, by purely psychological means. He lent me a riveting book by Dr Hank Tuke called *The influence of disease upon mind and body*. Even Dr Freud has abandoned the study of neurology because of the truly important influence that Charcot, almost alone, has demonstrated the mind can have on physical symptoms.

'I'm sorry, Estella, I'm speaking too much about myself.' Lindsey turned her eyes, almost reluctantly, from the fire and looked shyly at her sister. 'But, you see, there is a rather important reason. I may go to America quite soon. Mortimer wants me to marry him.'

'Oh Lindsey.' Estella, eyes shining, clasped both her hands. 'Oh Lindsey, that is *marvellous* news! I like him so much, and I hoped you did too.'

'I *like* him very much,' Lindsey said slowly, showing more caution than excitement. 'He is a very kind man as well as being so richly endowed intellectually. I think we are well suited. Mortimer is certainly as good as any . . .'

'"As good as *any*"!' Estella echoed, laughing. 'Whatever can that mean?'

'Well, he is as good as any man I'm likely to meet. I'm

twenty-eight and don't wish to remain unmarried. What can an unmarried woman do in life? Even if she has a career she is not respected.'

'It sounds a very – ' Estella groped for the right word, '*mundane* way in which to approach matrimony.'

'Mundane is correct,' Lindsey nodded, as though approving an accurate diagnosis. 'But what else is marriage? It is a contract, is it not? That's what father told me when he urged me to accept Wykeham St Clair. It is a contract between two people and has little to do with love, passion or even, apparently, inclination . . . '

'But you don't surely feel that way about Mortimer?'

Lindsey gazed thoughtfully at her well-kept hands, now more those of a lady than when she had assisted at operations at the women's hospital. They were long and white but still seemed so expressive of her personality: her capability, her self-control.

'In a way I do. I like him much more than Wykeham. But I fear I don't love him. Because I don't know what that sort of love is. I think I'm fundamentally cold, Estella. I have a burning love for you and your daughter and for poor dear Charlotte. I *like* Mortimer and respect him, very much; but I'm afraid. I'm afraid of showing too much emotion, of passion. Look what it did to you.'

She stared at her sister, her eyes troubled. 'I've seen too much of its results in the poor women I've treated. Men are so cruel, so base, so selfish . . . '

'But Mortimer is not like *that!* He's the nicest of men.'

'Yes, he's nice; but . . . ' Lindsey raised a hand towards her head and then lowered it. 'I can't explain. You know all about love, Estella. Don't you know what I mean?'

'I suppose I do,' Estella said thoughtfully. 'It's something we don't talk about, isn't it? Even as sisters? We can't mention that special relationship between men and women that is the undoing of so many of us.'

'I could never understand you and Tom. *I* saw him for

what he was, yet you never could because you loved him passionately. I didn't, and I think I still don't understand that at all. I'm too controlled, too cold. I can't think I would ever be a good wife.'

'Have you told Mortimer this?'

'Oh no!' Lindsey smiled. 'As if we could talk about such a thing! He loves me very much, he's told me. He never asks how I feel about him. I think he knows. He knows I'm cold.'

'Maybe he thinks it a very *proper* attitude in a young lady, his wife-to-be. We are not meant to feel passion, are we?'

'No,' Lindsey murmured, 'we are not meant to feel it or talk about it and when we know it exists we must disapprove of it. That's why I disapproved of you.' She bowed her head. 'I'm sorry to say it, but now I know it's true.'

Estella put an arm round her sister's shoulder and drew her to her. She felt both older and more motherly towards someone who, for all her learning, had very little real experience of life.

'You also disapprove of me now, although you don't say it, because I'm not a good mother and because I go to all the salons and have a lover. You're quite right in many ways, Lindsey. I'm not an admirable person. Marc flatters me by telling me I am too beautiful for my own good, but whether that's true or not I know I'm not beautiful inside. I'm ugly and hateful inside. I use people. I use you and Charlotte for my comfort, Marc as an escort to places that, as an unmarried woman, I could never go alone.'

'Does Marc never talk to you of marriage?'

Lindsey felt emboldened by their conversation to ask a question she would not have dreamed of posing before.

'Oh, Marc talks often of marriage! He would like nothing better. But I don't want to marry a man twenty years older than I am. Besides he is a very dull lover.'

242

Estella wrinkled her nose disdainfully and Lindsey laughed outright, clutching her hand.

'Oh I adore you, Estella, and I know why others do. You are very lovable, and you are certainly *not* ugly inside. But what will you do if I go to America?'

'You are really serious about going to America?'

'Yes. I am to tell Mortimer my decision this week. He would like us to be married in Boston and we shall sail together next month.'

'But what will our parents say? Will they not be terribly hurt and upset?'

Lindsey frowned. 'Could they be more than they are now? Mother and Father, and the way we treated them, remain a constant source of grief to me.'

'They aren't to me,' Estella said firmly.

'Then you're fortunate. I love my parents and I'm unhappy. I couldn't do more to make them approve of me.'

'I consider myself quite beyond the pale.'

'I don't. In many ways I'd still like to be the dutiful daughter. I'm sure they'd like Mortimer and welcome my marriage; but how could I have a wedding in Highgate without you? It would be more heartbreaking than if I do what I intend and marry in Boston. Then I can write and tell them and that will be that.'

'Oh dear, it all sounds so settled.' Estella pulled a face. 'I'm happy for you, but desperately unhappy for me. What shall I do without you?'

'That's what worries me,' Lindsey said gravely, 'because you don't really get on with Charlotte. That's why I brought all this up now.'

'And how will Charlotte react to your marriage to Mortimer?'

'Ah,' Lindsey twisted and untwisted her fingers. 'That, alas, is another problem altogether.'

243

CHAPTER TWELVE

If it hadn't been for Ellen, Charlotte would have gone back to her parents in Austria when Lindsey left for America with Mortimer in March of that year. For a period after she'd heard the news she was so overcome that she went to her room and stayed there for days, refusing to leave it. Meals were sent in, but they were returned uneaten and Lindsey grew seriously worried about her friend. All entertainment stopped and the parties and dinners that Charlotte was accustomed to give were cancelled.

For Charlotte loved Lindsey, had done for many years, and wanted to devote her life to her. She'd known that Lindsey did not return the love in the way that she wanted, and could not. Lindsey liked men too much and enjoyed their company and their admiration, though she might be reluctant to admit it, or not even aware of it. But Charlotte didn't like men at all and only tolerated them for the sake of Lindsey, for the sake of appearances.

She knew that, although it was not satisfactory to have a love such as hers unrequited, it was better than not loving at all. Just to have Lindsey present in the house was enough, to know that she would see the beloved face several times a day. Occasionally she would kiss her cheek or give her a little hug, but Lindsey did not like intimacy. It repelled her, and Charlotte sensed her withdrawal whenever she made physical contact with her. It had been like that for many years now and Charlotte accepted it and still loved her despite it.

But she had still hoped that, because she was so

unphysical, Lindsey would be content to devote her life to medicine and would never marry, that they could spend their lives together; but as soon as Mortimer Digby came over to Paris Charlotte knew what a threat he presented. He was so right for Lindsey; they had so much in common, and she soon saw how much he loved Lindsey even though she never spoke of her love for him.

Now was the day of Lindsey's marriage far away in Boston, and Charlotte sat in a corner of her bedroom with a shawl round her shoulders because she was so cold; yet it was May and quite warm. They had been in Paris over a year and Ellen had just celebrated her first birthday. And what a darling Ellen was! How providential that God had sent her to take Lindsey's place in her affections (or to take *a* place, because nothing could ever replace Lindsey). Even the thought of the little girl softened the harsh, sad lines on her face and made her lay her head back in her chair and smile. Yet the hours relentlessly ticked by. Lindsey was being married from the home of friends of the Digby family in Boston, Massachusetts, three thousand miles away. Maybe at this hour the ring was being placed on her finger. Charlotte shuddered. Although they had promised to return in the autumn, she knew Lindsey was lost for ever.

There was a knock at her door and, eyes still closed, Charlotte called 'Come in'. Estella was out and it was very quiet in the house, the sun filtering through the tiny burgeoning leaves of the tall trees in the garden, making a dappled pattern on the shiny polished floor of her room. She opened her eyes and saw Ellen's nurse agitatedly coming towards her, leaving the door half open. She sat up.

'What is it, Cécile?'

'If you please, madam,' Cécile bobbed. 'Mademoiselle Ellen is not well. She has a very hot body and she cries continually.'

Charlotte got rapidly to her feet and flew towards the door.

'Why did you not tell me this before? How long has she been like this?'

'Only since this morning, madam; but I thought I should tell you.'

'Of course and send for Dr Perrichot, at once, do you understand?' Charlotte felt so guilty because she had spent the day mooning in her room instead of playing with Ellen, as was her habit.

'Yes, madam.'

They had reached the hall and Cécile, as red-faced as her charge, ran down the stairs while Charlotte ran up a flight to the second-floor nursery suite. There in her cot baby Ellen was sobbing, with a sort of rasping sound that brought a feeling of panic to Charlotte's breast. She drew back the covers and felt the baby's limbs, which were burning while her clothes were drenched with sweat.

Charlotte fell to her knees and tried to grasp one of Ellen's hands, but there was no response, no chuckle as the baby's bright, feverish eyes alighted on the woman whom she seemed to think of as her mother, or maybe she was confused between her nurse and Charlotte.

Charlotte smoothed the hot brow, tucking the damp curls behind the ears of her darling and making gentle soothing noises; but Ellen's stricken eyes showed no spark of recognition and a fierce pulse throbbing at her neck struck terror into Charlotte's heart. She got to her feet and started pacing the room backwards and forward, backwards and forward, trying to stifle the panic, until the doctor's carriage stopped outside the door and, accompanied by a tearful Cécile, he hurried into the house.

'Scarlet fever,' Dr Perrichot said on completing his examination. 'Serious, but not invariably fatal.'

246

'Has she it badly, doctor?' Charlotte's ashen countenance made the doctor almost as concerned for her as he was for the child.

'Hard to say, Baronne. It takes time to develop. Time to reach its crisis and then . . . ' He shrugged his expressive hands and gesticulated in a helpless Gallic way. 'Is her mother here?'

'Oh surely it is not as serious as *that*?' Charlotte sank to the floor again, taking one of the hot little hands between hers.

'But her mother should be here in any case, Baronne. I'm not saying the child is going to die. Plenty of ventilation in the room, please, and do not overheat the body. I will send my boy with medicine and call again later in the day.' He put a hand under Charlotte's elbow and drew her up, looking at her kindly. 'Now, Baronne von Harden, I know you love the child as your own; but do not let this make you ill. The disease will take its course; but send for the mother, just in case.'

'I will *not* send for the mother,' Charlotte's face hardened. 'She has never been a mother to her and now she may not have the chance. I am her mother,' and she threw herself across the bed of the stricken child while the doctor tried in vain to comfort her.

Estella came home at five accompanied by Marc. Following an agreeable luncheon they had been to a matinée, with Madam Bernhardt playing the part of the Empress Theodora in Victorien Sardou's play of the same name at the Porte-St-Martin Theatre.

As soon as she came in the atmosphere of the house worried Estella, and the concern on the face of the maid who hurried to take their cloaks confirmed her fears.

'Is there anything the matter, Marie? Is the Baronne not well?'

'Oh, it is not the Baronne, Madame Abercrombie, it is the little one . . . '

'Ellen?' Estella, removing her hat, looked at Marc. 'There is something wrong with Ellen?'

'She has a fever, madam, the doctor came early this afternoon.'

'Oh, a fever . . . ' Estella walked slowly into the drawing room, Marc behind her. 'A fever is not very serious, is it, Marc?'

'It depends what sort of fever, my dear,' Marc Lagrange closed the door behind him. 'Should you not go up and see the little one?'

'Oh, if Charlotte is with her she will be all right. I'm sure there is no cause for concern. I'll pop in and see her later.'

Marc let himself into an easy chair and drew a cigar from a case in his top pocket. He examined it with care, sniffed it, cut off the top and then lit it with equal care, slowly and deliberately as though he had a lot of time on his hands. When it was drawing well he looked at the lighted tip and leaned back in the chair.

'My dear Estella, you really *are* a very unnatural mother, are you not?'

'Did I ever say differently? Did I ever pretend to be anything else?'

'No. No.' Marc examined his cigar again. 'But I find it hard to comprehend how the mother of a child, however unnatural she may be, can react with such callousness to its welfare.'

'Thank you, Monsieur Lagrange,' Estella snapped, swirling the bustle of her afternoon gown behind her as she sat upright in a chair opposite him. 'I'm *not* callous about Ellen's welfare, I assure you. It appears she has some trifling fever and is in good hands.'

'Who said it was "trifling"? I thought the maid looked very concerned. Should you not just go up, my dear, for your own sake?'

Estella stared at Marc Lagrange and momentarily felt

248

that she hated him. She had never loved him, so it was not the sort of hatred that follows love, but she liked him and needed his admiration. He was a tall, extremely slender man with black/grey hair and deeply set pale blue eyes. He was clean shaven and his face was very furrowed as though he had hewn a rough path through life. He had the entrée to all the best society in Paris, particularly that concerned with the arts, the theatre and music, and his influence was important to her; so was his opinion. But if she suddenly rose now and went to see Ellen Marc would think it was because she had a bad conscience, and she was determined to show him this was not the case; also that his influence over her was minimal, because she never intended a man to dominate her again as Tom had. She would go, but in her own good time.

'I will go up when I think it necessary, Marc. Would you like tea?'

'My dear, you know I can't *stand* this English custom of tea at five in the afternoon. I would like a brandy if I may.'

Estella got up and rang the bell and when the maid appeared ordered tea for herself and brandy for her guest. Then she waited, saying nothing but tapping her fingers upon the arms of the chaise-longue upon which she sat.

'I don't consider *Theodora* a very good play, do you?' she said conversationally.

Marc shrugged and tipped the ash from his cigar into a tray. 'It is a very good vehicle for Madame Bernhardt. I think . . .' There was the sound of the doorbell and he stopped speaking to listen, then remarked, 'Would that be the doctor?'

'How do I know?'

Estella continued the drumming of her fingers upon the arms. Marc got up and stood in front of the fire, which still burned, despite the mild weather.

'Really, my dear, I think you are carrying this indifference too far. I'm inclined to think *I* am more concerned than you.'

'You're wrong.' Estella stared at him. 'I *am* more concerned, but I don't want to make a fuss. If it were serious Charlotte would come and tell me.'

'But Charlotte does not like you very much at the moment, does she?'

'Charlotte has never liked me. She wishes I were either in England or dead. Anywhere but here.'

'Then why don't you come and live with me?' Marc smiled, his eyebrows raised interrogatively, sitting down again.

'You certainly would not give a place to my child.'

'Quite true; but you don't want her, do you?'

Estella ignored the question and folded her hands together on her lap, contemplating the rings on her fingers, one of which, a fine diamond, he had given her. 'If I came and lived with you I would be considered a kept woman, would I not? One who sells her favours for gain? I have no money, not a penny to my name. As it is I am kept by Charlotte; but that is not the same thing, and if you give me jewels from time to time is that not the prerogative of a lover towards his mistress?'

Marc chuckled and settled himself deeper in his chair. 'You're a funny one, my dear Estella. Now I see the reason for all this farce. And how long do you think Charlotte will put up with you?'

'As long as she can have my daughter. *That* is the reason she puts up with me. Formerly it was for Lindsey; now it's for Ellen.'

'Not a very nice picture,' Marc murmured and then smiled as the maid entered with a tray.

'Thank you, Marie. Has the doctor been?'

'He is upstairs with the Baronne, monsieur.'

'Then pray run up and see how the little girl is, and ask the good doctor to step in here on his way out would you?'

250

'Certainly monsieur.' Marie put the tray down, bobbed and, looking anxiously at Estella, made her way out.

'How *dare* you say that?' Estella rose and, pouring Marc a brandy, held it at arm's length as if inviting him to get up and come for it. Marc sat where he was and languidly crossed one leg over the other.

'As your lover may I not have a little liberty?'

'No, you may not; not of that sort.'

'I may have your body but not your mind, is that it?'

'What a coarse, a horrible thing to say.' Estella, quivering, still held out the glass, but he continued to sit where he was, contemplating her, his smile gone.

'I find you very difficult, Estella, unfathomable if I may say so. You are divine, a princess, a goddess; but as a woman I cannot understand you at all. Today you are positively alien to me. You have a daughter, you hardly ever see her and yet you will not part with her . . . I can't understand it.'

'It's my affair. Here's your brandy. Take it please.'

'Pray keep it if you cannot pass it to me in a civilized manner.'

'Take it.' Estella's hand shook and so, dangerously, did the glass and the amber liquid in it.

'No. Thank you.' Marc started quivering too. 'I don't know, furthermore, that I like the woman I see today; the unfeeling mother, the rather grasping goddess who does not mind being kept by another woman . . .'

'I said *take* it.' Estella moved over towards him, the glass tilting in her hand, and threw the contents in his face. Marc spluttered, shook himself, then, extracting a handkerchief from his pocket, carefully wiped his face and the front of his coat. Estella still held the empty glass in her hand, gazing at him, appalled yet not appalled by what she had done.

Marc rose, pocketed his handkerchief and, without looking at her, strode to the door. Estella wrenched the ring he had given her from her finger and flung it after him. It landed neatly at his feet and he stopped and gazed at it. Carefully he stepped round it and then turned to her, a sardonic smile on his face.

'If I were you, my dear, I'd keep it. One day, if you treat all your lovers like this, you may have need of it.' Then he shut the door behind him. Outside in the hall Estella could hear voices, that of the doctor, Marc and another female one, maybe the maid or Charlotte. She stood rigidly by the tea tray, her hand out in the act of pouring tea, as though paralysed by the force, and consequences, of her behaviour, her intemperate act in throwing the drink at Marc.

The murmurings in the hall went on for some time and then she heard the front door shut and soon after that the sounds of horse's hooves echoing out of earshot. Slowly she poured herself tea and, without sitting down, put the cup to her lips.

It was dusk and a solitary blackbird was singing in sharp urgent tones, as though the last thing it had on its mind was rest, when Estella crept into the darkened nursery. Charlotte sat crouched over the cot, her hand clasping that of the sleeping baby. Estella stood for a long time gazing down at the child, her mind a confusion of emotions: hope, fear, grief, despair, love. Much love. Thwarted, scared love. She bent down and timidly touched Ellen's head and the baby stirred, her eyes flickering.

'How is she?' she whispered.

'As you see, sleeping.'

'She doesn't seem very ill.'

'Doctor Perrichot sent a drug to calm her and make her sleep. She still has a high fever.'

Ellen's bedclothes were loose and her white linen nightdress was ruched above her legs showing the fat, sturdy little limbs, the pink feet with their chubby toes. Estella felt a sudden relief, gratitude surging through her and knew, now, how afraid she had been. She gave a sigh and knelt beside the cot taking one of the tiny pink feet in her hand. 'I was very afraid.'

She was aware of Charlotte's cool, hostile stare and she didn't dare meet her eyes. 'I really was afraid . . . to come up.'

'You haven't much courage about anything, have you?' Charlotte said, and a lump came into Estella's throat.

'I know it seems that way to you.'

'You can't face anything. There must always be someone around to take care of you. You are like a baby yourself.'

'Please, Charlotte,' Estella prayed, raising her troubled eyes, longing to be able to give the comfort that Charlotte could give to her child. Only Charlotte. Not she, the child's mother.

Charlotte tenderly tucked Ellen's hand by her side and got up, stretching as though her back were tired. 'I can't understand a woman like you, Estella. I must be honest because I can't. I have seen you so wretched and unhappy, when the only person in the world who could help you was Lindsey; and then I have seen you so self-contained, poised and remote when all you wanted was the adulation of other people. You have to be surrounded by admirers, don't you, as though life were a perpetual performance on the stage?

'Yet did you ever come to *me* when *I* needed comfort? Did you come to me when Lindsey told me she was leaving me? Did you realize, for example, that today is the day of her marriage when, three thousand miles away, she is giving herself to that man? Did you think how much that thought makes *me* suffer? And on this day, of all days, the only person I have left in the world becomes dangerously ill? What comfort have I ever had from you, Estella Abercrombie?'

'None.' Estella sank to the floor, her hand still clasping

253

the baby's foot. 'None at all. I'm sorry. I didn't realize how much you envied Lindsey her happiness.'

'Envy!' Charlotte's tone was shrill. '*Envy* did you say? Envy has nothing to do with it. Do you think Lindsey is happy to marry Mortimer Digby, do you think she really wanted to?'

'I don't know.' Estella gazed at the shadows made by the half light on the floor. 'Why would she marry him if it didn't make her happy?'

'Because she feels she *should* be married. An unmarried woman has no status in our society. Lindsey has seen too many clever women like herself, and she doesn't want to be one of them. She's marrying Mortimer Digby simply to be a married woman. It's a mere stepping stone so that she can embark on achievements of her own.'

'But Lindsey could have married any man she wished. She had many admirers.' Estella thought back to her conversation with her sister four months before.

'Of course she could marry anyone she wished. But she didn't want to marry any of them, any man. Do you think I don't know Lindsey, after living with her for so many years?'

'I suppose you wish Lindsey could have married you?' Estella let the baby's foot go and sat back, supporting herself on her hands. Charlotte went to the table and lit the lamp, then, blowing out the match, she came over until she stood above Estella, gazing contemptuously down at her.

'Yes I do. I have never made any secret of my feelings for Lindsey. I love her and I feel, in a way, wedded to her. I don't see why women shouldn't love as men and I'm not ashamed of my feelings. I can resist the pressures of society, but Lindsey can't. Besides,' Charlotte turned away, her shoulders curiously hunched as though she had suddenly become much older, 'she didn't return my love in that way. I knew she couldn't and I didn't press her.

But, whatever happens, Lindsey knows I love her and always will and that if she ever needs me I am here, always, ready to give her my support and my love – so much more reliable than that of men.'

'Do you hate men that much?' Estella felt she wanted to know.

'I don't hate them as people but as members of their sex, so, in that sense, I do. I hate the way they have taken over the world; they have made it their world in which we have only a secondary place, a minor, unimportant place. Look how hard women have had to struggle, not only to be allowed to study medicine, but to do anything they want, other than be the objects of men's lust.'

'Not only lust; love too,' Estella said sadly.

Charlotte stared fiercely at the bowl of the lamp which at that moment seemed to make her arresting face, with its strong, moulded features, look almost masculine. She would have made a fine man, Estella thought and, indeed, here was a woman who appeared to have missed out on much that was worthwhile in life. She had lived only for Lindsey and now was bound up in her passionate love for Estella's child. Had she no real identity, no purpose of her own? Was this, then, the fault of men?

'The love, I suppose, Tom showed for you,' Charlotte taunted. 'Did you call *that* love?'

'Yes I did. Love, very strong love. Not just lust.' Suddenly Estella felt suffused with tender memories of Tom, and the haunting scenery of the Lake District which had been so bound up with that love became so vivid that she could amost imagine herself to be there wandering among the hills with him, hand in hand. Slowly she got to her feet feeling strangely almost overwhelmingly tired, as though she were dragging her limbs, forcing herself to make some superhuman effort to propel them. She looked down at Ellen and realized that the product of that love, that good love, was there before her very eyes. She bent and embraced her child, taking her in her arms, raising her from her cot, and she knew she had never before felt the fierce, maternal love she felt now.

'Oh my darling,' she murmured, holding the hot little face to her own, 'please get well.'

Ellen gave a cry and opened her eyes, gazing feverishly at Estella. Then she started to struggle and began to cry, threshing about as though wishing to release herself from some alien embrace.

'Put her down!' Charlotte cried sharply, rushing over to the cot and attempting to take her from Estella's arms. 'It is too late now to be a mother, Estella. See, she is afraid of you.'

Limply Estella allowed Charlotte to take the baby from her and immediately Ellen grew quiet, stopped struggling and nestled contentedly against Charlotte's breast as she stroked her head, murmuring into her ears soft words of endearment.

'There, there my baby. Sleep.'

Coming so soon after that rush of pure, maternal love Estella felt the loss of her baby almost too acute to bear. She put out her arms again, vainly offering to take Ellen from Charlotte, trying to reclaim her property, but the expression in Charlotte's eyes stopped her. Charlotte seemed to be saying: 'This is my baby, not yours. You have no place here,' and she rocked Ellen gently, clutching her more firmly to her body as though she had borne her, fed her with her own milk, as though she and the child were one.

Then the tears gushed down Estella's face and her arms dropped helplessly to her sides. She turned and went slowly out of the room, her steps feeling as heavy as lead.

The Comtesse de Malle held a salon every Tuesday in her house on the Avenue des Champs-Élysées, a few doors along from the magnificent Hôtel Païva built by one of the most celebrated demi-mondaines of the Second Empire. From eight-thirty onwards a string of carriages drew up, depositing on her doorstep all the intellectual élite of Paris; the artists, writers, composers, politicians, men of affairs, and women too, whose presence formed an essential part of the *beau monde*.

Her salon was held on the first floor in a succession of drawing rooms which glittered with chandeliers and mirrors like a miniature Versailles. In one room there was music, in another a poet or writer was reading from his or her latest work. In another there was animated conversation and in yet another little tables were set with all kinds of delicious things to eat and drink. From about nine until well after midnight, sometimes until the early hours, up to a hundred people entertained and were entertained, meeting their friends, making new ones and discussing the latest book, play or musical offering.

Edmond de Goncourt was a frequent visitor to the salon, mischievously noting its activities in his celebrated diary; and the actresses Réjane, Léonide Leblanc, Elenora Duse and Madame Bernhardt herself had been known to make glittering but usually brief appearances, before being whisked off to some other exotic entertainment. There one could see at various times the novelists Emile Zola, Alphonse Daudet, Guy de Maupassant or Anatole France; the celebrated woman writer and journalist Séverine and her male counterparts Felix Fénénon, Leon Lebloy, Gayda of the *Figaro* or Blàvet looking for gossip for his *Parisis* column; and the painters Degas, Vuillard and Auguste Renoir. Socialites such as Robert de Montesquiou, the Comtesse de Greffulhe, the Princesse de Sagan, the Duc and Duchesse de Luynes, the Prince d'Orleans, Comte Eugène-Melchior de Vogüé and many others came and went as well as that great society beauty the Comtesse de Lynes who had been the mistress of both the critic Sainte-Beuve and Prince Jérôme Napoleon, who had encouraged her to set up her own *salon*. The Comtesse was not the only member, or ex- member, of the world of the demi-mondaine, those scandalous but celebrated women, many with the most elevated minds, who sold their bodies in order to acquire wealth, security and, surprisingly, the cachet or social status of being the mistress of a famous man. Also there were representatives of *Paris-Lesbos*, those bright, intelligent and charming women who preferred their own sex as lovers and made no secret of it. Many of these had belonged to the world of the demi-monde too.

Estella made her way carefully up the broad staircase towards the first floor, taking care not to trip over her elegant sequinned gown of oyster-coloured silk adorned with bows. It was the first time she had appeared in public alone and twice she had ordered the carriage to turn back to the house and twice ordered it to go on. The flunkey at the door had taken her cape looking round for her usual escort, but she had shaken her head and said she was alone.

She breathed deeply as she went up the stairs, closing her eyes and remembering those days just before the curtain rose when she stood alone, often on a darkened stage, conscious only of the restless stir of the audience and the clamorous beating of her own heart. It was nearly ten and the rooms at the top of the stairs milled with people, yet the tinkling soft strains of a piano piece by Schubert came clearly above the low cacophony of voices. She waved to Madame Daudet talking animatedly to M. Cadot the publisher, her son Léon hovering at her elbow. Many of the men present wore black armbands for Victor Hugo, who had recently died. She saw the Baron Paulet, M. Charpentier and the back of M. Rodin the celebrated sculptor who had once asked her to pose for him. However, she knew that, in return for immortality, he

258

expected favours from his young models. But, with his fleshy, sensuous nose and long yellow beard she found him repulsive and did not feel inclined to accept.

Christine de Malle was just emerging from the music room when she saw Estella and she opened her arms, embracing her theatrically on both cheeks.

'My dear . . . so lovely, and . . . alone?' She looked round, but Estella shook her head.

'He is not here.'

Christine gently tapped Estella's shoulder with her fan. 'A lovers' tiff or something more serious?'

'More serious,' Estella said, knowing she would not see Marc again.

'He was too old for you my dear anyway. I was always terrified you were going to *marry* him. I know how respectable you English women like, or *pretend*, to be. Now who can we find for you tonight?'

Christine looked around and, spying a young man alone, beckoned him over.

'Robert, permit me to introduce you to Estella Abercrombie. I am sure you'll have a lot to talk about. My dear, this is M. Caze the celebrated novelist and journalist.'

'We have met before.' Robert Caze, a friend of Edmond de Goncourt, kissed Estella's hand, but his eyes roamed around as though he were looking for someone.

'Oh excuse me, Comtesse, there is a friend . . . ' He hurried away and Christine shrugged her shoulders and smiled. Estella put a hand on her arm.

'Please don't trouble about me, Christine. I know so many people. I'm sure . . . '

'At least let me ask Baron Philippe to get you some refreshment, even though I know he is on his way out.' Christine stopped a man who was passing and once again performed introductions.

'Philippe de Valéry is such an old friend. He has a finger in every pie you could possibly imagine. May I leave Estella with you for a few minutes, my dear Philippe, perhaps to procure her a glass of champagne?'

The Baron, looking rather annoyed at first, was, however, too polite to refuse and bowed punctiliously to Estella, at the same time surreptitiously producing his watch from the pocket of his waistcoat and glancing at it. Estella, observing him, smiled at Christine as she hurried away. Then she said earnestly: 'Please M. le Baron, I am perfectly at home here. I can find my own way to the supper room.'

'Dear madame I would not dream of deserting you, a lady of such beauty entrusted to my care. Pray let me at least drink one glass of champagne with you before my next engagement.'

The Baron led the way through the throng and Estella, glancing to right and left, occasionally smiling or acknowledging someone she knew, followed him. She was not at all hungry, nor did she want wine; but she neither felt comfortable nor at home, and she determined to leave as soon as she decently could, probably in the wake of the Baron. She had been mistaken in coming alone.

The supper tables were crowded and Estella felt slightly dizzy, wondering if she had ever seen so many people in the room. The emotional scene of a few hours before was still with her, and she wondered, if it had not been for that, whether she would have come out at all. But the house, Charlotte's disapproval, were stifling, and she had decided on the spur of the moment to go on with the engagement to which she and Marc had been committed for the evening. Now she regretted her impulse.

The Baron drew out a chair for her and stopped a passing waiter, taking two glasses of champagne from a tray. One he handed to Estella, the other he put to his lips, still standing. Estella felt awkward, not knowing whether to drink, to attempt conversation with him from her disadvantageous position, sitting while he stood, or simply to sit and stare as so many others did.

'Have you know Christine long?' He bent down and put a hand behind his ear as though to aid his own hearing above the buzz of conversation.

'About a year.'

'She tells me you are an actress.'

'I have not acted for a long time.'

'Ah.' The Baron glanced at his watch again and Estella put her glass, untouched, on the table. Her feeling of agitation was getting the better of her and now she merely longed to be away from this crowd and alone. Suddenly she stood up and gazed at the Baron.

'I wonder, if you are leaving, if you would escort me to a carriage? I am not feeling well.'

'Oh my dear madame.' The Baron was all concern and, quickly setting his glass on the table, took Estella's arm. 'I thought you looked a trifle pale, but as I had not met you before, I thought maybe that it was your normal complexion. Please let me take you home.'

'I cannot . . .'

Estella clasped her fan and nervously waved it in front of her face.

'But you can. Come with me, dear madame. We will be in the open air in a moment.'

Carefully, skilfully, the Baron steered her through the throng, bowing here, smiling there; but Estella, looking neither to right nor left, saw no one. Her eyes were blurred by unshed tears and the vision that tormented her was of her little baby, Ellen, contentedly nestling against Charlotte's bosom as though to her real mother. Ellen had rejected her; she did not know her and, certainly, she did not love her.

Estella hurried down the stairs in the wake of the Baron, accepting her cloak from the footman, aware of the Baron's hands tenderly fastening it about her shoulders. The footman went out to summon his carriage, which stood with so many others in the street outside, the horses pawing the ground in the cold night. Suddenly Estella was reminded of that last meeting with Tom, that final, fateful meeting when she had flown out of the threatre across the street and into his arms. She choked, stumbled and those unshed tears now began to course freely down her cheeks. The Baron caught her arm, looked at her with concern and helped her into his carriage, which had swiftly been driven round to the portico of the house. She sank back against the seat, caring not where she was nor with whom, her eyes shut, the tears flowing freely, staining the front of her gown.

The Baron had given instructions to his coachman which she did not hear and slowly it set off; she knew not where. After a while, the gentle rhythm of the coach, the clipclopping of the horses' hooves, made her feel calmer and, sighing deeply, she opened her eyes. The Baron was leaning solicitously towards her, a large white handkerchief in his hand.

'Thank you,' she took it and wiped her eyes, dabbed her cheeks and looked helplessly at the front of her gown. 'I'm very sorry, Baron. If I'd known this would happen I would never have come. I thought it might distract me, but that was not the case.'

'I can see you are suffering, madame. Indeed I thought so when I met you. Is it, perhaps something to do with an affair of the heart?'

'Partly yes, and partly no. Partly it is to do with me and my inadequacies, the follies I have committed.'

'But have we not all committed follies?'

'Few as grave as mine. But I am more than sorry to have inconvenienced you in this way. I know you have an engagement. If you would take me to . . . '

'I am taking you to my home, madame, if you will

262

permit it, to give you time to recover. It is not far from here.'

'But your engagement . . . '

'It is cancelled, forgotten.' The Baron waved a hand and in the wan light of the street lamps she felt comforted by the kind, reassuring smile on his face. His abruptness had vanished completely and now, she felt, he had all the time in the world just for her.

PART III

CHAPTER THIRTEEN

The city of Boston, the intellectual and cultural pearl of America, with its spacious, well laid out streets, its notable public buildings, its many fine homes, had, nevertheless, its slums, as any great city has. These were situated on the south side near the docks and its mean dwellings housed the many immigrants from Europe and the Far East as well as the large negro population who provided the menial services on which the City and its population depended. They serviced the laundries, hotels and restaurants, worked in the docks, drove the horse-cars, emptied the sewers, collected the rubbish and otherwise disposed of the effluence of Boston which the well-to-do, of necessity, preferred to disregard. All these artisans had wives (many of whom worked themselves) and usually a number of children and, sometimes, the philanthrophy of Boston's great public institutions passed them by.

A clinic for women had been established in a small mean street near the harbour and every weekday, and half-day Saturdays, it was packed to the doors with those in need of medical attention which was provided free. Here Lindsey saw the women who had escaped the net of public care and, invariably, they were those who needed it most: the destitute, the deserted, the unmarried and those who were quite respectable but who came to the clinic, nevertheless, because of its reputation for care and compassion that many of the large institutions inevitably lacked.

Lindsey had been married three and a half years, and had worked in the clinic for two of them when, one Friday

267

late in the afternoon in September 1889, she sat listening to the frail, tired woman in front of her. Mrs Parker was only her age, yet she had already borne ten children and lived in dread of having an eleventh.

'You're a married woman yourself, Doctor. You'll know about men.' Her expression as she gazed at Lindsey was pathetic, yet not devoid of hope.

What a wealth of meaning there was in Mrs Parker's words, Lindsey thought as she lowered her eyes from the harassed face and gazed at her notes trying to decide what to say, what to do. Too much responsibility was put upon a physician, who had not only to make judgments on medical matters but on moral ones too. Mrs Parker had pleaded for a way of stopping the babies, a task which she deemed, naturally, to be up to her not to her uxorious spouse.

'I know what you mean, Mrs Parker, and believe me I sympathize. Have you talked to your husband?'

Mrs Parker snorted as if at the absurdity of the very idea. 'Much notice he'll take!'

'Men *do* have a way of obtaining contraceptives,' Lindsey said quietly. 'They get them from barbers' shops and so on. There is nothing I can do to help you here. If we started giving contraceptive advice we should become a scandal in Boston. We might be closed down. I deplore it, but it's true. This is really something for yourself and your husband. Surely he doesn't want more children?'

'He doesn't, Doctor; but he can't keep away from me; yet he doesn't seem to think it's anything to do with him.'

'Most men don't,' Lindsey said shortly. 'But I don't think you can go on having children without severely damaging your health. You're anaemic already. Could you not sleep in a separate room from your husband?'

'We only have two rooms. Already we have five of the children in with us.'

Lindsey wondered when they got the opportunity to

make love, but this was something she couldn't ask. She only saw the results of sex; how it happened and how its consequences could be prevented were strictly out of medical bounds. One of the consequences was too often seen in her clinic in septicaemia and the aftermath of botched attempted abortions. Too many women took the law into their own hands, as her own sister had once vainly tried to do, but many were not as lucky as she had been; some died and left their orphaned children to the care of the city.

'Well . . . ' She leaned back in her chair and looked gravely at Mrs Parker. 'It's very drastic, but I do think you have grounds for removal of the womb. You have fibroids and protracted, painful periods. Normally I would not suggest such a radical course, but . . . '

Mrs Parker's pale eyes gleamed with excitement as though someone were offering her a special treat, not mutilation.

'Oh, do you think so doctor? No womb, no babies! Is that it?'

'That's it. I don't like advising hysterectomy as a means of contraception, but in your case I'll see what I can do. There is a sympathetic gynaecologist to whom we refer patients at the hospital. I'm not sure he'll agree, but I'll make you an appointment.' She began to make notes on Mrs Parker's papers and the young woman got to her feet with agility, as though she had been given a new lease of life.

'Thank you, Doctor. I knew you'd understand.'

'Believe me I understand, Mrs Parker,' Lindsey smiled without looking up. 'I understand only too well.'

When the woman had gone she continued making notes, and then she put her patient's file on top of a pile of others that were being referred for surgery that was strictly unnecessary. She got to her feet, removed her stethoscope and washed her hands carefully in the steel basin in the corner of her consulting room. Mrs Parker had been the last patient for the day and two cleaning women were beginning to empty the bins full of soiled dressings, remove the sheets on the examination couches and swab the tiled floors with steaming water heavily laced with carbolic.

'Mrs Parker will definitely have to be referred to Massachusetts General for hysterectomy,' she said to her assistant Heather Ainsley as she came into the room. 'Medically I wouldn't recommend it, but psychologically I can't answer for the consequences. She has eight children under the age of twelve, and two others have died.' She looked round to see Heather gazing at her, a concerned expression on her face.

'Why don't you go home, Lindsey? You wear yourself out here.'

'No more so than anyone else,' Lindsey said firmly, drying her hands. 'If only we had more women medical staff we could think about expansion. I hear that in London Mrs Anderson is building a wonderful new hospital in the Euston Road. She has the support of the Prince and Princess of Wales, and the Princess has just laid the foundation stone. I wish we had her here.'

'Who needs Mrs Anderson when we have you? You've transformed this clinic. We never had the number of patients we have now. It is all due to you.'

'That's nonsense,' Lindsey said practically, taking her coat from the peg on the wall. 'But I'll talk to my husband about the possibility of raising funds. Will you share a hurdy with me Heather? I'll drop you off home.'

Heather Ainsley was not a qualified doctor. She had had some nursing experience and was married to a physician, but her attempts to enter medical school had failed when she was younger, Harvard emulating its European counterparts by refusing to admit women, and now she felt she was too old. She was nearly forty and had three teenaged children, two boys at the Latin School for boys and a girl at the High. Heather looked strong, but she tired easily and, consequently, only worked half days at the clinic. Lindsey had begun by working two days a week, but now worked five. On Saturdays only minor dressings were done which were carried out by orderlies and no doctor was present.

Lindsey locked the door of the clinic, pocketing the key, and the women walked a few blocks, away from the harbour towards the common, where they found a hurdy plying for hire.

The Ainsleys lived in the fashionable area known as Back Bay Lands off the Western Avenue which had been constructed on a substantial dam across the bay and contained some of the finest dwellings and public buildings in Boston. Lindsey often dropped Heather off before leaving Boston proper and crossing the Charles River to her home in the suburb, Cambridge.

Lindsey sank back onto the seat of the cab, leaning her head against the back, only now realizing how truly tired she was. 'Medicine is unending, isn't it? When you solve one problem a new one emerges. Sometimes I think we don't know the half of it.'

'You sound depressed today, Lindsey dear.' Heather put a hand on her arm. 'I've thought for some time you were looking peaky. Why don't you take a rest?'

'What good would a rest do me? What we all need are some breakthroughs in medical practice. We're using the same techniques now at the clinic that were used when I was a medical student nearly ten years ago. What these women really need is help to prevent them having babies to stop this terrible flow of self-induced abortions, and what progress have we made there?' Lindsey snorted with disgust and looked out of the window. 'We don't even like to *talk* about it. That was the one thing Mrs Anderson would not allow at the School, lectures in contraceptive techniques, and nothing has changed. It was and still is considered disgusting.'

'Well,' Heather withdrew her hand and primly considered her lap, 'it isn't really very nice, is it? I mean . . .'

'You've limited your own family, haven't you Heather?' Lindsey's eyes narrowed as she perceived the blush on her friend's face.

'Really Lindsey . . .' Heather plucked at the button on her glove. 'Is this *quite* the sort of conversation . . . Well,' she stared suddenly at her companion, her eyes unnaturally bright, 'there *is* such a thing as control. Unfortunately the working classes do not seem to have learned it.'

'The working class *men* have not learned it yet,' Lindsey said furiously. 'The women have to put up with it. But control is not the point. Oh, I don't know . . .' They passed Boston Common and above them loomed the cupola of the State House upon Beacon Hill. Its view was said to surpass anything in the United States. 'I get so *angry* at times,' Lindsey concluded and then smiled apologetically. 'Sorry, Heather; but have you noticed that, more than anything, the women like to talk? They seem to have no one to listen to them and, because of all the calls on our skills, we have not the time. If you ask me a sympathetic ear and understanding cures more ills than any amount of conventional medicine. I'd like to set up a clinic just to *listen*. Unfortunately it would only be attended by well-educated neurasthenic women who could afford to pay.'

Heather didn't reply and Lindsey contented herself with gazing out of the window at the elegant quarter through which they were now passing. Soon after she set Heather down outside her white low colonial-style house and told the driver to take her home.

Lindsey and Mortimer had lived since their marriage in Quincy Street, opposite Harvard College, in a narrow three-storeyed house built of red brick. They were looked after by a Negro couple, Beamie and her husband Noah, who lived in the basement, and by a young immigrant Irish maid who had a small room in the attic. Beamie cooked and did the hard cleaning, and Noah did odd jobs around the house, drove the coach and tended the garden. Eileen was Lindsey's personal maid, answered the door and waited on the table at mealtimes. Beamie now opened the door with her large cheerful smile, which had given her her nickname, and took Lindsey's hat and coat. She then ushered her solicitously into the pleasant drawing room which overlooked the large back garden enclosed by a high red brick wall covered with vines, honeysuckle and red and white camellias which made a beautiful show in the spring.

'Is Dr Digby home, Beamie?'

'He's upstairs in his study, Miz' Digby. You sure do look tired today Miz' Digby . . .'

'Fetch me some tea, Beamie, there's an angel.' Lindsey quickly tidied her hair, glancing in the mirror. 'We didn't have time this afternoon.'

'Ah was sayin' to Noah,' Beamie continued relentlessly, 'that you do too much in that clinic. T'ain't *no* place for a lady.'

'But it is for a doctor, and I'm a doctor. Tea Beamie, please.'

Lindsey sank onto the sofa and put her feet up, laying her head back for a few moments and closing her eyes. Yes she was very tired; she was exhausted. She knew she worked too hard but the main trouble was that she didn't sleep, so that she had difficulty getting the rest she needed to do her work. But there was a lot more to it than that. A lot more. Although she knew her work in the clinic was vital it was not really what she wanted to do, any more than it had been five years before, when she had decided to leave London for Paris to study with Dr Charcot. She felt as frustrated now as she had then. She was not so

273

much interested in women's illnesses as in the women themselves; or rather she was interested in their minds as the key to what, in many cases, made them organically ill. She felt that, now, she had personal experience to implement her purely medical knowledge.

Yet if she forsook the clinic to do the kind of work she wanted to do she knew how Cambridge society would talk, and how much that would add to the distress of Mortimer and his family who lived in the huge Digby mansion on a hill, commanding a fine view of the harbour and the sea, in Old Boston. The Digby family had not wanted their son to marry an unknown woman from London who had studied medicine in defiance of her parents' wishes and who had travelled to America with him, like some camp follower, they had observed to themselves, wondering what their fellow travellers on the boat thought – as people do who place undue emphasis on the opinions of others. A lady, surely, got married whether it was in Boston or London, from her parents' home with her parents' blessing and consent, and Lindsey had not even troubled to tell her family about her intentions. Why, Mortimer had not even met them. What sort of girl married a man her parents did not even know? Certainly no Digby girl would.

What sort of people were the Abercrombies then, the Digbys had asked themselves, who brought up a daughter in this manner? Who allowed her to travel freely abroad and decide for herself when she got married, where and to whom? Had she come from some well known, London family they would have welcomed an English bride for their son, but who had ever heard of the insignificant Abercrombies?

It was only when Mortimer and Lindsey were safely married and settled in Cambridge that they learned of yet another horrible secret; of a sister who was not only an actress who had left her husband and had a child, but who

274

now lived in Paris with a man to whom she was not married. A kept woman, quite plainly that was what she was. What a disgrace for the Digbys, who numbered themselves among the best families in Boston: the Lowells, the Jacksons, the Cabots, the Jameses and the Putnams.

It was the attitude of her in-laws that had prevented Lindsey from doing what she wanted to do, to pursue her studies in psychopathology, hopefully at Harvard. It was their attitude too that had made Mortimer decide to continue as a neurologist lecturing at the Harvard Medical School and practising at the Massachusetts General instead of experimenting with new psychological methods as he had wished.

The attitude of his family to Lindsey had unnerved him and awoken in him distant echoes of the pious, obedient son he had been brought up to be. Away from Europe and its liberalizing influences he was almost amazed to see how quickly, and with what little reluctance, he fitted into the familiar mould of his formative years. But at least they got married, and settled into a house of their own. At least they were able to do that much.

In time, after a year during which the Digbys had attempted in vain to turn Mortimer's odd wife into a genteel Bostonian, making social visits, joining sewing 'bees' and entertaining young married women like herself to tea, Lindsey had rebelled and found the sort of job that alone was acceptable to Boston society – unpaid work in a clinic devoted to poor women and their children, tucked well out of sight of the fashionable quarters.

Then there was the question of children. Why, the Digbys and their close friends asked themselves, did not Lindsey produce as a good wife was expected to? With a house full of children she would soon lose these ridiculous, pretentious notions that a woman's place was apparently not in the home but working outside it; not at her husband's side, but in some disease-ridden clinic in the Boston slums.

It was not that Boston women were strangers to learning or scholarship. Matters had progressed a little from thirty years before when Henry James Sr had written, concerning the ideal woman: 'Learning and wisdom do not become her. Even the Ten Commandments seem unamiable and superfluous on her lips . . . Her aim in life is . . . simply to love and bless man.' But in many true Bostonian hearts these sentiments still prevailed and, although there was an increasing number of distinguished women in various fields – the neurologist Mary Putnam Jacobi was one and the Bostonian novelist Louisa May Alcott was another – families such as the Digbys did not like to dislodge the angel in the house from her pedestal, or equate the sanctity of womanhood and motherhood with anything so defiling as paid work.

But Lindsey worked, harder and harder, and Lindsey had no children. What a disappointment she was to the Digbys. How quickly and accurately she fulfilled their forebodings. How they congratulated themselves on being right! What a mess poor Mortimer had made of his life.

Lindsey opened her eyes to find Mortimer gazing at her. He was in his shirtsleeves and his eyes behind his gold rimmed spectacles were red with fatigue.

'Beamie is bringing in some tea.' Lindsey struggled up, but Mortimer turned, pointing to the tray on the small table in the centre of the room.

'Beamie left this ten minutes ago. She didn't want to disturb you.'

'Heavens! I didn't think I *slept*.' She glanced at Mortimer's passive features. 'Please, now, don't tell me I'm too tired.' She got quickly to her feet, tucking her blouse into the waistband of her skirt, and began to pour the weak China tea into dainty Meissen cups. She gave one to Mortimer who sat on the sofa and crossed his legs, stirring his tea, gazing thoughtfully into his cup.

'I thought of going to Europe,' he said. 'We promised ourselves a visit, didn't we?'

'Europe?' Lindsey felt her tiredness vanish. 'Paris, for instance?'

'Paris, London, Vienna, Rome.' Mortimer nodded. 'I want to see Freud again in Vienna – he is doing some very interesting things – and you want to see Estella in Paris. I hope we can both meet your parents in London.'

'And in Rome? What have we there?'

'Why a holiday, my dear, I thought. We don't necessarily have to see anyone anywhere if you don't wish it.'

'Of course I want to see my parents and sister.' Lindsey sipped her tea standing up, looking out of the bay window at the oleander tree in the garden which was now beginning to shed its leaves. It was as though she could hear her own voice from a distance. Her clipped, abrupt English tones. Why did she always sound so brittle with Mortimer? When had they lost the ability to communicate with each other? How?

She knew how and why, but she was as reluctant to acknowledge it as any of her patients to confront the real reasons for their ills in her clinic in downtown Boston. The truth was that she and Mortimer had grown so apart because they had never really been together. The love she was beginning to feel for him on their journey to America, the sense of comradeliness and togetherness they shared on the boat, had vanished completely when she was confronted by the numerous members of his smart New England family, saw at once how they reacted to her, and how much their opinion of her mattered to him. She had felt an outsider from the beginning; had known with absolute certainty then and there that she would never become one of their number. She should have gone back to Paris – where she was loved and wanted – straight away, but she didn't. She was too proud to admit failure before she had given her marriage a chance to work, or herself to know his family better.

It was not that they were unkind to her; they were very civilized and polite, as behoved one of the best families in the State of Massachusetts. The men, almost uniformly elegant, cleanshaven and well dressed, well educated and well behaved, were the very epitome of punctilious politeness. The women were without exception gracious, well groomed and condescending, though not one of them had had one tenth of the education she had received. Yet her Cambridge degree, her medical qualifications, went for absolutely nothing. In Boston of the 1880s what mattered more than anything else was not what you had done or achieved, but who your parents were, and who theirs were, and who they had married and how long back the pedigree went. Money didn't matter, so long as it was plentiful, and was never referred to; but birth mattered enormously among the Bostonians, who, by their carefully cultivated English accents, even contrived to act and behave as though they were not American at all but citizens of some rarefied world acknowledging neither President nor Queen, but only God.

There were frequently long silences between Lindsey and Mortimer, as there was now, and the silences were informed not by hostility or indifference, but simply by an inability on the part of each to communicate with the other. To know what to say.

'My parents are coming for dinner, and Emmie. Had you forgotten?'

Lindsey clattered her cup on the saucer and gazed at him with consternation. 'Oh yes. I had.'

'I thought you might. Had I seen you this morning I would have reminded you then.'

'I had to leave early, Mortimer. Some of the women come before they go to work.'

'You leave earlier and earlier, Lindsey, and come home

278

later and later. Your work seems to have taken possession of you completely.'

Yes it had, Lindsey thought, setting the cup down on the table, wiping her lips on a hand embroidered linen napkin. It would absorb her all the time, weekends too, if she had her way. Anything to keep her out of the way of the Digbys, their relations and friends, and the silent but dignified and unspoken reproach of Mortimer whom she had so singularly failed to make happy.

'Beamie is a fine cook. How I envy you there,' Martha Digby said, delicately filleting her fine plaice which only that morning had reached Boston Harbour fresh from its Atlantic home. Yet even in the compliment she somehow contrived to convey that only in this one particular did she envy her daughter-in-law, by a subtle emphasis on the word 'there'. There was certainly nothing else, she seemed to imply, about Lindsey that she wished to emulate.

It was Martha Digby, with her genteel airs and snobbish prejudices, who had done most to influence the Digby family in its attitude towards Mortimer's wife. Related to the Lowells through her mother, she felt, even by this tenuous connection, that she had done much to enhance the social prestige of the Digbys. She was a tall, well built woman with no beauty but much charm; and she managed to hide her feelings about most people behind vague blue eyes and a seemingly benevolent expression. Lindsey had never been taken in by her for a moment.

'Why don't you borrow her from us, Mother, while we're away?'

'Away?' Martha looked at him and then at her husband. 'You're going away?'

'To Europe.'

'It isn't decided,' Lindsey said, crumbling a freshly baked roll on her plate. 'It was only mentioned this afternoon.'

'I thought we agreed?' Mortimer smiled at her. 'You

seemed to welcome the idea of visiting your parents and sister.'

'Europe,' Emmie Digby, Mortimer's sister, said, suppressing a shudder. 'Fancy. So far away.' She looked fearful at the thought of straying so far from the family hearth. But her mother glanced at her contemptuously, saying:

'I hope you're not thinking of going for good, Mortimer?'

'Certainly not, Mother.'

'You were away a long time on your last visit.' She raised her eyebrows and Lindsey knew what she was thinking. Her expression left no doubt in Lindsey's mind that her mother-in-law would like to have added, 'and look what happened then; look what you brought back with you.'

'It's a very difficult time for me to leave the clinic,' Lindsey said.

'*Any* time is difficult for you to leave the clinic.' Mortimer imperturbably helped himself to more potato.

'It's particularly difficult at the moment; we're so short of staff. I was wondering, Mortimer, whether it would be possible to raise funds for a larger building, start an appeal?'

'We'll consider it when we return, my dear. What you need at the moment is a rest.'

'Lindsey certainly *looks* very tired,' Newton Digby's expression was kind. 'You've lost weight and the shadows under your eyes are darker.'

'That's because she doesn't sleep,' Mortimer interjected.

'Lindsey doesn't sleep?' Emmie, perpetually pale and sallow-faced, visibly perked up immediately. 'Why Lindsey, I didn't think you had *any* weaknesses like us ordinary human beings.'

'Insomnia isn't a weakness,' Lindsey riposted, endeavouring to maintain an agreeable expression on her face even at the risk of cracking her skin. 'It's a disability.'

'But it's a disability *I* have too,' Emmie exclaimed. 'Then we do have something in common after all?'

'Evidently, though my insomnia is probably the result of overwork. The busy, crowded events of the day, the problems of my patients, prevent me from resting properly at night.'

'Which one could hardly say for you, Emmie.' Her brother smiled teasingly at her. He was the eldest and she the youngest. There was a brother and sister in between, both of whom were healthy, extrovert creatures, married with growing families. 'Overwork is not exactly your problem.'

At twenty-six Emmie was the youngest of the family, a timorous, rather bitter girl quite devoid of the charm with which the rest of the family made up for the lack of beauty. She was still unmarried and prey to nervous weakness, the specific causes for which remained undiagnosed by the many doctors she consulted. Emmie, though never exactly ill, was never completely well; and frequently sought treatment at fashionable establishments offering various cures by means of hydrotherapy, electricity, massage and rest.

'Don't be cruel to Emmie,' their father interjected mildly. 'Can she help it if her constitutional disposition gets the better of her at times? At least we seem to have proved that insomnia strikes indiscriminately, attacking those who work too hard as well as those who don't work at all. I have heard, however, that the make-up and temperament of women make them particularly unsuitable to exhausting physical or mental work . . . '

'That *canard* was disposed of years ago, Mr Digby,' Lindsey bestowed a smile upon him of great sweetness. 'It has no physiological or psychological basis, but was quite commonly put about when I was a girl by people, some of them quite eminent, who were against women leaving home. I . . .'

'I *think* we have the point Lindsey.' Mortimer frowned a warning at her. 'Whatever the cause of your insomnia, mental and physical rest in Europe for three months will do you the world of good.'

'Three *months*?' Lindsey stared at him. 'I couldn't possibly go for three months.'

'Or six,' Mortimer concluded, as though to himself. 'I haven't quite decided.'

'Would you close the house?' Martha Digby enquired this of Lindsey, domestic matters being clearly the concern of the wife.

'Well, however long we went, if we went, we certainly wouldn't like to lose Beamie and Noah and Eileen.'

'But you could borrow Beamie for dinner parties. Lindsey wouldn't mind at all. Would you dear?'

'Not at all,' Lindsey said graciously, fighting the urge to contradict him. She knew her nerves were on edge, and opposing Mortimer on matters she considered trivial wouldn't help her. Domesticity, to Lindsey, was very trivial indeed.

With the meat course the conversation became more generalized, although not so much so as to exclude intimate and animated discussion of their nearest and dearest friends. Gossip, Lindsey thought, permeated Boston in a way that it did not in London or Paris – even Paris – and, consequently, she felt both out of place and embarrassed by its prevalence. But Mortimer, too, was not immune to an interest in the affairs of his neighbours, the family of the eminent philosopher and psychologist William James, who had taught him at Harvard, and whose brother, the novelist Henry, lived in Europe; nor to tittle-tattle about the father of Emmie's best friend, Grace Dodge, who was rumoured to have left his wife and family for a woman twenty years his junior. On the other hand *some* said he was just on a protracted business visit to Europe. Half the fun of gossip, Lindsey decided, observing how animated the usually listless Emmie had become at this juncture, was speculation: not really knowing the truth. She guessed that at other dinner tables scattered about Boston and its suburbs – Concord, Brookline, Milton or Beverly – a sure topic of conversation, not much of it flattering, would be the strange Englishwoman poor Mortimer Digby had brought back with him, who not only worked as a doctor but had neglected to provide him with children as well.

As they gossiped and speculated, virtually excluding her, Lindsey contrived, as she usually did, surreptitiously to study the manners and habits of her in-laws.

On the whole she liked Newton Digby. He was a typical product of his class and age but, of them all, he had made her the most welcome and gone out of his way to be kind to her. He was a tall man, not handsome, but with a pleasant face, blue eyes and a firm humorous mouth. His iron-grey hair was neatly divided by a parting in the middle. Like her father he had never had to work, enjoying the fruits of earlier Digby labours. He was a man of learning, a philosopher and humanitarian, a member of many of Boston's most eminent academic societies. Lindsey thought that were he and her father ever to meet they would get on.

Lindsey could never recall having a proper conversation with Emmie and had nothing in common with her. They were antithetical because Emmie knew, or guessed, that Lindsey saw through her, and she doubtless envied the control she had over her life, her ability to lead an independent existence. Emmie sat glancing at her now and then from under her fair arched brows, and already Lindsey dreaded the half-hour she would have to spend with her and her mother in the drawing room after dinner.

When dinner was concluded the women rose, and the

men, retaining the old custom still prevalent at dinner parties, remained behind at the table to smoke and sample the port.

Newton Digby made a great play of lighting his cigar, pushing his chair away from the table and stretching his legs as he did.

'Europe.' He extinguished his match, depositing it in a large crystal ashtray that Eileen had placed in front of him when she brought in the port. 'Is Europe a *good* idea, Mortimer?'

'Why not, Father?' Mortimer had lit a cigarette, though his father always made him feel quite clearly that he considered cigars more masculine.

'You were away a long time before. Should you not settle down, my boy?'

'Settle down? Do you consider I am not settled? I have been married three and a half years; my lectureship at Harvard is secure. My work at the hospital has brought me both reputation and some private patients. I thought, when I returned from Europe, I would try and extend the private practice. It is largely because of this that I wish to study advanced methods of treatment that are rapidly being developed all over Europe. Morton Prince and Dr Putnam, among others, are very interested in them. I'm talking about the link between hypnosis and the development of systematic psychotherapy. Professor Dana at Cornell makes considerable use of hypnosis in his practice and so do Dr Starr at Columbia and Dr Osgood who is so interested in psychic research.

'I have discussed my plan with Professor James, who has given me a great deal of encouragement. But I particularly wish to see again Dr Sigmund Freud, with whom I regularly correspond. He has developed the most interesting theories concerning hysteria and hypnosis since his return to Vienna.'

'Mmm.' Newton sat back and gazed at his son, his

brows slightly furrowed, his fingers rapidly and nervously revolving the large ashtray which by now contained a good deal of the ash from his cigar. 'Well, I'm not a medical man and what you say is, of course, of interest. I know James thinks well of you as also do Prince and Putnam. I'm not really thinking of your medical work, Mortimer, so much as the personal, more intimate aspect of your life if I may be so bold as to refer to it. When I talk about "settling down" I'm thinking of a family. You were born within a year of my marriage to your mother.'

'Oh I see. I wondered when that would come up.' Mortimer extinguished his cigarette and immediately lit another.

'Well, Mortimer, I haven't mentioned the matter to you until now, considering it, properly speaking, no business of mine though your mother thinks differently. Your mother has been urging me to raise the matter for some time. We are both – in fact the whole family is – most concerned that you and Lindsey have not yet had children and show no signs of doing so. Is it wise for her to spend all her days at this clinic? Is there something amiss that you consider too delicate to talk about?'

Mortimer stubbed out his fresh cigarette, clenching and unclenching his hands. Then he pushed his chair from the table, as his father had done, before getting up and strolling to the sideboard where he helped himself to a nut.

'So the whole family are discussing my private life, are they? You distress me, Father.'

'My boy, it is only that we are all concerned. We don't intend to pry, or be prurient.'

'Nevertheless it *is* a delicate matter, Father. One which . . .'

'Travelling around Europe is no place if you have ideas of a family in mind. Your wife won't be a young woman for ever. She is past thirty.'

'I am perfectly aware of that.' Mortimer cracked the nut with silver nutcrackers, scattering the husk on the polished surface of the sideboard. 'In fact, in visiting Europe I had in mind the notion that some form of treatment might be available for Lindsey.'

'Oh, there *is* a problem?' Newton's voice dropped and his expression grew sympathetic. 'Is it something that doctors here can't cure? Have you seen them?'

'It's a *very* difficult, personal matter, Father; one that I would not have brought up had you not asked. But since you do . . . ' Mortimer put the pieces of nut in his mouth, chewed them slowly before selecting another. This he brought back to the table, resuming his seat, turning the nut round and round in his hand as if considering its shiny smoothness before submitting it to destruction. He didn't look at his father as he spoke. 'I believe Lindsey's trouble to be psychological rather than organic.'

'Psychological? You mean she's mad? She seems perfectly normal to me. Well, within limitations, shy and withdrawn certainly, at least in front of us, but not at all mad.'

'Oh Lindsey is not *mad*, Father.' Mortimer irritably cracked the nut, scattering the pieces on his lap. 'How little you know about psychology. Just because a person may have psychological problems that does not mean they are in any way deranged. I mean we all know that something is wrong with Emmie, and that the root of the matter is probably in her mind; but she's not at all mad.'

'Of course Emmie's not mad,' his father said testily. 'Just strange.'

'Then nor is Lindsey. But her problems are to do with those intimate aspects of marriage which are normally not discussed, even between father and son.'

'Oh, I'm sorry . . . ' Newton coughed with embarrassment and began hurriedly to relight the stub of his cold cigar.

'My wife has a repugnance for the marital act, such as to inhibit her from agreeing to its performance altogether. It is an ordeal for her, and consequently has become so for me. So that in fact we now seldom have relations, if at all.'

Mortimer gazed at the ceiling as though trying to remember when he last made love to his wife.

'But that's preposterous, my boy!' Newton sharply removed his cigar from his mouth. 'Repugnance or not, it is her *duty* to submit. Her duty to provide you with heirs. If that is all, it is of no consequence. She must submit, Mortimer, and you must make her. I'm sorry to say it, but I must.' Newton got up and went round to his son, standing behind his chair and putting a manly hand on his shoulder. 'You know, Mortimer, as man to man, it is not the function of women to enjoy the marital act. Most of them don't. It is not at all unnatural, I assure you. In fact, you might say it is perfectly proper that a woman of refinement and breeding should view such a procedure as she has to endure with abhorrence. The lot of women in matters pertaining to procreation is not, alas, a happy one. God knows why it should be thus – to torment us all, men as well as women. Happily those days, for me, are long over. But when she was younger, your poor mother . . .'

Mortimer put his hand on his father's and brushed it away. 'I don't wish in the least to hear about your relations with my mother, Father. That *is* deeply repugnant to me. After all, she has borne you four children and how that came about is no concern of mine . . .'

'I just said it to reassure you, son. As man to man. It is not an abnormal reaction on your wife's part; but it must be overcome . . .'

'Do you not think I have tried to overcome it, Father?' Mortimer leapt to his feet, his pale face burning, his eyes behind his spectacles gleaming feverishly. 'Do you think I have not done all that *I* could? Lindsey not only has a psychological aversion to the . . . the act; she has a physical one too. She experiences such pain and discomfort that actual intercourse is impossible. It is simply not *possible*!'

Mortimer crossed his arms and went and stood in a corner of the panelled dining room as though he were a schoolboy who had been sent there for some misdemeanour, thus perhaps subconsciously enacting the disgrace he felt.

His father, grave-faced, resumed his seat, his back to his son.

'That *is* very disturbing news, Mortimer, and I apologize again for being one to occasion such embarrassment. But at least there seems some medical reason for it. Maybe an operation . . . '

'You don't understand, Father, do you?' Mortimer unfolded his arms and pressed his hands against the wall. 'Whether because you won't or cannot I don't know. She has no need of an operation; there is no obstruction, as you appear to suggest, no impediment, nothing physically wrong with her at all.'

'But the pain . . . '

'The pain is caused in her mind, Father.' Mortimer patiently tapped his head, advancing again into the room. 'The apprehension of the act, whether natural or not, causes her to contract her limbs, her muscles, so that . . . '

'I understand, I understand, Mortimer. I'm not so foolish as all that.' His father put his hands over his ears, as though delicacy forbade him to hear more. 'There is no need to elaborate, seeing that this is causing such distress to you, and to me too I may say. It is a most unpleasant thing to have to discuss even with one's son. But is there not something . . . maybe on your own part? I mean some way of preparing your wife, making her relax . . . '

'You mean that I'm at fault too, Father?' Mortimer sat down again, his hands joined in front of him, his head

288

bowed. 'You're saying maybe I am deficient as a lover? Well, perhaps I am.' He raised his head and stared into Newton's eyes. 'I never had a mistress, Father. Never knew a woman's love before my marriage. I was a virgin too when Lindsey and I were wed.'

'Well, I didn't know that, Mortimer. I'm sorry.' It was his father's turn to look acutely embarrassed and now he hung his head. 'I naturally assumed that, like all full-blooded males, you had had some experience.'

'Why did you "naturally assume" it, Father?' Mortimer's tone was sarcastic. 'Did you bring me up with the idea of fornicating with women to whom I was not married . . . ?'

'Certainly not. I . . . well it is a weakness expected of males. I'm not saying I approve of it, but it is a fact.'

'Did you have mistresses before you were married?'

'Yes I did.' Newton clamped his unlit cigar once again between his teeth and stared at the ground. 'I'm not especially proud of it; but it was expected and, Goddam it, I wanted to know! I needed it from my teens.'

'But did you not consider the danger of disease from these women?'

'I'm not talking about brothels, Mortimer! The women I knew were mostly married women whose husbands were busy elsewhere. It was considered natural in my youth for a young man to be entertained, if he had the good fortune, by a well born married lady. I knew two or three such women so that when I married your mother at the age of twenty-six I had some experience. I'm sorry such knowledge passed you by.'

'You must have known I did not go with women.' Mortimer spoke so quietly and bitterly that his voice sounded close to tears.

'But in Europe. Surely . . . '

'I knew no women then either. I was so absorbed with my studies. Besides, unlike you, I did not feel the need.

My inclinations were not so strong. But when it came to my marriage I realized how inexperienced and uncouth I was. No wonder I disgusted my wife . . . '

'But your wife is a doctor! Goddam it man, you are *both* doctors. Surely between you . . . '

'Oh we knew the facts, Father. We knew all about the physiology of sex.'

'Then it should have been easy.'

'Well, it wasn't and it isn't, and I say that it is not a normal situation and that there are psychological reasons which account for Lindsey's attitude. I hope she will agree to have treatment, because her symptoms are similar to hysteria, and her aversion to sex *is* hysterical. It is nothing to do with her being a doctor and having the knowledge, which she has, but with her being a woman and being so overcome by fear that she experiences pain that is as real as anything you or I might feel. In fact, this condition is recognized in medicine and has a medical name. I have seen the agony on her face and I know it to be true. I cannot bear to put her through this time and time again. I cannot, I cannot, I cannot.'

There was a sudden knock on the door and when Newton called out Eileen popped her head in.

'The ladies say can you please join them, sir? It is getting very late.'

Mortimer, his hand raised, his face pale, turned away so that the maid should not see him. Newton hastily removed the stopper from the decanter, which had so far remained untouched, and poured himself and his son a large glass each of port.

'Here drink up,' he said. 'We both need it.'

The green creeper of Old Massachusetts Hall glowed in the light of the streetlamp. Lindsey was so used to studying it as she lay sleepless at night, her curtains open so that she had something to look at, that she felt familiar with every shiny leaf. Occasionally she lit the lamp and read, but tonight she was too exhausted by the visit of Mortimer's family, worried by the obvious bad temper with which he had returned to the drawing room. He'd said nothing to her afterwards and had gone straight to his own room after seeing his family out. The chasm between them seemed to grow bigger. Could a visit to Europe bridge it? Maybe she should stay there and let him return without her.

Lindsey thought back to her discussions with Estella, all those years ago, about marriage being a contract. In return for its advantages she had known she would have duties but, until the nature of those duties became explicit, she didn't know what to expect. Yet nothing, no amount of foreknowledge – which many brides lacked – had prepared her for the revulsion she felt when Mortimer made his first advances on their wedding night. Apart from a brief embrace they had never kissed, other than by touching each other lightly on the lips. She suspected she was cold, but had assumed that, when the time came, she would react as most women did to the unaccustomed familiarities of the marriage bed; if not with actual pleasure, then with resignation.

But she had not. His lips on hers disgusted her, his attempts to fondle her body filled her with loathing, and when he tried to insert himself, clumsily it was true, between her legs . . .

The disgust and horror of that moment still had the power to make her shudder, as did the memory of the many attempts since. Technically she was no longer a virgin; technically he had discharged himself in her – but at what cost – and, had the timing been right, technically she could have been a mother. So from a legal point of view they were married; the marriage had been consummated. The dreadful act had been performed several times with varying degrees of success, but with no satisfaction to either. But what a loathsome, disgusting business she considered it! How demeaning, both for a man and a woman. She didn't know how a well brought up, well educated, fastidious man like Mortimer could bring himself to do such a thing, or how any gently reared woman could be expected to respond.

Yet people did, apparently all the time, as the increasing population of the world bore witness. It astonished her that this was so; her sister, apparently, actually *enjoyed* it. It was very, very strange and something that Lindsey didn't understand at all. Yet she was quite able to divorce her private miseries from her professional life, and treat daily the women in her clinic who were either the willing or reluctant participants in an act which disgusted her to the extent that it caused her the most agonizing pain.

Suddenly a shaft of light intervened between her bed and the window out of which she was gazing. She sat up and jerked her head towards the door.

'Mortimer! What is it?'

'I wondered if you were asleep?'

She lay back on her pillow and drew her legs tightly together.

'No, I'm not sleeping.'

'Neither can I. Can we talk, Lindsey?'

'What about?' She put one hand nervously behind her head and continued to stare through the window.

'About us.'

'What is there to say about us?'

'Plenty. You know that. Only we can't seem to talk, can we? As we used to in London and Paris?'

'That was about medicine mostly, if I remember.'

'Did you *ever* love me, Lindsey?'

Lindsey didn't reply and he sat gingerly beside her on the bed.

'Why did you marry me if you didn't love me?' He timidly put a hand on hers.

Lindsey closed her eyes and started to tremble.

'Please don't,' she said.

'I'm not going to try and make love to you, Lindsey. I promise I won't touch you; but I do want to talk. I can't sleep for thinking how bad things are between us. And I love you very much. I still do, whatever's happened.'

'Is your father behind this?' Lindsey murmured, still feeling apprehensive.

'He wants to know why we don't have children.'

'I thought something had happened when I saw you looking so angry. Did you tell him?'

'In a way. He said I should have had a mistress before our marriage.'

Lindsey struggled to an upright position. 'You mean now your family knows all *this* about us? You discussed such intimate matters with *him* ?' Her voice was shrill; but she was so angry she felt like screaming. On edge, always on edge; always like this at home, nowadays.

'I had to tell him something, Lindsey. I told him that I thought your, our, problem was psychological. That it could be cured.'

Lindsey, breathing deeply, lay down again, but was still nervously aware of her husband's physical proximity. She wished he'd waited for the morning – a Saturday when they would have the whole day to themselves.

'I think Freud could help you, Lindsey. You must know that your trouble can be cured?'

'You've talked about *me* with Dr Freud too? Who else? Who else among your colleagues knows I'm frigid? Who? Who?'

'No one, Lindsey. Not even Freud. I just put the problem objectively to him, as though I were describing a patient of my own. Don't you want to be helped?'

'I don't think anything can help me,' Lindsey said, and she felt very small and insecure, like a young child in need of comfort, rather than a physician of mature years who gave solace to others.

'But darling, I want to help you. I want to love you.'

'But it hurts, Mortimer. It hurts so much.'

'It need not hurt, Lindsey, you *must* know that! I think much of the fault was due to me. I was a clumsy lover. I should have had experience, like my father had.'

Lindsey could see his face quite clearly now in the light from the streetlamp and suddenly she felt for him not anger nor disgust, but pity. Mortimer was a good, caring man; yet he was a product of his upbringing, as she was. She had married him and, surely, was it not her duty to try and understand him a little better than she did? 'You know not all the fault is due to you,' she said quietly. 'We were both too inexperienced, but too experienced too. I had honours in obstetrics and gynaecology. I am a specialist in diseases of women, yet I can't help myself. Oh Mortimer what *am* I to do?'

She reached out and took his hand and, at this first spontaneously intimate contact for many months, his heart lifted and he entrapped her palm between his own.

'Darling Lindsey, if you want to be cured you can be. You know all about the theory of hysteria, yet you need help to apply it to yourself. Freud is the man. He doesn't know you, or not as well as any psychotherapist here, and you can tell him everything. He has described cases to me, incredible cases, which he has cured. I have great faith in him and I want you to see him. I think he will be one of the really outstanding medical men of our time. And he can help me too. Why did I not need a mistress before I was thirty-six? What was it in my upbringing that made me able to do without that which most other men need from their teens? He can help us both explore our subconscious. And we can use what we learn about ourselves to help others. Can't you see it in that way?'

'Yes,' Lindsey murmured, still aware of the pressure of

his hands. 'Yes, I'm beginning to. If it doesn't work out, Mortimer, I'll release you from our marriage.'

'But I don't want to be released. I want you. I love you. And my greatest wish is for you to love me too.'

Suddenly, unexpectedly, her heart filled with such tenderness for him that she wanted to understand herself so that she could give him the love he so needed and deserved. If they had become strangers it was as much due to her as it was to him – though she blamed his family for much that had gone wrong between them. Their disapproval of her and their stereotyped attitudes about women had changed Mortimer in a way that he probably didn't realize. If Europe did succeed in bringing them together she would take good care to live away from them – probably in another town altogether.

'Thank you, Mortimer. Thank you for still wanting me. And I do love you. I think more than I realized. But it is not a love I can demonstrate – in a physical way. I have never been emotional, or able to show my affections. Poor Charlotte suffered much because of this.'

Mortimer stiffened at Charlotte's name. She wrote often, he knew, but was seldom mentioned between them. Sometimes he wondered if Lindsey's indisposition sprang from an attachment, albeit unconscious, to those of her own sex. But soon they would know. Freud would unravel many mysteries. 'I wish we'd talked before,' Lindsey continued. 'I meet all these problems and attitudes in my clinic. Why didn't I apply them to myself?'

'We'd let things go too far.' He bent and kissed her hand, aware, as he did so, that she trembled as though fearful he would wish to extend this intimacy. But he would not. Not until they'd seen Freud. He would give her no cause for concern before then. 'I'm to blame too. We'll go to Europe and begin a new life. Besides, darling, wouldn't you really *like* to have children?'

Lindsey clutched his hands, acutely, vividly aware of

what having children meant. Not only that pain, the particular pain, of intercourse; but the agony of childbirth which she had witnessed so often and been able to do so little about. She knew how terrible the pain could be, and sometimes how fatal too.

As if sensing her fear Mortimer bent over her, trying to convey to her the support he could give her, the partnership that was theirs to share. She felt the rough serge of his dressing gown on her face and then his arms were around her, hugging her to him, not sexually but lovingly, trying to infuse her with his strength and faith. Timidly she put her own thin arms round him, leaning her head against his chest. Yet still, despite his presence and the warmth of his embrace, she felt suffused not by hope or love, but by a paralysing cold, as if she had some foretaste of annihilation, of death.

CHAPTER FOURTEEN

In many ways it was as though she'd never left Paris, as though she and Charlotte had never ceased to live together, although now, in the late spring of 1890, Lindsey had been away over four years. She and Mortimer had arrived in London a month before, having delayed their departure from Boston in order to escape the Atlantic winter gales. Mortimer was a bad sailor, and they had found, after all, so many threads to tie up – a replacement for her at the clinic and someone to take Mortimer's classes at the Medical School. All these things took time, and so did arrangements to be made about the house and its staff and, surprisingly, farewells to be taken of the large clan of Digbys, including Mortimer's sister Elizabeth with her brood in Philadelphia and his brother John in New York, from which they'd finally sailed on the *Atlantic*. Suddenly the Digbys seemed to regret nothing about Lindsey so much as her leavetaking, because with her went Mortimer and it was felt that for them both the lure of Europe was strong. Lindsey was suddenly forgiven, welcomed on the very point of her departure and made to feel one of the family in a way she never had before. But so far as she was concerned it all came too late. When she returned, if she returned, and they gave no date for that, she would try and persuade Mortimer to sever his restrictive Boston roots and make their home elsewhere.

Despite their precautions the sea voyage was a stormy one and Mortimer spent much of it in his cabin bunk while Lindsey, who loved the sea, took long walks on deck and ate hearty meals, sleeping well despite the gales that at one stage made the boat heave to in mid-Atlantic until the worst was over.

Her parents had come to Southampton to meet her and the husband they had never seen and take them back to London, where they spent two nostalgic weeks. Lindsey had seen Mrs Anderson; had been shown round the newly completed hospital on Euston Road, not far from the School of Medicine for Women in Henrietta Street, and had tea with many of her old friends and colleagues, some of whom, like her, had since married.

Mary Scharlieb, who had returned from India because of ill heath, had succeeded Mrs Anderson as chief surgeon at the new Hospital. Mortimer and Lindsey lunched with her at her house in Harley Street.

Lindsey found her father much aged, her mother about the same; but both were at one in the joy with which they welcomed her and the affection they bestowed on her husband. There was only one occasion, late at night, when Estella had been mentioned, and her father had broken down in tears at the thought of the life she was now rumoured to lead in Paris while her mother remained dry-eyed, as stony-faced as ever. For her, Estella as a daughter had ceased to exist.

Mortimer had paused only briefly in Paris to see Lindsey settled with Charlotte while he went on to Berlin to meet a fellow neurologist with whom he had been corresponding. They were then to meet together in Vienna before the month was out for the consultation with Freud.

Freud. Lindsey lay back in her bed and gazed at the tree which had grown so since she last slept in this room that the top now disappeared from sight. Charlotte had given her her old room and nothing in it seemed to have changed, as though her return had been anticipated, as indeed it had. But four years was a long time for things to remain so familiar, so very much the same. The silver brush and comb set were on the dressing table, the same vases full of spring flowers on the tallboy and the table by the window. The curtains, newly starched, were the same and so was the wallpaper with its pretty light pattern of sharply etched pink rosebuds on a green background interspersed with vertical white stripes.

Lindsey put her hands behind her head and half closed her eyes. Peace. It was so peaceful. Why had she ever left here? What might she not have achieved had she never gone to America and married Mortimer? She might by now be one of the foremost neurologists in Europe instead of a harassed working doctor at a slum clinic dispensing medicines and, where she could, advice to other unhappily married women like herself.

Yet when had she ever admitted that she was unhappily married? When had she ever allowed herself a single honest moment to reflect on the true position? From a distance, now, it was easy to see how long and practised had been her ability for self-deception, with what reluctance she had ever desired, or been prepared, to admit the truth. She had simply gone about her work, taxing her diagnostic and therapeutic powers to the limit, and she might have continued that way had not Mortimer suggested Europe and they had their talk – the one and only intimate one then or since – on the night of his family's visit.

Since then she felt they were closer, but not intimate. They had resumed the easy friendship of the years before their marriage. The thought of physical intimacy still repelled her. Everywhere they went they were given separate rooms, because, she explained, of her insomnia, and so, in a sense, she had returned to the bosom of her adolescence and young womanhood by having her own room in Highgate and the one she had inhabited in the Parc Monceau house during her stay there.

Now it was very easy to forget that Mortimer had ever

299

been anything other than a valued friend and colleague. It was even possible – just remotely possible – to blot out the memory of his desperate attempts to be a husband altogether. They had certainly never referred to this aspect of their marriage again, although Lindsey knew that at the back of Mortimer's mind lurked the conviction that after Freud everything would change. But did she really want it to? Would it not be better to settle down again with Charlotte and bid goodbye to that dark, sad, unsatisfactory aspect of her life?

When she opened her eyes Charlotte was standing looking down at her. Lindsey didn't know how long she'd been there. In the old days she was quite accustomed to waking up and seeing Charlotte by her bedside, as though the mere fact of looking at her sleeping face gave her pleasure. But now, as then, she didn't comment on it, but smiled and stretched, sitting up in bed so that her full breasts were partly visible through the fastening in her nightdress. Her thick, long hair fell over her shoulders and her heavy-lidded eyes still bore traces of sleep. There was an innocence, a bloom on her face that seemed almost virginal, Charlotte thought, sitting gingerly beside her on the bed. Would, indeed, that this were so.

'Sleep well, darling?'

'Very well.'

'You look better already. How long has this insomnia afflicted you, Lindsey?'

'Oh, about three years. It's almost continual in Boston, but I slept very well on the boat when the ship bobbed and tossed all night! At home I didn't sleep too well, there was a lot of tension, really, with mother and father; they tried so hard, but the unseen presence of Estella, of my defection to America, always hovered as a sort of reproach between us. But last night I slept beautifully.' She put a hand on Charlotte's arm. 'Thank you. This house is very tranquil.'

'And he's gone.'

Lindsey laughed, removed her hand and began to braid her hair in a thick long plait.

'Poor Mortimer! He's not so bad. He was only here two hours anyway. You can't say he outstayed his welcome.'

'No he didn't.' Charlotte looked reflective, more acutely aware than she had ever been in the past of Lindsey's physical presence, so that, this time, she wondered if she could stop herself from touching her. The longer she remained away the more she wanted her. She wanted to reach out her arms and hold her. She wanted to tell her that her place was here in Paris by her side, for ever.

'Mortimer's a good soul.'

'That's a funny way to talk about a husband!' Charlotte said lightly, watching Lindsey plait her hair until it was finished and she tossed it back over her shoulder.

'Well, we've been married four years. You don't stay in love for ever. Do you know it's four years this month?' Lindsey looked momentarily as though she had forgotten the date of her own wedding anniversary, as, indeed, she had.

'I'm not likely to forget it,' Charlotte said bitterly. 'It was the very day Estella left home after seeing Ellen so ill.'

'Yes, I know.' Lindsey sat upright in bed and linked her arms round her knees. Charlotte wanted to take off the wedding band, the dull gold gleaming menacingly, threateningly in the sunlight, and throw it out of the window. 'I'm so nervous about meeting Estella. You say she's become quite a grand lady?'

'I hear she has. I scarcely see her. When she comes to see Ellen I take care to be out or remain in my room. But I did once, just out of curiosity, peep out of the window as she left and I saw her step into a beautiful carriage with a liveried postillion and a monogram on the door – doubtless that of her latest "protector".'

'I find it hard to believe that my sister leads the kind of

life you imply.' Lindsey looked severely at her friend. 'She may have a lover . . . '

'*A* lover! Just one? I hear rumours,' Charlotte primly pursed her lips.

'You shouldn't listen to them, not unless you know the facts. I don't say my sister is above reproach, and I know there was the Baron; but she never writes about her life to me.'

'She is still not a fit person for respectable people to consort with, and heaven knows how pernicious her influence will be on dearest Ellen.'

'I think you're prejudiced because you never liked her. I can believe much of her; she is headstrong, impulsive, but not what you suggest. If she has a weakness it is that she is too emotional, reckless in love . . .' Lindsey's voice dropped as she uttered the last word. For a moment there was a silence between the women as though each were considering its meaning.

'And you, do you like . . . love?' Charlotte whispered at last. She had a burning desire to know. The thought of Lindsey and Mortimer together gave her the most excruciating mental anguish, and how pleased she'd been when he said he wouldn't stay but was taking the night train to Berlin. She couldn't bear the thought of them together in her house. He had no place here.

'Oh Charlotte, I don't want to talk about all that,' Lindsey interjected with a weary smile. 'I hear enough about it at my clinic, worn old subject . . . '

'It's not worn to me . . . '

'Well, I don't want to talk about it. I want to see my niece. How is she this morning?'

Lindsey tossed back the sheets and flung her legs out of bed, her nightdress practically up to her thighs, her long bare legs lightly covered with blond hairs. She looked so vital and alive, the quintessence of femininity, of – though she would not acknowledge the word – sexuality, that

302

Charlotte turned her face abruptly away, punishing herself for her thoughts by depriving herself of what she so much wanted to gaze upon. But if she probed, if she annoyed or, worse, bored Lindsey, why, the beloved would leave her again and might never come back.

'Could I have a bath, Charlotte? The Americans are so clean. I take one every day.'

'Of course you may, dear. I'll run it for you myself.'

Little Ellen was at breakfast, sitting between her aunt and the woman she affectionately called 'Maman'. She saw her real mother only four times a year by an agreement that had been drawn up by lawyers between Charlotte and Estella when the latter was living with the Baron Philippe de Valéry. In exchange for custody and control Charlotte agreed to rear Ellen, to give her a home, feed and clothe her but not to make any decisions concerning her welfare without consultation with her real mother in the presence of lawyers. In exchange Estella was allowed to see her at a place chosen by mutual consent, was allowed to spend the day with her or take her to the zoo or for a drive or walk in the Bois or one of the parks. She was not allowed to remove her from Paris or take her on holiday.

All this came about not without much heartsearching on Estella's part, but by the practical realization that she could not care properly for a daughter who obviously didn't love her or need her. Yet she clung to the hope that when Ellen was older and could understand, she would realize the reason for what had happened and forgive her.

She was destitute, without a penny or home of her own and she realized that unless she could resume her stage career she would be dependent for a long time on men such as the baron who had the means to keep her; but not only to keep her. To make her rich. Estella knew then all about the scandalous women of the past, women such as Marie Duplessis who became the Countess de Perregaux

303

and whose death allegedly led Dumas *fils* to write *La Dame aux Camélias*; Aglaé Sabatiar – christened *La Présidente* by Gautier – who was the friend and lover of some of the most notable men of the age, and Anna Deslions (the inspiration of *Pommes de terre Anna* at the Café Anglais) who had been the mistress of Prince Napoleon.

Estella may not deliberately have considered the path her life would take when she embarked on her affair with the baron; but Lindsey did not yet know the whole of this story, as she chatted to Ellen, now five years old and pert, pretty and mature enough to appear much older. She was tall and very dark with black curly hair, brown skin and eyes that were practically black. If Lindsey had not been present at her birth, assisting the doctor who delivered Estella, she would have doubted that the girl could possibly have been her sister's, so dissimilar were they in looks as well as disposition so far as she could see. Estella was fair, pink-cheeked, blue-eyed; Ellen the antithesis. Estella was impulsive, temperamental, obstinate, loving, too loving; Ellen a little girl who seemed to have things worked out and well under control; obedient to her 'Maman', yet allowing her aunt to obtain a glimpse of considerable spirit, someone who was, even at this tender age, accomplished, self-possessed, bewitching everyone with her charm. It was in this latter aspect alone that mother and daughter resembled each other.

The aunt from America was very exciting for Ellen, who plied her with a number of questions about that country and its Red Indians. When Lindsey told her that she had, as yet, seen none Ellen looked as though she doubted her word, and turned to her 'Maman' for confirmation.

'America is a very civilized place, darling,' Charlotte smiled down at her. 'Especially Boston where your aunt comes from.'

Unfortunately Lindsey had bought her a doll in the

form of an Indian squaw, so the legend was rather hard to repudiate.

'How long are you staying for, Aunt Lindsey?'

'A few days,' Lindsey said.

'Will you see my mother?'

'Of course.'

'Then give her my love.'

'I will.'

'Ask her why she doesn't come more often.'

'You know why she doesn't come more often.' Charlotte's expression was pained. 'Your mother cannot keep you, and it was decided years ago that it was best for us to live as we do now.'

'But Mother always looks so rich!' Ellen stared wide-eyed at Lindsey. 'She wears the most beautiful clothes and she says her house is very large and one day she will take me there.'

'I'm sure she will, when "Maman" permits it. The main thing is that your mother loves you a great deal. Circumstances compel her to live as she does. And you must remember that.'

Ellen's eyes sidled towards Charlotte and Lindsey could see that, already, the sort of conflict she had hoped would be avoided was taking place in the young child's breast. Maybe if she herself had stayed in France it would have been avoided because Estella's break with Charlotte need not have taken place. Maybe, in a way, she was responsible for the life her sister led. But it was useless to reproach herself, or Mortimer, now, except that it would have been nice if a good marriage had come out of all this sacrifice.

The light French breakfast was finished and Ellen's nurse came to take her to her morning lessons with a governess whom Charlotte had recently engaged for her. Ellen stood on tiptoe to kiss her aunt, embraced her 'maman' and tucked her hand obediently into that of the nurse who had been with her since birth.

Lindsey, both hands curled round her bowl of coffee, savoured its fragrant aroma – that one could never re-capture anywhere else but Paris – as she watched her niece go out of the door.

'Did you *have* to tell her Estella was her mother?'

'Estella told her about a year ago. I nearly stopped her seeing Ellen then because she had broken our agreement, but my lawyer, who is wise as well as clever and expensive, said I would be foolish.'

'I wonder why Estella told her?'

'I think she was jealous of me and my influence.'

'She *does* love her daughter.'

'You call that love? I call it wanting to have your cake and eat it. I hope you didn't raise poor Ellen's hopes too high.'

'Yes, I call it love, knowing Estella. There are many kinds of love, Charlotte, and Estella was never deficient in any of them.'

Yet, for all her desire to see her sister, Lindsey delayed visiting her; she couldn't say why unless it was that the knowledge of what Estella had become frightened, as well as repelled, her. If anything she felt her duty was to Charlotte, because she knew how much she loved her and her own visit was – next to Ellen – the best thing that had happened to her in four long years. So she spent much of the next few days in the company of Charlotte, talking, visiting the *grands magasins*, going to the opera or theatre and then, one day, they took Ellen for a ride in the Bois de Boulogne, the fashionable meeting place of Paris.

The 'promenade' in the Bois attracted scores of sight-seers as well as participants, men and women who drove about in their phaetons and landaus, many with crests on the side, waving to acquaintances, calling or smiling to friends. Along the paths from the Grande-Cascade to the Place de la Concorde people came to stare, to applaud or

306

sometimes to catcall when a notorious *cocotte* drove past in the latest present from her lover, a dashing barouche.

This day, towards the end of May, the leaves were already so thick that it was scarcely possible to see through the trees to the other side, and the *beau monde* seemed to be playing a game of hide and seek as their carriages appeared through the foliage to disappear again a moment later.

Charlotte had intended that they would miss the *grande concourse*, which took place late in the afternoon, because its purpose, more often than not, was to serve as a meeting place for romantic encounters and too many undesirables, however rich and gorgeously dressed, were to be seen.

But Lindsey was fascinated by the colour and spectacle and did not wish to leave, declaring that she had never seen anything like it even in Hyde Park at the height of the season. Her eyes sparkling with excitement, she held onto the hand of her niece, who gave a running commentary about each one who passed even though they were quite unknown to her. Suddenly Ellen stopped talking in mid-sentence and, as Lindsey looked down to see why, she pointed.

'There is my mother! Oh Aunt Lindsey, do you see, in the yellow dress and a large white hat with that gentleman? Look, they are talking to a soldier.'

Lindsey gazed across from Charlotte's Victoria and saw, to her right, a small coupé driven by a gentleman in a grey suit and grey top hat. Next to him was Estella, as recognizable as if she had only seen her yesterday, and talking to them was a uniformed man on horseback.

'Oh!' Lindsey looked at Charlotte, who had promptly turned her face the other way. 'Oh I *must* speak to her, Charlotte.'

Before Charlotte could reply Lindsey descended from the carriage and ran back along the path, making her way

307

through the crowds that jostled around her. The man on horseback was raising his hat, evidently prior to departure, and Lindsey reached the coupé just in time to put her hands on its side and call:

'Estella!'

Estella grew suddenly rigid and then, glancing down, stared at Lindsey as if she could not believe the evidence of her own eyes. She turned quickly to her companion, who was about to flick the whip at the horse, whereupon he turned and stared too. Lindsey saw that he was about thirty-five with a pointed beard, Imperial style, and large moustaches; but Estella, without any regard for dignity, had already opened the door and, within a second, she was in her sister's arms, the two of them laughing, yet crying, as though tears had simultaneously sprung to their eyes.

'Oh *Lindsey*. How long have you been in Paris?'

'Only a few days.'

'But no word . . . ' Estella looked past her shoulder to the Victoria which stood discreetly in the shade of a large oak. Her smile left her face and her eyes clouded. 'It's Charlotte, of course.'

'I had to spend some time with her.' Lindsey, seeing her anguished expression, put a hand placatingly on Estella's arm.

'And Ellen too. She's with you.'

'Yes; but don't go and see her now.'

'I must. She's my daughter.'

'You have an arrangement . . . '

'Which is very convenient for Charlotte . . . '

'Please Estella . . . '

'No . . . '

Estella broke away and ran in the direction that Lindsey had come, pushing past the men who made an immediate path for her as they stopped to gawp and admire. Her yellow walking out costume was really quite spectacular.

The jacket, figure hugging, had a high 'officer' satin collar, and the skirt, fitting closely over the hips, fell in folds to the ground. Her small bonnet was trimmed with accordion pleated lace meeting in a bow at the centre. A sable wrap was worn rather nonchalantly over her shoulder as though she either did not know, or did not care, about its worth.

Charlotte sat bolt upright in the Victoria, poised in the act of giving an order to the driver, when Estella stopped beside it, her hand reaching over to seize Ellen's which was outstretched towards her.

'Hello darling. What a lovely surprise to see you here, and to see Aunt Lindsey!'

Ellen shyly took her mother's hand, blushing as she nervously looked at 'maman'.

'How are you, Charlotte?' Estella proffered her free hand, which Charlotte ignored, securing her own fur wrap more firmly about her shoulder. 'I didn't plan this meeting, Charlotte. May I not say "hello" to my daughter? I see so little of her. Would I could see more.'

'But Mother you *can* see me more . . . ' Ellen leaned over the rim of the carriage pathetically hanging onto her mother's hand, and Lindsey, rapidly coming up behind them, feared a scene.

'Why don't I ask "maman" if I may take you to see your mother as a special treat? Let me try and arrange it when I get home. Yes? To celebrate my visit to Paris? After all, I shan't be here very long.' Lindsey turned to Estella, offering her cheek. 'Estella, I can't wait to talk to you and hear your news. When may I call?'

'Come tonight!' Estella said.

'No I can't. We're going to the opera.'

'Then tomorrow. I will be free any time you wish. I would love to see Ellen at my home if you can prevail upon the ogress to let you, but in the meantime come yourself. Come soon. Come for lunch tomorrow.'

'Yes.'

Lindsey felt the soft familiar cheek against hers, damp as hers was too. Her nostrils were assailed by a beautiful fragrance that seemed part of Estella's flawless beauty and, if Lindsey had expected to see depravity and corruption in her eyes, she did not. Estella looked as pure and beautiful as she always had, even when she was living in the slums of Manchester with Tom and, later, carrying his child with so much misery in London.

The sisters hugged each other as if not wishing even a brief time to part them and Estella whispered: 'You can't think how I want to see you. Please.'

'I'll be there tomorrow.' Lindsey gently disengaged her arm. 'Expect me at noon.'

Sadly she climbed back into the Victoria, never glancing back, only aware of the bereft expression in Ellen's eyes and the unmitigated look of hatred in those of Charlotte.

Nothing in her sister's letters, nor in the whispered snippets of accounts of her life, had prepared Lindsey for the splendour of her house in the Rue de Grenelle. This was just off the fashionable Faubourg Saint Germain, where the old aristocracy, the last surviving members of the *ancien régime*, the true blue blood of France, lived. There, with might and main, they strove to retain their exclusivity, as well as their contempt for the nobility created since Napoleon, such as his niece the Princesse Mathilde, who had once declared that, but for her uncle, she would still be selling oranges on the streets of Ajaccio.

The house, tall, narrow, five storeys high, was not outwardly distinguished from its neighbours by anything particular; it was made of stone, double fronted, and its imposing doorway was approached by three stone steps that led directly from the pavement.

But once inside what a transformation occurred, lifting it from uniformity to a very special place in the accomplishments of the decorative arts. There was a wide tiled hall dotted with priceless oriental rugs, and off this were rooms to right and left with kitchen and servants' quarters in the rear. A central staircase also branched to right and left leading onto the first floor, where there were three principal drawing rooms, one of which stretched from the front of the house to the back affording a view of a small but sumptuous, well-stocked garden with a gazebo and a sunken lily pond. On the next floor were the principal bedrooms, including Estella's, and a recently installed bathroom; on the third floor were lesser bedrooms, a laundry room, and what could pass for a nursery suite, while the top floor was reserved for servants, who descended to the basement by means of a back staircase.

On the ground floor, at the rear of the main dining room, was a small sitting room with double doors which led onto the paved terrace overlooking the garden. It was in here that Estella spent much of her time and where she led her sister after taking her on a tour of the house, all of which, needless to say, was furnished with the most priceless furniture and *objets d'art* from the best periods of all the main European countries: eighteenth-century English, early-nineteenth-century Viennese, and Louis Quinze and Second Empire French.

As they passed through the house servants magically appeared discreetly to open and close doors, and when they were ensconced in the parlour a manservant placed before them a silver tray on which were jugs of cordial and a crystal decanter of chilled white wine.

'I am quite dumbfounded by such elegance,' Lindsey said when the servant had withdrawn. 'You never hinted as much. Is it your own?'

Estella, dressed in an enchanting spring dress of white muslin with a long blue sash around her waist and ribbons of the same colour in her hair, took Lindsey's hand and drew her to a Récamier sofa placed by a window which was open to show an entrancing view of the garden.

311

'My very own.'

'But how, how did it come about?' Lindsey, thinking back to her conversation with Charlotte, wondered if she wanted to know the truth.

'Ah, my dear sister, that is a long story.' Estella tucked her feet under the sofa and drew the table with the silver tray nearer to her. 'Wine or cordial?'

'A glass of cordial please.'

'You know Philippe, the Baron de Valéry, was my saviour during that hard, sad time just after you went away and, due to Charlotte's behaviour, I felt myself alone and homeless?'

'Yes, you wrote to me.' Lindsey's expression was sombre.

'Well, alas, poor Philippe was a sick man and although I did not know it – and nor did he realize then the gravity of his illness – he had not long to live. He was a widower and his only daughter had become estranged from him for family reasons that I never fully understood. I was his solace in his last year and he said he could never be sufficiently grateful to me. Indeed, I loved him for his sweet self, though he was very much older than I, and wanted neither gratitude nor thanks. However, although the bulk of his fortune was entailed for his daughter, and he was devoted to his grandchildren, he begged me to accept this house and its contents, which he loved and had collected over many years, as security after he had gone. He even wanted to marry me and give me his name but, sadly, the formalities were not completed by the time he died quite suddenly in his sleep one night.

'So I found myself with this beautiful house but really with insufficient means to maintain it and, once again, I was alone; but . . . ' Estella handed Lindsey a cut glass full of raspberry cordial and smiled at her with an unaccustomed timidity, 'I had, by that time, made a number of new friends thanks to my dear Philippe, who knew well

312

the lot of unattached women like me, and many of them were subsequently very kind to me. I soon had a new "protector" – if you like that word, I don't – Conte Vassili, an Italian who had a wife and family in Rome, but who enjoyed the opera and was passionately attached to the theatre. We became lovers, and he showered me with gifts because he was almost as generous as my dear Philippe whom I so sadly missed. He was also a man of the utmost fastidiousness and elegance. A perfect gentleman, at home in every branch of the arts; a friend of Zola. But he was a diplomat by profession and was sent to the Italian Embassy in St Petersberg, and after him . . . well, there were a number. I now it may not seem very estimable to you, my dear Lindsey, but it is the only way a woman like me can exist on her own. It is an acceptable way of existence, acknowledged by society, though we do not have its counterpart in England, nor in America I dare say.'

'In other words, you became a courtesan?'

'Well, yes, if you like. I'll make no bones about it but, like the stage, it is part of a long and honourable tradition. I never had more than one lover at a time but I was fortunate in that each was, if possible, more generous than the one before. I was able to maintain this house in the way that Philippe would have approved, and to make for myself a life of some comfort such as I would not have been able to enjoy otherwise.'

'Did you not think of *marriage* with any of these men?' Lindsey acidly enquired, wondering how she would face Charlotte now. 'Or were none of them free?'

'Well *some* of them were.' Estella entwined the fingers of one hand nervously with the other. 'But I only really considered marriage with Philippe, whom I loved, though maybe like a father rather than a husband.'

'I suppose you wouldn't make as much money with one man, nor get so many jewels.' Lindsey looked at her contemptuously, and Estella raised her chin, her eyes glistening.

'I see I should not have told you the truth, Lindsey.'

'It *is* very hard to take.'

'Still, I hoped you'd understand. I could easily have lied to you. What I really wanted to do was resume my career on the stage, but I was not successful. I hadn't and still don't have enough facility with the language to enable me to make a name for myself in France. Besides, there is so much jealously and rivalry upon the French stage – worse than England – that parts which might have been available were snatched from me by others with better connections or more important lovers. Madame Bernhardt finally gave me a *very* small walk-on part with her company; but she was always suspicious of me, fearing that I had my eyes on her current lover, which was very far from being the case.' Estella attempted a smile.

'And the man I saw in the Bois?'

'Oh, that is Prince Alexis Maximov, a member of a house allied to the Romanovs. He is a third cousin of the Emperor. The coupé you saw him driving was his latest gift to me, and he was teaching me how to use it.'

'I ask you frankly, are you happy leading this sort of life?' As she spoke Lindsey abruptly put her glass on the table, untouched, and getting up went over to the open window and leaned against the sill.

Estella gazed after her anxiously. 'Well, in a way. Why should I not be? I am only really unhappy that I can't give a home to my daughter; but Charlotte has me too much enmeshed in legal red tape to make that possible.'

'Would you like Ellen to see how you live, with lovers coming and going, one succeeding the other?'

'No.' Estella rose and came slowly to stand behind her sister. 'No I would not. That's why I would like so much to succeed on the stage and, believe me, I don't give up trying. Why tomorrow I have an audition . . . '

'If that's true why don't you go back to England?'

Lindsey turned and gazed at her so fiercely that Estella lowered her eyes, seeming engrossed by the polished parquet surface of the floor.

'To give up all this?'

'Yes, to give up this life! You *cannot* enjoy it. What sort of existence is it, merely to *please* men and accumulate wealth you no longer need? What happens when you grow old and lose your looks, or catch some terrible disease and, believe me, I've seen many of them.'

'I beg you not to think I consort with men who do not take the greatest care in matters of that kind – fastidious, careful men to whom cleanliness and hygiene are important,' Estella said with some *hauteur*; then, dropping her voice, she added, 'As to losing my looks, that is a long way away, is it not? I seldom think of the future. I never have. My only regret about the past is Tom; but I don't even regret that too much now. I had a child whom I only grew to love when it was too late. But if I do think of the future I think of her; and the fortune I'm accumulating, this house, are all for her. I want to be independent for myself and Ellen alone.'

'And do you suppose she will be pleased that it all came from a mother who was a prostitute?'

'Oh Lindsey, don't use that word.'

'But it's true.'

'It is *not* true! I do not roam the streets. I do not entertain men I don't know, or see them one after the other.'

'But you sell your body, don't you? It's much the same to me.'

Lindsey was now deeply sorry she'd come and wished that she'd gone on to Berlin with Mortimer, thus avoiding the reproaches of Charlotte, this humiliating, agonizing encounter with her sister. Although in some ways it was better than she'd feared – Estella lived in style and comfort and looked very well – it was also worse too. She was dependent for her lifestyle on the lust of wealthy men. She admitted it. What she declined to admit was that she was a member of the oldest profession: a woman who sold her body for gain. Rank herself with the great *demimondaines* of the past she might, but basically she was no better, in Lindsey's eyes, than a common woman of the street.

Estella went to the doors and flung them open, taking deep breaths of the pure spring air, trying desperately to retain her equilibrium. Much as she had wanted to see Lindsey, relying on her sisterly understanding, she had dreaded seeing her too. Now she wished she had not come; that their lives had remained for ever separate. She had forgotten how stern and unbending, how censorious Lindsey could be.

'The men who are my lovers I . . . like. Among their number are writers, poets, diplomats. They are men of refinement and charm.'

'And wealth!'

'One was a poor actor I met at Bernhardt's theatre. He actually took money from *me* and proved much worse, in his treatment of me, than all the others. I have always liked love, Lindsey; it is, if you like, my weakness. I have always been in particular need of the kind of support and affection only men can give.'

'Don't I know it!'

'Oh now you wish to revile me . . .'

'I don't revile you, Estella.' Lindsey joined her by the open door and together they strolled out onto the terrace. 'I love you. But you are my father's daughter, a member of an old, honourable English family and, yes, I grieve to see you living like this.'

'I have a *salon* to which some of the best known people in Paris come. Many say it is as elegant as that of the Princesse de Metternich, who lives just round the corner, and far less stuffy than that of the Comtesse de Lévis-Mirepoix whose husband is a member of one of the oldest families of France. They too live in the Faubourg; I am very discreet, Lindsey, I assure you. I do not flaunt myself or give my favours easily.'

'Still, people must know what you are. I wonder what the aristocrats you mention think of having *you* as a neighbour?'

Estella looked as though she'd been struck by a blow in the face. 'That's cruel, Lindsey. Very cruel. Not *who* I am, but *what*? I see. Then, there is nothing more to be said.'

The sisters, separated now by a gulf that grew wider as the minutes passed, both stared ahead while above them the green fronds of a magnificent oak, its leaves barely open, waved majestically in the breeze.

'I won't stay for lunch after all.' Lindsey turned to go. 'I'm more upset than I can say.'

'But Lindsey, you've told me nothing of yourself, your husband . . . ' Estella timidly touched her arm but Lindsey pushed her hand away.

'I find we've nothing in common, Estella, nothing left.'

'You've married into a proud Boston family . . . '

'The Digbys have nothing to do with this. I don't even like them.'

'Then you've got a contract, like me.'

'How do you mean?' Lindsey, one foot across the threshold of the door, turned and looked at her.

'You remember we've talked about a contract?'

'Yes I remember.'

'It's the same. You've contracted to marry to suit your own ends. You admitted you didn't want to remain a single woman and, because of that, you married without love. I call that prostitution of a kind.'

'You can't compare my life with Mortimer to the one you lead!'

'Oh no, at least yours is respectable, yours is socially

317

acceptable whatever the motives that inspired it. I know I'm beyond the pale, and I don't mind. I've said so before. I hope your conformity has made you happy. To me it doesn't appear that it has.'

'How do you know I'm not happy?'

'You don't look it. You're very thin and desperately pale. You've large shadows under your eyes.'

'I suffer from insomnia.'

'There you are! At least I sleep very well.'

'Perhaps it's all the exercise you get before you go to sleep.'

'Maybe *you* should try it then!' Estella raised her voice and the expression on her face was animated, her colour high. 'You don't look like a woman who is fulfilled to me! Are you, perhaps, not happily married, Lindsey? Does Mortimer not satisfy you? Is that it?'

'Don't judge others by your own lamentable standards!' Lindsey shouted back, aware that they were beginning to behave like two fishwives in a French seaport. 'I have a very caring, loving husband. I have great satisfaction in my work. I . . .'

'Then why don't you sleep?' Estella's face was an inch from hers, taunting her, and Lindsey felt that, given a chance, she would hit her. All the disagreements, all the rows of their childhood and young womanhood, seemed just a preparation for this moment. They loved each other, but their natures were too dissimilar. How could she possibly understand a woman who earned her keep by prostitution, whatever name Estella liked to disguise it with? How could she possibly *still* love someone who stooped as low as that?

Suddenly her life with Mortimer seemed preferable to anything she'd heard today, and his family positively benign.

'The trouble with you, Estella, is that you have no fine feelings . . .'

318

'And the trouble with *you*, Lindsey Digby, is that you're bourgeois and mediocre. You've always considered yourself better than me. I wonder you're not triumphant now. You must feel *very* superior indeed.'

'I don't. I feel humiliated. I feel that, if my family – Mortimer's family or any of the Abercrombies – ever knew about you they'd think I had tainted blood. If your father knew just what you were, he'd die of shame.'

Lindsey now found herself alone in the room, Estella having remained outside. She opened the door and went into the hall where a butler stood very rigidly beside the newell post at the bottom of the staircase. He bowed, betraying not by the flicker of an eyelash that anything appeared to be amiss.

'Would Madame Abercrombie be requiring luncheon to be served, Madame?'

'I know nothing of Madame Abercrombie's intentions.' Lindsey took her parasol from a stand in the hall and shook it. 'Kindly show me to the door.'

Charlotte was playing on the lawn with Ellen, pretending to give a tea party outside a large dolls' house she had had specially built for her. How happy and relaxed she looked in the child's company, Lindsey thought. Yes, she was a mother to Ellen in the way that her own mother could never be. Knowing what she now knew, Lindsey hoped never would be. It was the first day of June and the blue Parisian sky had subtle tones of azure, like that of the south of France. Lindsey lay in a wicker chair and, for some reason, she imagined that there was croquet on the lawn; that, instead of Charlotte, Ellen and the nurse, she could see herself and Estella playing with Rayner Brook and Wykeham St Clair all those years ago at home in Highgate.

'How did you find your sister?' her father had asked in a letter received that morning, and how would she ever answer it? 'Quite well, Papa'; 'Very well, Papa'; 'Bloom-ing, Papa'; 'Surrounded by luxury, Papa, that she has purchased with her body'.

'Come back ten years,' Lindsey closed her eyes, letting the past live again; 'but change it so that . . . so that Estella never meets Tom, does not go on to the stage but marries Rayner and becomes a good wife and mother, living happily ever after. Change it so that I . . . never study medicine but agree with the wishes of my parents and marry Wykeham St Clair, maybe going with him to India, becoming a Memsahib with a brood of children and twice their number of servants . . .'

'Of what are you thinking, dearest?' Charlotte asked, handing Lindsey a minute cup of tea. 'The tea's real. We just made it.'

Lindsey opened her eyes and took the tiny cup with a delighted smile.

'I was thinking I wish one could live the past again, but differently. That's not possible, is it?'

Charlotte grimaced. 'You're thinking of Estella, of course.'

'I'm always thinking of Estella; I can think of nothing but her since I saw her. She haunts me day and night. Oh Charlotte, was I wrong to speak as I did . . .'

'Of course you *weren't* wrong.' Charlotte glanced at Ellen, who was giving tea to all her dolls arranged in a circle on the grass. 'What else could you have said to her? You're her elder sister. Someone has to affirm there are standards in this world. The pity is that you went at all.'

'Yes, the pity is I went. You shouldn't have let me go.'

'How could I stop you?' Charlotte sipped her tea, puckering her lips to fit to the rim of the tiny cup. 'Would you have taken any notice of me? You wanted to know. You had to know. Well, now you know. Forget all about her. She's not worth the time.'

'Still I think I was wrong to show my disapproval so strongly. I should at least have tried to be more understanding. She is my sister. She has, you know, no one else close in the world.'

Charlotte snorted and put her cup and saucer on the ground. 'She has her many lovers, she has the Russian Prince. I'm sure they're understanding and certainly *very* close. Besides, they have the advantage of having lots and lots of money which your sister craves.'

'She never used to be like that.'

'I never used to be like this.' Charlotte gazed fondly at Ellen. 'We all change. I never thought I'd have such fierce maternal feelings.'

'One thing to thank Estella for.'

'The *only* thing to thank Estella for.' Charlotte sat back on the grass supporting herself with her hands. 'I wish you weren't going tonight, Lindsey. Can't you stay and cut out Vienna?'

Lindsey avoided her friend's eyes, not wanting to reveal more. She was too proud to tell Charlotte, in so many words, that her marriage was on the brink of failure. She was too fastidious, too inhibited, even to hint at the reasons for this failure. She had told Charlotte that she was going to Vienna to study; no mention had ever been made of the man she had met briefly in Paris a few years before. How could Charlotte possibly understand about Freud and his unorthodox methods? She could hardly understand them herself, scarcely believed in them, despite her medical training.

Shading her eyes against the sun which was now shining directly into her eyes, she gazed across at Ellen playing with her nurse on the lawn, at her friend sitting by her side, and she thought of her sister on the other side of the river in her elegant house on the left bank and of the life she led there. Regrets, regrets, too many regrets.

'I wish I could. Sometimes I think I should; but I can't. I'll be back, dearest Charlotte,' she said softly, at last. 'I have too much that is precious to me in Paris not to want to return as often as I can.'

CHAPTER FIFTEEN

Estella's salon was not by invitation. People knew she kept open house on Thursday evenings and she usually expected up to fifty guests, some of whom she didn't know, brought by friends. This way she met many new and interesting people, men and women, including the writer Rachilde, whose novel *Monsieur Vénus* had made her instantly famous in 1884, just before Estella had come to France. She was sentenced in Brussels to imprisonment for two years on account of the novel's scandalous nature, but escaped by living in Paris.

Rachilde, who liked to dress as a man and had inscribed on her card *homme de lettres*, had flattered Estella by telling her she had heard of her. 'You are becoming a celebrity, Madame,' she'd said. 'Maybe you should write your autobiography.'

But Estella didn't want to write her autobiography, or put anything about her life down in writing. Her scene with Lindsey had distressed her so much that she had sent Prince Maximov away and, in a gesture not without significance, returned his gifts which included a large emerald that tradition said his family had acquired from Catherine the Great for unspecified services rendered. For days after Lindsey's abrupt departure, Estella had remained in the house, confined to her bedroom or small sitting room, receiving no callers, eating little, brooding.

How often did she dream that Lindsey would come back, would return to make up as they did when they were girls. For Lindsey was the elder sister and, if Estella had not been aware previously of the power that gave her over her, she was now. She wanted Lindsey's approval and love, and wanted it more than anything else on earth so that for a while she even prayed for it.

But then she knew Lindsey had left Paris, having sent a servant to make discreet enquiries at Charlotte's house. Lindsey had gone, she knew not where, and she would not ask. For with the passage of time, her guilt and self-pity were replaced by anger against and resentment of the sister who had embraced a compassionate profession – the healing of the sick – and yet was evidently unable to extend that compassion to her own kin. With her vivid sense of the dramatic Estella saw herself as a victim of circumstances, a waif tossed about on the tide of life, now retreating, now advancing, now disturbed, now serene. She felt that very little of what had happened to her could be helped, and that at no time could she have done very much to avoid it. Blame was laid at the doors of other people – Tom, Charlotte, Lindsey, her parents, but never her own.

But with a certain childishness of outlook went the resilience of the young, and Estella's way of life, her introspection, soon bored her. She threw open the doors of her retreat and sallied forth into the Paris streets to arm herself with a fresh wardrobe, as she had in days long gone by, in which once more to confront the world. Clothes symbolized to Estella a sense of inner renewal; a visible, outward sign of the fresh hope and resolution that had been born within.

It was too late to recall Prince Maximov; but it was not too late to hold a Thursday salon, which she had cancelled for the duration of her brief period of introspection and mourning. She had put it about that she was indisposed; but now she was well again, and she sat on a brocade chair in her green drawing room teasing those gathered around her as to the exact nature of her malady. Most people assumed she had had an abortion, but no matter. In the life she led abortions were quite a respectable method of birth control and certainly they were expected once, twice, if not three times a year for those who were careless.

As her guests came up the stairs she felt a resurgence of life, a return of that old vitality and zest that made it worth living. The candles in their silver sconces glittered, throwing shadows on the gold brocaded walls, reflected in the curls and whorls, the gleaming inlaid marquetry of the priceless Louis Quinze pieces – because the green drawing room was devoted to eighteenth-century French furniture and that monarch had dominated his age.

There was the novelist Catulles Mendès, who had brought Rachilde to her last *salon*, and there was Félix Fénénon, one of the most respected of contemporary critics who did so much to publicize the work of artists such as Seurat and Pissaro; who had defended the music of Richard Wagner and now did the same with the plays of the Norwegian dramatist, currently scandalizing London too, Henrik Ibsen. But behind Fénénon was someone else; someone she recognized, but whose face instantly brought back memories of the past. Someone . . .

He was smiling as he came over to her, his arms outstretched. She half rose from her chair, but the crowd surrounding her made movement impossible. He bent and kissed her hand and, as he raised his head, looked into her eyes.

'What a long time it has been, chère Madame.'

'Rayner Brook.'

She held onto his hand and at last succeeded in rising, her friends looking at her curiously, making way for the tall Englishman who was obviously a friend of their hostess, maybe a new lover.

'You remember me, Estella?'

'Of course I remember you! Oh Rayner it *is* marvellous to see you!'

'And for me to see you. When Félix said he was going to

see you tonight I couldn't believe my ears. "Abercrombie," I said, "are you sure? She has a sister." But Estella Abercrombie, he assured me, it was. A very charming hostess, known to all Paris . . . '

He raised his eyebrows but his expression was not disapproving. 'I congratulate you, Estella, on your success, on the distinguished gathering of people you have here.'

'My success . . . ' Estella stared at him and then, throwing back her head, began to laugh. 'Oh, it does me good to hear you say that.'

'Oh why?'

'Don't you know?'

'Know? Know what?'

'Oh nothing.' She took his arm and began to move with him across the room, aware of the envious eyes of the men. 'Come, let's have a glass of champagne to celebrate this meeting and then I'll introduce you to some interesting people.'

When most of the company had left – it was nearly two – Rayner was still there. He had hardly left her side as though he couldn't believe his good fortune in finding her again. He still had his dark looks, but his face was leaner and just a little lined as though suffering had put her mark on him.

'You must be, what is it now . . . ' Estella started counting on her fingers.

'I'm thirty-five. I haven't seen you for six years. I can't believe it.'

'Do I look much older?'

'Much more beautiful. But I hear you no longer act.'

'What else do you hear?' She looked at him nervously.

'You keep on saying that, Estella. I've heard nothing. When Félix mentioned your name today it was for the first time. I came to Paris to see Antoine's Théâtre Libre which Félix supports. He and I are old friends. What is it you're

326

nervous about, Estella. This? All this wealth?' He looked around, but his eyes quickly turned to search hers.

'Don't you want to know how I got it?'

He leaned forward and wagged a finger at her. 'I suspect from some man who became infatuated by you. And why not? I was infatuated myself and, had I a house like this, I'd have given it to you.'

Estella laughed, aware now that all her guests were departing one by one and she and Rayner were alone in a corner of the room, sitting comfortably side by side like the old friends that they were.

'Go on Rayner Brook! *When* were you infatuated by me?'

'When I realized I'd lost you. When you went off with Tom Shipley.'

'But you were madly in love with . . . , what was her name?'

'Harriet Leadbetter. Yes I was very much in love with her. But with you I felt I had no chance, anyway. Then I was so inexperienced I needed older women. Maybe too I was a little jealous of you; you were much more successful than I. A man doesn't like a woman to be better than him, you know. Well, now I have had some little success . . .'

'And I have none.' Estella stared sadly at her glass, feeling a little drunk, excited by the presence of Rayner yet increasingly nervous of what he would think of her if he found out 'what', as Lindsey had said, she was.

'Why did you leave the stage Estella? You were on the brink of such success . . . It was all such a mystery to me, but I had problems at the time of my own.' Rayner put down his glass and studied her face with an intensity that made her avert her eyes.

'There were many reasons – restlessness, lack of ambition, maybe . . . the return of Tom Shipley.'

'That above all, I think,' Rayner said quietly, continuing to gaze at her while she hesitated before replying.

327

If she told him about Ellen now . . . it was surely the right moment? He would understand because he was unconventional, a man of the theatre, a Bohemian. Ah, but *would* he understand? Was he not, by upbringing, a Victorian English gentleman, like her father? She glanced at him nervously, as if seeking guidance from the expression in his eyes. Yet all she saw was friendship, admiration, perhaps a man yet again on the brink of love.

How could she – a woman who, above all things, craved admiration and love – disillusion someone she needed so badly as a friend; that link with the past which at times seemed like a stretch of barren land and yet was so precious to her? And was there not something even more dreadful than a bastard child that she wished to conceal from him: the life of pleasure she led now?

'Tom is in the past,' she murmured at last, observing that they were alone in the room and the servants were discreetly moving about. 'He had married a woman in Australia and, as far as I am aware, he returned to her. He deceived me most horribly, and it was to erase all memory of him and his treachery that I decided to accompany my sister and her friend to Paris.'

'And forgo Irving, Terry and the Lyceum?'

'To forgo all that.'

'Oh, my dearest Estella, what a swine that fellow was! How unworthy of anyone as good, as pure, as beautiful as you are.'

Rayner seized her hand and brought it to his lips, but she wrenched it away and placed it instead against her burning cheek.

'I am not good and pure, Rayner. You misunderstand . . .'

'I don't care about your past. To me you are those things.'

'But I'm not. Oh, if you knew . . .'

'Knew what Estella?'

328

'Everything.'

She described an arc with her foot on the floor, but when she looked at him again she had mastered her feelings and, with a smile that replaced the anguish he had briefly seen on her face, held out her hand. The art of the actress was very obvious to him now, filling him with disquiet.

'See, Rayner, it's nearly dawn. For how long are you here? I do hope I'll see you again. You are part of the past that is very precious to me. Precious indeed.'

Rayner took her hand and put his lips to her ear. She smiled and shook her head, but her hand lingered in his. Together they went slowly down the stairs and at the bottom Rayner paused and, looking round to make sure they were unobserved, took her in his arms pressing his lips again to her ear.

'You've no idea how beautiful you are, Estella. Of course I'll see you again. And again. Do you think, now that I've found you, I'll let you get so easily away?' He gazed tenderly into her eyes, lowering his mouth to hers, but she put a hand on his chest and abruptly pushed him away.

'Please,' she said. 'Not now.'

Then she walked quickly upstairs, not waiting to see him out.

The next day, after failing to sleep for what was left of the night, she had her maid pack her bags and left for the south of France.

His hands were firm but cold, as though he had just come in from the snow, although it was June in Vienna and pleasantly warm. She felt the pressure of his fingers on either side of her head and he spoke very softly in his heavily accented English: 'Now why is it, do you think, that you don't sleep? Under the pressure of my hand you will begin to think, and when I relax the pressure memor-

329

ies will come back to you, will come flooding back maybe. Do not resist them, however irrelevant you consider them to be.'

Lindsey closed her eyes and realized that the reason his fingers seemed so cold was the burning, throbbing sensation inside her skull as images whirled around, recollections, pictures of the past, people, places, croquet on the lawn.

'I can't think,' she lied. 'I can't make any sense out of anything.' She felt, somehow, that it was important to keep the truth from him, not to let him think he could control her life.

'Try.' Freud slightly eased the pressure on his fingers. 'Now what do you see?'

'Nothing.'

'Yes, you do. Tell me about it.'

She sighed. 'All right, then, it's not important, but I see myself playing croquet on the lawn with my sister.'

'Alone with your sister? How old were you?'

'I was twenty-two. It was the summer of 1880, just ten years ago. No, we were not alone; there were two men whom our parents wanted us to marry.'

'Tell me about the one they wanted *you* to marry.'

She told him about Wykeham St Clair (it could do no harm); she described him in every detail: his age, his appearance. She'd known for some time that he was interested in her but she resisted him.

'Why?'

'Because I wanted to study medicine.'

'And he would have stopped you?'

Now his fingers were no longer there and she knew that he was sitting behind her out of sight, seeing but not being seen.

This was her third session with Dr Freud. The first time she'd sat opposite him talking, trying to establish an equality as one physician to another. He had said very little, nodding, studying her with his dark intense eyes, telling her little about his method, and nothing about himself. If ever she asked a personal question he ignored it; she thought him rather rude.

The next time he'd asked her to lie down, saying that, in his experience, the presence of the physician could be a bar to the free association of ideas that he wanted his patient to express; so he would remain out of sight.

'Say whatever comes into your head, however absurd or irrelevant it may seem. Hold nothing back.'

She'd thought it was absurd and said so, and he replied by telling her about the patients he had helped by this method, whose efficacy he was really only just discovering for himself.

But today was the first time he'd applied pressure to her head and then invited, not commanded, her to tell him what immediately came to mind.

'And he would have stopped you?' Freud asked again, interrupting the reverie which she knew had come about because she was so reluctant to tell him anything, anything at all.

'No. He said he would support me, that I could study if I wished.'

'Why didn't you accept him then?'

'I don't know.'

'Think. You do know; it is there somewhere in the dark recesses of your mind.'

'I didn't love him. What's the point of all this, Dr Freud?'

'We'll see. Was he not suitable?'

'Very suitable. I liked him; but I felt he would interfere, whatever he said. I passionately wanted to be a doctor.'

'Passionately. I see. Think of the word "passion" Frau Digby, and tell me where it leads you.'

Lindsey felt the heat going from her head to her body, suffusing her limbs. She struggled, uncomfortably aware

331

of lying on a couch while a strange man, a relatively strange man, stared at her body. She felt resentful and annoyed, embarrassed, and involuntarily she squeezed her thighs together, crossing one leg over the other. She didn't reply.

'Tell me what you're thinking now.'

'I'm thinking . . . nothing.'

'Yes?'

'I can't tell you.'

'You must tell me,' his voice was gentle, persuasive, persistent. 'You must tell me everything that comes into your head if you want to be well.'

'I am well.'

'Then why are you here?'

'Because . . . '

'Yes?'

'You know why, because my husband wanted me to come.'

'Why?'

'Because . . . '

'Yes, go on.'

'I don't enjoy sexual intercourse. You know quite well, he told you. Why do you also want to hear it from me?' He was obviously a prurient man, she thought, and her resentment of him grew. He ignored her question and continued:

'So passion *did* have a connection. You passionately wanted to be a doctor. It is an important word to you.'

'That's nonsense.'

'Nevertheless I think it's relevant. Concentrate on the word "passion". What does it convey to you?'

'I can't think.'

'Try . . . '

'I don't want to try. I don't want to go on with this, this nonsense.' Lindsey sat up and swung her legs over the side of the couch, aware that she was panting and her face was covered with sweat. She unbuttoned the top of her dress and fanned herself with her hand. Bearded and remote, Freud gazed at her impassively. 'I can't go on with this, Dr Freud. It's getting us nowhere. I thought you were going to hypnotize me?'

'Why do you want to be hypnotized?'

'Well . . . I thought it was the way you worked.'

Freud leaned back in his chair and looked at the ceiling, tapping the tips of his fingers lightly together. Then he leaned forward and mechanically straightened the cloth on which she had rested her head at the top of the couch. He glanced at his watch and stood up.

'That must end our therapy today, Frau Digby. Come again tomorrow. We are getting somewhere, gradually.'

He made his way to the door and, resentfully, she struggled to her feet.

'Dr Freud!'

He turned and looked at her, his expression benign. 'Yes, what is it?'

'I don't want to continue this treatment, if you call it treatment. It's not what I expected.'

He sighed and returned to his chair, motioning her to take a seat opposite him. The room was full of heavy old-fashioned Viennese furniture, the atmosphere oppressive.

'Frau Digby, sit down please.'

Lindsey sat on the edge of a chair clutching her bag. She felt ruffled and undignified, like a small girl having some elementary point of etiquette explained to her.

'Yes Dr Freud?' Her tone was peremptory, sharp. She too was a physician, after all. Sometimes when patients were recalcitrant she addressed them sharply to indicate that her time was precious, and she didn't want to waste it. Now she wanted him to know that she wasn't going to waste time here in Vienna, in this nonsense talking about the past.

'Frau Digby, you have come a long way to see me. It now appears you didn't want to. Am I right?'

'Yes.'

'You think it a waste of time?'

'Frankly, I do.'

'Because I have no magic method,' he waved a hand in the air and she was briefly aware of a twinkle in his eyes, 'no potions or pills or electrical machines, no hypnosis.'

'Well . . . ' she stared at him, refusing to be cowed by his considerable personality. Although she had only met him briefly five years before she was aware of how much he had changed.

'Frau Digby, believe me if I thought they worked I would use them. In fact I have and discarded them. I have massaged patients and applied electric currents to their limbs, as Charcot did. I have hypnotized them, though not always successfully. I am now changing my methods because I believe what I am doing now is better. In fact I don't think hypnosis is as successful as we once thought, because it relies too much on the suggestion on the part of the physician. I am of the opinion that it is up to the patient to make the changes in his or her psyche, not the doctor. This method is better, believe me.'

'What *method*?' Lindsey taunted. 'Just letting people talk. You call that a method?'

'I do; but not just to "talk", as when you have a conversation with someone, making everything neat and to the point, the sentences carefully put together. I want you to talk completely at random, saying exactly what comes into your mind.'

'And what will that do, pray?'

'I believe it will unlock the secrets in your past. I believe it will tell you the reason why you don't sleep and why the marital act is so repugnant to you. We were nearly there today and I observed how you squeezed your legs together

334

as though you were frightened that I might try and prise them apart . . . '

'Dr Freud!'

'It is very shocking, Frau Digby, is it not, to say that?'

'I think it's indecent.'

'It *is* indecent. Quite. I agree, and many of the things that lurk in the unconscious part of your mind are indecent too – so indecent you're unwilling to admit they're there. I want to discover what those indecent things are and release you from your hysterical symptoms. I want to make you sleep well again.' He got up and smiled at her. 'Now I have another patient. Will you trust me, Frau Digby? Your husband wants you to trust me; but you don't for reasons of your own. You don't want to unlock the secrets of the past, those unpleasant secrets. I do. Please come again tomorrow.'

He led the way to the door and, bowing, extended a hand as she passed through without saying another word.

Lindsey, who had pretended to be rather amused about the whole thing, certainly apathetic and above it all, found her detachment turning quickly to resentment as she decided that Professor Charcot's old pupil was resorting to quackery to achieve his ends. There was certainly nothing that she considered the least bit conventional or medical about his methods, although she knew he was not unique in thinking he could cure mental illness by talk alone; neurologists of an advanced turn of mind in Europe and America were trying this too. She certainly agreed, always had, that talking about problems helped; had she not said so in Boston to Heather Ainsley? She considered herself an enlightened and progressive physician, as Mortimer was. Unfortunately she failed to see herself in the role of patient, being helped by methods which she was quite happy to accept could be applied to other people; just as she was reluctant to discuss with her husband the reasons for the sexual maladjustment of their marriage. It was

335

indeed this sexual connotation of her latest encounter with Dr Freud that she found so upsetting, because it seemed to introduce a personal element that she found both dangerous and disturbing.

Freud's consulting room which was also his residence – the noise made by his children being heard from other rooms – was in the Kaiserliches Stiftungshaus, a new apartment block built on the site of the old Ring Theatre which had been burned down with great loss of life in 1881. Consequently many people had been too superstitious to live there, but Freud and his wife, Martha, had no such misgivings and moved there after their marriage in 1886.

His block was in the Maria Theresien Strasse, opposite the Schotten Ring and not far from Lindsey's hotel in the centre of Old Vienna in the shadow of the great Gothic cathedral of St Stephen. Despite many modern improvements to the city the Innerstadt, or Old City of Vienna, was enchanting with crooked, narrow streets and timber-fronted houses. It was surrounded now by the relatively new Ringstrasse, which had replaced the broad glacis devised by Joseph II, the 'people's Emperor', as a recreational area insulating the inner city from its suburbs.

Now it was four o'clock in the afternoon, and Lindsey, feeling the English need for tea at that hour, entered a small crowded café. There she ordered not tea but the Viennese equivalent, 'Jause', a large cup of hot chocolate with whipped cream and a piece of succulent Sachertorte. Tea-time was a favourite hour in Vienna as in England, and the café was full of university students with their peaked caps, hotly debating in loud, excited voices. Perhaps they were discussing the huge demonstration on May Day, the previous month, when thousands of workers had marched through the streets of Vienna demanding an eight-hour day, and shopkeepers had boarded their shops so that the populace began hoarding food. For a moment the stability of the Austro-Hungarian Empire had seemed threatened, but nothing further happened. However, undoubtedly it was a portent. There were middle-aged matrons with bulging shopping baskets gossiping to their friends and elderly Jews with full beards, round black hats and a twisted plait by the side of each ear signifying orthodoxy, reading the papers which, as in all Viennese cafés, were freely available.

Yet, despite the company around her, Lindsey felt lonely and afraid; or perhaps the guttural German language, of which she didn't understand a word, contributed to her sense of isolation. She felt she had embarked on an intolerable experience, or rather it had been thrust on her by a husband who now seemed as strange and as alien, certainly more remote, as these citizens of a foreign land.

Freud was foreign; his methods were alarming, unmedical, unscientific, salacious. She couldn't imagine what someone as prosaic and practical as Mrs Anderson would think about the set-up if she were told, which God forbid. These probing, intimate questions were not at all in the tradition of medicine in which both she and Lindsey had been trained. She would write and tell Mortimer as much and, why, she would telegraph Charlotte this very day that she was returning to Paris – Paris, that home from home, more of a home than Boston, certainly much more of a home than Vienna, where she felt she had been deserted.

Lindsey finished her 'Jause' and hurried out of the café, making her way through the old streets until she came in sight of the beautiful cathedral of St Stephen with its four lofty towers, one of which was the highest in Europe. Her hotel was in the Schuler Strasse, just behind the cathedral and not far from the tiny River Wien on the east side of the Old City, which was once notorious for its pollution and said to have contributed to the high death rate in the city to which it had given its name. But since 1870 many improvements had been made and Vienna had been supplied with fresh water from the nearby Alpine streams.

There was a letter from Mortimer which did little to allay her feeling of despondency. He seemed to be having a good time in Berlin and never once referred to her treatment with Freud or said that he missed her. Lindsey read it twice lying on the bed in her second-floor room, which was large but dark with heavy Viennese furniture and thick velour drapes at the window which did much to keep out the light. It reminded her a little of Freud's consulting room and she shivered as she put aside the letter – having failed to find any comfort in it – and drew the thick quilt over her.

Freud; she couldn't get his face out of her mind. It seemed to hover over her, suspended from some remote, invisible point in the ceiling. Well, she would see him no more; she would write and ask for his bill. She would tell him that his methods were nonsense and enough was enough. She, after all, was a qualified medical practitioner too.

After a while Lindsey rose, washed her face, did her hair and sat down to write a long letter to Mortimer telling him all about the failure of the treatment yet reluctant to mention why, to say anything about the nature of Freud's questions. Apart from that it was more like a medical report from one physician to another than a letter from wife to husband, containing no endearments or personal reflections. She sealed the envelope but having no stamp decided to post it the next day, when she would telegraph Charlotte. She was not hungry, but she went down to the hotel restaurant to have something to eat, toying with her Schnitzel, drinking half a glass of wine, anxious, nervous, troubled in her mind.

And later in trying to sleep she had the old problem for, tired as she was, the balm of unconsciousness eluded her; sleep would not come. Instead Freud's face hovered there, almost beyond the periphery of her vision, menacing, dangerous, accusatory, his eyes full of secrets; knowing things about her that he would not share, things she didn't know herself.

At four in the morning she rose, washed her face and sat in a chair by the window, covered by the quilt, watching the towers of the cathedral slowly outline themselves against the horizon as dawn came. Then finally, she got back into bed and, at last, slept.

'I have only come to say goodbye,' she said, carefully skirting the couch with the neat lace cloth on which she was supposed to lay her head. She stood in the centre of the room holding out some notes. 'I'd like to pay my bill.'

Freud, looking very formal, went to his desk and began writing on a small piece of paper. When at last he looked up he didn't render her account as she had expected, but pointed to the couch.

'When you're ready,' he said, returning to the note he was making. Lindsey felt exasperated.

'Dr Freud, I'm not staying. You can't – force me.'

'I'm not forcing you, Frau Digby.' Freud sounded just very slightly amused. 'You came back of your own volition.'

'I came merely to say goodbye. I considered it polite.'

'Oh no,' Freud said firmly, 'it wasn't mere politeness. You could have sent a note. You came because you wanted to see me, but your resistance is so strong, my dear Frau. Please lie down and tell me why you're resisting me.'

'I can't. I won't lie down.'

'Then tell me from the chair. Please, sit down. Sit there.' He pointed kindly to a chair and turned to face her, folding his hands and waiting for her to speak. She sat down gingerly on the edge again, clutching her bag.

'Dr Freud, you can't treat me if I don't wish it.'

339

'That's true. But I want to know why you came back.'

'I've told you.'

'It's not the truth. Is it?'

'No.' She shook her head firmly, staring back at him, when a curious, totally unexpected thing happened: his face underwent a startling metamorphosis. Instead of being stern, accusatory, even cruel, it looked, by contrast, as if he cared, cared deeply, about her. About Lindsey. He was, after all, she realized then, a compassionate man concerned about her here alone in Vienna, isolated from her family, from her friends, perhaps isolated from herself. He cared, as a person not a doctor, just about her.

She continued to stare at him, wondering for a moment if he were hypnotizing her. A large old-fashioned clock on the mantelpiece ticked away – Freud collected antiques – and the sounds of the Viennese traffic seemed miles away instead of just outside. She knew then that she must trust him, must surrender herself to him, tell him everything he wanted to know because that way she would be released from herself.

'I feel very tired,' she murmured, her eyelids heavy. 'Maybe I *will* lie down.'

'That's good,' Freud replied, getting up to take his place at the head of the couch. 'Lie down please. Tell me why you're so tired.'

Wearily she went to the couch and sank onto it, aware, as she was so often, of total exhaustion because of the difficulty she had during the night of closing her eyes in sleep. The couch with its heavy decorated cover seemed a familiar place, like her bed at home, and she snuggled on her side, nestling her head on the palm of one hand, her legs slightly bent in the comfortable position she assumed at bedtime before falling – or trying to fall – asleep.

Once again she felt the gentle, insistent pressure of both his hands on her forehead, twisting her head, making her more comfortable.

'Relax,' he said gently, stroking her head, 'and think of all the pleasant things you can. Tell me what they are, what comes into your mind about pleasure and relaxation? What was the happiest time you had?'

'When I was a girl, alone with my father in his library.'

'You had him all to yourself?'

'Yes.' She turned, her body flat now on the couch, her eyes open at the ceiling. 'My sister was only a baby. She took my mother's whole attention, and father and I were often alone. He loved to read to me.'

'Why was it so pleasant just to be alone with your father?'

'Because I hated my sister . . . ' she stopped and put her hand to her mouth, swivelling her eyes round to stare at him. 'I mean I didn't hate her *really*. Don't think I hated her, please . . . '

'Go on, go on. Don't think about me. Imagine I'm not here and you're alone, reliving your memories aloud.'

And oh the memories, how they came flooding back now that the pressure of his hands on her head had gone, now that she was alone. Yes, she *had* hated her sister, resented her arrival. Suddenly the house had seemed to revolve only around the small squalling baby in the cot. She'd hated that baby, really wanted to harm her, was afraid, eventually, to go near the pram in case she put her hands on its neck and strangled it. She always, she remembered, thought of the baby as 'it' and never 'she' or 'Estella'. Once she'd come so near to doing what she dreaded that only the intervention of Estella's nurse had stopped her. If the nurse hadn't come . . . Estella wouldn't be alive. Oh my God. The tears welled up in her throat and choked her. Oh my God what *had* she done? What a memory to live with, something to bury deep down and try and forget; to expunge completely from her mind so that never, never would father know what wicked thoughts she had entertained about her small sister, about 'it'.

Then the tears were streaming down her face because, finally, he knew; she had confessed, at last, everything to him that she'd suppressed all those years ago.

'Oh *father*,' she cried as he leaned over her, 'I really didn't mean . . . I would *never* have done it. I love Estella. How could I possibly have wanted to harm her?'

She felt his hand on her brow, stroking, soothing, his face hovering over her. But it was smiling now and so forgiving, not stern, not accusatory, full of compassion because of the knowledge that she didn't have.

'There,' he said. 'There, Frau Digby. When I release the pressure you will feel calm again because you didn't kill your baby sister, but all your life you have been terrified by that rage inside yourself, that resentment of her that you suppressed so many years ago.'

He removed his hand and Lindsey dug frantically in her pocket for her handkerchief, raising it to her face to blot away those telltale tears. Had she let herself down? Betrayed herself? Why had she done it and what, indeed, had she done? There was scarcely a sound at all in the room and her head felt heavy, about to burst. She raised her head and blinked her eyes, turning round to find Dr Freud at the head of the sofa looking at her, nodding his head. He seemed so wise, so full of forgiveness, just like father. What she had felt was not so very serious, not so very naughty after all.

'I think we have many things to discover,' Freud said quietly. 'Things which you would rather not remember, which you have locked in your mind and which have made you ill.'

'I'm not ill,' Lindsey protested still, her voice, however, very faint.

'No, but when we have discovered all those secrets, when the cupboard is bare, you will feel much much better.' Freud looked at his watch. 'Now it is time. Please come again tomorrow.'

Lindsey got up and put on her hat, feeling rather shaky, taking care to avoid his eyes as he opened the door and showed her out.

CHAPTER SIXTEEN

For the next six months Lindsey applied herself with passionate dedication to her treatment with Freud, so much so that it seemed at times almost as though he were the patient and she the doctor. She studied her treatment; she thought about it, examined it in retrospect, analysed it. She read all the books and papers she could get her hands on that dealt with this new science of psychological medicine.

Although Sigmund Freud was ultimately to hold a unique place in the history of psychiatric medicine, in 1890 he was not a pioneer. Many doctors in Europe and America had tried an approximation of his methods before him: Morton Prince, George Beard and Weir Mitchell in America; Pierre Janet, Hippolyte Bernheim, Auguste Liébeault in France and, not the least, Freud's own colleague in Vienna, Josef Breuer, who stumbled on the technique of catharsis by free association with his patient known to history as Anne O, but in reality Bertha Pappenheim.

This curious amalgam of truths and half-truths, of groping in the deep recesses of the mind which had various practitioners as yet had no name. It was not hypnosis, it was not psychology, nor was it psychiatry, and some people scarcely considered it medicine. It had far more detractors than it had defenders. Six more years were to pass before Freud would call it psycho-analysis and, for the foreseeable future, it would remain controversial. In 1890 Freud was an experimentalist, a physician turned neurologist, almost permanently hard up, convinced nevertheless that destiny had a part for him to play, a great part, but not all all clear at that point as to what it was.

When he realized the extent of his patient's interest and involvement, her excitement at this method of mental catharsis, Freud dropped some of his detachment and began to regard Lindsey as a colleague, broadening his sessions with her and discussing them afterwards in a way that was not possible with the other middle-class Viennese women – for women they mostly were – suffering from a variety of neurotic and hysterical manifestations. After all, he conceded, was she not a trained physician and one who, although exhibiting the usual attitudes of indignation, astonishment, denials and resistance, had more insight into her condition than most?

Every day, during the early part of that summer, Lindsey went to the apartment in the Kaiserliches Stiftungshaus for her daily sessions and sometimes, if there was no other patient, she would discuss her treatment with him as if they were in consultation about a third party. Often in those days Freud was short of patients because, soon after his visit to Charcot in Paris in 1885, he had established himself as a controversial figure, one who displeased the Viennese medical establishment, including his old teacher Professor Theodor Meynart, head of the psychiatric department at the General Hospital in Vienna and one of Europe's most celebrated brain anatomists. First of all he had advocated the use of hypnotism, which Meynart thought was humbug, and then he started lecturing and writing about the sexual basis of hysteria and the fact that it was not confined to women but also to be found in men. Even though he was still a Lecturer in Neuropathology ('Dozent') at the University, he was thought odd; his views and methods were considered suspect and the private patients subsequently sent to him were few. Thus, to find a congenial, sympathetic soul like Lindsey, even if she was a woman, was almost irresistible to

345

someone as enquiring, as inquisitive and as talkative as Freud, who felt himself ostracized by his colleagues except for a few friends, and isolated by the domestic trivia of his growing family and a wife whom he loved but who was largely uninterested in his work.

Lindsey usually saw Freud in the morning, after which she would eat a light lunch at a nearby café and then spend the afternoon reading, either in her room or at the University library, having gained admission by virtue of her professional qualifications to which was added her desire to learn German as quickly as possible. A young impecunious Austrian medical student was engaged to tutor her and she soon made rapid progress, aided by her desire to discover as much as she could.

And what of Mortimer in all this? The man for whose benefit the treatment had originally been designed became so remote from her life as to be almost excluded completely. He shared with many people an infelicity in communication with others via the written word, and his letters were stilted and perfunctory; containing mere items of news like a diary. Lindsey found she had very little to say to him, and not much interest in what he did, so her letters back were as short and cursory. She was far from ready to reveal to him the startling results of her daily researches into her own unconscious, the store of repressed memories she was unlocking about the past.

In August Freud took his customary holiday with his young family, and Lindsey and Mortimer met for the first time for two months. It was not an easy meeting and not a happy holiday, part of it spent in the Swiss mountains and part in Mortimer's beloved Rome, where he had hoped so much to rediscover his bride of four years before. But Lindsey was restless, remote, and a prey once again to vague anxiety, depression and the sleepless nights which had practically disappeared during the two months of her treatment with Freud.

'I find no change in you at all,' Mortimer said disconsolately one night towards the end of the holiday as they sat on the balcony of their hotel room overlooking the Piazza Navona. 'In fact, if anything, you seem more unhappy than before.'

'I'm not unhappy,' Lindsey gazed in front of her. 'I'm different. I *am* changing, but I don't know in what direction.'

'I wish I'd talked to Freud.'

'Freud can't tell you anything either. This is as much a new exploration for him as it is for me. He's discovering himself too, finding new ways, perfecting his method. It's an adventure for both of us.'

'But what do you *do*?'

'Do?' Lindsey smiled at him. 'We talk. Just talk.'

'And to what purpose is this talk?' Mortimer felt uneasy.

'Towards a discovery of the mental conflicts that have been forgotten, that have been repressed in the unconscious. Many of them only come to light in our dreams.'

'Dreams?' Mortimer looked startled. 'You talk about your *dreams*?'

'Freud is very interested in dreams; he finds links between what I dream and what I may be trying to hide.'

'I think Freud's going too far,' Mortimer said testily, getting up to return to the bedroom and reappearing with a cigarette in his mouth. 'I have heard that some people think he's decidedly eccentric. I'd expected by now all this treatment would be over. I had great faith in Freud. Now I wonder.'

'You do well to wonder; but not in the way you think. It is wonderful, exciting . . . ' Lindsey rose abruptly and went and stood at the balcony, looking down to where the local inhabitants of this old crowded part of Rome had sauntered out to take the night air, sitting at the many cafés in the square, on the rims of its famous fountains.

347

Children of all ages played up and down, dogs barked and babies bawled, either in the arms of their parents or from the uncongenial prison of their prams. 'Freud has a *most* alert, original mind. At first I thought I hated him because he was so dogmatic. He had his fixed ideas and I . . . ' Lindsey turned to face Mortimer. 'I had mine. I resented him. But now I think that what he, *we*, are doing is very important. If this treatment is successful, or if it only partly succeeds, it will give me great insights into the workings of my own mind and, ultimately, those of other people, my patients for example, that I never had before. It might explain a lot of things to me that I didn't understand or don't care, maybe dare, to explore. It is what you wanted, Mortimer, isn't it?'

'I don't know,' Mortimer stubbed his cigarette out on the balcony. 'It's not quite what I thought would happen. You know I'm interested in the psychological basis of neurology too; I realize we've a lot to learn. The old concepts of the causes of neurosis are suspect, many of them outdated. It is true we must try and find new ways, but I always thought they would be in the regions of conventional medicine; new methods of treatment that would have some objective criteria, which is why I pursue my researches into the structure of the nervous system. I think I really feel the cure to nervous and mental illness is primarily physiological, though I don't altogether exclude psychological factors. Freud seems to have abandoned physiology altogether – you'd think he'd know better – purely for speculative investigations into something you can't really investigate – the unconscious.'

'Freud has turned away from Charcot and hypnosis,' Lindsey said patiently. 'It is too suggestive to the patient and does not allow him the opportunity to find his own cure for himself; it lacks permanency. Now I agree with Freud, reluctantly at first, about the sexual basis for hysteria, the importance of the unconscious.'

'But Freud isn't the first one to discover the unconscious,' Mortimer expostulated, lighting a fresh cigarette. 'I read Hartmann's *Philosophy of the Unconscious* in London in the early 1880s. Lipps was writing about unconscious processes about that time too. We all *know* the unconscious exists and its importance; what I am not convinced about is the underlying assumption on Freud's part of a sexual basis for all this.' He turned his back on her, as though resenting her as well as Freud, angrily puffing away at his cigarette as he stared at the darkening sky.

Sex. It was a profound, mysterious thing; disturbing and unpleasant in its connotations. Even though sexual difficulties had been the problem element in their marriage, Mortimer was still reluctant to acknowledge that Freud's methods might be the right ones. Looking with sympathy yet detachment at her husband's back, Lindsey acknowledged to herself that she still hadn't really come to terms with Freud's supposition that, in her infancy, some sexual trauma had caused her instinctive aversion to sex which persisted in a mature woman of more than thirty. Didn't one grow up and overcome childish things? 'No,' Freud seemed to be saying; 'in parts you are still yet a child. Once you discover what you feared as a child you will understand yourself as a woman.' But how hard it was to attempt to explain all this to poor Mortimer now. There were too many unhappy experiences between them, now dividing them, to allow her to have the rapport she enjoyed with Freud. She could talk to Freud, still not easily but with less inhibition than before, but not to her husband. They had shocked each other too much in the elemental privacy of the bedroom, and that shock still had to be openly analysed and understood. The time was not yet.

Sadly she knew she could still not be a wife to Mortimer, nor explain to him why, because she did not yet

know why. Maybe she never would; it had to be acknowledged Freud might fail. She knew Mortimer was disappointed with the holiday; as restless now to return to his
studies into physical neurology in Berlin as she was to go
back to Freud.

Freud. As she turned once again to study the people in
the square, standing silently next to Mortimer, inhaling
the warm scent of a Roman summer, she still seemed to
see his face. The thought of him was comforting, troub-
ling, very exciting, like being in love. She felt thrilled,
raised apart from normal life, quite indifferent, really, to
Mortimer's suffering. She wanted therefore to get back to
Freud, who understood her, and away from Mortimer,
who didn't. Compared to Freud he seemed a shallow
product of the New World, lacking the deep mysterious
links that bound Freud with an older civilization and
myths of the past. Mortimer as a man disappointed her.
The thought of Freud made her ache with a longing that,
she feared, was partly sexual.

Once again, she was obsessed by her mentor and
tormentor – because the way Freud had unsettled her was
a sort of torment. Her only desire now was to see him
again, lie on the couch and be aware of his nearness beside
her, out of sight but not far away; within reach, but
untouchable.

That night in her separate bed she dreamed continually
of Freud, and the next day they packed their bags for their
journey north – she and Mortimer as far apart as they
were when they had met again.

'You asked me to tell you everything that went on in my
mind,' Lindsey said. 'To hold nothing back.'

Freud didn't reply. She stared at the ceiling, blinking
her eyes, feeling isolated despite his presence behind
her – seeing and not being seen. She wriggled round to try
and look at him but his face seemed to have merged in the

350

shadows with the rest of his personality, that haunting, disturbing personality. She had almost felt like that timid young girl again, shyly entering his room, her heartbeat rather fast, her steps tentative. How would he greet her? What would he say? He'd merely pointed to the couch, and she'd felt rebuffed.

'I feel I love you and not Mortimer,' she blurted out. 'The holiday was a disaster. I thought of you the whole time. It's as though I'm sick with you. Sick with love.'

'Did you make love to Mortimer?'

'No.'

'Did he try?'

'No.'

'What would you have done if he had tried?'

'I would have resisted him.'

'Would you resist me?'

Lindsey was confused and afraid again, unnerved by his questions. She put her hands over her face.

'I don't know.'

'Love with me is impossible,' Freud said, after a while, almost gently. 'I see it distresses you, but that's not the point. Think of someone you would like to make love to, who is also unattainable.'

'I can't. No one . . . '

'No one?'

'No.'

'No man that you've loved very much; that you wanted to be with all the time? Not your father?'

'My father!' Lindsey sat up. 'That's a terrible suggestion.'

'But you love your father.'

'Not to *make* love to.'

'Are you sure?'

'Of course I'm sure. It's a disgusting suggestion.'

'I'm going too far again, aren't I? I'm getting close to those regions which you want to forget; how you wanted

351

your father to make love to you and not your mother. How you resented your mother. You knew they made love because your sister was born, and you hated her. *You* wanted to have a baby by your father.'

Lindsey jumped off the couch and stood over him as he sat, solitary, aloof, almost unconcerned by her behaviour, in his armchair at the head of the couch.

'I think you're perverted,' she shouted. 'You really are. Mortimer said he'd heard bad reports about you, that you'd become eccentric and he's right. You're dirty, twisted and horrible. How could I *possibly* have wanted to make love to my father? You are obsessed with sex. No wonder you have a reputation, that you have so few patients! All you're after is money, Dr Freud. Well, you won't get any more of mine! You can send your bill to my hotel. I shan't see you, you twisted, perverted man, again.'

Lindsey jammed her hat on her head as Freud listened impassively, not smiling, not angry, almost indifferent. Nor did he attempt to get out of his chair to show her out.

In the hallway Lindsey bumped into Frau Freud, who was carrying a large basket of clothes apparently from one room to the other. Martha Freud was not beautiful, with rather an impassive peasant-like face. Lindsey had never seen her face to face before; she'd usually been a figure partly observed in the distance, busy, always busy, with her children, her household affairs. Now she didn't smile at Lindsey, but stared past her towards the door where her husband saw his patients, the basket clasped to a belly that was slightly swollen, as though she had seen indignant patients rushing out too often. Did anything surprise Frau Freud? Did she know what went on behind those closed doors? Frau Freud didn't say a word to Lindsey, who stood back to let her past, but went on her way, closing the door of the room she entered behind her, not glancing at Lindsey again.

Lindsey went swiftly out of the apartment – how glad she was she wouldn't see it again – and hurried back to the hotel, her chest puffed out with indignation. In imagination she could amost see herself hurrying along like a determined *Hausfrau* who has been insulted by the butcher, her rather unfashionable hat on her head, her lips pursed with repressed fury.

What was so humiliating was to think how she'd longed to see Freud – approaching him like a timid bride, confident he would take care of her, not offend her susceptibilities. The parallel of this attitude with her approach to her marriage did not seem to occur to her and, when she got back to her hotel, she threw herself on the bed, panting because she'd been walking so fast.

Freud was an imposter, a charlatan. Mortimer was quite right about him. He was a loathsome, revolting man. She thought of her kind silver-haired father, and the disgusting thing Freud had suggested . . . what would her *father* say if he knew about this? Of course she loved her father, but not in that way. The thought was evil, ugly and very disturbing; the clamour of her heart in her breast didn't lessen even though she was no longer hurrying. She found she was sweating profusely although it was a little chilly in the room. Evil, ugly, loathsome . . . these and many more adjectives came to her mind when she considered that tormentor who sat smugly in his room not a mile away, probably having forgotten all about her.

By night-time she was exhausted. The mental turbulence was worse than anything she'd ever known; the range of emotions she passed through conflicting and fearful. She got up and sluiced her face with water then examined it in the mirror. Her appearance shocked her – she looked haggard, haunted. Behind her then she saw Freud's face. She turned round searching for him, but of course he wasn't there. Convinced that she was going insane she threw herself again on the bed and wept.

Freud said talk was cathartic; tears were too. Maybe she wept for an hour or more; but no one came to comfort her. The cure was in herself. Shame, a sense of inadequacy, began to take the place of rage and then another emotion intervened whose primacy she reluctantly recognized. Jealousy.

Frau Freud had been about five months pregnant, almost flaunting herself, in Lindsey's mind, as she clasped the basket of clothes in front of her. 'Look,' she'd seemed to be saying to Lindsey, 'what he does to me? You who are barren, don't you envy me?' She imagined Freud making love to his wife and wondered what they felt. Did Frau Freud enjoy it really, or did she pretend? Had she been reluctant, unwilling like Lindsey, or had she been eager to be possessed by him? She looked a very curious woman to enjoy love, not like Estella, not like Lindsey either.

Was Freud very physical? She didn't like to think of it, any more than she liked to think of her father making love to her mother . . . yet Dr and Frau Freud and Mr and Mrs Abercrombie paired for this disgusting ritual, maybe time and time again. They all had children to prove it; yet she, Lindsey Digby, a fully qualified medical practitioner, gold medallist, married woman, had none. Something terrible had intervened to stop her being normal, like other women. What was it? Why her? Perhaps Freud really did want to make love to her which was why he made her lie down; he'd sit there, probably, staring at her body, watching her move about; she had a large bosom and maybe looking at it gave him pleasure.

No, she would never go back. She would put this experience out of her mind and resume normal practice among women who suffered from various complaints that had only organic origins. But how did one *know*? Her own complaint was organic too; she experienced pain in intercourse. Many women did; it was purely a muscular thing, but she had been tricked into thinking it was psychological. Yet why should it be? No, maybe treating other women would remind her of herself; so perhaps she would resume those long-abandoned neurological studies into the pathology of the human brain. She would go back to Paris, as she should have done months before, and return to Charlotte. Return home.

'It took you a long time to return,' Freud said, closing the door.

'But you knew I would.'

'I hoped you would.'

Freud pointed politely to the couch and Lindsey lay on it carefully, reluctantly, taking good care not to meet his eyes.

'I've had a crisis,' she said. 'I thought I was going mad. I lay on my bed for nearly a week neither eating, nor sleeping.'

'Then what did you do?'

'I got up and looked for an apartment.'

'Did you find one?'

'Near here, next to the Bourse. I'll pay you for all the sessions I missed.'

'Why is money so important to you? You talk about it a lot.'

'It isn't important to me. I thought it was important to *you*?'

'You like to pay me as though I were a prostitute. You pay me for my services.'

'I felt so terribly angry, jealous of Frau Freud. I couldn't bear to think she's having a baby. I realized I hated the noises made by the children here in the apartment.'

'The children you'd like to have by your father . . . '

Lindsey, to her surprise, didn't feel angry, although he'd immediately returned to the subject of sex; but she'd

355

gone through too much to get up and go away again. She had gradually adjusted herself to the fact that Freud was necessary to her; that he alone possessed the key to the puzzle that was her mind. That was why she was here.

'The thought of relations with my father *is* abhorrent.'

'Yet you'd like his children, not Mortimer's. Why should you give Mortimer children when you want to give them to your father? I want you to tell me about your father.'

Lindsey's head felt swollen again, feverish. She closed her eyes.

'I've told you.'

'Tell me again. Tell me what comes into your head.'

Once again she felt the pressure of Freud's fingers and she closed her eyes, letting her mind roam freely down the past, as far back as she could go, to the days when she was very small, running through the house which she had to herself. Everyone waited on her, Mother and the servants, and Father was always there to gather her up in his arms. She was his darling, he told her, his baby. In this little kingdom she was queen. Then one night, she woke up feeling very frightened. It was dark and she couldn't light the lamp. She cried for her nurse but no one came so she got up and tiptoed very quietly to her parents' room, pushed open the door . . .

Lindsey put her hand to her burning head, longing for the cool of Freud's hands, his palms pressed against her burning skin. Something terrible was happening inside that room. She didn't know what it was because it was dark and she couldn't see; but she could hear, hear terrible things. Her mother was groaning; a strange noise was coming from the bed and, as her eyes got accustomed to the dark, she could make out violent movement. Her father seemed to be attacking her mother, stabbing something into her, again and again and again.

Paralysed by shock and fear, she couldn't move,

couldn't do anything to help her mother, anything to stop Papa . . .

Suddenly her father cried out; the movement stopped and the silence in the room was almost more frightening than the noise. Had Father killed her mother? Was he dead too? Fearfully she approached; she had to know what had happened. Timidly she went up to the bed and stretched out her hand. She could feel her mother's fingers hanging over the bed. Then she could see her father lying on top of Mama, who had her legs spread out, her nightgown ruffled up past her waist.

Then she knew that something evil, something obscene, had happened . . .

'Why did you think it was evil?' Dr Freud asked as she paused.

'Because it was to do with death. Then I realized my parents were both still breathing. There was a slight movement and Papa raised himself. I saw that his night-shirt was right over his buttocks too . . . I ran. I ran all the way back to my room. I put my head under the bed-clothes. What I had seen made me much more afraid than I was of the dark . . . '

'Because it was primeval. It came from the place where ghosts and spirits come from; fear of the unknown. But you knew nothing about love, did you?'

'Of course I didn't.'

'The things we don't understand are much more frightening than the things we do. Fantasy is more dreadful than reality, however bad that might be. You thought your father was killing your mother; that was frightening, but you could understand it. The thing you didn't understand – why your venerated parents had their lower parts bare, were engaged in that strange, grotesque position – frightened you more. It lodged itself in your mind. You couldn't find an explanation for it.'

'I never went to their room again. Any horror I had in

my bed alone was preferable to that, to seeing and hearing things I didn't understand.'

'That was before your sister was born, wasn't it?'

'Yes.'

'Tell me what comes into your mind now?'

Lindsey was aware of an extraordinary feeling of calm, as though she had rid herself of an impossible burden she had unknowingly carried alone for years. At last she had told somebody of that horrifying suspicion that her parents had done something unmentionable. Yet, strangely, she had never thought about it again until now; had forgotten it completely. But as she had been talking it was so vivid, so clear, so real – as though she were a little girl of four or five again, hearing the noise, seeing the sight, hugging that horrible secret all to herself.

'Soon after, my sister was born. I don't know how soon, maybe a few months, I felt jealous of her from the beginning.'

'Did you associate it in your mind with what you'd seen in your parents' room?'

'I don't know.'

'I think you did. You thought your father was killing your mother; but he was giving her life. To you death and copulation were the same.'

'How could I possibly know that as a child?'

'Because you were afraid to ask, weren't you?'

'How do you mean?'

'Well, you didn't say "What were you and Mama doing in bed last night, Papa?"'

'No, it would have been unthinkable.'

'Exactly. Anything else that might puzzle you, you would ask about. But not that. Why do you think you didn't ask about that?' As Lindsey didn't reply he continued. 'Because the unthinkable had at last happened. Even as children we know instinctively about the process of creation, but we shut it completely out of our minds. It

358

means violence – violence by the beloved to the beloved. It causes pain. It is too complex for us to understand even if we wished to. Because the tenderness of sexual love is something we cannot then comprehend. Your parents' behaviour that night did not seem to convey to you the joy and fulfilment of mutually shared adult, sexual love. You still cannot comprehend it, can you Frau Digby?'

'I don't know what you mean?'

'I think you do,' Freud's voice was very soothing as if he were taking care to explain to her something that was painful to him too. 'For you sex and violence are indistinguishable, which is why you do not want your husband to make love to you – in case he destroys you, in case he gives you a baby which will bring you the pain it brought to your mother, giving you in the process something you didn't want: a little sister, a rival for your father's affections. No wonder you wanted to kill that sister, intrusive little thing; but you suppressed those violent, shameful feelings and have to this day. But now it has all come out, as I promised you it would; it is over.'

Freud lapsed into silence; Lindsey lay upon the couch loath to get up. She felt quite drained, as though she had lived through an emotional and physical experience whose own violence and power overwhelmed her. She had gone back in time nearly thirty years; she had seen herself as a child, a small frightened little girl overcome by fear of the dark whose search for refuge and reassurance in her parents' room had unleashed, instead, further terrors.

Slowly she swung herself off the couch and, as she stood up, Freud rose too and turned to her, his face beaming as if in a greeting.

'This calls for a celebration, Frau Digby,' he said. 'I must smoke a cigar.'

By Christmas time Lindsey was ready to see Mortimer again. It wasn't that she felt she was cured, but she understood the reason for the nausea that the sexual act gave her. She knew now that her cramps and pain were hysterical; they arose from that far-off trauma of seeing her parents making love and equating the act with suffering, maybe death. She wanted to apologize to Mortimer and explain to him why; to tell him that she was now a pupil of Freud and that he was training her to take his work to America.

Mortimer saw at once that she was different. She'd put on weight and the dark shadows had gone from under her eyes. She had a small two-roomed apartment in the Helferst Strasse which was comfortable enough, but crammed with papers and books, not really a home. Mortimer, however, remembered the summer and had taken care to book into the hotel where they'd stayed before.

'I'm not much of a cook,' Lindsey said. 'You know that.'

'We could have eaten out,' Mortimer pretended gratification as she placed a plate with a pork chop and cabbage before him. 'I didn't expect this.'

'Poor Mortimer. You don't expect much from me, do you?'

'What right have I to expect anything from you?' He quietly fastened his napkin into the top of his waistcoat. 'I put you through this ordeal with Freud. All I can say is that now, unlike the summer, you look well.'

'It's a terrible readjustment to one's life. I know myself better, that's all.' Lindsey sat opposite him, passing him the bottle of wine he'd brought so that he could pour. 'I was always attracted to psychological medicine, but not for myself. I could see how others needed help, but not me. Yet how can I help others without helping myself?'

'How indeed?' Mortimer, at a loss to reply, smiled as he filled her glass. 'And now *do* you know yourself?'

'I know enough to know how little I know. I have discovered a lot about the sexual jealousies of my parents that tormented me as a child, but which remained buried in my unconscious mind until now. With this was joined a resentment of Estella who was so much more feminine than I was, even when she was tiny. The men, my father's friends, always admired Estella because she was pretty and made up to them, whereas they ignored me because I was too grave and serious and stood on one side while they petted her.'

'You underestimate yourself.'

'I knew I wasn't like Estella; so I wanted to be something quite different. I haven't been happy with myself as I was, or am. That's what I'm discovering now. The reason, in Freud's theory, seems to be that I was physically in love with my father, and I resented Estella because he had inseminated my mother. Remaining in love with my father made it very difficult for me to love anyone else.'

'But you left your father years ago!' Mortimer protested. 'I noticed no excessive love for him when we were with your parents in London; filial respect, but no more.'

Lindsey joined her hands and gazed at him over the tips of her fingers. 'Love and fear. I don't understand it myself.'

Mortimer leaned back and wiped his lips. What she said troubled him. He knew she had changed but did he want that change? Had things better been left? No . . .

He reached across the table for her hand, but it lay in his like a limp bird, timid, unresponsive. It seemed as though Lindsey too was fearful of change. She lowered her eyes. The theory was one thing but, now that Mortimer was here, her customary diffidence returned, her reluctance to discuss anything personal with him. She could talk to Freud about anything; but Mortimer . . .

'I don't know how it will be with us, Mortimer,' she said frankly. 'I have so many bad habits and attitudes to unlearn I don't really know that I can change very much, so soon.'

'I've booked a room at the Büren,' he said. 'I don't expect you to . . .'

361

She met his eyes, pushing her plate away. She'd been so nervous that she'd ruined the meat. But that was unimportant. 'Maybe you *should* expect something from me, Mortimer? Maybe you should assert your rights . . .'

She lay in the crook of his arm, comfortable and at ease. At peace. He had on his nightshirt and her nightgown was carefully tucked tightly around her ankles.

'It doesn't matter,' Mortimer said.

'I'd hoped it would be all right.'

'You've a lifetime of fear to overcome. You can't overcome it just like that.'

'You're terribly understanding.' Lindsey timidly stroked his hand which rested lightly on her shoulder.

'I love you,' he kissed her forehead. 'I love you as you, and not for anything else.'

'I can't think why I deserve you.'

'You've done so much for me, for us. What you've been through is as hard as anything in life, any illness.'

'Harder. There are so many conflicting moods and emotions. I even thought I'd lose my reason.'

'I like cuddling with you like this anyway.'

As long as she knew he wouldn't do anything else she didn't mind either. He was a nice, solid, dependable person. Good to be with. Now that he was here, she realized how much she'd missed him.

Freud said it would take a lot of time and it did. It took months of patience on Mortimer's part and effort on Lindsey's. Mortimer had to learn skills as a lover he didn't automatically possess. He was a clumsy, unsure man and he had to attempt to awaken Lindsey's desire by gentle persuasion. Lindsey's trouble had become partly physical because organs that had not been receptive to love took time, like unused machinery, to become so. She didn't have the power, the inclination or the natural feeling to make them become so, despite her growing love for her kind, generous husband. It was hard to express this love for him in a physical way. She lacked desire.

Freud helped them both because they both became his pupils, as well as his patients. He enjoyed working with the Digbys, finding them an interesting, stimulating couple, well able to convert their own subjective experience into objective fields for study. Freud was often to say that he was not so much interested in the therapeutic aspects of his work as the opportunity it gave him to break through intellectual barriers, to extend the sum of man's knowledge of the unconscious. Although he was not by any means the first to discover this, few before him had examined it and its implications, not only for healing but strictly as an intellectual exercise. He was convinced that he had touched upon 'one of the great secrets of nature'.

The Digbys were not sick; they were intellectually alert, psychologically aware physicians, also interested in the extension of knowledge for its own sake. To Freud, with their new ideas and open minds, they were refreshing. Freud, who was in his late thirties, had spent so many of his professional years on the wrong track that he was in a hurry to make up for lost time. He was also anxious that he should be recognized as the pioneer he was, the first to put the primacy of sexuality in its place in the etiology of hysterical and neurotic illness. He was also vain about his discoveries, impatient both of criticism and competition. But Lindsey and Mortimer Digby, the better they got to know him, became uncritical and devoted followers of a man they knew to be not only fearless, but so far ahead of his time.

They stayed in Vienna, living together in the small apartment in the Helferst Strasse until the following summer. They both agreed that their time with Freud was the most seminal, most extraordinary experience of their lives, struggling with their unconscious, bringing into the open fears which had for so long been repressed. Freud showed Mortimer that his own feelings about sex were not dissimilar from Lindsey's and had made him able to contain what, to others, were natural, uncontainable urges quite easily until he was a man of thirty-six. He came to realize that sex had disgusted him too, but for different reasons; the reasons given by his father that women of refinement were not supposed to enjoy the marital act, the corollary being that, to take them in this way was to abuse them, and to demean a man by bringing out his base nature.

In the process of learning to make love, to please him and respond to his caresses, Lindsey gradually fell in love with her husband; she couldn't have wished for a gentler, better natured man. They would never be great lovers, and she personally felt she would never enjoy the act *per se*, even after if had ceased to cause her pain. That was part of her nature, her constitution, and Freud's gift to her was to help her realize it. She was not a very sexual person and it would be artificial to try to make her one. She was scarred by her life-long repressions, but not permanently damaged. She and Mortimer could love each other by sharing mutual interests, the same way of life. Freud called it sublimation – canalizing wishes and desires into other things that made life together meaningful and enjoyable.

In the course of those months there were many moments when they came close to despair, and many when they could see progress, both in their sexual lives and their spiritual or natural ones. They learned to live together.

The degree of self-knowledge that they eventually came to possess helped constructively to reorientate their own lives and, eventually, would help to change the lives of others, many of them not yet born.

CHAPTER SEVENTEEN

The curtains were drawn in the large bedroom, though neither the light nor its lack affected Edmund Abercrombie, who lay pretty much as he had done when he was lifted onto this very bed after his stroke, completely unresponsive to the world.

Lindsey checked her watch and took her father's pulse. She and Mortimer had arrived five days before, having been hastily summoned from Vienna. Estella, who had been in the South of France, was expected any moment, much against the wishes of Minnie, who had not seen her daughter for nearly ten years.

'I do not *wish* it,' Minnie had protested tearfully.

'Hush Mama. She has a right to see Father. Besides, you may need her.'

'How could I possibly?'

Lindsey had avoided her mother's gaze and turned away to do something else.

'Nevertheless, you may.'

Lindsey herself felt she needed her sister. The presence of Mortimer was not sufficient to cushion her against the terrible blow not only of their father's seizure, but of that fact which had contributed to it: he was facing bankruptcy.

Occasionally Edmund opened his eyes and seemed to look straight at her, but Lindsey didn't know whether he saw her or not. There was certainly more movement than before and, although the prognosis was poor, the doctors did not give up hope altogether that he might show some degree of recovery, for here was a well-preserved man of only fifty-six, years during which he had taken good care of himself.

She tucked his hand back under his bedclothes, straightened his sheets and was about to sit down again when she heard the sound of a carriage stopping outside the gate. She rushed to the window and there was Mortimer standing on the pavement, helping a very beautiful, elegant woman to alight from the hackney cab, from the back of which the cabbie was producing a large number of valises, baskets and hatboxes.

Lindsey glanced at her father and then, leaving the door open, rushed downstairs to greet her sister who, by that time, was standing in the hall, the cases round her feet, betraying, despite her poise, the fact that she was uneasy.

'Oh thank God you're here,' Estella said as Lindsey, feeling rather nervous too, approached her. 'I did not want to meet Mama first.'

The sisters gazed at each other, each, maybe, reliving the memory of that last bitter encounter. Then suddenly they ran into each other's arms, embracing, remaining thus for some time.

Lindsey's reaction on first seeing her sister was that she looked older; that, despite the obvious sadness due to the occasion for her visit, she wore an air of melancholy. If anything this enhanced her beauty, giving it a maturity she had lacked before. People on whom fortune smiles seldom have the character in their faces of those who have known vicissitude. Lindsey guessed that her style of life worried her more than she had cared to admit. They were too close for her rejection of Estella in Paris eighteen months before not to have had some effect. But Lindsey also knew that the warring emotions within her sister had produced this air of spiritual suffering.

When Estella finally removed her cheek from Lindsey's she had tears in her eyes. Lindsey could sense the strain of the homecoming, knowing not only that Father was so ill but that she had to face her mother once again.

'How is Father?' Estella whispered.

'Pretty much as he was. Would you like to see him?'

'Where is Mama?' Estella looked round, removing the pins from her wide-brimmed hat, whose central feature was a pair of stuffed birds with outstretched wings, and giving it to the maid.

'Madam's upstairs, mum,' the maid mumbled, feeling quite faint, wondering if perhaps royalty had come to call; for anything like this grand, regal apparition she had never seen within these walls before. For, to her training as an actress and her career as *grande cocotte,* Estella had added an elusive air of quiet distinction which made most people, wherever they were and whatever they were doing, stop and look at her. It was not only that she spent hours at her toilette, but she exhibited that indefinable poise which women who are much admired by men seem instinctively to acquire. Many women of her kind – actresses, members of the *demi-monde*, what have you – maybe because they came from humble origins, also acquired with their riches, an air of vulgarity, be it ever so slight, which gave them away. Not so Estella.

In France she was taken by many who didn't know who she was to be at least a member of the old aristocracy; one who lived off the Faubourg by right not conquest. She also managed – heaven knows how – an air of almost tragic innocence, with her pale skin and brilliant blue eyes, which were at the same time not those of an ingénue, but of a woman of experience. Hence, she presented an intriguing combination.

Today her blond hair was beautifully dressed and she had on a long walking out ensemble, made of rose silk, with full bell-shaped skirt, short blouse and a tight-fitting jacket with leg o'mutton sleeves and large turned back cuffs with a velvet trim. The maid cowered back against the wall clasping the exotic hat to her flat bosom, saucer-eyed with admiration.

'Pray take care of my bonnet,' Estella said, smiling at

367

her kindly. 'It cost me a fortune. May I go and see Father, Lindsey?'

'Would you like to see your room first? Your old room? Mortimer, dear, would you like to see to Estella's things?'

Mortimer was only too glad to obey. He had failed to recognize Estella when she had waved to him from the window of the Flèche d'Or as it steamed into Victoria. Already, as her door opened, a number of gentlemen who had travelled in her compartment vied with one another to help her alight. Mortimer had thought she must be some minor member of the European royalty and, ignoring the wave which he could not suppose to be directed at him, had run along the platform, looking into the windows of the rest of the carriages. A clear voice had again hailed him and Estella, to the chagrin and envy of the rest of her admirers, had planted an affectionate kiss on his cheek and tucked his hand in hers. From that minute Mortimer was her slave, scarcely able to take his eyes from her during their journey to Highgate, listening to everything she said as though he were in receipt of a personal message from heaven.

'Mortimer's quite besotted, I can see,' Lindsey whispered with a smile, preceding Estella up the stairs and along the corridor to her room.

'He said he didn't recognize me! He walked straight by, though after looking into my eyes, and began to search the windows of the other carriages.'

'You're very different. He hasn't seen you for six years remember.'

'Have I changed all that much?' Estella sounded wistful.

Lindsey didn't reply, thinking the answer must be obvious, and flung open the door of Estella's old room which had been prepared for her. Bright vases of flowers stood by the bed and on the dressing table, and the late winter sun sparkled on the bare trees outside the windows.

'Oh!' Estella clasped her hands together pausing at the threshold. 'Oh Lindsey, to be *home* again.' She advanced slowly into the room, her hands solemnly joined beneath her chin as though in a prayer of thanksgiving. She stood at the window looking out at the well-cut turf of the lawn and when she turned her eyes once again were full of tears.

'I seem to be crying rather a lot these days,' she said, attempting to brush them away. 'This is a very emotional moment for me. Lindsey, what a *long* time has passed since we used to share our girlish confidences in this room. What a lot has happened. How I regret so much of it.'

She held out her hands and Lindsey took them, enclosing them firmly between her own.

'Do you think I don't have regrets too? My behaviour towards you in Paris was unpardonable. As you said, I lacked the compassion, the understanding, that you, as a sister, had the right to expect of me. I showed less charity towards you than I would to one of my patients in similar circumstances.'

Estella drew Lindsey's hands to her bosom and her eyes filled with tears again.

'Oh, darling, I forgive you! Of course I was hurt, but you were right! I was selfish, immature. In many ways I still am. I have always thought of myself first and others second. Even Ellen's happiness I put after mine . . .'

'But you could not help . . .'

'I could. I could.' Estella released Lindsey's hands and extracted a handkerchief, a wisp of a thing exquisitely perfumed, from the sleeve of her gown, dabbing her eyes with it. 'Was I not always at the beck and call of fortune, obeying its commands, never attempting to steer myself? Did I not first rely on Mama and Papa, then on Tom, then on Uncle and Aunt, then on you, again, and Charlotte? As soon as the first man who could provide for me came along in Paris did I not throw myself into his arms? The odious Marc Lagrange.' Estella sniffed imperiously and thrust her handkerchief into her sleeve, her lips curled as

369

though in self-contempt. 'It was you who showed me to myself, fleetingly it's true, as I was, and I did not like the picture. As you said, I could have returned to London and sought work taking Ellen with me; but the life of ease that she had with Charlotte appealed to me too. I consider Charlotte a hard unemotional woman – I cannot bring myself to love her – but I acknowledge the extent of her affection for Ellen. Yes she wanted Ellen for her ends – she wanted a child – and they suited me. I was too young and silly to realize my own responsibilities. How I have suffered for this . . . '

As Estella began to weep again Lindsey clasped her emotional sister in her arms and stroked her hair, being careful not to disarrange the elaborate coiffure.

'My dearest sister, I am past thirty and I have just discovered things about myself that make my own recent behaviour seem childlike. You are an actress; you have always had a nervous, excitable temperament. How can you blame yourself for decisions that you made when there seemed no alternative? I was not of much help to you. We are too close.' Lindsey rested her head against Estella's for a moment and then she drew back. 'Now that we are together again we have so many problems that we need each other's help and support. Mama is very stricken by Father's illness.'

'Do you think Mama will speak to me?'

'I think so. She does spend a lot of time in her room. Father's sudden illness was such a shock to her.'

'She didn't want me to come, did she?'

Lindsey studied the floor. 'No.'

'I knew because you were here before I was sent for and you had a long way to come. You persuaded her to send for me?'

'I thought it was only fair that you should have the opportunity to see Father . . . also, well, something else very serious has happened too· which requires a family council, whatever Mama thinks.' Lindsey sat down on the bed, but Estella remained by the window. 'Father has lost a great deal of money on some speculative business venture in South America.'

'But the trustees . . . '

'Well, of course it is the fault of the trustees, but that doesn't help matters. It is father's, our, money. There was some question of prospecting for diamonds or gold and the forecast was so good that the trustees thought it worth taking money out of investments which, though safe, yielded little income and money has to be made to grow. I saw the lawyers yesterday with Mortimer, and the point they made was that one can't live for ever on inherited wealth. Money must be changed and moved about. No Abercrombie has really worked for two generations, and Father had no interest in business, trusting others to guide him.'

'But can *they* not be held responsible for their bad advice?'

Lindsey sighed and smoothed the cover on the bed. 'Unfortunately it seems they can't. They took the best advice and many other trusts, as well as a bank or two, are in trouble too. Father received this news only a week before his stroke. It weighed very heavily on his mind, the thought of selling this house, having nowhere to go. Mother says he didn't sleep for nights; she had never seen him so agitated.'

'Nowhere to go! Sell the house? Is it possible?'

'I'm afraid so. All the money has gone. There are, moreover, debts. It's doubtful if even selling the house will settle all the bills. Father is faced with bankruptcy. There's no doubt about that. Ruin.'

'Oh Lindsey!' Estella went quickly to her side and took her hand. 'That is the most terrible news I've ever heard.'

'Mortimer and I discussed taking them to the States with us. But, alas, our plans are very fluid too. I don't want to continue to live in Boston and Mortimer has agreed to move to New York soon, so we too shall be without a home, for a time anyway. Besides, unless Father were to die and Mother come with us alone, how could we get him there?'

'Oh no it's not to be thought of. There's my home, of course . . . ' Estella fell silent and gazed at her sister.

'I think your lifestyle might . . . surprise Mama,' Lindsey tried to choose her words with care. 'I mean, she's bound to wonder, to ask how you came by such wealth. If you do not tell her she'll find out. The shock might kill her.'

'I can sell some jewels . . . '

Lindsey shook her head. 'The sums I have heard mentioned are too vast to be covered by such a gesture, however generous on your part. I thought . . . I thought of asking Charlotte if they could be given a temporary home in the house her family still retain in Museum Street.'

'Oh no we can't ask Charlotte! Certainly not!' Estella, a high colour suddenly sprung to her cheeks, flew up from the bed and started agitatedly to pace the floor. 'I would never permit that!'

'*You* would not permit it?'

'No, I would not. Charlotte has enough hold on our family as it is.'

'Charlotte has given a home to your daughter.'

'And that's quite enough. Don't you think I would like to have my daughter back from her? Don't you think I *bitterly* regret the circumstances that forced me to allow her legally to assume complete maternal care?'

'In those days there wasn't much alternative.'

'Well, in this case there *is* an alternative. We shall think of something. We *must* think . . . '

'Come and see Father.' Lindsey rose and gently took her sister's hand. 'But be prepared for a shock; he won't show any recognition. We're not sure how much he hears and feels. Then later we shall all think hard what is the best course to take about the future.'

Estella knocked quietly on her mother's door and, without awaiting her summons, opened it. Minnie Abercrombie sat in a chair by the window, and Estella, thinking she was asleep, tiptoed across the room and stood timidly by the chair looking down at her.

'Mama?' she said.

Minnie didn't reply and Estella bent to see whether or not her eyes were open. They were, gazing in front of her, and two large tears stole silently down her cheeks.

'Oh *Mama*,' Estella threw herself on her knees and reached for one of her mother's hands, but Minnie firmly tucked them under the shawl that she had round her legs and, still kneeling, Estella dejectedly clasped her hands in front of her, head bowed.

'I have come home, Mama. It is I. Estella, your daughter.'

'I know who it is quite well,' Minnie said with surprising sharpness. 'I didn't wish to see you and I still don't. I consider you no daughter of mine. No daughter of mine,' she repeated.

'But I *am* your daughter, Mama, and I love you.'

'You didn't show much love over the past ten years.'

'Nor did you, Mama! You sent word I was not to come home again. But my love was always there, in my heart – much as I resented your attitude.'

'You opposed me and your father at every turn. You were a stubborn, disobedient daughter from the start, always wanting your own way. An actress! Now what have you become – an unmarried woman with a child, a strumpet! You have brought shame on this family and I wish to God you had stayed in Paris where you belong. You have no place here, Estella. No place with me.'

Minnie's tone grew firmer and at last, when she looked into her daughter's eyes, her tears had gone, her expression was hard and unforgiving. 'Your father and I have lived all these years without the love and consolation of the two daughters I bore. You have been most unnatural, both of you and, if we were not in such extremities, I doubt if I would have called either of you now.'

'But Lindsey . . .'

'Lindsey has been a trifle better than you, but only a trifle. She too has always insisted on her own way, rejecting parental guidance and, if she has not brought upon us as much shame as you, she has given us both scant happiness. Imagine, marrying a man we didn't even know! Taking the law into her own hands, as always. Yet we welcomed this husband, whom we had never met, last year but even then they only stayed a short time with us. We haven't seen them since, though they have been not far from us, on the Continent.'

'Studying, I understand . . .'

'*Studying*! What use is study when parents are getting older and need the support of children and grandchildren? I hoped that, with this clever husband of hers, Lindsey would at last settle down and raise a family. Your father has been very agitated about financial matters for some time and to whom could he turn? No one, no daughters or sons-in-law, no close member of his family, only a few remote cousins who implied that he had got what he deserved. We can hardly go to them in our extremity. This collapse of the South American mine was only the last, the final straw; there were lots of warnings before then. His cousin Robert Abercrombie – the one who owns whisky distilleries in Scotland (whisky, I ask you!) – had the impudence to tell your father he was lazy! He wrote him a long letter on the subject of thrift and hard work. Another person we shall not speak to again.' Minnie puckered her lips, her eyes contracting with spite.

374

Estella thought how much her mother seemed to have shrunk, gone into herself, become prematurely old and pinched, like a mollusc retreating into its shell. She had scarcely any vestige of beauty left, and, if Estella had rejected remorse before she felt it then. Seeing the physical degeneration made concrete fears that she had hitherto dismissed from her mind. Now, based on reality, she knew her past behaviour, however justified, would haunt her.

'I'm sure if you had written to Lindsey she would have come at once; and so should I. We are family, Mama; we are your blood, yours and Papa's.' Estella knew she would have an uphill task in trying to woo her mother's love.

'Such family!' Minnie leaned back in her chair. 'I'm very tired, Estella, and I don't wish to continue this talk, which I find upsets me. I feel a nervous fluttering of the heart. I fear my own health is not good. Please leave me alone. Do what you have to do, see your father and then, please, go.'

'Right away, Mama?'

'Yes, for good. I would not wish to see you again, were I left on the streets and destitute. I would not ask you for shelter. That is how I feel about you, Estella Abercrombie.'

Minnie firmly closed her eyes, signifying that the most painful interview of her daughter's life was at an end.

Back in her room, sitting in front of the mirror on her dressing table, Estella gazed earnestly at herself, lightly tracing the contours of her face with her finger. In the old days, before she used to make up for the stage, she would do just this, sit for a moment as if appraising herself, trying to see, perhaps, beyond the skin, to find out what sort of person she was underneath. She had never really succeeded.

Now, as she used to in those days long ago, she rubbed a little rouge high up on her cheekbones to hide the pallor of her skin and she carefully combed the tiny curls over her brow as if to conceal the infinitesimal wrinkles she saw there. Her clear blue eyes gazed back at her; and suddenly she thought she saw a stranger. Her eyes widened in dismay and slowly, thoughtfully, she drew away from the dressing table and rose from her chair, crossing to the window and looking onto that beloved scene of the back garden leading into Highgate Woods. Often, in imagination, she had returned here over the years.

Since she'd heard about her father's misfortune and resolution, an extraordinary notion had been forming itself at the back of her mind which seemed to offer ways of both expiation and liberation. Was not to give up everything to free oneself? Was it not easier for a camel to pass through the eye of a needle than a rich man to enter heaven? What about a rich, fallen woman? A woman who – however much she minced her words – had sold her body for gain? What peace, what pleasure had it given her?

Looking in that mirror, trying to discover her soul, she had realized as she dipped a finger in the rouge to rub on her cheeks that the call to a new life was stronger than any hold the old one had on her. The rouge, the greasepaint, the smell of sawdust on the stage, the lights, the sudden darkness as the curtain rose. No, sacrifice would not be hard at all, and in the mirror she might one day see someone she recognized rather than a stranger she disliked.

Estella raised her hands above her head stretching wide her arms as though greeting an imaginary audience. Then she hurried from the room.

Mortimer and Lindsey sat waiting in the drawing room for Estella to emerge from what they had all guessed would be a difficult meeting with her mother. After the distressing experience of seeing her father she had said she wanted to be alone for a while to compose herself, and then she would see her mother alone. Lindsey had wanted to come with her; but Estella had refused.

'She *is* a long time,' Lindsey looked up from her book.

'They have much to say,' Mortimer murmured.

'Well, at least I'm glad it's not a monologue. Mama said she wouldn't talk to her at all. Still, I wish I'd gone too.'

'It is best, my dear, that you let her do as she wished. This is a very stressful time for Estella . . . and for you too. I know how agonized you were about the thought of your meeting. But it went off very well didn't it?'

'I love her,' Lindsey said simply. 'She has such a generous heart, a generosity of spirit, Mortimer. How I regretted the way I spoke to her in Paris. That was a lack of generosity in me.'

Mortimer bent over and took her hand. 'You know much more than you did then, my darling. Your experiences with Freud have clarified your attitude to your sister.'

'Yes, there was no hate, only love. When I saw her my heart wanted to burst with joy – no envy, no malice . . . just tenderness.'

Mortimer kissed her hand, restoring it tenderly to her lap, and she only pretended to resume her reading, feeling warmed by his love, buttressed by his strength. What a tower of strength Mortimer had become; how rapidly he'd taken charge in this house full of women. She was only too aware that this feminine feeling of needing the support of a man was something she was unused to, something she'd rather despised. But since she'd fallen in love with him she'd realized that support in marriage was a mutual thing; that one gave and took, and that sometimes Mortimer needed her and at others she needed him. She'd needed him very much since the news about her father's illness had made them pack and leave Vienna immediately. He'd organized the whole

377

thing, taken control, and he'd also been so very good with Mother, assuming just the right degree of authority, tempered with understanding and compassion.

Mortimer too had a book in his hand, but his eyes did not see the printed pages. His mind was running over the events of the day, the impact Estella had made on him at the station, surrounded as she was by the men she had already enslaved on her journey and the bevy of porters who vied with one another to carry her bags. His memory of his sister-in-law had been of an attractive but subdued and depressed young woman carrying a baby which she did not want, dependent very much on the care of her sister, wounded in soul, still frightened and alarmed by events she did not understand and couldn't control.

Mortimer, considering the two sisters, thought how alike they were not only in looks, but also temperament, though each might have denied this. They were both rebels – yet each had chosen a very different path towards freedom. Lindsey had fought bitterly for a career, had put it before parents and, indeed, before her marriage. Both he and her parents had been the victims of her non-conformity. But he would not have had it otherwise, now that they were achieving so much together, finding new dimensions in themselves and in their marriage, new paths towards happiness, new fulfilment in their professions.

But Estella – what did he really think of Estella? Was he not, perhaps, shocked by her, in awe of her, maybe a little frightened of her? Whereas Lindsey was over-controlled, Estella seemed entirely swayed by her passions. He didn't know what he honestly felt about a woman who had lived as she did; yet he couldn't condemn her. She was too vital, exciting and alive. Estella's impact on him was such that she appeared to transcend sin, if sinful her life had been and it seemed it had. But it made him think, not for the first time, about what sin meant. If it meant evil and wickedness then he considered Estella neither evil nor wicked. He was, it is true, quite bowled over by her; yet at the same time protective towards her, anxious to help. He understood now, in view of the effect she had on him, this curious quality of vulnerability that made her a prey to men and hence, too, a hostage to fortune. Yet were they not all three, in various ways, hostages to fortune? He felt very much at one, at that moment, with his wife and his wife's turbulent sister.

As the door opened and Estella entered Lindsey and Mortimer got simultaneously to their feet, their books dropping on the floor. Estella looked pale but calm. Lindsey, reaching for her hand, led her to the sofa, and Mortimer picked up the books and put them on the table. Then he stood before them, his spectacles on the end of his nose, the blue eyes peering over the rims, bright yet benign, with the expression of a physician pondering a difficult but not yet fatal case.

'Mama has not forgiven me,' Estella said. 'She considers me a stranger and wishes I hadn't come. She has no love for me in her heart. She has had too much to bear alone with Father. I may never know either whether in his heart he has forgiven me.' Estella groped for her handkerchief, crumpling it in her hand, prepared for tears. 'It is what I deserve. I went to my room and looked at my face in the mirror. Do you know what I saw?' As both shook their heads she continued. 'I saw a woman who has taken too many wrong turnings in life. I thought that to make mistakes is one thing, but to be rejected by one's parents is possibly one of the worst things in life, because there is such a store of love for us in their hearts from when we were born. I have whittled away at that store and now it is empty. I thought, then, the only worse thing that could happen to me would be to be rejected by my daughter, and who knows when that will happen?'

She looked up at them, her limpid eyes rimmed with tears.

'*We* love you,' Lindsey pressed her hand. 'Mortimer and I; Ellen loves you too. The store is not empty there. We will make sure it never empties.'

Mortimer bent over her from his great height, conscious that Lindsey had included him in her love for her sister and grateful for it. Now they were truly one: he was family. He was now part of the Abercrombies, and had a large measure of responsibility for their welfare. The emotion engendered by this realization made him acutely aware of how lonely he had been, cut off at one time not only from the understanding of his own family but the love of his wife. Now he basked in her love and was invited to share it with her stricken family. He would. He pulled a chair up and sat down, facing the sisters, aware of how trustfully they regarded him. How much they depended on him.

'Your Mama is shocked. You must not have too much regard for her attitude, Estella. She is, after all, heart-broken about your father, and this sad turn in the family fortunes has made her bitter. She will take her grief out on you.' His cultured Bostonian accent, now almost completely Europeanized, made his voice sound authoritative, reassuring.

'Mortimer,' Estella looked at him gratefully, 'I know you are a kind man and you mean well; but Mama has wanted to say this to me for years. She means it, every word. How much she knows of my life in Paris I don't know; but she talks of my daughter without even asking after her welfare . . . '

'She *knows* she's with Charlotte,' Lindsey said gently, 'but thinks it is only because you can't afford to keep her.'

'Then what does she think I do?' Estella looked piercingly at her sister.

'I suppose she realizes you do have a . . . someone who protects and looks after you. I have told her nothing, I assure you, except that you've had some work on the stage. I have told her often how very much you regret all that has happened. But she blames me for much too.'

'Parents are very reluctant to move with the times,' Mortimer said. 'They have given us our problems too in America, Estella, which is why Lindsey and I are moving our home to New York. We think we shall have more chance there of living our lives undisturbed. You too have your own life to live away from your parents.'

'Have I?' Estella didn't disguise her bitterness. 'What life? Have I not lived my life away from my parents and what has it brought me? Dishonour; the loss of a daughter. Lacking courage and confidence to resume my career I assumed an easy life that has only brought me shame. Don't think now that I don't regret it. But it's too late for regrets. Meanwhile I have decided what to do . . . ' The colour had returned to her face and her eyes resumed their customary animation. Estella still unconsciously lived her life as though it were a continual role: one moment dejected, the next sanguine, the next elated, as the various scenes of the play she enacted in her mind (with herself in the starring part) proceeded. In a way she had never left the stage; she belonged on it in life as in art.

'I will stay here for a few days longer,' she said, 'not seeing Mama if she doesn't wish it. But I wish to talk to the lawyers. I want to know exactly what Father's liabilities are. I have property now in the south of France as well as Paris. If the sale of all I possess will cover Father's debts, then sell I shall, so that he can stay in the home he has lived in all his life and in his last days, years – we don't know what is left to him – have some modicum of peace.'

'But what will you do?' Mortimer regarded her frankly. 'Lindsey tells me that all you've done has been with your daughter's welfare in mind. Is it wise that you should be bankrupt as well as your father? He may not have long to live; surely your mother can be taken care of?'

'*If* it can be avoided I am determined the shame of

bankruptcy, added to my misdeeds, will not further stain our family name,' Estella replied. 'If I have sinned against my parents – and I have – this is the only small way I can think of making recompense to them.'

'But are you *that* wealthy . . . ' Lindsey stared rather disbelievingly at her.

'I have some wealth, more than you think. I have rather enjoyed business, you know. I study the *Bourse*.' Estella gave them a rather arch smile as though it were even more of a fall from grace to be familiar with the movements of the stock market than to entertain lovers in bed. 'But what there is, is theirs, or rather Father's creditors. Having wiped the slate clean I may start my life again; not as in the past. I will return to live in London – Mama may consent to let me come here after you've gone, but if she doesn't no matter – and see what opportunity there is for me on the English stage. At all events I want to be near Father – just to let him know, merely by my presence if nothing else, that I'm sorry.

'Then, if I can do that, maybe I'll be able to live with an easier conscience than I have now.'

CHAPTER EIGHTEEN

In the last two decades of the nineteenth century Europe was enjoying an unprecedented boom of peace and prosperity. True, the last major war had seen the end of the Empire in France, but otherwise it was a Europe governed by monarchs. A few sat on the throne with ease, but most with varying, and justified, degrees of trepidation. On the whole, however, monarchy did not feel itself intrinsically threatened despite what had happened in France in 1870, when the last Emperor of the French, nephew of the great Napoleon, had fled to England to be welcomed by that most secure monarch of all, Queen Victoria.

In Italy Umberto I continued the rule of the recently founded House of Savoy; in Spain Alfonso XIII of the restored House of Bourbons, had held sway since birth and was still a boy. In Russia Alexander III was probably less certain of dying in his bed after the assassination of his father, and in Berlin that aggressive grandson of Queen Victoria, Kaiser Wilhelm II, was plotting dreams of Prussian expansion. In the Austria of Dr Freud the Emperor Franz Josef II was building a Carmelite convent on the spot where his heir, Crown Prince Rudolf, had killed his mistress and then himself. And throughout the Austro-Hungarian Empire all sorts of minor royalty, dukes and princelings clung desperately to the notion that the institution of monarchy was an undying one, regardless of what others might have to say or what vicissitudes the politicians might bring.

In Paris that populist President Marie-Francois Carnot had opened the Universal Exposition of 1889, its site dominated by the enormous tower erected by Monsieur

Eiffel; at 984 feet it was the highest structure in the world. As with the Crystal Palace, which had been built in London for the Great Exhibition in 1851, there were many who had prophesied disaster for it but, like the house of glass, it survived.

These years also saw spectacular advances in science and medicine, innovations of all kinds in art and music, of incredible inventions such as the moving picture, the electric light (it had been installed in the Parc Monceau in 1889) and the development of that suspicious contraption which would eventually displace the horse, but still have its speed measured in horse power, the motor car.

Despite her remorse – she was, after all, not the first woman to repent a life of pleasure – Estella had been very much at home in the world of *La Belle Époque*. Gay, elegant Paris, the pleasure capital of the world, was most congenial to her flamboyant and extravagant temperament, which was pleasure-loving too. For as well as riches she loved art and music, the theatre, the latest novels and stimulating conversation with men and women of talent.

She also found the business world fascinating and studied the transactions of the *Bourse*, regarding the financial columns of the paper every morning in bed over her *petit déjeuner*. She enjoyed the art of making her own money grow. Some went into stocks and shares, some into property, much into jewels and antiques. In financial matters she was advised by an old friend of the Baron Philippe's, Roger Laurier, whom she occasionally repaid in kind though he was a cautious man very much in love with, and in awe of, his wife.

It was her trusted adviser and occasional lover who listened with horror as she explained, on her return to Paris, her plan to liquidate all her assets, realize every last franc she possibly could. Moreover, she told him, she was a changed woman; from henceforward she would

384

devote her life to repenting the past and caring for her old sick father. It was an extraordinary statement.

'But how did this come about, my dear Estella?' he enquired in his vast room on the Quai d'Orsay overlooking the Île St Louis. 'Have you been converted to religion?'

'Not at all.' She smiled serenely at him, the last word in beauty and fashion, exuding confidence and distinct sexual allure. 'I have merely decided to change my life. Circumstances forced me to look at myself and I did not like what I saw. It is that, rather than any religious conversion, which has made me ashamed of my past.'

'And your daughter? Did you not wish her to be a woman of wealth?'

'I wished more than *anything* to have my daughter with me. Maybe now, when I am no longer a *cocotte* and no longer rich, that wish may come true. However, I am going back to work. My mother has agreed, reluctantly, to let me live at home. My sister has returned to America and I think my mother would rather have one daughter there, than none at all. I am going to try and return to the English stage. Who knows, Roger, I may make another fortune yet.'

Her smile was so brave, so confident, that Roger Laurier felt only admiration for her. He felt even envious. He had misjudged her. He had imagined her too much in love with the life she led. No other woman he could think of would be willing to abandon such a life and, in attempting to save family honour, restore her own.

For a time, after the houses were sold – the Paris house as well as the beautiful villa overlooking Monte Carlo Bay that had been bought for her by a lovesick American, Eustace Chessington – Estella once again experienced a feeling of rootlessness. But this time it was worse than when she'd left Tom. There was no Lindsey, she and her husband having returned to the States and, although

Minnie Abercrombie had said her daughter could live at the house she had saved, it was only as a lodger.

Minnie had taken very little interest in the settlement of her husband's debts, other than to express relief, but to Lindsey not Estella, that they were to retain the family home. It was almost as though she considered it the duty of someone, no matter who, to come to their rescue. She made no enquiries as to details and maintained towards her younger daughter the same chilly remoteness, the same unforgiving stance she had shown from the beginning; remaining ungrateful and aloof.

It was Lindsey who smoothed things over, Mortimer who made all the arrangements, visiting the trustees and bankers and acting as go-between.

When the debts were settled the Abercrombies were seen to have very little left, but enough if they were careful. There was nothing to invest on a large scale, only small sums placed in gilt-edged securities that would yield a small income. By the standards of many people in England at that time, they were comfortably off, but by their former standards they were poor. Minnie had to make economies she objected to and, instead of thanking Estella, she blamed her for them. She pleaded with Lindsey to come back and live in England, but now Lindsey felt her duty was to Mortimer, who had already given up so much for her. Nor were they well off because Lindsey's income from her father was no more, and the Digbys had already told Mortimer it was time he supported himself and his wife. They had their own life to make together.

Lindsey and Mortimer did as much as they could to settle things before they left for New York, although in her heart Lindsey was full of foreboding for the future and the mutual happiness of her mother and sister.

Estella, however, saw little of her mother. Once her mind was made up she became very industrious, practical

386

and busy, travelling between London and Paris, attending sales of her possessions and finally, one poignant day, walking alone around the grand empty house in the Rue de Grenelle. For an hour or two she relived some of her triumphs there, her salons, her parties, her loves. Above all, she thought in retrospect, she had been secure. Now she felt that once again she was sailing out alone onto uncharted seas.

Charlotte permitted her a brief, unscheduled meeting with Ellen, who was called from her lessons with her governess to see her mother. After greeting each other they sat together on the sofa in the drawing room, and Estella explained that she was leaving Paris to resume her acting career in England.

Ellen worshipped her mother because she was not only so beautiful but also so remote. It was not that her personality was remote; it was warm and generous; but her absences made her seem remote and, as with many things in life, the less one sees of a person the more one sometimes desires them. The more difficult they are to know the more one wishes to. Ellen thought continually about her mother, speculating about where she lived, what she was doing, that mysterious woman who was always so elegant, dressed *à la mode*. She thought she must lead a very glamorous life away from the Parc Monceau which, for some reason, she couldn't share. That brief meeting in the Bois remained firmly in her mind – her mother like a breathtaking vision in yellow silk accompanied by a handsome man driving a dashing coupé.

Today because it was cold Estella wore a fur cape over her blue travelling dress and a little hat on her head, a toque with fur trimmings and a veil that almost covered her eyes. She removed the cape but not the hat and Ellen found she was mesmerized by the little pieces of fur which decorated the hat so that her eyes kept wandering from her mother's face to her head.

'Are they real?' she interrupted.

'What darling?' Estella, disconcerted, paused in her explanation and nervously touched her hair.

'The furs in your hat?'

'I thought you meant my hair! Yes the fur is quite real; it came from Alaska, or so my milliner says. Now Ellen have you been attending to what I've been saying?'

The little girl nodded gravely, her dark curls bobbing, a wistful far-away look in her eyes.

'May I not come with you, Mama? I would so like that.'

'I'm afraid not, Ellen.'

'But why may I not know where you live?'

Estella placed one of her long beringed hands tenderly over one of the tiny ones next to her.

'There are reasons my sweet which, one day, you will understand. In the meantime you must remain here with "Maman" who has been so good to you. You love her, don't you?'

'I love you better.' Ellen suddenly put her arms round her mother's waist and burst into tears. 'I don't understand why you leave me like this. I want to be with you always.'

Estella pressed her close, that little body that she had scarcely ever seen, never bathed or dressed or suckled at her breast as a mother should. God was punishing her for the treatment of her innocent baby so long ago, by making her love the child more now than she could ever have believed was possible. Hugging her, she vowed to herself that one day she would make reparation to God and Ellen, as she had to her parents. She would work so hard, become so famous that Ellen would be proud of her and, at last, she would not be ashamed to give her a home.

'Soon darling. If I am a very successful actress like Miss Terry, after whom you are named, I'll have a lovely home for us in London. But just now I have no money and I couldn't have you with me even if I wanted to and, believe me, I do. Will you pray hard for Mama that she succeeds?'

388

'I will.' Ellen, her eyes still glistening with tears, gazed up at her, thinking she would retain the memory of how lovely her mother looked at this moment all her life – her beauty tinged with sadness, an expression of melancholy in her large blue eyes.

The door opened and the governess came in, Mademoiselle d'Argent, a brisk but pleasant young woman from Limoges. She smiled at Estella and held out her hand.

'Come along now, Ellen, we must resume our lessons.'

'May I not stay a moment longer, mademoiselle . . .'

Estella rose and took her fur cape off a chair, shivering as she looked at the bare trees of the Parc Monceau, their branches swaying mournfully in the wind.

'*I* must go my darling. I've a train to catch. My bags are all ready and waiting in the *fiacre* outside.' She felt she must be as brisk and practical as Mademoiselle d'Argent or she would break down. She avoided Ellen's eyes as she put her cape round her shoulders and adjusted her hat in the mirror, pulling the veil over her eyes to hide the tears that had gathered there.

'Now darling. Goodbye . . .'

She stooped and kissed her and, taking Ellen's hand, led her firmly to the door. 'Come and see me off. Wave to me?'

Ellen tucked her hand in her mother's and Estella was aware how hot it was and sticky because her little girl was nervous and afraid, as she was, of being alone. Yet Ellen was not alone. Charlotte loved her. But who loved Estella? It was hard to realize that for so many years she had existed with desire taking the place of love; passion replacing deep affection.

Ellen came alone with her to the door and briefly they embraced again, Estella kissing the hot little hand and gently disengaging her daughter who clung to her. Her lips lightly brushed her forehead once more and then she turned quickly away, trusting that her veil obscured the despair in her eyes as she said goodbye to the only person she truly loved in the world and whom she was now leaving.

Shakespeare's *Henry VIII*, which Irving staged at the Lyceum in 1892, was one of the most lavish of all his productions. It had fourteen scenes of unparalleled magnificence which showed in authentic detail the Palace of Bridewell, royal apartments, the King's stairs at Westminster, gardens filled with real trees, shrubs and flowers and a London street complete with latticed-windowed Tudor buildings through which passed the triumphal bridal procession of Anne Boleyn, carried shoulder high above the crowds under a rich pallium. Seymour Lucas had seen to the correctness of every detail of Alice Comyn-Carr's costumes, which were based in turn on the etchings of Hans Holbein, court painter to the King.

It was a costly, gorgeous, lavish pageant as, Irving said, Shakespeare had intended it. Had he not, after all, burnt down the Globe Theatre in his attempt to make it realistic by letting off a live cannon? The production costs were nearly £12,000 and the theatre was packed during the whole of the seven months' run.

In addition to Irving's celebrated impersonation of the great Cardinal Wolsey, there was William Terriss – some said he was the most handsome man on the London stage – playing the King, Johnston Forbes-Robertson as the Duke of Buckingham and Ellen Terry's twenty-year old son Teddy as the Cardinal's secretary. But the talking point behind the scenes, the thing that kept the cast going throughout the long run, was the scarcely veiled hostility between Ellen Terry who played the ageing Queen Katharine, and young Violet Vanbrugh who gave her all as the lovely yet wilful Anne Boleyn who replaced Katharine in the affections of the King.

Ellen, although at the vulnerable age of forty-four, objected to being relegated to the role of a white-haired old lady, an opinion that was shared by a number of her male admirers including the critic Bernard Shaw, who told her she was wasting her talents. Ellen loudly informed everyone who would listen that she neither liked the play nor her part in it but, as usual, she played the Queen with the same sort of gusto that she gave to all her roles be they mad Lucy in *Ravenswood* or the noble Portia in *The Merchant*.

Her famous second-act scene with Henry –

> Sir, I desire you do me right and justice,
> And bestow your pity on me; for
> I am a most poor woman . . .

moved many in her audience to tears. Those who remained untouched by this, finally succumbed as she lay dying on a bier perched over by an unlikely band of angels who, to gasps of admiration from the audience, floated realistically down from on high clutching harps, lilies and assorted angelic paraphernalia. These included a chaplet of flowers which, once safely on the ground, they presented to the white-haired old Queen, nightly breathing her last to rapturous applause from the crowd:

> I was a chaste wife to my grave: embalm me,
> Then lay me forth; although unqueen'd, yet like
> A queen, and daughter to a king inter me.

For Estella too it was a magnificent spectacle, but her part, or parts, were as unrewarding to her as Terry considered hers.

She doubled up in the roles of Patience, woman to the old Queen with, admittedly, six lines to speak, and one of the dancing ladies in the scene where Henry chooses Anne Boleyn.

> . . . I have half a dozen healths
> To drink to these fair ladies, and a measure
> To lead 'em once again . . .

Yet it was work, it was the theatre and she was fortunate to be there. This time Miss Terry had not made a special visit to persuade her to join the company, but gave her a few minutes in her dressing room before the matinée. She immediately recalled Estella and, with her celebrated charm, could not have been more kind, but she pointed out that her years of absence from the stage were irretrievably lost. Acting was not something that improved with rest. Miss Terry even seemed doubtful about the possibility of engaging her, but Irving took to her immediately. He liked pretty women and Estella reminded him, although he did not tell her, of Ellen Terry when they had first worked together. Irving, with his mane of thick hair, firm mouth and high-bridged nose appealed to Estella too, and it was because of this rapport that he engaged her for the run of *Henry VIII*.

'Though not, alas, as Anne Boleyn,' he'd said, smiling at her regretfully. 'I may give you Patience which, at least, is a speaking part. Shakespeare was not very kind to women in *Henry VIII*.'

And, true to his promise, he gave her Patience, as well as one of the ladies who danced before the King.

As Patience, Estella had to take a curtain call, but slipped away as soon as she had removed her make-up and hung her clothes on the rail in the crowded dressing room she shared with the rest of the supporting cast. Every night the routine was the same and she was one of the first to leave by the stage door and look for a cab in the busy streets of Covent Garden. Sometimes she had to walk to Bloomsbury or farther before she found one, hurrying through the crowds that flocked from Drury Lane and Covent Garden Opera House, scurrying along the crowded back streets packed with theatregoers, urchins, pickpockets, and men about town looking for a woman with whom to pass the night.

One evening she left the theatre as usual, dodging past those who thronged the stage door in the hope of seeing one of the stars. Suddenly she felt a hand on her arm and tried brusquely to brush it away without looking because this was not an unusual occurrence, some man hopefully mistaking her for a woman of the streets.

'F—ella!'

She turned, startled, and stared at the dark, familiar face lit by the light of the street lamp.

'Rayner Brook . . . ' she paused, lost for words.

'May I walk with you?'

She felt unnerved by the unexpected encounter, frightened without knowing why.

'Why certainly you may walk if you care to. I'm looking for a cab to take me home.'

'Then let me help you find one.'

'I'm in a hurry.'

'We'll try and find one quickly. May I?' He took her arm and hurried along with her, guiding her through the throng. 'I've waited for you for several nights outside the stage door. I've seen the performance six times. Do you go out by another exit?'

'No, but I slip away as soon as I can. It's hard to find a cab. Why did you choose this way to see me, Rayner?'

'Because I thought you might not receive me at your home. I've only been back in London a short time. Why did you leave Paris without a word to me two years ago? I tried desperately to find out where you'd gone.'

'Surely you know the reason.' She darted across Bow Street, dodging through the traffic.

'What reason? There was someone else?'

She didn't reply but turned into Broad Court opposite the Opera House, walking rapidly past the dwellings and

393

into Drury Lane. A hackney passed, followed by another which Rayner attempted to hail, but both were occupied. They stood on the pavement looking at the backs of the cabs and Rayner shook his head.

'Do you *ever* get a cab at this time of night?'

'Sometimes I have to walk half-way home. I usually get one round about Camden Town if all else fails.'

'Isn't it unwise to be alone and abroad so late at night?'

'What can I do about it? I'm a working actress.'

'I hear you paid off all your father's debts.'

'Yes and incurred even more opprobrium from my mother's friends. "How *could* she do it?" they asked. "She must have been a woman of the streets".'

'They don't think that. They think you had a very wealthy lover.'

'Still, a creature of shame.'

'Estella, don't torment yourself.'

They were now walking along Queen Street, past restaurants full of people eating after the theatre. Rayner tugged at her arm. 'Won't you eat with me? Aren't you hungry?'

'I'm starving. I usually eat at home.'

'Let's eat now. Or will your mother worry?'

Estella grimaced. 'My mother cares not what I do nor what happens to me, nor what time I get home. I usually sit with my father anyway. Sometimes he wakes up and likes to know I'm there.'

'But he can't speak?'

'He is a little better, and he does understand. We just sit there holding hands and I tell him about the theatre. I think he enjoys it but, yes, it is a one-way conversation. He can only nod his head and show in his eyes that he understands.'

'It must be a very lonely life for you, Estella.'

'It's certainly different.' She stopped and, disengaging her arm, faced him. What was she hurrying away from?

Him? Why? He had gone out of his way to see her and, as she looked into his eyes, she saw only hope and friendship, no reproach. Yet he had every reason to reproach her for the way she'd treated him. 'If you like, I'll eat with you; but we mustn't be long.'

He seized her arm again, and, after studying one or two menus, they entered one of the less crowded restaurants, slightly dowdy but pleasantly small and intimate, the tables covered with crisp linen cloths, the dainty gilt chairs well worn with red plush seats. A black-coated waiter, his few sparse black hairs carefully plastered across an otherwise gleaming bald pate, hurried up and offered them a table next to the window. As he took her cloak and held back a chair for her Estella gratefully sat down, aware now how tired she was as well as hungry. Rayner expansively asked the waiter to bring a bottle of champagne and, at last, she smiled at him.

'Are you now a man of wealth?'

'This is a celebration. At last I've got you to myself.' He leaned across the table and stared hard at her. 'You're still very beautiful, Estella. Your presence on the stage almost eclipses Terry's!'

'Oh come!' She blushed, the colour enhancing her looks, her deep blue eyes, her wide mouth painted red. She still had some greasepaint and make-up on her face, and little wisps of blond hair adhered to her brow. He thought she looked adorable.

'You're completely wasted where you are.'

'I'm lucky to get a part. They didn't really want me or need me. Mr Irving was particularly kind to take me. I had to tell him something of my story, but not all.' Her blush deepened. 'There was no need to tell him everything.'

Rayner lowered his eyes too. He was only too aware of her vulnerability, her reluctance to be questioned about the past. The waiter brought the champagne and opened it with a flourish, pouring it into the twin glasses from a great height.

'An occasion?' he enquired kindly.

'Of a sort.' Rayner took his glass and raised it towards Estella. 'To you. Success.'

As he drank she raised hers and when he'd finished she said, 'And to you, for understanding. I was very bad to you in Paris and I'm sorry. There was no one else; but there were difficulties. I often regretted the way I behaved towards you. But I behaved very strangely in those days altogether. What did you do, after Paris?'

'I went back to America. I've been restless here. The managers don't understand my plays; they say they're too modern. You know Shaw, the music and drama critic? He's read them and he likes them. He says I'm like Ibsen, but I think I'm better.'

'Miss Terry *detests* Ibsen! You should hear her on the subject.'

Estella could almost feel the cool champagne slipping through her body and she began to relax. Rayner Brook was still very attractive, his pale face and dark eyes surmounted by his untidy black hair. His velvet suit and blue bow tie proclaimed him some sort of artist, a writer or a painter. Quite a few people were surreptitiously looking at them as if they stood out in the crowd. Rayner had the air of a man who'd lived hard and, perhaps, loved well. He'd known suffering, and traces of this too showed on his face and in the sombre light of his beautiful velvety brown eyes. He'd travelled a lot and struggled with failure, as she had. Maybe success would elude them both, and their fate was to be for ever cast in the roles of those who had not quite made it in the world. Yet they had much in common; they were fighters. He seemed to be bursting with energy and she knew that, despite her weariness induced by conditions at home, on stage she was known for her vitality and professionalism. Irving was pleased with her and had already promised her better parts.

But, more than that, they'd known each other for years. They were old familiars, friends, past colleagues on the stage and, in this hard life of hers, it was good to feel at ease with someone she had known for so much of her life. She settled more easily into her chair, aware of a renewed intimacy between them.

The waiter reappeared with the menu and they ordered: fresh prawns and rare roast beef. Rayner poured more champagne, sensing the change in her manner.

'Miss Terry would be marvellous in Ibsen; but so would you. You would, however, be much better in the play I'm presently writing.'

'I could never leave the security of the Lyceum, Rayner, though it's kind of you to think of me.'

'But this play is written especially for you. I've watched you on the stage at night and, my head full of ideas, I've gone home and written all the following day. It's nearly finished. Couldn't you take a chance with me, Estella?'

'Would Mr Irving like the play?'

'I doubt it very much. Irving is a great actor but he's so conventional, so safe. Apart from Shakespeare he's quite happy with the rubbish other playwrights put out as drama these days. You have to reach out in this world, Estella, and grab your chances. We've missed so many. I have a real feeling that this play could make you and, perhaps, me.'

'Is there a part for you too?'

'Of course,' he smiled at her. 'As your lover. We both, in the play, defy convention.'

'Then it sounds as though it will not be successful.'

The waiter returned with a dish of prawns, plates and finger bowls. He fussed about, exclaiming on the quality of the prawns, and when they were served Estella began hungrily to prise the shells away from the flesh.

'These look marvellous! I didn't mean to be hurtful about your play, but I need money.'

'We'll find money. There's a new independent theatre group started by a man called Grein which is supported by Hardy and Meredith as well as Shaw, Pinero and Henry Jones. They produced *Ghosts* at the Royalty last year.'

'I heard about the fuss,' Estella murmured, sprinkling her prawns with pepper. 'The critics were very cruel to it. I believe the management of the Royalty told them they were unlikely to be given the threatre again.'

'That won't happen to me,' Rayner said loftily. 'But believe me, Ibsen will be a great man and so shall I.'

'When can I read your play?'

'Very soon.'

'And the part is for *me*, and no one else?' She smiled, reminding him of the time he'd given the lead in his play to another. 'That started my acting career. I have you, really to thank for that.'

'And you'll thank me again,' Rayner said unabashed. 'I promise you that.'

She was intrigued and she asked him about the part but he wouldn't tell her. Instead he talked entertainingly about America and his travels. Then they reminisced about the old days in Manchester and the north; and thus an hour or two slipped by as they ate good food and finished the champagne. When they left they were the last people in the restaurant. The waiters were already removing the white cloths from the tables and putting the chairs on top of them, ready for the cleaners who would come at dawn in the morning. Their smiling waiter, a little frayed now, saw them to the door, pocketing his tip as he let them out.

'Good night, sir, madam. Do call again.' Then he shut the door and thankfully hung up the sign saying: CLOSED.

Outside the street was almost deserted and Rayner tucked his arm through Estella's, guiding her towards Kingsway where they were now easily able to hail a cab.

'Father will be worried.' Estella sank back in her seat, feeling slightly drunk but very happy.

'You sit up with your father all night?'

'No, just an hour or two while I unwind after the play. But tonight I'm very unwound. Thank you, Rayner.'

As she looked at him he took her hand, holding it lightly as the cab jogged up towards Camden Town, passing St Pancras Church, Euston Square and the station.

'I'm glad we're together,' he whispered. 'Don't run away from me this time, will you?'

'I've nowhere to run except to the Lyceum,' she chuckled. 'If I ran away from that it would be the end.'

'I love you, Estella.'

She'd been half expecting him to say something because of the mood the evening had engendered between them. He would tell her he loved her and ask her to go to bed. She'd been expecting it. He knew about her reputation and thought it would be easy. Even the boldest lover had to make some sort of endearment before coming out with the proposition. It was not an unfamiliar situation in which to find herself. She wasn't even offended. But she knew how to deal with it too. She'd had years of experience.

'You don't love me, Rayner,' she briskly replied. 'You want to sleep with me.'

He withdrew his hand and moved up the seat to the corner by the window, looking out.

'That's very cruel, Estella.'

'I'm afraid I've grown cynical about men. I know what they want. It was a nice evening and this sort of thing usually follows it.'

'Don't you think anyone can love you without wanting that? Aren't you sure enough of yourself to recognize any real emotion?'

'*Now* who's being unfair?' She glanced at him sharply, but his profile was still turned away from her.

'You're not, are you Estella?' He turned and looked into

her eyes. 'You think your beauty is like a shop front which men only want to enter for what's inside. You are beautiful and I do want you; I don't tell people I care for them lightly; and certainly I don't say it if I just want to go to bed with them.'

Estella stared at him for a moment or two while it dawned on her that he was serious. He looked so hurt and withdrawn that she half expected him to stop the carriage and get out. She felt rather bewildered and not a little ashamed of herself, so she answered him slowly.

'I'm sorry. I'm very conscious of my past. I've had numerous offers from men; they called it "love", but meant something else.'

'You should know me. I'm not a stranger, after all. It's not a thing I'd easily say to a woman I'd known for years, and known well, unless I meant it. I intended to tell you in Paris if you'd given me the chance. When I heard you were back in London I was so excited I couldn't sleep. I didn't know how to approach you for fear of being turned away. I've watched you for nights on the stage like some lovelorn schoolboy. Now I feel ridiculous.'

'I'll say it again: I'm sorry. I really am.'

'I thought you felt something tonight for me too, or did I mistake the looks you gave me. Were they merely those of a professional whore?'

Estella hit him across the face but he caught her in his arms and pressed his lips to hers. She experienced such shock that at first she had no chance to struggle, and then she didn't want to. She'd been kissed by many men, but there was something about this first embrace with Rayner that left her astounded, that left her wanting more. But his expression remained savage and, seizing hold of her shoulders, he shook her.

'How much did *that* kiss cost?'

His words stung. Before she could reply he kissed her mouth again, and she half drowned in the sweetness of a totally new sensation. Then, as he kissed her chin and her throat and between her breasts, she murmured slyly into his hair: 'It will cost you a great deal if you go any farther.' Rayner released her, shook himself and smoothed back his hair with both hands.

'I feel terribly ashamed,' he muttered.

'And well you might,' Estella said reprovingly, attempting to draw her cloak more tightly round her neck like some decorous young maiden who, rather late in the day, remembers her modesty. 'To refer to *me* as a professional whore is insulting . . . '

'I didn't mean . . . '

'But you *did* mean. It is evidently at the back of your mind. I ask you, are there not many respectable married women who, in fact, exchange their bodies not for love, but for status, comfort, security and wealth – far far baser than ever I was. I have always worn my heart on my sleeve, being too susceptible to men, too honest with them and, I think, not unattractive to them.'

She lowered her eyes, glancing at Rayner as she did, and he took her hand and drew it to his lips.

'You know how attractive, you witch.'

Impulsively she encircled his head with her arm, drawing his cheek against hers. To his consternation he felt it wet with tears.

'My darling, what is it?' He held her face away from his, staring at it in dismay. Her soulful, tear-filled eyes gazed back at him.

'But I *was* weak, Rayner. I am not proud of my past. That's why I ran away from you. I'll confess, I was ashamed. I preferred that you remembered me as a young actress, and not as a . . . '

'Shh, don't say it.' He drew her once more into his arms, only this time more tenderly, but with no less passion, murmuring endearments and telling her again and again that he loved her.

401

The cab was beginning to climb Highgate Hill and the driver called for instructions, which Rayner gave him, leaning out of the window. Then he sat back and clasped her hand.

'What are we to do? You know I love you. I've written you dozens of letters in the past two years and torn them all up. I tried so hard to look for you when you left Paris, but no one would tell me where you'd gone. That's how I found out,' he paused and looked at her anxiously, 'a bit more about you.'

Did he know about Ellen? And if he didn't, what would he think when he did?

She looked at him speculatively, not quite knowing what to say. 'You found out I was a *cocotte*?'

'I found out that . . . well, yes, but people spoke of you with admiration. They said you were very selective, extremely discreet.'

'And it didn't deter you?'

'No, not a bit. I mean, I'm glad now that you've given it up. I wouldn't like to one of a number.'

'There were never a *number*,' Estella said a little haughtily, 'only one at a time. But please don't let's talk about it now.'

'I won't ever talk about it again.'

Estella looked at him and, placing a finger against his lips, kissed it.

'Yes you will, when we quarrel. You'll accuse me of being a tramp, because you'll always have it on your mind.'

'You talk as though we had a future.' He leaned towards her.

'I think I'd like that; but we both need time.'

'We've *plenty* of time now,' Rayner said eagerly. 'I have no plans to go away again.'

'And nor have I.'

'Then?'

She kissed him gently on the lips and, as the cab stopped outside her house, she opened the door before he had the chance. She stepped onto the pavement and saw that the lamp was still on in her father's room.

'Then we'll see. First show me your play!' Her tone was teasing, but her expression solemn. She blew him a kiss and darted through the garden gate.

CHAPTER NINETEEN

This is the year for fallen women. (wrote the theatre critic of *The Pall Mall Gazette*) After the scandal of Arthur Wing Pinero's *The Second Mrs Tanqueray,* which Mr Alexander put on at the St James's in May, Rayner Brook has startled us with *A Woman's Wiles* which we saw last night at the Lincoln Theatre in Kingsway. Yet the star of this play, Estella Abercrombie, is no Mrs Patrick Campbell. That is not to say she is inferior – she is in every way her peer. But whereas Mrs Pat's interpretation of Paula Tanqueray makes us feel the shame of that woman when confronted with her past, Miss Abercrombie has no shame at all. She shocks us all with her boldness. Far from bowing down under the weight of her misdeeds her Lilah Martin actually seems proud of them. What makes this play unique in contemporary drama is that we are shown a woman learning from her past mistakes to establish for herself a happier, more independent life. She gets the better of them, not they of her. In this play there is no moralizing, no final tragic ending. Lilah Martin doesn't crawl away to shoot herself as Paula does; but, as the curtain falls, she is left alone on the stage, alive, confident – looking forward, with apparent equanimity, to the rest of her life which may be no distinct improvement on what has gone before.

Whether we agree with Mr Brook's account of *A Woman's Wiles* or not; whether we think she deserves to suffer, the play is, in its way, a triumph because, for once, it has no clear moralistic message. Whether we approve of the sentiments thus proclaimed for two hours upon the London stage or not, the impact leaves us breathless. It also makes us unsure of our previously held values. It leaves us thinking.

Rayner Brook threw down the paper on top of a pile already resting on the floor at his feet. He sat for a moment with his eyes closed and then, stooping, he gathered all the papers in his arms and raced upstairs, flinging open the door of his bedroom and throwing them on top of the recumbent figure in the bed.

'We've done it, we've done it, we've done it, Estella.' He bent down and shook her. 'Wake up, my darling, we have a great success! I told you we would. Estella, wake up.'

Estella, who had not gone to bed until three, lay with her face to the pillow and opened her eyes. She could feel the added weight on her body, and the rough edge of a newspaper tickled the nape of her neck. Rayner bent down and kissed her and, turning over, she reached up for him and pulled him down beside her, staring with some stupefaction at the papers which began to fall off the bed. She was still half-asleep.

'Estella, the reviews are marvellous. Not only Archer and Shaw, and Yates of the *Saturday Review*, but all the others except Clement Scott, who is as sniffy as he usually is about anything he doesn't understand. My darling, you've done it. *We've* done it. They say you're a new star and I'm the English Ibsen. Now, what do you think of that?'

Estella raised herself on her pillows and, releasing Rayner, rubbed the sleep from her eyes, gazing disbelievingly at him.

'They *all* say it?'

'Yes, yes, except Scott but he's of no account. I told you the audience loved it, my darling; but these reviews . . .' his arms swept over the papers that still lay on the bed. 'I've never read anything like them. They compare you to Mrs Pat, and there is even a flattering comparison with Terry.'

Estella slumped back on the pillows and stared at the ceiling. Although the applause at the end of the play had been rapturous and she and Rayner had taken curtain after curtain, she had still dreaded the verdict of the critics. They could have killed the play, as they still tried, with varying degrees of success, to kill Ibsen. Rayner had wanted her to see the papers before they went to bed after a late-night celebration with the rest of the small cast at Rules, but she was too frightened. Critics had damned plays applauded by enthusiastic audiences before.

'I'm so pleased for you, Rayner,' she said at last. 'It is your triumph too, my dear, and how well you deserve it.'

She gently stroked his face, noting the lines that the struggles of the past year had etched more deeply on his brow and at each side of his mouth. At first they had been able to find no backer for the play; even the Independent Group, chastened by their misfortunes with Ibsen, wouldn't look at it. Mr Irving, the first one to see it, had said it was the greatest rubbish it had ever been his misfortune to read, and Ellen Terry, at her most gracious, had warned Estella about the consequences of forsaking the Lyceum to appear in a bad play by a relatively unknown, and so far comparatively unsuccessful, author. Both Irving and Terry had indicated that if she left them she might, to their regret, not be hired to play for the Lyceum Company again.

But Shaw had liked the play and so had William Archer, Shaw's friend and fellow critic. However, this was not enough to secure backing, because they espoused so many lost causes connected with the new drama. If he did succeed in putting it on, Shaw and Archer warned him, Rayner should use an established actress such as the American Elizabeth Robins, who had played with Rayner years before with the Boston Museum Company, or the gifted Janet Achurch, despite her luckless partnership with her husband Charles Charrington. Charrington always seemed an awful warning to Rayner because, despite his energy and talents, with him one failure succeeded another.

In March the Lyceum company had appeared at Windsor before the Queen and her Court and Her Majesty had spoken kindly afterwards to Estella. Irving promised her the role of Jessica in *The Merchant* in their forthcoming American tour.

'My dear Estella,' Miss Terry had cautioned her yet again, 'you have ruined your career before on account of your emotional nature. You are too headstrong, my dear. If you wish to succeed on the stage, and I think you may yet, you must put your career first before love. Career first, love second.'

But, once again, Estella let her heart rule her head. Even Shaw thought it might be the end of her, and warned them that they would be like the Charringtons, perpetually hard up, talented but luckless. After all, neither of them was in the first spring of youth.

Then came the success of *The Second Mrs Tanqueray* which had a theme so similar to Rayner's play that he almost despaired. The only difference was, as the critics noted, that in his play an immoral life was not equated with vice and, instead of the pistol which finished poor Paula Tanqueray, Lilah Martin was given a new chance in the form of her understanding lover, Peter Osborn, played by Rayner Brook.

In their case real life and drama were almost interchangeable, and in *A Woman's Wiles* they re-enacted the story of their own lives. Lilah Martin, after a disastrous marriage, goes to Paris where she acquires lovers and riches as a member of the *demi-monde*. The illness and death of her father makes her ashamed of her life and she is about to give in to despair when her old lover, Peter Osborn, returns to tell her that life is worth living and, by learning from her past mistakes, there is a future for them both. The only point where fiction parted from truth was that in the play the heroine was not an actress, but a well brought up, rather literary, young woman of leisure.

Getting the play put on was not the first of their difficulties. Getting Estella to agree to play the story of her life was a formidable hurdle which Rayner, only with difficulty and the force of his real-life love, was able to overcome. Estella was at first affronted and indignant that

407

he had used so little of his imagination for the drama with which he finally hoped to make his name on the stage, that he had used her story for his own ends. For this he was asking her to give up a tour of America after appearing at Windsor in front of the Queen.

But by that time she not only returned his love; they were lovers. He had rented a house in Doughty Street in Bloomsbury, and Estella spent as much of her time there as she did at Highgate, where, since the death of her father the Christmas before, she had felt barely tolerated.

In agreeing to play Lilah Martin and forsake her career at the Lyceum Estella had no doubt about the risks she was taking. She was once again openly living with a man to whom she was not married; neither of them had any money, and they were seeking to join the ranks of all the unknowns who jostled for position on the London stage. Most of them failed. It seemed to everyone who knew them very apparent that Rayner and Estella would fail too.

And then to the rescue had come Harriet Leadbetter, that old love of Rayner's who was now a widow and had the considerable fortune left to her by her husband Jack with which to do as she liked. She had a flat in London and she'd renewed her acquaintance with Estella after seeing her as Patience at the end of the run of *Henry VIII*. Estella led to Rayner, and Harriet proved herself the friend that she had been in the past. She was undemanding, supportive, eager and able to lease the small Lincoln Theatre, on their behalf – although it was considered almost as unlucky as the Novelty where the Charringtons had had a critical success but a financial disaster with *A Doll's House*, which they blamed largely on the dingy theatre in Great Queen Street. However, Harriet spared no expense in refurbishing the Lincoln, which was conveniently, if not fashionably or centrally, placed between Lincoln's Inn Fields and Kingsway. There had been great women managers in the past and she saw herself as another. She threw herself with typical flair and energy into her new career. In case *A Woman's Wiles* failed she had laid plans to put on a succession of drawing room comedies which would be sure to draw the crowds, and in which she promised herself some small, interesting parts.

Rayner and Estella breakfasted together that morning surrounded by papers. Harriet arrived at noon and was invited to have breakfast but she declared she had eaten it at seven. Nothing – late nights or even sleepless ones – tired Harriet. She was still a handsome woman, despite ths fact she was in her fifties, and had arrived in her own carriage accompanied by her lover Sergei, whom she had picked up when he danced in London with a Russian ballet company. Sergei far preferred the luxury of life with Harriet to the rigours of the ballet. Besides, he had theatrical ambitions himself and had assisted Jonathan Moore, who had carried out the redecoration to the Lincoln and designed the sets for *A Woman's Wiles*.

Sergei was a small neat man of about twenty-eight who was willing, polite and anxious to please but virtually inarticulate. His command of the English language was poor. He also liked his food and eagerly accepted a second breakfast, sitting down to tuck into chops, sausages and eggs with Rayner. Estella toyed, as usual at breakfast time, with tea and toast.

They read the papers again and Sergei began carefully to cut out the clippings to preserve for posterity. Harriet declared that she would give Rayner the most expensive blank book for his press cuttings that money would buy, bound in real leather.

It was a happy time. Rayner opened champagne and they toasted one another until they were all slightly tipsy. Estella looked pale but radiant in a pale gold robe that Rayner had given her as a thirtieth birthday present the previous March, which also marked the occasion of her appearance before the Queen. Rayner had hoped then that it would be a talisman of success, and a talisman it had proved to be.

'Estella mustn't tire herself out or have too much to drink,' Harriet said anxiously. 'We want a good performance tonight too.'

'I shall sleep all afternoon,' Estella replied. 'I had very little last night.'

'But, my darling, I *told* you at Rules it would be all right.' Regardless of her warning to Estella, or, perhaps, because of it, Harriet felt free to accept more champagne. 'I saw the way the critics rushed out to file their reviews. If they intend to blast a play they always linger overlong at the bar to fortify themselves though, heaven knows, some seem to get fortification enough merely by being unpleasant. I expected Clement Scott to write as he did in the *Telegraph*. I think he's in the pay of Irving. Talking about pay,' she sipped her champagne and looked at Rayner and Estella, whose hands were linked across the table, 'do you realize you will now be able to afford to get married?'

Estella sharply withdrew her hand from Rayner's. 'Married?'

'Married, my dear. Is it not what you intend?' She looked about her ostentatiously, the osprey feathers in her hat waving gracefully, as though to remark on the size of the house which was sufficient to accommodate two, perhaps more.

'If Rayner and I intended to get married, Harriet, we should have done so before now. We did not need success or fortune to make us marry.'

'But I can't understand why you don't marry, now that your father is no longer with us.' Harriet sighed with exaggerated sympathy – she had never even met Estella's father – and pulled the fox fur draped across one shoulder closer to her neck as though to conceal her insincerity.

410

Although a big fire blazed in the grate it was October and very cold. In fact it had been a good time to open her new theatre, because the bitter evenings made Londoners wish for somewhere warm to be entertained at night. Like Irving at the Lyceum, she had enlarged the pit, which was proving very popular with the masses. 'You could be one of the most famous theatrical partnerships of all time – marriage is no bar to that, as the Bancrofts and Kendals have shown us, not to name a host of others alive and dead. Besides, you *need* marriage to make you respectable.'

Estella rose abruptly from the table, drawing her robe with its long train in a wide arc around her legs in a gesture that would have been more suited to the stage.

'I'm going to have my bath now. Shall we see you tonight at the theatre, Harriet?'

'Of course, darling, no one could stop me,' Harriet blew her a kiss and smiled. 'Pray don't be angry about what I said. I only meant well, *and* I'm planning a lavish party to celebrate your success. Depend upon it, I will have the Prince of Wales there too.'

Harriet watched Estella go out and then turned to Rayner. 'Why, pray, are you so much against marriage?'

'*I'm* not against marriage. Estella is,' Rayner said shortly, drinking coffee and buttering a piece of toast while Sergei and Harriet emptied the bottle of champagne between them. 'But we have had so much on our minds I didn't want to bring that up.'

'But I can't understand it. Does she not *love* you?'

'Of course she loves me! I am the most fortunate of men. Do we not live together, well . . . most of the time? Marriage has nothing to do with love, as Estella is fond of telling me. I think she feels we will love better if we don't marry.'

'Oh she *is* a modern woman!'

'Yes she is,' Rayner replied defensively. 'She is very

411

modern. She has had a very unhappy marriage, don't forget . . . '

'That was *no* marriage!'

'Well, legally it may not have been; but to her it was. She has told me often how much she loved Tom, to be so bitterly hurt by him. Even though it happened long ago the memory is fresh in her mind. She says she wants to be free.'

As he was talking Harriet was peering through her lorgnette at the cuttings handed her one after the other by Sergei, accepting them from him with a kindly smile as though he were a little dog. Indeed there was something of the pet about Sergei, who, trained for the ballet, was a small light man with neat moustaches, his sleek black hair parted in the centre. Were he not a ballet dancer, some thought he might have made an admirable ringmaster in the circus, for there was much of the Latin temperament about him, though he'd been born in St Petersburg.

'Hmm,' Harriet murmured, 'they're very good, Sergei darling, aren't they?' Then she let her lorgnette drop and looked frankly at Rayner.

'Rayner dear, yesterday you and Estella were unknown. Today you are better known. Tomorrow you may be famous. Have you thought of the effect on her reputation if it is known that you and she live in sin?'

'I think Estella doesn't care about reputations.'

'Oh, but she will. Miss Terry cared enough to marry again in order to give a name to her bastard children.'

'We have no bastard children.'

'No that is *not* the point, Rayner. Appearances *are* important which is why I referred to Miss Terry. I know people live in sin all the time, especially theatrical ones, but not quite so openly. Although one *supposes* an affair between Irving and Terry no one is *sure*. For years and years they have maintained the utmost discretion. But you two live together under the same roof . . . '

412

'Officially Estella still lives with her Mama.'

'Officially or not, in actual fact she lives here. London may accept your play; but I don't know that it will accept your living openly as you are. The gossips, hitherto indifferent to Estella, will now become interested in her. She will be photographed and famous like Langtry, Sarah Campbell, Terry and the rest. You have succeeded with a scandalous play, Rayner dear. I beg you not to tempt fortune with a scandalous life. Try and persuade dearest Estella, for all our sakes, to walk to the altar with you and put official blessing, if not that of God, on your union.'

But, despite Harriet's well-meaning efforts, the last thing Estella had on her mind was marriage. At thirty her star had risen and in the next three years she became the darling of London. Managements who had previously ignored her sought to woo her away from Harriet Leadbetter. Beerbohm Tree tried to persuade her to do a Shakespeare season with him at the Haymarket. Johnston Forbes-Robertson, with whom she had acted in *Henry VIII*, wanted her to do a short season with him, touring the provinces, and promised her all the leading roles.

But Estella could not be wooed. She said she owed her success to Harriet Leadbetter and Rayner Brook and with them she would stay, happy to let them share in her ever increasing aura of fame.

Lindsey put down the letter and sat for a moment looking out of the window of her pleasant consulting room, which overlooked the garden of the house she and Mortimer had shared happily together now for nearly six years. The room was furnished in contemporary style, but the major feature was the analytical couch with the comfortable chair at its head, a tradition started by Freud and which all his disciples adopted.

By the spring of 1897 Freud was still little known, even

413

in Vienna; but his adherents were increasing and in America the Digbys were numbered among the foremost. Mortimer combined his practice as a psychotherapist with a lectureship in neurology at Columbia University, because in those early days psychoanalytic techniques had not yet had the success they were later to achieve. The analysis of unconscious motivation, especially the sexual origins not only of much mental and nervous illness but of much behaviour considered normal, was still regarded with the gravest suspicion by the conventional medical world, who used a number of unflattering words to describe it. But among those who welcomed these methods, many of which were not new, were many respected physicians such as Morton Prince, James Jackson Putnam and William James, all of whom the Digbys had known in Boston. It was Morton Prince who had founded the *Journal of Abnormal Psychology* in Boston, in which the word 'psychoanalysis' first appeared in America in 1896.

But Lindsey, with her singlemindedness, ignored the violent criticism that the evolving methods of treating neuroses and those suffering from emotional disorders attracted and would continue to attract for generations. She had living proof of the success of Freud's methods and, with her annual visit to Vienna, renewed contact with the Master and underwent with him a refresher course of analysis to bring herself up to date.

Despite the vigorous opposition of the Digby family, who expected them to settle down to pursue conventional medicine and, hopefully, produce a conventional family, she and Mortimer had moved to New York on their return home in the autumn of 1891. Lindsey had persuaded Mortimer that there was no hope for them or their marriage in Boston – a marriage that was still fragile, but growing in strength. Once back in the bosom of his family they would be subject to the old pressures, which would prise them apart again. Mortimer was realistic enough, and had sufficient faith in his wife, to agree. But it was hard, because Boston was the centre of many cultural activities, of much enlightened medical practice, as well as the place where he had his roots.

But roots had to be dug up and re-examined – they both knew that then. New York was an exciting place too, with Columbia and a number of large hospitals and small specialist clinics. It was the home of many foreigners, which gave it a much more cosmopolitan air than Boston. The international flavour reminded Lindsey of Paris and London, and she had started her own practice there in the spring of 1892 as soon as they were settled in Washington Square. At first she attracted few patients, like her master in Vienna who was experiencing what he would later call his years of 'splendid isolation', shunned by most of his colleagues and misunderstood, if not actually reviled, by those who knew of his work. Like Freud, Lindsey was forced to take patients suffering from all kinds of normal physical maladies, and became part general physician and part psychotherapist. She corresponded regularly with Freud and the other enlightened doctors she and Mortimer had met in Vienna, Paris and Berlin; and Freud sent her early copies of his works which she read in German.

In 1893, together with Josef Breuer, Freud had published *A Preliminary Communication on the Psychical Mechanism of Hysterical Phenomena*, upon which William James, Professor of Psychology at Harvard and former neighbour of the Digbys in Cambridge, had commented favourably in the first issue of *The Psychological Review* of 1894. This had initiated a correspondence between Lindsey and Professor James which had developed from an acquaintanceship into friendship. In 1895, again with Breuer, Freud had published his *Studies in Hysteria* and these formed the basis of a lecture in the same year by Dr Robert Edes to the Massachusetts Medical Society, on 'nervous invalidism'. Also in that year, 1895, Dr Bronis-law Onuf, a neurologist in the New York State Hospital and colleague of Mortimer's, had abstracted Freud's *The Neuro Psychoses of Defence* for the *Journal of Nervous and Mental Disease.*

Lindsey felt that she was as much on a voyage of exploration as her patients. In this journey, often an uncomfortable one, she shed many of her formerly held truths, much of her dogmatism, most of the authoritarian airs of the physician trained in the conventional schools. It was later to be said of Freud that he became more authoritarian, more certain of his beliefs; but Lindsey didn't. She found she questioned everything.

Her own experiences in Vienna; the startling revelations of her violent but hitherto unconscious desires and fears, suppressed for so many years, had made her more receptive to what, in the old days, she might have considered weaknesses in others. But no longer. In this process, in her continuing struggles with herself, she became, so imperceptibly that only those close to her noticed it, gentler. Although she had never lacked compassion she grew more understanding, particularly in the areas where no organic causes to suffering could be found. As she had wanted to years before, she listened to her patients, encouraging them to talk, even if they came to her with a severe head cold or a stomach ailment for which normally one would have prescribed medicines. Often the symptoms went away without treatment; and what was thought of as a simple cold or a persistent cough was found to have its origins in the behaviour of the spouse, the unpredictable reactions of children, the normal strains, stresses and conflicts of everyday life.

But as for psychoanalysis itself, and those who came to her specifically for this long and expensive treatment, who had tried many other methods of relief for nervous debility, while some appeared to benefit from it many did not. It was difficult to say with truth that anyone had actually been cured in the same way, say, that an operation cured an inflamed appendix by removing the cause of the trouble, or the way the amputation of a limb cured gangrene.

With the neuroses it was difficult to get at the *cause* of the trouble because, without meaning to, the patient often went to great pains to conceal the causes, to repress them, as Lindsey knew from her own treatment with Freud. Patients were ready to lie on the couch and practise free association by talking about anything which came to mind; but it often took weeks, sometimes months, for anything significant to emerge. There were no short cuts, and Lindsey knew that in the dark realms of the unconscious she was still a novice herself.

There were heartrending times when a patient abruptly discontinued his or her visits. Others when patients stormed out because they objected to the personal, sexual nature of some of her questions and were not seen again. Nor did they pay their bills, perhaps in indignation, despite repeated reminders. It was difficult to sue a patient for small unpaid bills, and she gradually realized why doctors had a reputation for greed if they wanted payment in advance. Lindsey suffered much from the withholding of fees at a time when – again like Freud – she and Mortimer were not well off.

The practice of this new psychoanalysis, therefore, was not an easy process either for patient or practitioner; and Lindsey was discovering this for herself in New York with its large, mixed, sometimes itinerant population, in the same way that Freud, painfully, was finding it out in Vienna.

But Lindsey never despaired. She was fired by her psychotherapeutic practice and each case taught her something new, whether it was partly successful, or whether it ended in disaster. She found her life interesting, fulfilling and she had, at last, achieved some measure of real peace.

The satisfaction that her work gave her was of more importance to Lindsey as she came to accept that she and Mortimer would never have children. Although their intimate life was not a paramount feature of their now very happy marriage, it was not the disaster it once had been. Having overcome her initial difficulties, thanks to her own analysis, she was able to accept her limited enjoyment of sex or, to be honest, the fact that she really didn't enjoy it at all; but not to allow her feelings to mar her husband's pleasure. For neither of them was it as important a part of their marriage as their intellectual harmony, the many other things they enjoyed sharing together. If Freud's analysis had only been partly successful in one respect, in another it had succeeded beyond their expectations, because it had brought them together by helping them to identify similar attitudes and objects of interest from which their feelings developed into a binding, most satisfying form of love.

It made them both accept too the great sorrow that Lindsey, due to reasons no one could identify, could not conceive. For one trained in gynaecology Lindsey was curiously reticent about submitting herself for examination. But such cursory investigations as she permitted seemed to suggest that there was nothing organically wrong with her, though the inability to conceive was one that no one had yet attributed to psychological causes; one day that would be attempted too.

Lindsey had hoped for a baby, but not passionately. Her main wish had been to please Mortimer, who loved children. She was not domesticated and she knew that no fierce maternal fires burned inside her. She had delivered many babies but never envied the mothers, never yearned to hold one of her own in her arms. So, as the years passed and there remained just the two of them, she was content, because it enabled her to pass the benefits of thwarted motherhood to the care of her patients. Even with servants children were demanding and, as a woman, Lindsey doubted whether she would have found her work as rewarding as she did if she'd been the mother of a family. Mortimer too seemed to acquiesce in his childless role, absorbed by his work, by his hobbies of reading and walking – sailing in summer – and by their happy life together. It was also a fact, noticed by many of their friends, that their childlessness seemed to make them a particularly devoted couple. It was rather as though they gave to each other in abundance the share of love and affection that might otherwise have been disseminated among their offspring.

Yes, she was content; but the contents of the letter which had triggered her ruminations disturbed her and, looking at the watch she wore suspended on a chain around her neck, she went along the ground-floor corridor of the house and knocked on Mortimer's door. When he replied she went in and shut it behind her.

Mortimer, writing at his desk, looked up as she entered, extending his hand in greeting.

He had never become a perfunctory husband, the sort who takes his wife for granted. His appreciation of Lindsey had grown over the years, and showed in all the courtesies and little attentions rather to be expected in a newly married husband madly in love. Indeed his love for Lindsey had increased with each setback they had been called upon to share, their mutual disappointment – his in particular – about their failure to have children. But for him she was, and continued to be, the perfect partner, and the longer he knew her the greater he appreciated her, the more dearly he loved her.

'Sit down, my dear,' he got up, solicitously shaking the cushions on the comfortable chair next to the fire. 'Not bad news I hope?' He indicated the letter in her hand and sat down again at his desk, attentively looking at her.

'It *is* bad news, dearest.' Lindsey's eyes flew quickly

419

over the first page of the letter. 'Charlotte has advanced heart failure. She of course has been ailing for years – I have always suspected mild neurasthenia myself – but now the doctors diagnose something more serious. She would, I feel, like me to go and see her.'

'Oh that is very sad. May I read the letter?'

Lindsey passed it to Mortimer and as he read she sat with her chin resting in the palm of her hand watching him. Mortimer, at forty-six, exactly filled his role of eminent physician. His fair hair was nicely greying, and he had only a tiny little tuft of it left on the crown of his head. Yet there was a generous growth at the back which enhanced his air of distinction. His myopia had worsened and he wore spectacles all the time, but they served to impress his patients. Without them his blue eyes were too merry, lacking the *gravitas* expected of a learned member of his exacting profession. His face was even kinder now, more in repose, were that possible, than when she had first met him, and she knew that much of the happiness in it was due to their mutual marital and professional harmony.

Mortimer gravely put the letter on his desk and gazed at Lindsey. 'And will you go?'

'I feel I must. There is the question of Ellen.'

'Let me see, how old is Ellen?' Mortimer started to count on his fingers.

'She's nearly twelve. As you see, Charlotte fears the effect of her continued ill health on her.'

'But would you like to have Ellen here?'

'That's quite out of the question, my dear.' Lindsey got up and walked over to the fireplace, staring into the embers, because it was a warm day and the fire, lit by the maid in the morning to warm the room, had been left to die. 'When Estella knows how ill Charlotte is she will wish to have her daughter with her. You know she has always wanted that. That's what I must persuade Charlotte to allow. It might not be easy.'

420

'I see Charlotte's point. Ellen hardly ever sees her mother.'

'That's scarcely Estella's fault,' Lindsey riposted with more spirit than she normally used when speaking to her mate, although they did argue a good deal on medico-psychological matters. 'Charlotte has *never* allowed Ellen to visit her in England, and my dear sister has been so busy cementing her successful career – and who can blame her? – that she scarcely ever has time to go to Paris. But I know she thinks of Ellen constantly. In every letter she mentions her.'

'Thinking is one thing, doing another.' Mortimer got up and put an arm round her. 'You know, my dearest, I will support you in anything you consider right. Would you like to bring poor Charlotte to visit us here? We could get a proper diagnosis of her condition and, in that light, see what is the best thing to be done.'

Lindsey rested her head against his shoulder. 'Dear Mortimer, what an angel you are to think of such a thing. I had it in mind too; but didn't know how you'd react.' She quickly glanced at him, then lowered her head again. 'Charlotte might be here for years, you know.'

'Oh yes, I know; that old feeling that Charlotte had, and still has, for you burns as brightly as ever I guess.'

'Well, it is a good feeling, a loving feeling. There was never anything bad or evil in it.'

'Never?' His voice in her ear sounded as a whisper and she clasped him compulsively round the waist.

'Never ever. There was never anything at all physical about it, though I know some thought differently. Mrs Anderson was one and, I believe, many of our fellow students talked about us; but I didn't care. Nor did dear Charlotte. We were completely impervious to the insinuations of others. I was quite glad to go to Paris, though. One of the reasons I went, apart from Estella's condition.'

'In my young days in Boston they referred to such

relationships, and there were quite a few, probably still are, as "Boston marriages". But I'm glad you married me and not Charlotte.'

Mortimer's tone was only half-bantering. Lindsey removed her hand from around his waist and, leaving his side, went to the window, straightening the curtains which had the appearance of having been hastily drawn.

'There was never *any* question of a marrriage, though deep feeling, especially on Charlotte's part. I am glad I married you, my dearest. How little I deserve you.' Satisfied with the curtains she turned round. 'You have made me so happy and God grant that may continue for many, many years yet. But I do love Charlotte in the way that women can love each other, that's nothing to do with sexual passion and, if I can make her happy in what time is left to her, I'd like that. It would be a good and generous thing to do.'

'Then do it, my dear. You have all my support.'

'As for Estella, I know the presence of Ellen will be all she needs to make her life complete. At last, I believe, she is happy, and thank God for that too.'

'Amen,' Mortimer said.

CHAPTER TWENTY

BENEDICK:	Do not you love me?
BEATRICE:	Why, no, no more than reason.
BENEDICK:	Why then your uncle, and the Prince, and Claudio
	Have been deceived – they swore you did.

The audience rustled with amusement. As the play drew to its climax Estella had never experienced such a feeling of being at one with a vast number of people; knowing that everything she said or did, every gesture would meet with their approval. For the first night of *Much Ado* at the Lincoln she and Rayner had pulled out all the stops, playing the tempestuous lovers with just the right mixture of passion, mock-tragedy and farce. It was a highly spirited, professional performance. They had chosen it as a kind of self-indulgent tease, because it was now seventeen years since they had read it together in the amateurs' hall in Highgate. Although it was not a particular anniversary, the play was very close to Estella's heart and she had wanted to do it with him on the stage.

Rayner looked magnificent as Benedick – swaggering, vain, uncertain, slightly pompous and then, at the end, like a man foolishly, but still nobly, head over heels in love.

> Peace! I will stop your mouth.

As they were lovers in real life as well as on the stage, they kissed, pausing just fractionally longer than mere stage lovers would and the audience stirred again and one or two started murmuring. Then Rayner drew apart from her, still holding her hand and, with a dramatic flourish called:

Strike up, pipers!

The entire auditorium rose spontaneously to their feet as Estella sank into a deep curtsey before rising again and exiting with Benedick.

Once in the wings he took her in his arms, completing the kiss he'd begun on the stage. Estella half-laughing tried to push him away.

'If the curtain goes up and they see us like this . . . '

'They'll love it.'

'Rayner . . . these things are all right on stage. Come. Be serious!'

He tried to kiss her again but, though excited by his embrace, she stepped aside and, taking his hand, kept it firmly by her side as they waited for their cue. The curtain rose and the minor characters started to go on at first in threes and fours, then in pairs and finally, with the actor who'd played Dogberry, singly. He got a huge cheer, but the crowd saved its frenzy for Rayner and Estella, who emerged together, hands still clasped, both with their free hands extended in a salute to the audience, maybe their mutual passion, as well as their excitement from the play, showing on their faces. Estella curtsied to the ground, Rayner bowed low. Flowers rained upon the stage from the auditorium, and then footmen staggered from the wings with huge bouquets which they piled into Estella's arms and laid at her feet.

'Bravo! Bravo!'

She had never known such applause, not even when the Prince of Wales attended *A Woman's Wiles* with Lady Brooke. He had returned again a fortnight later, and that time one of the bouquets had been from him. Knowing the reputation of the Prince, Rayner had been uneasy but no invitations to private supper parties had followed the bouquet. Estella had assured Rayner that he had nothing to fear from a portly old man in his fifties, even if he was the heir to the throne. But from then on Bertie saw all her performances, and once she and Rayner had been invited to meet him at one of Irving's celebrated private supper parties held in the Beefsteak Room at the rear of the Lyceum Theatre.

Heady years they had been. Four of them had now passed since *A Woman's Wiles* had had such a reception; and maybe they chose *Much Ado* for that reason, as well as to celebrate the Queen's Jubilee and the fact that, although Rayner swore he couldn't remember speaking it with her, the play had such power to move Estella.

'Come home with me tonight,' Rayner whispered, still on stage. 'There is a little dinner for us just *à deux*.'

She glanced at him and pressed his hand. The curtain fell, rose again and fell and, finally, they took their last bow and retired to congratulate the cast.

Harriet Leadbetter came round with Sergei, Sir Squire and Lady Bancroft popped in and soon Estella's dressing room was full of people clamouring to congratulate her. Laughingly she attempted to remove her make-up, speak to a dozen people and read her telegrams all at the same time.

'I thought we'd have a little supper,' Harriet said. 'I've a table at Gatti's.'

'Thanks, Harriet, but Rayner wants us to dine alone. He has something prepared.'

'Is there an *occasion*, may I ask?' Harriet wrinkled her nose conspiratorially.

'*Much Ado* is very special for us.'

'It was a beautiful performance, darling. It is because you are still in love that you both played it so well. The audience knew. They *know* these things. Besides, Beatrice and Benedick are very like you and Rayner, the way you quarrel so much – always quarrelling and always

425

making up. Nice though.' Harriet looked a trifle wistful as though some little storms with Sergei would liven things up a bit. Sergei, however, who smiled continually, didn't move a muscle, largely because he mostly didn't understand what was being said.

Estella smiled and rubbed cold cream on her face, examining her glistening eyes and white teeth speculatively in the mirror.

'Do you know, Harriet, I'm thirty-four?'

'Well darling. I'm fifty-four and I never felt younger.'

'Yes, but still.' Estella touched her skin and then rapidly removed the rest of her make-up while her dresser read her telegrams, including one from the Prince, one from Irving and Terry and another from George Alexander.

Yes, they'd been heady years; happy ones.

'There is no such fulfilment as success,' she said to Rayner as the carriage bore them the short distance across Bloomsbury from the theatre to Doughty Street.

'Why do you say that, darling?'

'Well, I was thinking how happy I am. I am happy in life and in love. What more could a woman want?'

'A child?'

'A child?' Estella's heart bounded unpleasantly and she looked at him. 'Whatever made you say that?'

'Well, wouldn't you like a child?'

Estella leaned back. She had never told Rayner about Ellen. Why it was hard to say, except that it was the one thing about which she was still ashamed, that could still draw from her as nothing else could feelings of guilt and remorse.

'You mean *you* would like a child, Rayner?'

His arm circled her waist and he put his lips to her ear. 'More than anything I would like a child by you. Darling, why don't we get married now? There is nothing in the world to prevent us. We are a couple and we always will

426

be. I think it would only do us good, enhance our status with our public.'

'Oh that's what you're thinking of.'

'You know it's not only that, Estella! But since we have become so well known you hardly ever stay all night with me in case someone finds out.'

'Ellen Terry always warned me to be discreet about love.'

'Well, if we're married you can be discreet. I think this is a ridiculous and absurd situation. I, for one, am tired of it.'

He folded his arms and looked angrily in front of him, his large nose almost touching his aggressively, exaggeratedly pouting mouth. Estella didn't know whether he was serious or acting.

'Oh darling, you *are* cross!' She touched his arm but he shook her hand away.

'Haven't I proved myself to you, Estella? Do you think I will *ever* love anyone else? Why cannot we be married and live as married people do, in the same house? We have sufficient money to buy one and enough for you to take a year off and have a child. You are not getting any younger, my darling.'

Now Estella felt angry and stared hard at his profile. 'Thank you very much indeed, Rayner Brook. Why this very night I was examining the lines of age on my face.'

'I don't mean that! I mean the fact that the child-bearing life of women is very limited. I mean . . . '

'Well, I'm not yet forty. I've heard some women have progeny at fifty.'

'I said I don't mean that, I mean . . . ' he fumbled for words, knowing he'd been clumsy. As an actress and a beautiful, and inevitably vain, woman, Estella took the passage of time both seriously and personally. 'Look, Estella, I'm tired of this and I wonder you aren't too. Do you not *wish* to live with me?'

'I wish to live with you, darling, but . . . ' She clasped his hand and looked anxiously out of the window. 'There are so many "buts" Rayner. So many problems.'

'Problems, Estella? What can possibly trouble you? You are at the peak of your career. You are loved by everyone, but specially by me. Is not that enough?'

He made to take her in his arms, but she drew her cloak tightly around her, feeling cold, alone. Puzzled, he sat back and they completed the journey in silence.

When Estella awoke in the morning she had no idea of the time. The place beside her in the bed was empty and the curtains were still drawn. She put her arms round the pillow where he had laid his head and held it against her cheek. The memory of their conversation in the coach troubled her, and yet they had not referred to it again. They had dined quietly together by candlelight, talking about the performance, confident, yet a little nervous as performers always are about what the critics would say. Rayner made no attempt to draw her about her problems, but had shown her by his words and later his actions the extent of his love.

Why, then, did she feel alone? Why did she simply not do as he wished and agree to marry him?

Ellen. That was the reason. The secret she had kept from him lay between them, an invisible presence, which she wished to share with him but could not. Could she go through her whole life, a life perhaps eventually shared with him, and not tell him about her daughter? How cowardly and foolish she'd been! Why this very day, she resolved, she would make everything right between them.

She sat on the edge of the bed, shivering in her light nightgown and, reaching for his robe, drew it on; but she knew that the cold she felt came not merely from the chill air in the unheated room. It came from the fear in her heart. If Rayner loved her he would understand and, once this burden was shared, surely it could trouble her no longer? Her very resolution seemed to strengthen her. No longer feeling the cold, she got up and marched firmly towards the door. There was no one about, but she could hear sounds from the basement and smell coffee. She went quickly downstairs and found Rayner in the drawing room, sitting by the window reading the papers, a cup of coffee by his side. She was about to exclaim, but the expression on his face stopped her.

'Bad reviews?' she whispered. 'Oh, not *bad* reviews?'

Rayner put down the paper and got up to kiss her. His action was rather mechanical. He looked pale, but they'd had a busy, energetic night and she'd heard the first blackbirds in Mecklenburgh Square before they'd gone to sleep.

She touched his face tenderly and ruffled his tousled hair.

'Darling, you look delicious crumpled,' she said. 'But why are you so serious? Where did we go wrong?'

He passed her the paper, making room for her beside him. Estella glanced at the paper, frowned and turned to the front page.

'*Some Say* . . . What's this?'

'It's a gossip sheet. Read what it says.' He pointed to a few paragraphs in bold type and Estella lowered her head obediently.

There was, once again, a rapturous reception for Estella Abercrombie and Rayner Brook at the first night of *Much Ado About Nothing* at the Lincoln last night. The usual gathering of celebrities was there to applaud the stars and their excellent choice of this witty play. There were those who thought that the love between Beatrice and Benedick has its real life counterpart, and some say the two share Mr Brook's cosy little house in Doughty Street, Bloomsbury where another scribbler, Charles Dickens, once lived. Perhaps the literary connection suits the talented Mr Brook who, some say, is working on a new play.

Readers might recall his first success with Miss Abercrombie in *A Woman's Wiles*, which is frequently revived at the Lincoln because of the success it first enjoyed four years ago when it ran for almost a year.

Some say Mr Brook based the play on the real life of a certain person who played the female lead in the same play. No names mentioned yet, *but* some say that she went to Paris to hide because she had a child by a man to whom she was not married. In order to support the child she took to the life of a courtesan and amassed a great deal of money. Some say that, in order to pay off debts accumulated by her father, she sold all she had and returned to London to resume a stage career she had forsaken years before. Some say the lady in question is Miss Abercrombie. Or is she a *lady* after all?

As Rayner gently removed the paper, Estella started to tremble. He took her in his arms, wrapping them round her. Her teeth began to chatter and he quickly called for Giles and told him to bring some fresh, hot coffee.

'Don't worry, darling, I'll sue. I'll sue him for so much . . . '

'But how . . . ?'

'They make up any lies. I suppose a number of people know you were in Paris . . . '

'But how . . . ?'

'I'll sue them, I tell you. I'll get hold of my lawyer this very morning and a writ will be served today. These scandal rags are the bane of London. They vilify innocent people the whole time. I shan't be the first to make the scoundrels pay.'

Giles came in with the coffee and quickly poured a cup which he put by Estella's side. She still trembled so much that she was afraid to pick it up, and Rayner gently took it from the table and put it to her lips.

'There darling. Drink up and then go back to bed. The reviews are excellent, of course. Clement Scott especially ecstatic, now that he thinks we have abandoned "experimental drama". He thinks! Little does he know what I'm working on now. Harriet sent the papers round early this

430

morning and also this scandal sheet, which she told me to read first before I showed it to you.'

Gradually Estella felt the blood returning to her numb body and she clasped the cup in her own hands and drank from it. As the hot liquid warmed her she realized that the shame she had refused to face before was now facing her. She replaced her cup, brushed back her hair which had fallen over her face and got up, clasping Rayner's large dressing gown around her and walking slowly over to the fire where she bent to warm her hands.

'It's all true, Rayner. If you sued we'd be a laughing stock.'

'True?' Rayner got up and put an arm around her. 'How can that thing about a child be true? You have no child.'

'But I *have*, a daughter. I never told you because I was ashamed. I started to several times, but every time I began I couldn't go on.' She turned and faced him, but when she saw his expression she turned away again. 'I had a child by Tom Shipley. That's why I left London. I thought you might have known; but it was something I managed to keep very secret.'

'You had a child in that house with you?' Rayner withdrew his arm from her and sat abruptly down again as though he'd had a shock.

'No, no. Ellen stayed with Charlotte, Lindsey's friend. Charlotte adopted her and brought her up. I made over my claim to Ellen so that she could have a good upbringing. She's called Ellen, my little girl, after Ellen Terry. I was a very bad mother in those early days, Rayner, because I was frightened and didn't know what to do. Then Lindsey went to America and married Mortimer, and I was left with no money and no home. I didn't like my baby very much then, but how that thought still haunts me – because I grew to love her desperately. It was for her sake that I wanted to have money, and for her sake

431

that I wanted to be famous. I think of Ellen constantly and last night when you talked of a child I wanted to tell you then. It was also why I felt I couldn't marry you, because then you'd have to know.'

'But Estella, I would have to have known *one* day.'

'Well, I postponed it for as long as I could. I *am* ashamed. I have a lovely daughter whom I only see now about once a year when I can slip secretly over to Paris, and I have never been a mother to her. She loves me, but she should hate me.'

Estella dropped to the floor and knelt beside him. 'I have been a miserable coward, Rayner, and just this very morning, troubled by our conversation last night, I resolved to tell you all. Now it's too late. You won't believe me.' She looked anxiously up at him, but he turned his face away. 'Do you believe me?'

Still not looking at her, Rayner got up and walked slowly over to the window, staring out at the grey wintry scene, the deserted street, the bare branches of the trees in Mecklenburgh Square over to his right.

'If you say it I believe you, Estella. But I wish you'd told me before. This was the problem you referred to, this the reason you wouldn't marry me. Yet all the time I could have known, could have shared your burden with you.' He turned and gazed at her. Now, still kneeling on the floor, it was she who would not meet his eyes. 'Estella, I don't think you can have ever realized the extent of my love if you could keep something so important from me.'

'I promised Charlotte I would never regard myself as Ellen's mother. I said it would be a secret that no one else should know.'

'Then Charlotte was a monster to make such a request! She had no right.'

'Charlotte did what she thought was best. She despised me and I thought I was not fit to be a mother, and I wasn't. Oh Rayner, I wasn't.'

432

In an agony of remorse Estella knelt right over and put her head on the floor, her lovely hair tumbling over her face, concealing it from him. Seeing her thus, Rayner thought that the penitent Magdalen must have resembled her, and it seemed that his love was momentarily displaced by pity and also something much stronger and more destructive: jealousy. All these years Estella had preferred to keep something so important from him; so, surely, she loved Ellen more than she loved him?

Slowly Estella straightened up, brushing her hair away from her face, and saw him there before her, upright, stern, like an admonitory father. If only he would reach down and take her in his arms . . . She put her hands up to him, but he ignored her gesture and sat down, crossing his legs and gazing at her.

'It seems you were, indeed, not fit to be a mother, doing what you did. Maybe it is as well we did not have a child, now that I know what you did with the one you had.'

'Oh Rayner, cruel . . . ' She could see her father now, as he used to be, reprimanding her for some childish misdeed – the expression on his face causing terror but never remorse. She realized she had now made herself look ridiculous, and rose to her feet without awkwardness, being the actress she was, finally standing so that she could look down at him. 'Cruel, Rayner, to say that.'

'Nevertheless it's true.' He began to drum his fingers upon the arm of his chair, his gaze still cold. 'I think you want no commitment, Estella – you can't give your heart to anybody; not to me, your daughter, your sister or your parents. I should have realized that your talents as an actress made you impervious to real feeling. You love only yourself. Even now you look as though you're playing a part, that we are engaged in some macabre drama. That's why you always act so naturally on stage, because you can't tell the difference between life and art . . . '

Estella raised a hand threateningly towards him, stared at him and then abruptly lowered her arm, aware how violently she was trembling. He had gazed at her unflinchingly, as though prepared for the blow, maybe welcoming it.

'No,' Estella said, 'no. I will not hit you, Rayner. I can't hit you, because that is how children behave and your cold behaviour, your disdain, make me realize that all you wish to do is to humiliate me, mortify me, make me feel like a child. In the old days I would have hit you, but not now.'

'Hit me if it makes you feel better,' Rayner said imperturbably, uncrossing his legs and crossing them again. 'I think you *are* still a child at heart and that you don't wish to grow up. Your daughter is a rival, so you keep her in wraps.'

'*That's* not true either.'

Estella felt the hammering of her heart grow quieter and, glancing at herself in the mirror, she drew her hair back on either side of her face and, with one hand, knotted it loosely behind her so that a long thick curl hung down her back.

'I can see that you don't understand me Rayner. Maybe that's why I didn't tell you about Ellen before, because I knew you wouldn't understand. Maybe I was too afraid of losing you and now . . . '

'Now?' his voice faltered and she, too, swallowed but continued in a firm tone.

'Now I am stronger.'

'But you're not going to lose me.' He weakly attempted to smile as though to convince them both that the situation hadn't changed; but both knew better.

'I hope I will not lose you, but I think the feeling you had for me, which you called love, was not love at all. Not real love.'

'You're being dramatic again, Estella.'

'But then I'm an actress, aren't I? A player?' She tossed

434

her head provocatively and took a few steps away from him. 'You just said I couldn't tell the difference between real life and the stage. Well, I can tell the difference between a love that is true and one that's false.'

'Just because I said . . .'

She felt the temper rising within her again and struggled to control herself, continuing in a voice that was only slightly raised. 'You said that I wanted no commitment, that I was a poor mother, impervious to real feeling. I mean that *is* what you said, after all. Now that you know about Ellen your attitude towards me *has* changed.'

'It was the shock of discovery. Maybe if you had told me yourself it would have been different.'

'That we shall never know,' Estella said bitterly. 'You say I should have told you, but look how you've behaved today. Where is your eternal love, your compassion now?'

'Still there, I assure you.'

'You have a funny way of showing it. Will you believe me, Rayner, when I tell you that last night in the coach I suddenly felt very alone. I was lonely too when I woke this morning even though we had passed the night together, loving each other. Maybe it was some instinct about what would happen today. Maybe I had some foreknowledge. I realize now that I was right. I am alone and, as far as your so-called "love" is concerned, I think I always have been.'

Her gaze was level, controlled, proud, and, as she finished, Rayner started to rise. But before he could get to his feet she had gone swiftly to the door and let herself out, never glancing back. Slowly he sat down again and, realizing that his own hands were trembling, he joined them in his lap, squeezing them tightly together, aware of the sudden desperate ache in his heart.

Upstairs Estella dressed quickly, taking her usual care about her appearance. Her composure and the fact that she had remained dry eyed throughout the ordeal, while it surprised her, also seemed a sudden unexpected sign of her maturity. Had she finally taken control of emotions that had caused such havoc throughout her life? In the old days she and Rayner would have struck each other, maybe rolled on the floor in a frenzy of anger which later would, inevitably, have turned to passion. But passion solved nothing. It merely postponed the process that made some people mature, while others continued to behave like children.

Well she, Estella Abercrombie, was now a woman, a mother, an actress of distinction. Yet her real life was not on the stage. One day, not too far distant, she would go to Paris and claim her daughter, making a fresh start in life for herself, for them. If she had lost a lover she would gain a daughter. It was indeed high time that she realized her responsibilities and took command of her life. Maybe one day, in her heart, she would thank Rayner for making her finally recognize her priorities.

In the hall downstairs stood Mr Giles, an apron covering his morning suit, polishing the brass ornaments in the hall. He looked at her with surprise, then up the stairs, as though expecting to see Rayner.

'Going, Miss Estella?'

'Would you call a cab for me, Mr Giles?'

He took her cloak from the hallstand and looked around for her hat. She still had on the evening dress she had worn the night before, and she suddenly realized the irony and comedy of the situation, as if she were a cocotte leaving the house of a man who had used her for a night's pleasure. Briefly she smiled as Mr Giles wrapped her cloak tenderly around her shoulders.

'No hat, Mr Giles.'

'It's very cold outside, Miss Abercrombie.'

'I'll take care.'

She looked towards the stairs and Mr Giles glanced with her; then he gazed at her, his face inscrutable.

'If you wait here, Madam, I'll . . . '

436

'I'll come with you, Mr Giles. We'll easily find one on the Gray's Inn Road.'

Mr Giles divested himself of his leather apron and then opened the door, standing aside for her to precede him. Swiftly they walked along the pavement, turning left into Guildford Street which led to the busy main thoroughfare. Estella hadn't looked up at the first-floor window to see if Rayner was standing there; nor, now, did she look back at the house. She walked with a cheerful swing, chatting to Mr Giles as if she hadn't a care in the world.

Her critics and admirers, seeing her then, supposing they had known the emotions in her heart, might have thought that, perhaps, it was the best piece of acting she had ever done.

January in Paris was probably the bleakest month of the year – in Paris, or any city. People hurried along the boulevards muffled against the cold, but many of them still found time to stop and talk about the latest sensation in the Dreyfus Affair. Émile Zola had just published his open letter to the President of the Republic on the front page of *L'Aurore* denouncing top-level government officials and high-ranking army officers for complicity in the affair. J'ACCUSE was a sensation and 300,000 copies of *L'Aurore* had already been sold in the streets.

But, in the quiet house in the Parc Monceau, the scandal that threatened not only the government but the very stability of France was not a topic of conversation.

The matter that preoccupied the household was Charlotte's health, which had deteriorated even since she had written to Lindsey. She now lay for most of the day on a couch in the first-floor salon. Through the wide bay window she could see all that went on in the little world outside bounded by the perimeters of the garden and the park.

'My world has become so small; just this,' she said,

reaching up for Estella's hand and, with the other, gesticulating towards the window. 'You are very welcome, Estella.'

Shocked by her appearance, yet doing her best to conceal it, Estella clasped Charlotte's thin hand between her gloved ones, wondering if she dared bend to kiss her. No, she decided, she dared not. Despite her emaciation, the tired smile of the chronic sick, Charlotte's personality remained forbidding, reminding her of the old robust adversary who had kept her daughter from her. Too much troubled history lay between them, as yet, to allow even this perfunctory intimacy.

'Lindsey wrote that you were ill.' Estella remained standing. 'So I came at once. Yet even now I was fearful you would not see me.' She let fall Charlotte's hand and began drawing off her gloves.

Charlotte pointed to a chair by the side of her couch. 'Lindsey is on her way here. You must stay until she comes. You'll want to see Ellen.'

'Alas, I can't stay long,' Estella shook her head. 'I'm rehearsing for a play. Only a few days at the most.'

'You have become very successful.' Charlotte sank back against her pillows with a sigh. 'Ellen follows every stage of your career, keeps every notice. She is very proud of her mother.'

'I'm glad . . . ' Estella paused. 'I'm glad that now she has *reason* to be proud.'

Charlotte's eyes wandered for a moment to the static scene outside the window. 'I know you've thought me a very hard woman, Estella, but what I did I thought was for the best. It seemed to me that a settled, secure environment was the wisest thing that you, or I, could give Ellen.'

'Those days being what they were, I think you were probably right.'

Charlotte slowly turned her head away from the window and her eyes met Estella's.

438

'You're very generous, in the circumstances.'

'Now I can afford to be. Then I couldn't. Sometimes when I think what a selfish immature young woman I was I tremble.'

Charlotte nodded, her eyes roving over Estella's face, her elegant, fashionable attire.

'You've changed. I can see you've matured. It has made you even more beautiful. How I envy you your youth and beauty, especially your health. How I envy you that.'

'But you will be well again, Charlotte. Lindsey hopes to persuade you to go with her to America. She says the sea voyage and the expertise of the doctors there will cure you.'

'We have very good doctors in Paris. There is nothing that any doctor can do. All I want now is peace of mind.' Charlotte closed her eyes as if overcome by weariness, or conscious of something that Estella couldn't see or apprehend. 'I want you to take Ellen back with you to England. I have done all I can for her and it does her no good to share a house with an ill woman. This is a dismal place for Ellen to grow up in. I know she's only young, but she is an entrancing child – your child – and now her place is with you. That you are not the woman you were I see quite clearly.'

Although she knew the criticism was just Estella felt her composure threatened by Charlotte's manner. She had tried very hard to prepare herself for what she considered an ordeal, thinking that she would have to persuade Charlotte to let her have Ellen. Charlotte's changed circumstances now rendered her demeanour less threatening; yet she still had the power to wound – apparently the inclination too.

'I always loved my daughter, Charlotte,' she replied firmly.

'Not always,' Charlotte said with equal firmness. 'You've a short memory, Estella. You did *not* love her at

439

the beginning. I was so fearful that you would take her away, have her removed from me and adopted by someone else, that I made those very stringent demands of you. I wanted to tie you down and I did. Whatever you've become, you were not always thus.'

Estella struggled with her resentment of Charlotte's imperious manner, forcibly reminding herself that she was in the presence of a very sick woman – mortally sick, according to Lindsey.

'The past is the past, Charlotte,' she said gravely. 'But at the time if your own manner had been more gentle I would have given in with better grace . . . ' To Estella's embarrassment and concern Charlotte abruptly lowered her head, and groping for her handkerchief brought it to her eyes, clearly close to tears. Estella hastily knelt by the sick bed, but Charlotte turned her face away, her hands continually dabbing at her eyes. 'Please Charlotte, I didn't mean . . . '

'Oh it's not you.' It was Charlotte's turn to struggle for composure and, after a short while, she tucked her handkerchief in the sleeve of her dress and, her eyes artificially bright, the tip of her nose pink, gazed again at Estella. 'Don't you think, my dear, as my life nears its end, how *I* repent of my attitude, not only towards you but your sister, Ellen, everyone I've ever loved. I've always been cold, Estella, afraid of showing emotion. I can confess it now. I had, you know, a not very happy childhood and it threw me too much on my own. Knowing that I was unloved by my parents, who kept me continually in the care of nursemaids, made me feel I was indeed unlovable. I was afraid of love and, until I met your sister, I never knew strong emotion. I suppose, in the light of hindsight, one could say I was jealous of you – a strong-willed, beautiful creature who had known love, passion, heartbreak, maternity. Unwittingly, perhaps, I wanted to deprive you of something and have Ellen for

440

myself. I know I was completely unconcerned about you. Well . . . ' Charlotte leaned back once again, her hands falling to her sides. 'I have not succeeded in that either. Though she respects me, she doesn't love me and never has. She keeps all that love for the absent mother . . . ' Charlotte looked wistfully ahead of her and then, abruptly, straightened herself, leaning slightly forward. 'And now, my dear, for us both let bygones be bygones. I am near death and you are on the threshold of world-wide fame. You have many, many years ahead of you in which to enjoy your success, indulge your love of life. Go to Ellen now, she's waiting for you.'

'Does she know?' Estella rose from her knees, gently taking one of Charlotte's hands and holding it again between hers as though it were in her power to infuse the invalid with her own vitality. Charlotte, as if responding to the gesture, smiled, shaking her head.

'I wasn't sure if you'd be willing, not being *au fait* with your circumstances. I'm glad you are. From now on, you and your daughter must mean a great deal to each other. Look after her. Look after her for me.'

'Oh I *will*.' Estella, overwhelmed by the emotion of the moment, was about to fall on her knees again, but Charlotte's hand in hers seemed to preclude anything so dramatic. 'And when you're better, you'll come and stay with us, for a long time . . . '

Wordlessly Charlotte shook her head and, gently withdrawing her hand from Estella's, waved it towards the door. 'Go now and let me sleep a little. I'm very tired. Very, very tired.' As Charlotte's head sank upon her chest Estella tiptoed towards the door, quietly letting herself out.

Ellen Abercrombie would be thirteen that May. She was a tall composed young woman who was already fulfilling her early promise of exceptional beauty. Her dark curls were shoulder length, her blue eyes were that special colour which characterizes the rarest sapphires, and her pale complexion was highlighted by twin blushes on each cheek which grew rosier when she was excited.

But Ellen was not often excited. Like her aunt she was controlled. Mademoiselle d'Argent had remained with her as her governess, and much of this detachment had been acquired from that self-contained, unemotional spinster from Limoges. It did not do, Mademoiselle had insisted, to forget that one was a lady and demonstrate too much excitement like the common people.

Though uncertain about her origins, puzzled about her parentage, Ellen had, indeed, been brought up with the manners and the disposition of a lady of quality. She lacked nothing in the way of money or cultural interests to be anything but a *jeune fille bien élevée*. She did, it's true, look a lot older than her tender years, and two small breasts had recently formed which already gave a pleasing fullness to her graceful figure.

'How you've grown, my darling,' Estella said, first holding Ellen at arm's length and then drawing her towards her. 'And it's true you *are* a beauty!'

Ellen laughed and wriggled away from her mother's embrace, nervous now that the moment so eagerly awaited had come. They had last seen each other in the summer, when Estella, *en route* to the south of France, had spent several days in Paris seeing many old friends with whom she still kept in touch, including one or two faithful old lovers. 'You can't call me a beauty compared to you, Mama.' Ellen gazed deprecatingly at the floor, the twin spots on her cheeks grown a violent pink. 'I'm too dark. Someone asked me the other day if my parents were gipsies!'

'Gip . . . ' Estella put a hand to her mouth uncertain whether to laugh or be appalled. 'Oh my darling, your father was an actor. Never a gipsy.'

'But why do I resemble him so much?'

'I wish I knew.' Estella looked towards the fire and Ellen, surreptitiously gazing at her, excited by her presence, saw sadness in her face.

'Did you *hate* my papa, Mama? I know so little about him.'

'I never hated him, my darling.' Estella reached out a hand and drew Ellen down on the sofa beside her. Her mother looked so wonderful, so elegant, smelt so beautiful that Ellen wondered if she would ever overcome her awe of her. 'It is just that he . . . didn't treat me very well. He left me, you see, for another woman and then I found I was expecting you and was too proud to tell him. There now, darling.' Estella patted the hand of the girl beside her. 'You are a little too young to know these things. When you are older I'll tell you the whole story.'

'But why am I too young?'

'Because you are. Please don't argue with me,' Estella said sternly as if the question brooked no argument. Then she realized that for the first time she was reprimanding her daughter. On those brief visits it had always seemed very important to let nothing untoward mar the occasion, to conceal her feelings in order to secure Ellen's affections. As a mother she had never been able to be natural. Now that she could, and they were to live together, would their relationship become more real? And how would Ellen respond to these maternal reprimands? She resembled Tom not only in looks, but in a rather rebellious, obstinate temperament. However, unlike Tom, she had the advantage of a genteel upbringing and a good education. How her mother hoped that these advantages would outweigh the drawbacks of her paternal inheritance.

Estella rose suddenly to her feet and wandered over to the fire, recalling that, in this same room and on a day not unlike this one, she had had her final interview with Charlotte before she left the house for good. How painful

443

that had been, agreeing to Charlotte's conditions, signing the document the lawyer had drawn up giving Charlotte custody and control. Now in this very same room she was reclaiming her daughter. She wished in a way that Charlotte had prepared her for it. 'Darling,' she looked at Ellen sitting rather abashed on the sofa, gazing at her knees. 'How would you like to come back to London with me?'

Ellen started, looked up, her eyes shining as if by her mother's words she had been transformed from a subdued, well-brought-up young miss to something very like the gipsy her friends had supposed her to be. Mother and daughter looked into each other's eyes.

'Mama, you don't *mean* it?'

'But I do.' Estella laughed with relief, realizing only then how nervous she had been.

'Oh Mama, it is the most wonderful thing that ever happened to me . . . ' Ellen paused. 'For a visit . . . ?'

'For good, if you like it.'

'Mama, I like it. I do.' Ellen clasped her hands together and burst into tears, and Estella, quickly sitting down beside her again, took her daughter's head and leaned it on her bosom, stroking her dark curls.

'Charlotte is very ill, as you know, Ellen. She has agreed to let me give you a home now that I am in a position to offer you one. At first it will be with your grandmother with whom I live in Highgate. She is very anxious to meet you. It is the house in which I and your Aunt Lindsey grew up and I think you will love it.'

'Oh, think of the people I shall meet. Sir Henry and Miss Terry, Mr Brook . . . '

'Mr Brook is not in England any more, darling,' Estella said quietly, still stroking Ellen's hair as though calming a frightened animal. 'He went to America last summer and, as far as I know, has no plans to return.'

Ellen raised her head, no longer tearful, her expression

444

quizzical. 'I thought Mr Brook was a *special* friend of yours.'

'He was . . . he is.' Estella gave an affected little laugh. 'But we've acted together for a long time. We felt we needed a change. There are lots of exciting things for me to do on the London stage without him.'

'I would love to have seen your *Much Ado*.'

'Well, one day you might, darling.' Estella choked slightly as she spoke. 'But certainly there are no plans at the moment to revive it. In time, Ellen, I thought I might buy a house of my own; but first you must see how you like your grandmama.'

'And school? Shall I go to school?'

'Why certainly.'

'And I'll have lots of friends? Girls of my own age?'

'Of course.'

Estella gazed at her daughter's excited face, aware that here was a being who had been starved of all the things she most craved – her mother, friends of her own age, a school to go to. She had been brought up by a governess, she had never really known her mother, she had very few friends of her own. Despite Charlotte's well-meaning attempt to do the right thing, had she succeeded?

Estella drew Ellen more closely against her, leaning her own cheek against that other, younger one; flesh of her flesh. 'Darling Ellen, I have so much to make up for, and I will, I will.'

For a long time the coast of France remained in sight, growing fainter until they were out in the open sea. Charlotte had remained in her comfortable stateroom, which had a door onto the deck, and would do so for the rest of the voyage. Lindsey, in an adjoining room, had energetically unpacked their trunks, and already familiarized herself with the boat and some of the people on it.

'They seem a nice crowd,' she said in answer to a query of Charlotte's. 'The Fishers from Boston are on board. No doubt they will report back on the curious situation that I travel without my husband and spend most of my time closeted with a mysterious female companion.'

Charlotte laughed, extending her hand. 'You're so *good*, dearest. Even if I were to live ten more years I could never repay you for this particular kindness.'

'Already you look better.' Lindsey, carefully smoothing her dress, sat by Charlotte's side. 'You will live another ten years and many more. You were weighed down by sickness, worry and the uncertainty about Ellen.'

'She was so *happy* to see her mother. She went off with hardly a backward glance. Even Mademoiselle d'Argent appeared moved at the leavetaking, and she has never been a lady to show emotion. I don't think, you know, that Ellen really cared anything at all for me. It hurt in the end.'

'That's not true.' But Lindsey had already received an excited letter from Estella saying how well Ellen had settled down with only a passing reference to Charlotte.

'It is true, my dear,' Charlotte sighed. 'I did everything for her from love, but was not loved in return. Estella did nothing and was adored. Is it fair?'

'Not fair maybe, but, as you say, a fact.' Lindsey drew the rug more carefully over her friend's thin frame, puffing up the cushions behind her. 'Although I am sure Ellen loved you, there is nothing as strong as blood, Charlotte. I'm sorry to say it but it's true. One day, though, Ellen will realize all that you did for her and will love you as you deserve.'

'Only I shan't live to see it.'

'All her life she will be grateful to you, and you can be sure Estella won't let her forget you. She has a strong sense of duty. I'm so glad that at last you two made up. How sorry I am though that I missed her.' Lindsey had

446

arrived in Paris two days after Estella left, taking Ellen, and forced home by the need to rehearse her new play with George Alexander at the St James's.

'She looked lovely.' Charlotte smiled her thanks as Lindsey finished seeing to her comfort, 'but a little sad about the eyes, I thought, when one caught her in an unguarded moment, as if she had a secret.'

'I thought that she would marry Rayner Brook. He was a sweetheart of her girlhood and, from her return to London until the summer, they were inseparable. She merely wrote and told me the partnership was now severed and he'd gone to America. I asked her to tell me more but she evaded my request. Actors are very unstable people, I'm afraid, dominated by strong emotions. However much she has matured Estella always was and always will be subject to fluctuations in her private life. I'm sorry I didn't see her to learn the truth. Never mind, we shall return to Europe in the summer with you, and see her then, and Ellen.'

Charlotte shook her head, gazing towards the porthole which showed nothing now but the shining expanse of ocean. 'I doubt I shall see Europe again. I have left a very careful will, you know, about the house and my possessions. I shall give you all the details so that if I die you'll know what to do. You may be sure that everything is as it should be.' She looked up to see Lindsey gazing severely down at her, arms akimbo.

'Charlotte, I want no more talk about death and wills. You are to have a holiday with us, see the best doctors and take a well-deserved rest.'

'You are so good, dearest Lindsey,' Charlotte said, tears starting to her eyes. 'Who knows what I would have done without you? To come all this way, and then to take me home with you. I wonder Mortimer didn't object.'

'Mortimer is an angel. It was *he* who suggested you should come and stay with us. Mortimer knows all the best physicians in New York. Heart failure is very amenable to cure, you know.'

'You've cured my heart already.' Charlotte reached up and tenderly touched Lindsey's cheek as she bent forward. 'Just to see you again is worth dying for.'

Lindsey once more energetically tucked the rug, which had come away, under her friend. 'We'll have such lovely days together on the boat alone and when we're in New York. It will be like when we were young women again. Remember?'

'Oh, I *remember*.' Charlotte gazed into her eyes. 'They were the best years of my life.'

'Well, they'll come again.' Lindsey straightened the short jacket she wore with her smart, functional travelling dress made of brown alpaca.

Charlotte leaned resignedly back against her cushions. Her face had grown so thin that the effect was skeletal, and Lindsey wondered, not for the first time, whether more ailed her than trouble with her heart. But her grey eyes were still luminous, the best feature, now as before, of a handsome rather than beautiful face. Her brown hair was heavily streaked with grey.

'Just to be with you is all I need,' Charlotte murmured. 'To have you near when I die is all I ask. Next to Ellen you are my life, Lindsey, and now that I no longer have her you're all I've got. Can't you understand what that means to me? I said to Estella I've never been loved and I haven't; but I have loved. You know that don't you?'

'Yes, I know it.' Lindsey interrupted her brisk tidying up to stand still for a moment. 'Be sure I know it, and be sure that you are loved too. Very much.'

Charlotte sighed deeply, closing her eyes, and Lindsey gazed at her anxiously. Then Charlotte's eyelids flickered, her mouth curving serenely in a smile as if she had beautiful dreams. Satisfied, Lindsey bent down, knowing that

448

what she had said had given her friend the joy and peace she needed to face the days of illness and uncertainty which undoubtedly lay ahead.

'Very, very much loved,' she whispered, stroking the invalid's brow and, from under the rug, Charlotte's hand reached for hers and held it.

CHAPTER TWENTY-ONE

From the shade of the overhanging branches of the great oak tree Minnie Abercrombie watched her granddaughter and a group of friends playing at croquet on the lawn. Beside her the table was set for afternoon tea, and the maids went back and forth busily adding to it – plates of cucumber sandwiches, layered sponge, little iced fairy cakes and jugs of cordial.

'Call Miss Abercrombie, would you Dora?' Minnie said over her shoulder. 'She went up to rest.'

'Yes'm.' Dora bobbed and scurried away.

Minnie clapped her hands and beckoned to the players, but they went on with their game which was dominated by Ellen, who was not only the most skilful, but also the most bossy in the way she directed the play of the others, telling them exactly where to stand and what to do. The curious thing, Minnie thought, was that none of her peers ever resented Ellen or answered her back. She managed to be bossy without being belligerent and, in this curious way, she seemed to earn the veneration of male and female alike.

Young people flocked to the house in the way they used to when Lindsey and Estella were girls and, in the last eighteen months, since Ellen's arrival, Minnie had felt years fall away – years of suffering, sorrow and resentment, years that, despite Estella's success, had never entirely been forgotten and never would be. But if Estella had atoned for her past it was not by her success, nor by saving them from bankruptcy – but in this provision, late in her life, of a granddaughter for Minnie who had always yearned to be a grandmother.

Jeremy St Clair was the son of that Wykeham who had once courted Lindsey. Gazing at them, Minnie contentedly remembered that summer, a hot one just like this, when Wykeham had proposed to Lindsey and the whole sad business of the disobedience and betrayal of her daughters had begun – one terrible event following on another. Jeremy at seventeen was a pupil at Highgate School just up the road, and Ellen was one of the stars, as her aunt had been, of the North London Collegiate, now in other hands than that of the celebrated Miss Buss, but still an excellent school for girls. The other two were a brother and sister – the girl at school with Ellen – whose names Minnie could never remember,

Watching them play, half closing her eyes, the thought passed her mind that one day Wykeham's son and Lindsey's niece would make a very good pair; they were just the right ages, three years apart, and both of scholarly disposition. Minnie accepted the fact that scholarship in women was an evil that ran in a branch of her family and one that, unfortunately, was here to stay. Ellen was going to Cambridge and then to the Medical School like her aunt and her late, lamented 'Maman' whom Minnie remembered well. Ellen had no doubts about her future and never had. Even Lindsey had never been as positive, as ruthlessly determined to get her own way, as Ellen.

Ellen had contrived in this subtle, pleasant manner of hers to rule the house since her arrival. She had established an immediate bond with her maternal grandmother, but failed to hit it off with the mother she had always idolized and idealized.

Minnie soon perceived that Ellen liked to be the centre of the stage too, and having a glamorous mother already in that position didn't make her desire to relinquish it any the more. Metaphorically speaking, they were continually elbowing each other out of the way. Minnie was more than glad to assume the maternal mantle, as Charlotte had before her; taking Ellen to the school for her interview, buying her clothes and doing all the things that the girl had expected her mother would do. So, resentment slowly built up, mutual resentment based on mutual misunderstanding. It suited Minnie quite well to play off mother and daughter, getting her own back. It made her feel important; a pivotal point in that stormy and insecure relationship.

There was a rustling sound behind her and Estella appeared in a teagown of pale blue voile with billowing sleeves and a low scalloped front at which Minnie stared disappovingly as Estella sat down.

'Only an actress would wear a gown *that* low.'

'Really, Mother?' Estella parted her lips showing her even teeth in a mirthless smile. She never contradicted her mother. She either ignored her or made some nondescript comment. Her mother scarcely ever saw her without some derogatory remark or other springing to her lips, but Estella contrived to turn a deaf ear to them all. She had her own world where she was the star; not an inner but a real world, another life. Her mother's taunts no longer affected her. 'Is that young Jeremy St Clair with Ellen?'

She shaded her eyes with her hand, and just then the foursome put down their mallets and came over to the two women under the oak.

'Hello Jeremy,' Estella extended a hand. 'You're beginning to look very like your father. How is he, by the way?'

'Very well thank you, Miss Abercrombie. He sent you his regards, should I have the good fortune to see you today.'

'*Good* fortune? Ah!' Estella, pretending to be amazed, smiled at her mother and daughter. 'How kind of you to say that, Jeremy. I am completely without honour in my own country, you know.'

'How do you mean, Miss Abercrombie?' Jeremy accepted a glass of cordial then took his place on the grass beside his friends, gazing at her worshipfully.

'If you don't know, I can't tell you . . . '

'Mother means,' Ellen paused with a cucumber sandwich deliberately half-way to her lips, 'that we take no notice of her airs and graces here.'

'Ellen!' Minnie remonstrated glancing at Estella, but looking rather pleased all the same.

'That was a trifle rude, Ellen dear,' Estella reprimanded mildly. 'Not *quite* what I intended. I must say that when I was at your school they thought good manners and respect of one's parents just as important as learning.'

Minnie opened her mouth as if to defend her grand-daughter, but quickly closed it again as she saw the expression on Estella's face. Mother and daughter were always at loggerheads; they were too alike and Ellen seemed to resent her mother's fame, perhaps from envy, and did all she could to belittle it in front of her. Yet when her mother went on tour she missed her, and Minnie knew that in her heart she was very proud of her. She had a huge cutting book of notices of every play Estella had done since *A Woman's Wiles* had established her reputation.

'I saw your Portia with Sir Henry,' the young man whose name Minnie could never remember said. (It was in fact Angus Mackintosh and his sister Maud was Ellen's best friend.) 'My mother said it was better than Miss Terry's.'

'Oh dear, did she say that? I don't think *any* interpretation could better Miss Terry's; but mine was *different*.'

'Didn't Miss Terry mind you taking her part?' Maud enquired, awestruck by the close proximity of such a famous actress, even if she was her friend's mother.

'No.' Estella shook her head and accepted a cup of tea from Minnie. 'Thank you, Mama. No, dear. Miss Terry and I are *such* close friends. She was having a welcome holiday and was very pleased for me to act with Sir Henry Irving, and I must say it was a great honour for me to play the part. Do you know once at the Lyceum I was only one of the ladies dancing at the court of Henry VIII?'

'*Really*, Miss Abercrombie?' Maud joined her fingers prayerfully before her.

'Yes, really.'

'What Mama is saying,' Ellen said patronizingly, 'is that success does not come easily, even to stars.'

'Quite, darling.' From Estella's smile one would never have guessed that her daughter was a constant irritation, even though she loved her so passionately and missed her when they were apart. As soon as they got together they grated and the sparring started. Estella didn't know why. It was a source of grief to her that something she had longed for for so many years had misfired. But still she would not lose Ellen for the world; she was only sad that she had not got to know her sooner, because then she might have understood her better.

'I was named for Miss Terry,' Ellen said grandly. 'Was I not, Mama?'

'You were indeed darling.' Estella looked at the fob watch hanging on a thin gold chain round her neck. 'Now I must get ready to go to the theatre.'

'What is it tonight, Miss Abercrombie?' Every time Jeremy addressed her he blushed.

'I am playing in *The Prisoner of Zenda* with Mr Alexander at the St James's. It is absolutely *ridiculous*, but very amusing and brings in a lot of money. That reminds me, Mother,' Estella turned to Minnie. 'Speaking of money, I have seen the dearest little house in Bayswater and something tells me I should buy it.'

'For *what*?' Minnie's question was more of a bark than a query.

'To live in.'

'But what is wrong with this house?'

'Nothing. Only I feel it is time I had a place of my own.'

'And what about me?' Ellen said petulantly. 'I have *no* intention of leaving Grandmama.'

Estella got up slowly, rearranging her long bell skirt.

454

'And *I* have no intention of asking you to if you do not wish it. Good-bye my dears. Give my regards to your Mama and Papa, Jeremy, and do pray tell them that, if at any time they should wish to see one of my performances, to be sure to allow me the pleasure of presenting them with tickets.'

'Oh thank you, Miss Abercrombie.' Jeremy, scarlet-faced by this time, rushed ahead of Estella to fling open the door for her, bowing as she swept past with a queenly smile, a word of thanks in her lilting, musical voice – memories that he would treasure for days.

Estella ran up the stairs, aware of an intense, irrational feeling of irritation. It was expected that Ellen would make a fuss about coming to live with her, and did she even want her? Yes, of course she did, she immediately reproved herself; they were mother and daughter, the same flesh and blood. But she wanted a house of her own. She was thirty-six and at times she felt like a schoolgirl living at home.

She took off her dress and started vigorously brushing her hair, going over towards the window which over-looked the lawn where the croquet game had been resumed. Ellen had a mallet stretched imperiously in front of her, directing a willing Jeremy who obediently took up the position she wanted him to play. Ellen, tall and regal with her long dark hair tied back by a flaming red bow, was not unaware of her looks, despite her alleged prefer-ence for cerebral activities. She was not a flirt, but she was already aware of her power over the male sex. She would dominate them as she was quite determined to dominate everything else.

Estella turned away, carefully combing the curls of her 'doormat' fringe over her forehead, securing her coiffure at the back with a large tortoiseshell comb. Yes, Ellen would dominate men in the way her mother never had. Or, rather, she could dominate the men who did not interest her; but not the one man she wanted and who still occupied that special place in her heart: Rayner Brook.

Some Say had certainly done the damage it intended; but maybe not in the way it had hoped; if, that is, gossip writers wish to do anything more except irritate by titillation. The public flocked to see her and Rayner act together, but only for a while. They invariably played to full houses anyway, and as actors were above, or beyond, scandal; it had, by the 1890s, no real power to affect their lives as it would, say, that of a politician. It couldn't harm them as it could to others like Dilke or Charles Stewart Parnell, whose lives had been ruined by scandal.

If Estella had one bastard child or ten the public would still love her, or perhaps they were glad to know that she had one, and that her impersonations on the stage had a real-life foundation. It did not disturb them to find that their idol had feet of clay; they were delighted to find a person like them – warm, human, loving. Yet who else had her talent? She was of the people, yet superior to them by virtue of her art, and they acknowledged it and still loved her. Meanwhile Estella had remained smilingly discreet, silent, refusing to be interviewed by newspaper hacks and leaving by another entrance when they hovered by the stage door.

People soon forgot; but neither Rayner nor she forgot what had happened between them. He tried to make amends, she rebuffed him; she tried to make amends, he rebuffed her. Their attempts at reconciliation never occurred when they were both in a mood to forgive. Each harboured resentment – he that she hadn't trusted him; she that he hadn't shown sufficient sympathy or understanding: he'd been shocked. He denied it; and so on. Maybe they were tired of each other. Their performances together lost the special sparkle that audiences expected of Abercrombie and Brook, and they minded that more than any whiff of scandal between them or talk of illegitimate children.

Finally Rayner abruptly sailed for America, leaving Harriet to find a new leading man for the Lincoln. One day he was there and the next day he was gone and Estella, who had never expected anything so dramatic, nearly broke down. But she had to go on. She could show no one especially her public how much she was suffering. The rules of the game didn't permit it.

Finally she too broke with Harriet, affectionately and certainly not finally. She wanted to accept some of the many other offers she'd had, and Harriet understood. She acted with Irving, now Sir Henry, at the Lyceum – he and Terry had almost reached the end of their fabulous partnership, but the public didn't know it. She toured the provinces with Frank Benson, adding to her repertoire the role of Volumnia to his Coriolanus. Shaw tried to entice her into being his Candida. Now she was again playing with George Alexander at a light-hearted season at the St James's.

She was extremely busy, but when her mind wasn't occupied with a thousand other things, when she had time to think about herself, she thought of him: Rayner. She knew they belonged together and, although the break between them was artificial, feared only that it might be too late to repair it.

Estella changed into a fresh dress, carefully put on her hat so as not to disturb her hair, and went downstairs to await the carriage that Alexander always sent to take her to the theatre.

Rayner sat awkwardly upon the chair, his legs crossed, attempting to balance a cup and plate at the same time. Lindsey put a little table in front of him and took his plate from his hand.

'There, that's better, Rayner. Is it not a perfect day?'

'Perfect.' Rayner looked up at the sun through the trees and was reminded of England. It was a very English house, an English scene, English tea and cakes upon the lawn at the back of the well-proportioned house in Washington Square, New York City. Mortimer, in a biscuit-coloured linen suit, a linen hat on his head, slumped in a lounger and Lindsey, dressed in white, dispensed tea from a silver pot, a large straw hat shading her eyes from the sun.

'I'm so glad you got in touch with us,' Lindsey said. 'You should have done it sooner.'

'I forgot your married name. Then I had a letter from Harriet Leadbetter reminding me that you lived in New York and giving me your address.'

'I'm so glad she did. Estella must have given it to her.'

'Estella?' Rayner gulped and coughed on a crumb of cake that had lodged in his throat.

'Of course. How else would Harriet know where you were?'

'Of course.' Rayner cleared his throat and brushed more crumbs from his knee.

'You were lucky to find us here. We like to go to Newport for the summer where we have a little house. Mortimer enjoys sailing. But, as my practice grows, I find it more difficult to leave my patients, many of whom are in the process of analysis.'

'Analysis?' Rayner looked politely curious.

'Psychoanalysis. Have you not heard of Dr Freud?'

'I'm afraid I haven't.'

'He has evolved a new method of treating nervous illness. I am helping to pioneer his methods in the United States. He's a most brilliant man. He's writing a book now on dreams, and I send him mine and my patients'.'

'Dreams?' Rayner wasn't really very interested.

'They play a part in the subconscious, you know. Freud thinks a very important part. Mortimer gave a lecture on

Dr Freud the other night to the American Psychological Association. Professor Putnam was in the chair. The place was packed.'

'But we had the usual storm,' Mortimer chuckled. 'We expect them when the name of Dr Freud is mentioned. The audience is invariably divided between those who hate him and those who admire him. His critics are most vehement. But we enjoy a scrap, don't we Lindsey?'

'We don't exactly *enjoy* it, Mortimer dear, but yes, it has its own curious way of stimulating us.'

Lindsey smiled brightly at Rayner and offered him more cake. He thought she must be over forty now, but she was an extraordinarily handsome woman, beautifully dressed as she always had been. He had never known her very well, but he recalled her vividly as a young woman and there was no doubt that now she had lost much of the severity that had dominated her youthful looks, made her rather awesome. Her eyes behind her gold-rimmed spectacles were kind, if slightly daunting; she still looked at one with the percipience of the trained physician, as she had even before she became one.

Her resemblance to Estella, which he'd forgotten, had startled him when he was first brought out onto the lawn by the maid. Yet the sisters were not immediately alike; they shared the same features, they were undoubtedly related but it was, he thought, their characters that made them so essentially dissimilar. Estella was beautiful, a woman intensely aware of herself *as* a woman; a very feminine, sexual creature. She moved like an actress because of this self-awareness; she expected people to look at her and they did. Her hair was always beautifully coiffured, her clothes exquisite, she invariably had a smile on her face.

Lindsey looked what she was – a middle-aged physician whose mind was perpetually on higher things. Her hair was carelessly drawn back without any attempt at a style, and her figure, though still graceful, was a little dumpy around the middle. Yet her summer clothes were elegant because Lindsey had always dressed well; and she held herself well. She was tall with a firm bust. Looking at her reminded Rayner of Estella and, in a vivid way that he hadn't expected, of that still aching gap in his heart. He wished he hadn't come.

'Do you remember that day,' he said suddenly, perhaps because he'd been thinking about the two sisters, 'oh it must have been 1880 or 81 when we played croquet with Estella and Wykeham St Clair on the lawn?'

'I remember it.' Lindsey, watching him closely, had seemed to follow his thoughts, and now clasped her hands together, leaning forward. 'How funny you should mention it, Rayner. I was only thinking of it the other day. We had guests here for a small summer party and they called for the croquet set. As they played I watched them and the very next day I had a letter from Estella recalling the very same event and saying that Wykeham's son, Jeremy, is much around the house attending upon her daughter, Ellen. Isn't that singular?'

'Very.' Rayner swallowed more tea and replaced his cup on the table.

'We shall be seeing them all quite soon. We try and visit Vienna every year or so and in the winter, maybe around Christmas time, we're going over for a month. We shall dock in Southampton and hope to spend Christmas at Highgate before going to Austria. Alas, poor Charlotte died. Did you know that, Rayner?'

'No. I'm sorry. I never met her, but of course I heard a lot about her.'

'Not many nice things, I'm sure. She and Estella didn't get on, although I'm happy to say they came together in a sort of mutual apology before Charlotte died; but she was a very good soul. Ellen owes much to Charlotte – stability, which is so important in the young. We hoped to find a cure for her here; but, alas, she had cancer as well as heart trouble.' Lindsey folded her hands in her lap. 'I like to think her last days were very peaceful.'

'They were, my darling, and happy too.' Mortimer peeped at her from under the rim of his hat. 'Thanks to you.'

'Mortimer and I were *both* only too happy to do all we could for Charlotte in her last days,' Lindsey said quietly. Then, thoughtfully, as if to change the subject: 'Estella doesn't find Ellen . . . easy. She's a very spirited young woman.'

'She needs a man,' Mortimer declared firmly. 'Or rather, a father. Someone strong in that house of women.'

'Does Estella have anyone in mind . . . do you know?' Rayner's voice was deliberately casual.

'You mean any strong man?' Lindsey smiled and poured fresh tea into his cup. 'Well, I don't know that there's anyone in particular . . . '

'Some lord she was talking about,' Mortimer settled more comfortably into his lounger. 'Who knows, she might be Lady Whatsit . . . ?'

'Dugdale,' Lindsey picked up her embroidery from the grass where it had lain while she poured tea. 'Lord Alfred Dugdale. Does that ring a bell, Rayner?'

'No.' Rayner looked at his watch, then rose abruptly, as if he'd heard enough. 'I must go.'

'So soon? Are you acting tonight?'

'No, I'm writing a play. I've never had the success in America I had in England. I may take this play back with me. Harriet is keen to see it.'

'Oh *you're* going home too?' As Rayner rose Lindsey put aside her embroidery once again and got up with him. 'I'll see you out.'

'Well, I have to go home some time.' Rayner stooped to shake Mortimer's hand and murmur a few formal words, and then accompanied Lindsey back to the house.

'As I was saying, I have to go home some time. I feel like an exile here.'

'Of *course* you do.' Lindsey removed her spectacles and put them in a pouch she carried in her pocket. Her sympathetic expression seemed to invite confidences. Rayner could understand why patients should want to pour out their troubled feelings to her. Even though she was not a mother there was a motherly quality about her. She was, he decided, a good woman who lived a good, satisfying life. 'I was very sorry you and Estella parted, Rayner,' she went on. 'I think you were very good for her.'

'*I* good for her!' Rayner pretended consternation. 'We quarrelled the whole time.'

'Still, there was something in your relationship that suited both of you. You were together for a long time.'

'Yes, we were,' Rayner dusted imaginary specks from the brim of his white Homburg hat that he had taken from the hall stand. 'But we never really got on.'

'Didn't you?' Lindsey raised her eyebrows. 'I must say that remark surprises me. I think you did, and I think you know it. I also think Estella misses you very much.'

'Misses me?' Rayner snorted. 'I don't believe it. She has never attempted to get in touch with me.'

'Perhaps she didn't know how.'

'Of course she knew how. Well, she could have tried . . . ' Rayner appeared less certain and his expression showed his confusion.

'Did *you* try and get in touch with her?'

'No.'

'But she did.' Lindsey waved a letter she had drawn from her pocket. 'Why do you think Harriet wrote to you?'

Rayner shrugged, his eyes on the letter. 'Harriet keeps in touch.'

'Oh yes, but this time she wrote because Estella *asked* her. See here.' Lindsey put on her spectacles again and shook out the pages of the letter, reading in a low, clear voice.

'I still long for Rayner, my dearest Lindsey, and I think you know it. Nothing in my life has been the same since he left, though I continue as successful professionally as ever. Lord Alfred bores me to death with his attentions – he fills the house with gifts – but please, I beg you, do not think I have resumed my old ways. Not only in thought but in deed I am faithful to Rayner. I would to God that we had not been so stubborn towards each other a year ago. When Rayner disappeared to America, I felt he would quickly return. But he stays away.

'Do you think he has married someone else? If I knew, perhaps I'd have some peace. I have written to Harriet and asked her if she knows his whereabouts. Meanwhile, if you should see his name in the paper or on a billboard perhaps you would let me know . . .'

Lindsey adjusted her spectacles and turned the page, scanning it rapidly. 'There she goes on about Mama. She has seen a house she likes. She . . . ' Lindsey regarded him frankly peering at him over her spectacles. 'She wants you very much, Rayner. If you still feel as she does it seems to me ridiculous that you should remain apart.'

Rayner suddenly threw his hat high into the air and his arms round Lindsey's neck.

'Lindsey, you are the most darling woman. I love *you*!' He planted a kiss on her cheek and, groping for his hat, now on the floor, raced for the door, pausing to wave as he opened it.

Lindsey watched him, smiling, and raised her hand. 'See you in London,' she said.

Lord Alfred always had the same table in the corner of the grill room at the Café Royal. He discussed the menu with the chef in person in the course of a day in which he had not much else to do, and the meal that was served after the theatre contained all the rare and expensive dishes which that pampered gastronome could find to delight his beloved: asparagus and strawberries out of season, quail, plovers' eggs, caviare from the Baltic, salmon caught in the rivers of his lordship's Ducal father's rivers in Scotland and smoked by experts in the East End of London.

Estella toyed with her food, played with her wine, avoided Lord Alfred's eyes.

'But you *may* continue your career, my darling. I would never stand between you and the stage.'

'No, of course,' Estella plonked a half-eaten asparagus back on its plate. She was not in a graceful mood. 'But would you really like an independent woman for a wife?'

'Of course, my darling.'

'But I'm *five* years older than you.'

'Of what consequence is that?' Lord Alfred pressed her hand. 'Anyway, it's only four. I checked your age in the reference books.'

Estella smiled. He was very sweet; he was also quite handsome, with waving fair hair and large moustaches. He could not be called dashing, but he was kind and very thoughtful – attributes that made up a lot for the absence of Rayner. She had never had a cross word with Lord Alfred; she could say what she liked to him and he never complained. Yet he would be more of a brother than a father to Ellen, whom he liked and who appeared to like him. Ellen definitely needed a father, as Lindsey had stressed. It was something to do with the importance of a father figure in one's life, which was one of the tenets, apparently, of this new psychoanalysis. Yet could one *see* Lord Alfred as a father? Although he was thirty, in manner as well as appearance he seemed younger. She had never been tempted at all to go to bed with him; but kept him rather as a pet, in the way Harriet Leadbetter treated Sergei.

It was true that Lord Alfred was extraordinarily rich. Not that Estella had money problems any more, but she was extravagant. She was now used to luxury and she liked it; Alfred would give her anything in the world she wanted. His family had houses in London and Scotland – a huge mansion there, with forests and moorland and rivers full of salmon. It belonged to his father the Duke and Lord Alfred, being a younger son, would never succeed to the title; which made him still very rich, but rather carefree and irresponsible. He would have too much time for her. He would get on her nerves. Yet, *Lady* Alfred Dugdale . . . ? His family had seemed to expect it. She had spent a holiday with them in the summer – and had been bored to death.

Both Alfred and his Ducal family were very boring. She looked at him candidly, but only saw love in his eyes.

'You really are very boring, Alfred,' she said, and Lord Alfred smiled with pleasure.

'My darling, if it amuses you, say anything you want. I'm your slave. Is the asparagus not cooked the way you like it?'

'Not really.'

'Oh!' Lord Alfred put his hand to his mouth in consternation and beckoned to the waiter. Estella immediately put a hand over his.

'I was *teasing* Alfred. Please don't blame the chef. It's just that, as everything you say and do is boring, I have to create some diversion.'

Lord Alfred joined his hands together and rested them under his chin, perfectly content.

'Estella, you are *so* divine. Every hour spent with you is like heaven. Your wit is as flamboyant as your presence. How could a man ever have a single dull moment with a wife like you? Do you not *wish* to be a peeress?'

'Titles have no attraction for me,' Estella murmured, not altogether truthfully. If she married Alfred it would be for both his money and title – nothing else. A waiter approached the table carrying a silver tray. 'I play too many titled ladies on the stage. For me?' She stared at the waiter, who indicated a note on the tray.

465

'If his lordship permits, Madam. A message for you.'

'His lordship may pay the bill, but messages for me are messages for me whether his lordship permits it or no.'

Estella looked at the waiter severely. 'Pray tip him, Alfred.' Then she gave him her gorgeous smile. The waiter, looking first abashed then confused and, finally, gratified, bowed and put the coin in his pocket, backing away from the formidable presence of the greatest attraction on the London stage. She had more temperament, as the staff all knew, than Mrs Pat, Miss Terry and Lillie Langtry put together. Yet Estella had, unusually that night, been rude to one of the staff. By taunting Lord Alfred she had broken one of her own canons of good manners. Temperamental she could be and was, but not with her inferiors. It was a rule. Waiters, stage hands, scenery shifters, cabbies, chambermaids – she identified too much with the depressed classes to want to do anything but treat them with respect. Fanciful, maybe, but in many ways she saw herself as one of them, but for luck that had twice rescued her from poverty and humiliation. She made a mental note to be specially nice to the waiter when she saw him again. She knew he would forgive her. Everyone did. She slid a knife through the envelope and opened the note.

There were simply seven words on it. Seven words and an initial:

I have written a play for you. R.

Estella rose immediately from her chair and excitedly looked round the room, scanning the tables, clasping the letter to her breast.

From a table in the far corner Rayner smiled.

It wasn't necessary for *Some Say* to notify everyone that Rayner Brook was back in London. *Some Say* did report the fact, of course, along with a few other conjectures.

But even the *Daily Telegraph* had a tiny paragraph describing the scene when Miss Estella Abercrombie dashed across the Grill Room of the Café Royal, upsetting a waiter with a tray full of *hors d'oeuvres* in her haste, to embrace her former partner.

Everyone seemed glad that Rayner Brook had returned. Parties were given to welcome him back and managements made plans to lure him to act with Miss Abercrombie. But Rayner had his own plans, and his own play. He read it to a select audience consisting of Estella, Ellen, Minnie, Harriet Leadbetter and Sergei in the Highgate house soon after his return.

It was a tremendous play with a dazzling part for a woman. But this time it was tragic. The woman deserted her family for a much younger man who ended up abandoning her in a Chicago slum. She had her *Just Deserts*, the title of the play. By setting it in Chicago, too, he hoped it would be successful in America. Everyone shivered at the end.

'It is a little bit shocking,' Minnie said. 'Just a little bit.'

'It's really *tremendous*.' Harriet frowned at Sergei, indicating that he should immediately agree with her. 'Such *depth* of degradation, Rayner dear.'

Rayner, very debonair in a new suit of grey barathea and a spotted blue necktie, looked round with as much anxiety as he felt on a real first night.

'I can just *see* Mama in the part,' Ellen remarked graciously, at her best behaviour in the presence of the man she had wanted so much to meet: the stormy, gifted, talented Rayner Brook. Estella smiled to herself. If Rayner hadn't been there the comment would have been very different; it would have had some barb. But she didn't mind. She had sat slightly behind the others on an upright chair, her chin balanced on the palm of one hand, her blue eyes gazing at him.

She felt so at home with him; at home with love. How

easily they had slipped into their old ways. How familiar too, yet how uniquely thrilling, had been their reunion in his dear, deep, familiar bed.

It was difficult to believe they'd been apart for so long. They were already like an old married couple, and Harriet was reopening the Lincoln for *Just Deserts* which would herald the new year, the new century. For this was October 1899, and the year 1900 was approached without trepidation by all those who thought the future would be as safe as the past; that the accustomed peace, harmony and enterprise of the gay nineties, *La Belle Époque*, could not possibly end. There were inventions and new discoveries all the time; but surely they would only pave the way to an even safer, more exciting world? It was true there was the slight matter of a war in South Africa; but that was thousands of miles away – the British simply establishing their ascendancy over the Boers, as they had every right to do.

'Estella hasn't said a word.' Rayner looked at her anxiously. He'd been too nervous to read the play alone with her. Estella got up and sat beside her daughter, putting an arm round her dainty waist.

'Ellen's spoken for me,' she said. 'It really *is* a tremendous part for her mama. Your exile has done you good, Rayner dear.' In front of Ellen she always took care to keep her tone even with Rayner; not to betray a hint of the excitement she felt continually in his presence. 'It has certainly sharpened your talents. It is very nice, too, that a husband for once is seen in his true colours, and not as a wronged hero. It was because of his behaviour that she left.'

'It's still not quite *proper*, is it Estella dear?' Minnie looked nervously at her granddaughter. 'I always considered it the duty of a wife to stick by her husband, no matter what. It's old-fashioned, I know.'

'I really must go.' Harriet picked up her gloves and gave

Sergei a little kick which made him immediately jump to attention. 'Give me the word and the bills will be printed. I'm going to try and get H. R. H. to come. I'm a particular friend of Mrs Keppell, you know, his new lady love. She's much younger than I am, of course, and much younger than he is . . . but still she's a dear.'

'*Pas devant l'enfant*,' Estella smiled mysteriously at her daughter, who stamped her foot.

'Oh Mama, I know about *these* things. I can also speak French, as if you didn't know. I must go and do my maths homework.'

Rayner raised an eyebrow and lit a cigarette.

'Another Lindsey in the family I see.'

'Oh yes, I'd like to be a doctor too. Did you know that Aunt Lindsey is coming over soon?'

'She said something to me in New York. Ask her to try and be here for the opening. After all, she was responsible for it.'

'She's going to take me to meet Mrs Anderson! Imagine, *the* Mrs Garrett Anderson. Although she's retired she's still terribly influential in medical circles.'

'That's exciting for you,' Rayner said, smiling. He seemed genuinely interested. Ellen smiled back. She approved of Rayner. In fact, she adored him. He was exciting, very masculine, unlike Lord Alfred whom Mama had threatened to marry. Ellen hadn't taken to him at all. Yet Rayner wasn't a threat. He was, of course, quite old; older than Mama, nearly as old as Aunt Lindsey, and so no rival between her and her mother. She particularly liked the way he had her mother under control, not in a nasty domineering way, but firmly and kindly. Mother'd had fewer moods since Rayner had been back. She appeared to find life – even the cold autumn of 1899 as the troops went off to the war in South Africa – perpetually full of sunshine. He seemed to make her mother very happy. Ellen was glad, because she felt that if Estella were happy it would make her happy too. To her surprise she wasn't jealous at all.

This was the Rayner Brook whose name appeared in all the cuttings she'd collected over the years about her mother's successes. *The* Rayner Brook, author of *A Woman's Wiles*. She liked him enormously and was glad he'd come back.

'I must see to the dinner,' Minnie said, getting up with Harriet. 'I haven't had a moment all day to talk to cook. You're sure you and Mr . . . '

'Call him Sergei,' Harriet filled in.

'Mr Sergei won't stay to dinner?'

'No thank you, dear Mrs Abercrombie. I'm having a little party next week for Rayner and Estella. Be sure to be there. And Ellen too.' She took Ellen's arm and they all went out together, leaving Estella and Rayner alone. The wind blew a flurry of leaves against the window; Estella shivered and drew the curtains.

'She's awfully like you,' Rayner said.

'But awfully different too,' Estella replied. 'Could I have one of your cigarettes?'

Rayner passed her his case, selected a fresh cigarette for himself and then lit them both.

'Lindsey said Ellen needed a father.'

'Did Lindsey say that? She's a bit old for one I'd have thought.' Estella looked at him slyly and blew smoke away from his face. She wore a black skirt and a white blouse with a high frilled neckline and the effect was to make her look both chaste and alluring.

'I though of offering myself as Ellen's father.'

'What a very roundabout way you have of putting things, Rayner.'

'Well, you make it difficult, you're so modern. I felt that if I came out with a straight proposal you'd flatten me with one of your remarks.'

'Dearest, are you by any chance proposing? I tried to

470

put Lord Alfred off by similar remarks, but nothing could stop him either. I like my independence, Rayner. I'm used to it. I'm buying my own house, and investing money on the Stock Exchange. It's *quite* as exciting as the *Bourse*. Luckily I just sold some South African mining shares. I've quite a gift for finance.'

Rayner slid an arm around her waist. 'Listen to me . . . '

But she placed a hand on his chest, gently, but firmly too. 'I'm listening, Rayner; but I want you to know that, happy as I am to have you back again, I mean what I say. I *am* a new woman. I approve of the new woman. I'm on the London Suffragette Committee and, believe me, we shall get more militant if things don't improve.'

'I'm for the vote too, but I would still like to marry you . . . some time.' He smiled into her eyes and kissed her and, impulsively she put her arms around him and pressed him close.

'Please don't leave me again, Rayner. I couldn't bear it. I nearly didn't last time, and next time I won't be able to. Let's remain, always, friends as well as lovers. Please, whatever happens.'

Rayner put his mouth close to her ear and whispered: '*Friends*? Very difficult. Can lovers be friends? I'm not sure.

> Friendship is constant in all other things
> Save in the office and affairs of love.

Claudio: Act 2, scene 2.'

'I'm aware of the context, my darling. *Much Ado* once brought us together and *Much Ado* once drove us apart.'

'It wasn't *Much Ado*. It was this uncertainty about us. We can't just be friends, Estella, and we can't just remain lovers. The idea of marriage seems dull to you but it needn't be. Frankly, I can't see our lives together ever deteriorating into boredom.'

471

'Frankly,' Estella said, 'neither can I. But you'll have to give me time.'

'Time!' Rayner said explosively. 'Time is what we don't have.'

'*If* you're talking about my age . . . '

'Your age has nothing to do with it.'

'We're not going to quarrel, are we Rayner?' She looked at him petulantly, provocatively, her mouth half open.

'Quarrel? When did we ever quarrel?' Rayner tightened his hands behind her back, almost lifting her off her feet. She started to struggle, but her efforts somehow lacked conviction. ' "Peace," ' he murmured, gazing at her, as she grew quiet in his arms. ' "I will stop your mouth".'

And he kissed her.

Martha Warner, an empty bottle by her side, contemplated the ruins of her life.

'Alone, all alone,' she exclaimed bitterly, slowly raising her arms above her head. 'No one left to love . . . no one to love me.'

She stood upright, her hair dishevelled, her skimpy dress a symbol of her abject poverty, her hands clawing emptily at the air. For a moment she stood there, a woman importuning heaven; but there was nothing left. Then, slowly, she sank upon the floor and lay without moving, her face upon the bare boards.

The curtain fell. For a moment the theatre was silent too. Then came applause from the back, then more and more and soon the packed auditorium was applauding, feet stamping, seats banging as most of the first-night audience rose to its feet.

The curtain rose again and Martha, still alone but upright, only now radiant, bowed deeply from the waist, looking first at the stalls, then at the circle and finally at her faithful friends who had stormed the gallery and the pit, queueing for hours before the theatre opened to get in.

'Bravo! Bravo!'

Lindsey had tears in her eyes and Mortimer was unashamedly mopping his face with a large handkerchief, his spectacles in his hand. Ellen, her eyes shining, her heart bursting with pride, was on her feet too, clapping frantically, while Minnie remained slumped, exhausted in her seat, a handkerchief pressed to her eyes. Now Rayner joined Estella on the stage and the assembly roared again. The critics made a mass exit for the door, jostling with one another to be the first down to Fleet Street to write their reports.

The rest of the small cast came onto the stage and made their bows. Harriet Leadbetter had played Martha's old mother, trying to save her from ruin, and she got a special burst of applause. The curtain came down, and quickly rose again . . . again, and again, and again.

Another triumph had arrived on the London stage.

Later when the audience had reluctantly departed there was a small party on the stage for the cast and friends, the curtain raised to show the dark, empty theatre. Champagne corks were popping and perspiring waiters moved about the throng, carrying trays of *canapés* and glasses of the sparkling white wine.

Estella, in a long white evening dress, the halter neckline emphasizing her peerless bosom, a circlet of diamonds around her neck, looked the antithesis of a woman who, a short while before, had succumbed to the consequences of dissipation and a misspent life. By her side Rayner, splendidly handsome in white tie and tails, received congratulations both for his playing of the part of Martha's husband – not a very sympathetic character – and the strength of his play. Shyly Ellen approached him.

'You were wonderful,' she said. 'How *glad* I am you came back to act with Mama.'

'You look pretty,' he stooped and kissed her. 'You're your mother's daughter. I'm glad I came too.' Then he looked past her and put out his arms.

'Lindsey, how wonderul that you could be here. The architect of my happiness.'

Lindsey, still in the grip of the strong emotions induced by the play, the thrill of seeing her sister in another success, acting together again with Rayner, embraced him warmly. 'I'm so *glad*, and congratulations too. It really *is* a wonderful play.'

'Most moving,' Mortimer shook his hand. 'I quite surprised myself by caring. Do you know Chicago?'

'Not well, but . . . '

From somewhere off-stage a gong sounded and everyone suddenly stopped talking.

'It's midnight,' the stage manager cried, rushing to the centre of the floor. 'You can hear Big Ben clearly from the stage door. Happy New Year everybody.'

'Happy New Year. Here's to 1900! Happy New Year.' Glasses were raised, toasts drunk, kisses exchanged.

'Happy New Year darlings,' Estella put one arm through Rayner's and another through that of her daughter, drawing them close. 'What a lovely party. Oh and Lindsey and Mortimer, and Mama too, isn't it marvellous that we can all be together here, on this night of nights? It can't happen for another hundred years . . . and who knows where we'll all be then?'

As everyone bursts out laughing the scene fades on a family grouped apart on the stage: a grandmother, a granddaughter, two sisters, the husband of one, the lover – perhaps soon to be the husband too, who can tell? – of another. It is a happy family, united at last after years of unhappiness, discord, loneliness, misunderstanding, disunity, much striving – but, finally, fulfilment and success.

Not many stories end like this, and who can say how long

474